LETTERS F[
AMERICAN [

J. HECTOR ST JOHN DE CRÈVECŒUR (1735–1813) was born in Caen to a family of minor French nobility. Rigorously educated by Jesuits, he resisted both a military profession and a career as a missionary. An extended visit to England in 1754, led him to develop strong and lasting Anglophile feelings. Crèvecœur subsequently travelled to Canada, where he joined a French regiment involved in the Anglo–French War. Leaving the army, he travelled as a surveyor in uncharted American territories. In 1769, he married and settled down to farm in the Hudson Valley. His peaceful, prosperous life there (described in the *Letters from an American Farmer*) was abruptly shattered by the Revolutionary War of Independence between England and America. Unable to take sides, he fled to France to try to establish his children's inheritance in French law. He returned in 1783 at the end of the war to find his farm burned by Indians, his wife murdered, and his children gone. Recovering his surviving family, he settled in New York as consul of Louis XVI, and established a career in business. He continued to correspond with literati on both sides of the Atlantic, and was elected to the American Philosophical Society. Ill health forced his return to France in 1790, where he evaded involvement in the French Revolution, and composed his *Voyage dans la Haute Pennsylvanie et dans l'État de New York* (1801). Other literary manuscripts including the *Sketches of Eighteenth-Century America*, remained unpublished until after his death. Crèvecœur's eventful transatlantic life and cosmopolitan sympathies make him both a representative figure of the Revolutionary years and an acute observer of the topographical, social, and political nature of the new nation. At once documentary and prophetic, the *Letters from an American Farmer* remains a classic of early American Literature.

SUSAN MANNING is a Grierson Professor of English Literature and Director of the Institute for Advanced Studies at the University of Edinburgh. She has published widely on eighteenth- and nineteenth-century American and Scottish writing, and her critical study *The Puritan-Provincial Vision* (1990) compares the two literatures in relation to an English tradition. Her editions of Walter Scott's *Quentin Durward* and Washington Irving's *The Sketch-Book of Geoffrey Crayon, Gent.* are available in the Oxford World's Classics series.

OXFORD WORLD'S CLASSICS

*For over 100 years Oxford World's Classics have brought
readers closer to the world's great literature. Now with over 700
titles—from the 4,000-year-old myths of Mesopotamia to the
twentieth century's greatest novels—the series makes available
lesser-known as well as celebrated writing.*

*The pocket-sized hardbacks of the early years contained
introductions by Virginia Woolf, T. S. Eliot, Graham Greene,
and other literary figures which enriched the experience of reading.
Today the series is recognized for its fine scholarship and
reliability in texts that span world literature, drama and poetry,
religion, philosophy and politics. Each edition includes perceptive
commentary and essential background information to meet the
changing needs of readers.*

OXFORD WORLD'S CLASSICS

J. HECTOR ST JOHN DE CRÈVECŒUR

*Letters from an
American Farmer*

Edited with an Introduction and Notes by
SUSAN MANNING

OXFORD
UNIVERSITY PRESS

OXFORD
UNIVERSITY PRESS

Great Clarendon Street, Oxford OX2 6DP

Oxford University Press is a department of the University of Oxford.
It furthers the University's objective of excellence in research, scholarship,
and education by publishing worldwide in

Oxford New York

Athens Auckland Bangkok Bogotá Buenos Aires Calcutta
Cape Town Chennai Dar es Salaam Delhi Florence Hong Kong Istanbul
Karachi Kuala Lumpur Madrid Melbourne Mexico City Mumbai
Nairobi Paris São Paulo Shanghai Singapore Taipei Tokyo Toronto Warsaw

with associated companies in Berlin Ibadan

Oxford is a registered trade mark of Oxford University Press
in the UK and in certain other countries

Published in the United States
by Oxford University Press Inc., New York

First published as a World's Classics paperback 1997
Reissued as an Oxford World's Classics paperback 1998
Reissued 2009

British Library Cataloguing in Publication Data

Data available

Library of Congress Cataloging in Publication Data
St. John de Crèvecœur, J. Hector, 1735–1813.
Letters from an American farmer / Hector St. John de Crèvecœur;
edited with an introduction and notes by Susan Manning.
(Oxford world's classics)
Includes bibliographical references.
1. United States—Social life and customs—1775–1783. 2. United
States—Description and travel—Early works to 1800. 3. St. John de
Crèvecœur, J. Hector, 1735–1813. I. Manning, Susan. II. Title.
III. Series.
E163.S73 1997 973′.3—dc21 97–5795

ISBN 978–0–19–955474–4

13

Printed in Great Britain by
Clays Ltd, Elcograf S.p.A

CONTENTS

INTRODUCTION

Ban, Ban, Cacaliban
Has a new master—get a new man!
Freedom, high-day! High-day, freedom! Freedom,
high-day, freedom!
> (Shakespeare, *The Tempest*, II. ii)

What, then, is the American, this new man?
> (*Letters from an American Farmer*)

Mr Heartbreak, the New Man,
come to farm a crazy land . . .
(John Berryman, *The Dream Songs*, i. 5)

The *Letters from an American Farmer* is a book about
identity—specifically American identity—struggling into being.
When it was published in 1782 its author was no adolescent,
nor even a young man searching for an adult self; but something about the exigency around him prompted fundamental
reassessment of a previously settled world view. The book
that took shape in the years before and during the American
Revolution embodies the personal crisis induced by momentous political events. It is at once the fullest literary expression of America's coming into being (D. H. Lawrence called
Crèvecœur the 'emotional . . . prototype of the American'),
and a moving exploration of the meaning of 'revolution' in
the personality of any previously established self.[1] The peculiar power of the *Letters* is quite different from that of the
novel of youthful identity-formation or adolescent angst: this
is no *Catcher in the Rye* or *Bildungsroman* on the lines of
Goethe's *Wilhelm Meister*, but rather the painful record of
a mature, well-informed individual with a consistent outlook

[1] *Studies in Classic American Literature* (1924; rpt. Harmondsworth, 1971), 29.

on life facing an inescapable convulsion of all the facts as he
has known them. What begins to emerge from the narrative
of Crèvecœur's 'American Farmer' is something like a fatal
flaw—akin to the crack in Henry James's Golden Bowl—in
the nature of reality, and it proves to inhere equally in the
individual and in the world around him. In this sense, the
Letters are at once a celebration of America, and its tragedy;
Crèvecœur writes the requiem for the new nation as it comes
into being, and his book is deservedly known as the first
work of American literature.

Some of nascent America's most pressing concerns are
adumbrated in the *Letters*: in addition to the question of
American identity, the largeness and fertility of the land are
celebrated, as is personal determination and freedom from
institutional oppression. From the beginning of the book it is
apparent that the physical enormity of America forces a complete revision of perspective by the newly arrived European
settler; he 'suddenly alters his scale . . . he no sooner breathes
our air than he forms schemes and embarks in designs he
would never have thought of in his own country' (Letter III).
The reassessment enjoined by the size of the land itself prompts
a corresponding internal adjustment in the immigrant; the
Letters, as Stephen Fender has recently put it, 'gave America
its first moral geography'.[2] A single reading will release both
the charm of Crèvecœur's portrayal of colonial life and the
horror of its overturning. To absorb the design which makes
the book more than the sum of these parts, we need to know
something of its author, something of the philosophical ideas
which structured his understanding of pre-Revolutionary life
in America, and something of his reaction to the events which
shattered this apparently harmonious existence. Together,
these provide the emotional logic for the quiddity of the
narrator Farmer James, and the shape of his narrative.

---

[2] Stephen Fender, *Sea Changes: British Emigration and American Literature* (Cambridge, 1992), 12.

One can give a straightforward and reasonably satisfactory account of the life of the author of *Letters from an American Farmer*. Michel-Guillaume Hector St John de Crèvecœur (1735–1813) was born at Caen in Normandy, into an ancient and respectable family in reduced circumstances. A Jesuit education left him well-tutored, cultured, and sceptical; an extended visit to relatives in England in 1754 marked the beginning of his abiding admiration for English political freedoms and culture. He subsequently joined a French regiment in Canada, rose to the rank of lieutenant, and took part in the battles at Lake George and the Plains of Abraham in the French and Indian Wars. Following the defeat of France, Crèvecœur resigned his commission and settled in New York State as a naturalized subject of George III. As a cartographer and surveyor he travelled widely in the American colonies before (in 1769) settling at the age of 34 to marriage and life as a New York farmer and man of letters. The following years were —at least as he wrote of them in retrospect—a kind of idyll of colonial American life. In 1776 agrarian calm and prosperity were shattered by the outbreak of the Revolutionary War of Independence; seeking to return to France, Crèvecœur was separated from his family, imprisoned, and suffered nervous collapse before finally being permitted to leave for Europe. Back in France, following the publication in England of the *Letters from an American Farmer* in 1782 he became a minor celebrity, enjoying the company of Mme d'Houdetot and her salon, engaging in extensive correspondence with the duc de la Rochefoucauld on such matters as the establishment of a botanical garden and other civic amenities in New York, and translating American articles for the *Mercure de France*. Crèvecœur became known to the American leaders Benjamin Franklin and Thomas Jefferson, and corresponded with both on matters of public interest. He reported on the American colonies for the French government, and when the Revolutionary War came to an end in 1783 returned to New York as the official representative of Louis XVI. He arrived to discover his home, Pine Hill, burned in an Indian raid, his wife murdered, and his children gone. Subsequently reunited with what remained of his family, Crèvecœur occupied a prominent agricultural, commercial, diplomatic, and literary position in the newly independent nation. He died in France in 1813.

This is an account of a public career which suggests a successful and substantial figure of the Establishment rather than a shape-changing 'new man'. But the outlines of the story begin to blur as soon as we subject them to scrutiny. For one thing, there is a recurrent confusion about dates: Crèvecœur's marriage, his visit to Niagara, and his naturalization are all questionably and variously located. How much of this may have been vagueness or even deliberate obfuscation on Crèvecœur's part, and how much the product of the unsettled years in which the events took place, is unrecoverable now. More significant is the repeated evidence of ambiguous behaviour under pressure which troubled his contemporaries. Crèvecœur's biography is punctuated by episodes of silence alternating with passages of sustained self-fashioning which amount almost to serial identities. Refusal to declare his sympathies openly made him suspect to both patriots and loyalists; in time of revolution, neutrality was the most dangerous position of all, and non-combatants were maligned and harassed by both sides. Additionally, however, Crèvecœur's behaviour during 1778 (following his abandonment of Pine Hill) does seem to have been, if not positively duplicitous, certainly questionable, and it is hardly surprising that both his literary and surveying activities at that time gave rise to unease about his true loyalties. It is indeed hard to make sense of his decision to leave the family and the farm on which his stability, his livelihood, and his ideas of ethical behaviour were based. A report drafted in 1779 for the information of the British governor Sir Henry Clinton by Peter Dubois, a magistrate of the New York City police, characterized the suspect in the following terms:

He appears to be a Man of Extensive knowledge, Well Read in Phisic, Skilled in Botany and the Mathematics; Indeed in the Arts and Sciences, Nothing is new to him. But it is said in his Temper and Disposition he is often Violent, as well as Capricious, and will at some times affect an Ignorance of what he Realy knows; Many Occurences in Which he has been Consulted, have proved him to be a Man of Penetration, Art and Stratagem.[3]

Nor was this the first time Crèvecœur's conduct under fire had given rise to suspicion. In 1759, serving as a young lieutenant under French command against the British in Canada, something (whose details will probably forever remain obscure) happened to cause his fellow officers to demand that he resign his commission and leave the area. Crèvecœur made his way from Quebec to New York, changed his name to the English-sounding Hector St John, and began a new life as a travelling merchant. It was under this bellicose *nom de plume* that the *Letters* were published. Whatever the original circumstances which prompted this change of identity, their memory was apparently sufficiently traumatic years later to cause Crèvecœur extreme disquiet when the possibility arose of meeting a man who had been an officer in the same regiment. His French compatriot Brissot de Warville, who knew Crèvecœur both in America and France during the 1780s, described him as one labouring under a burden of fear and secrecy: 'Crèvecœur portait partout un front sombre, un air unquiet ... Jamais il ne se livrait aux épanchements, il paraissait même quelquefois effrayé du succès de son ouvrage, il semblait enfin qu'il eût un secret qui lui pesât sur l'âme et dont il craignait la révélation.'[4]

---

[3] Quoted by Bernard Chevignard, 'St. John de Crèvecœur in the Looking Glass: *Letters from an American Farmer* and the Making of a Man of Letters', *Early American Literature*, 2 (Fall 1984), 175.

[4] 'Crèvecœur always wore a melancholy aspect and an air of disquiet ... He never allowed himself any outpouring of feeling, he even sometimes seemed frightened by the success of his work, a man, in short, with a secret

To a certain extent the evasions and duplicities in Crèvecœur's life story may be explained by the observation that he was a peaceable man born at a time of crisis, and thrown against his will into public events of the most momentous kind. In this respect his plight, and his confusion of identities, may represent that of every non-partisan colonist. No politician, but a man of ideas and a writer, his primary loyalties were to a set of philosophical ideals, and it was far from clear in the confused political and military wranglings of the late 1780s which (if either) of the sides which claimed America would be more likely to uphold them. Crèvecœur's life encompassed the Anglo-French war over Canada, the American Revolution, the French Revolution and its subsequent 'Reign of Terror', and the rise of Napoleon. In all of these he was a reluctant participant who tried to remain an observer. Furthermore, he was a farmer and the frightened father of a family, and his peaceful existence had been overwhelmed and all but annihilated by a public turmoil whose progress seemed to presage only destruction for everything he valued. His most recent biographers describe him as 'condemned to be a Janus, looking toward the future and America when in France, and turned toward the past and France when in America'.[5] Inevitably, the assumption and discarding of names caused confusion. It was directly responsible for a delay in his first meeting with Benjamin Franklin, who (expecting to encounter 'Hector St John') was obliged eventually to write in puzzlement, but with characteristic directness: 'Madame la Comtesse d'Houdetot had warmly recommended to me a M. Crèvecœur who had been long in America. Please inform me if you are the same

which weighed on his soul and whose disclosure he dreaded.' Brissot de Warville, quoted by Howard Rice, in *Le Cultivateur américain: étude sur l'œuvre de Saint John de Crèvecœur* (Paris, 1933), 43 n.

[5] Gay Wilson Allen and Roger Asselineau, *St. John de Crèvecœur: The Life of an American Farmer* (New York, 1987), 214.

person.' Crèvecœur's embarrassment is as evident as his reply is intriguing:

> Yes Sir I am the same person . . . the reason for this mistake proceeds from the singularity of ye french customs, which renders their names almost arbitrary, and often leads them to forget their family ones; it is in consequence of this that there are more alias dictums in this than in any other country in Europe. The name of our family is St. Jean, in English St. John . . .
>
> I am so great a stranger to the manners of this tho' my native country having quitted it very young that I never dreamt I had any other than the old family name. I was greatly astonished when at my late return, I saw myself under the necessity of being called by that of Crèvecœur.[6]

As French consul in America following the Revolutionary War (and having reassumed his patronymic), Crèvecœur still found himself under suspicion from both sides: neither French enough for the one, nor sufficiently American for the other. He christened his first child, symbolically, América-Francès; she lived up to her name and married a brilliant young French diplomat, their union appropriately blessed by the presence of Thomas Jefferson at the ceremony. But the optative nominal synthesis which he wished to confer on his daughter would not hold in reality for Crèvecœur himself: as he wrote to Jefferson in July 1794, 'I am at once an American by adoption and law, and a Frenchman by birth'.[7] And, he might have added, an Englishman by emotional allegiances. His experience bridged two cultures—French and British—and witnessed the violent emergence of a third. It was an experience, as he wrote it into the *Letters from an American Farmer*, of fragmentation and severance rather than of union.

Crèvecœur's less than transparent behaviour in crisis might properly remain in the realms of biographical speculation and historical contingency, were it not for the light it casts on some aspects of the *Letters*. (It is worth noting that the book

---

[6] Ibid. 90–1.   [7] Ibid. 213.

was written in Crèvecœur's adopted language of English before it was translated into French, which he had almost to re-learn for the purpose; and that in the process the *Letters* became to all intents and purposes quite a different work.) His reaction to the pressure of events seems to have been to remake himself, repeatedly, with a kind of chameleon adaptability aimed at rendering him inconspicuous in every situation. In terms of its literary resonance in the book's many faces and voices, we might see the author himself as a prototypical 'American', a 'new man' in the Melvillean sense: polymorphic, protean, assuming and discarding identities to meet the occasion. This was neither a game nor the product of whim or vanity; it may in fact have been essential for survival in the shifting sands that were America in these early years. Franklin, the most famous autobiographer of the period, whose composed 'Life' became a different kind of representative text of the new country, himself created a narrative in which he assumes a series of provisional identities. His *Autobiography* writes about this process, and its significance in the success story of becoming an American: it is part of the capacity of *this* new man simply to leave behind his past—including his past selves—when they no longer suit his purposes.

What Herman Melville would later call these 'avatars' of selfhood are integral to the structure of Crèvecœur's work and its status as a representative text in a much more troubled and troubling way than is Franklin's opportunistic assumption of advantageous roles.[8] Among the 'Arts and Stratagems' described in Peter Dubois's report were 'Some Boxes' brought by Crèvecœur to New York, 'in which he had curious Botanical plants and at the Bottom of those Boxes under the Earth in which these plants were, he had private Drawers or Cases in which he had his papers'.[9] These hidden papers included the essays which Crèvecœur would, on

---

[8] See Melville's *The Confidence-Man: His Masquerade* (1857).
[9] Chevignard, 'Crèvecœur in the Looking Glass', 175.

his arrival in London, sell to the booksellers Davies and Davis as the *Letters from an American Farmer*. The anecdote may serve as an apt symbolic image of the complex artfulness of the *Letters*: natural specimens of American life collected by the farmer from the land have some perplexing and politically dangerous material concealed within their rustic medium. The exuberant physical description of America holds the germinating seed of America's literary utterance, and this turns out to be a much more complicated and ambiguous florescence than ideologues of either persuasion would be able to countenance. In the *Letters* both personal identity and group loyalties are not fixed principles but mutable products of environment and circumstance. Crèvecœur's adaptiveness in life was not casual but costly, and the distress finds an artistic voice in the book. One of the narrative's most striking qualities is its ability to catch the distraught, confused voice of the man in the middle, neither loyalist nor patriot, in a world where he is daily called upon to declare himself one or the other. By the close of the *Letters* Farmer James has become every private man whose life has been caught up and swept into public events with whose magnitude he is neither able nor willing to engage.

To understand the nature of the havoc wrought by the Revolution as it is exemplified in the *Letters*, we need to trace some of the ideas (and their destabilizing internal contradictions) held by Crèvecœur and expressed through the book's various points of view, most notably that of the narrator Farmer James himself. The *Letters* belong to a European tradition of epistolary fiction, reworked to encompass a totally new environment. In addition to their obvious documentary and empirical interest, they are also an exercise and an experiment in theory: the thinking of French Enlightenment writing translated into fiction in an American context. James has many available models of order to help him make sense of the plenitude of American life; it is the progressive failure of these models to deal not only with irreducible brute realities but

with his reactions to them that leads his narrative into ideological confusion. The honesty and fullness with which James is
able to register the disorientating effects on the personality of
this intellectual revolution is what makes his work more than
a documentary record of colonial life in the years surrounding the American War of Independence.[10]

First and foremost, however, this is what it appears to be,
and the way it was received by the majority of its contempor-
ary readers. It describes itself as by 'a genuine farmer', James,
who lives in the Quaker colony (later state) of Pennsylvania
just inland from the eastern seaboard of America. Crèvecœur
himself farmed further north at Pine Hill in New York State,
and we may assume that many of the details of farming life
in the second and third Letters were drawn from his own
experience. Moving on from this local agricultural documentary (which became a valued source of information about
ordinary life in the colonies), later Letters take up a more
dispassionately 'philosophical' (in the eighteenth-century sense)
stance of observation to describe in almost sociological or
anthropological fashion the 'Island of Martha's Vineyard', and
'Manners and Customs at Nantucket' (an island off the colony

[10] Much of Crèvecœur's initial success may be attributed to the timeli-
ness of his work. The *Letters* were received by their first European readers
(many of whom would have been familiar with its French Enlightenment
philosophical underpinnings) as the best single source of information about
America. Apart from the Marquis François-Jean de Chastellux, who had
visited America during the War of Independence as a major-general in
Rochambeau's army and subsequently published *Voyage dans l'Amérique
septentrionale* (Travel in North America) in 1780, there were as yet scarcely
any attempts to describe the nature of this new nation struggling into being.
The *Letters* make an important counterpart to Thomas Jefferson's *Notes on
the State of Virginia* (written 1781–2; published 1787), which were composed in response to a set of queries constructed by Barbé-Marbois, the
French *chargé d'affaires*, to inquire on behalf of his government into the
geographical, social, and political conditions of all the newly independent
colonies. Barbé-Marbois, being French consul-general in America, was not
only Crèvecœur's close acquaintance but his immediate superior during the
1780s, and his questionnaire was heavily influenced, if not actually formu-
lated, by the French *philosophes* of the Jardin du Roi who also stand closely
behind the *Letters from an American Farmer*.

of Massachusetts and the site, with 'Martha's Vineyard', of early America's important whaling industry). The narrative then ranges further afield to consider the southern city of Charles Town and broach the vexed question of slavery (Letter IX); another letter adopts a conventional technique of eighteenth-century travel narratives to give an account, as from 'Mr Iw——n Al——z', of a visit to John Bartram (here called Bertram), the famous Quaker naturalist. Throughout, documentary and what we should now call sociological observations are interspersed with meditations and questions which reflect not only the farmer's direct experience but Europe's urgent inquiries of America, most notably 'What is an American?' Although none of these should be taken simply as records of the author's own agricultural experiences, all contribute to the charming and largely harmonious celebration of colonial America for which Crèvecœur's work is justly famous. We should not be misled, however, into believing this to be the only level on which the book works for its reader.

The narrative starts out propitiously enough, in a serio-comic discussion between James, his wife, and their minister about the practicalities and proprieties of 'Mr F.B.'s' request that James should correspond with him on matters relating to farming life in America. James's lack of learning, says the minister, will be made up for by the novelty of his information; the richness of his matter will more than compensate for the awkwardness of his manner, the true voice of the American farmer being its own guarantee of sincerity. 'Remember', says James to his reader, 'that I am neither philosopher, politician, divine, or naturalist, but a simple farmer.'[11] Much more is at issue here than the potential embarrassment

---

[11] It is worth noting that in addition to being a farmer, James is the 'surveyor' both of the new settlements and of the progress of recent emigrants, as he charts and estimates their steps to success. Surveying and map-making (Crèvecœur's own profession before he became a farmer) were important practical pursuits which represent quintessentially American activities in the early literature of the new land. William Byrd's *History of the Dividing*

of an inelegant stylist: a number of cardinal presumptions about the nature and virtue of life in the New World are already under discussion. First of all there is James's occupation. The practice of agriculture in the colonies was quite literally a matter of survival in a fragile patch of cultivation hewn from a 'crazy land', a powerful natural environment ready at every moment to reclaim its territorial wilderness. But even the term 'farmer'—as Crèvecœur's narrator is at pains to point out—meant something rather specific in America in the late eighteenth century. He was not, as in Europe, a tenant owing taxes and paying tithes, but a freeholder, a man without a master. It was an important distinction in the evolving definition of what it meant to be an American. In 1794 the English traveller Thomas Cooper claimed that nine-tenths of American legislators were farmers.[12] More than this, however, the farmer represented a rhetorical and philosophical ideal to certain writers of the Enlightenment, and this ideal carried stylistic implications for a distinctive American idiom.

The adjective 'physiocratic' was coined by Pierre-Samuel Du Pont de Nemours, a French friend of Thomas Jefferson and disciple of the political economist François Quesnay. It describes the belief that the wealth and virtue of nations resides in the cultivation of land, and that agrarian nations are the most contented. Jefferson famously praised farmers as 'the chosen people of God', and adapted physiocratic ideals to the American environment.[13] Writing to John Jay

Line (1729; publ. 1741), and the *Journals* of Lewis and Clark (1814), like Crèvecœur's *Letters*, developed the idiom of narrators who charted the land, its people, and its possibilities. But in the *Letters* Crèvecœur is a tricky surveyor: the map references he gives for Nantucket, for example, are not only wildly wrong but nonsensical, and contribute to the work's destabilizing of any kind of simple documentary purpose.

[12] See his *Some Information Respecting America, &c.* (London, 1794), 73.
[13] *Notes on the State of Virginia* (New York, Evanston, and London, 1964), 157. For more information on the physiocrats, see *The Correspondence of Jefferson and Du Pont de Nemours*, with an Introduction on Jefferson and the Physiocrats by Gilbert Chinard (Baltimore, 1931).

in 1785, he declared: 'Cultivators of the earth are the most valuable citizens. They are the most vigorous, the most independent, the most virtuous, and they are tied to their country and wedded to it's [*sic*] liberty and interests by the most lasting bands.'[14] Crèvecœur's distant relative and sponsor Étienne-François Turgot was a leading French physiocrat who encouraged his protégé to write on farming matters, both as philosophical correspondent and as practical farmer. The Farmer James of the *Letters* is a 'farmer of feelings' (p. 26), whose occupation is a complex mixture of what we might call 'genuine' and 'philosophic' farming; in Letter II, for example, he gives tips on making good mead along with advocacy of the virtues of simple agrarian life. Both strands are united in his observations in the same letter on his livestock, practical detail seamlessly woven into meditative reflection on his duty as master and superior: 'the law is to us precisely what I am in my barnyard, a bridle and check to prompt the strong and greedy from oppressing the timid and weak.' The world-famous Quaker naturalist John Bartram, too, describes himself in Letter XI as 'but a ploughman'.

Behind both the practical farmer and the physiocratic theory lies a sustained tradition of agrarian literary reference going back to Virgil's *Georgics*; Crèvecœur's *Letters* renew the symbolic currency of the plough in an enlightened American context. The minister declares that he has 'composed many a good sermon' while following the plough; in Letter II this quintessentially agricultural occupation becomes an ethical standard of universal application:

Often when I plough my low ground, I place my little boy on a chair which screws to the beam of the plough . . . I am now doing for him, I say, what my father formerly did for me; may God enable him to live that he may perform the same operations for the same purposes when I am worn out and old! . . . the odoriferous furrow

---

[14] *The Papers of Thomas Jefferson*, edited by Julian P. Boyd and others (Princeton, 1950–), vol. 8 (1953), 426.

exhilarates his spirits and seems to do the child a great deal of good, for he looks more blooming since I have adopted that practice; can more pleasure, more dignity be added to that primary occupation? The father thus ploughing with his child, and to feed his family, is inferior only to the Emperor of China ploughing as an example to his kingdom.

This is a myth of stability: the good society is guaranteed by the recurrent, unchanging cycle of life in harmony with the land. Jefferson wrote to Peter Carr in August 1787,

Man was destined for society. His morality therefore was to be formed to this object. He was endowed with a sense of right and wrong merely relative to this. This sense is as much a part of his nature as the sense of hearing, seeing, feeling; it is the true foundation of morality . . . State a moral case to a ploughman and a professor. The former will decide it as well, and often better than the latter, because he has not been led astray by artificial rules.[15]

'Metaphysics' became a derogatory term in the empirically based ideology of the Enlightenment, 'not', as the historian Daniel Boorstin has put it, 'a branch of philosophy, but a mental disorder'.[16] Observation-based knowledge implied an equality of facts against the hierarchical fictions of the speculative metaphysician; it also posited (in principle) equal access to this knowledge to every rational individual. 'Candour' and 'candid' are recurrent terms in James's self-characterization, words which would surely resonate with an audience which had recently heard the unforgettable first paragraph of Thomas Jefferson's *Declaration of Independence*: 'let facts be submitted to a candid world.' Candour, in the eighteenth century, retained the meaning of its Latin root, newly appropriated by John Locke to describe the receptivity of the mind of a child (and thence any human being not blinded by partiality and prejudice): white, clean, open to evidence, and therefore virtuous. But—and here is the first flaw in the Arcadian image—to

---

[15] *The Papers of Thomas Jefferson*, vol. 12 (1955), 15.
[16] *The Lost World of Thomas Jefferson* (New York, 1948), 133.

insist, as James does, on one's candour with all that powerful philosophic freight, is to invite ambiguity: the truly candid man (like the truly innocent one) would not know himself to be so. It is one of those words which can only be defined with reference to its opposite. Both the text's empirical and its moral authority derive from the authenticity of the farmer's voice, but that authenticity is necessarily compromised by the enlightened framework of its expression, and indeed by the very fact of that expression in printed form.

Writing is itself suspect in a moral environment dedicated to the tilling of the earth, and the book has a voice for this too in Farmer James's wife. She gives early and vigorous expression to what later comes to seem a characteristically American opposition (fully exemplified, for example, in Hawthorne) of writing as 'useful labour', and a corresponding distrust of all art. She makes the more specific point of contrast too, that in England men 'live by writing', which they may well do because 'they have no trees to cut down, no fences to make, no Negroes to buy and to clothe'. In America, 'it is not by writing that we shall pay the blacksmith, the minister, the weaver, the tailor, and the English shop'. John Bartram in Letter XI endures similar doubts from *his* wife about his new vocation to document the natural life of the New World. Once again, in the very evocation of a stable existence of simple agrarian virtue lie the rhetorical seeds of its disruption. Right from the beginning an element of slippage and uncertainty characterizes even the work's most straightforwardly optimistic utterances. Whose voice speaks through Farmer James? Are these 'real' observations, or are they fictions? Whose are the queries which structure the text? None of these questions, of course, have single or simple answers.

For one thing, in the early 1780s the 'new man' of America was not and could not be a single being. John Shy has described how, even at the end of the decade, the United States was 'an improbable political construct' of sectional, class, and racial interests whose differences frequently seemed stronger and more numerous than the common cause that kept them together.[17] Indeed, as late as the 1750s Franklin and Washington had each fought for the interests of his own colony (Pennsylvania and Virginia, respectively) against the competing demands of the other. In that sense, Farmer James's instinct that the common interest of all was membership of the British Empire—though it may have been outrun by the late 1770s—was strongly founded in recent history. It is more the case that, when the 'world turned upside down', he (like his creator Crèvecœur) was among those who were slow to make a matching somersault.

An additional source of tension (inherent from the beginning, but which becomes overt and pressing in the straitened circumstances of the final chapter), is that the physiocratic ideal of unchanging stability pulls against another, equally powerful but opposed principle in the text: the imperative to counter the theory of species degeneration in America. In his gigantic and influential fifteen-volume *Histoire naturelle* (1749–67), the French comte de Buffon had advanced the theory that the soil and climate of the New World were inhospitable to growth and that plants, animals, and men would therefore degenerate in America. The theory of degeneration was supported and furthered by the writings of his fellow *philosophes*, the Abbé Raynal and the Abbé Du Pauw, and continued influential in Paris up to the time when Franklin and Jefferson made their appearance in the salons. Crèvecœur's *Letters* not only purported to supply much-needed information on the issue, but also to provide the indisputable empirical authority of a qualified working observer. The text's recurrent motif of regeneration and rebirth is radically opposed to Buffon's theory of degeneration: 'In Europe they were as so many useless plants, wanting vegetative mould, and refreshing showers; they withered, and were mowed down

---

[17] 'Franklin, Washington and a New Nation', *Proceedings of the American Philosophical Society*, 131: 3 (1987), 315.

by want, hunger, and war; but now by the power of transplantation, like all other plants they have taken root and
flourished!' (Letter III). Crucially, though, both negative and
positive versions depend on a model of change through time
which is at odds with the universal virtues of agrarian life as
advanced by the physiocrats. Crèvecœur's narrative cannot
make such contradictions square; they are presented, rather,
as serial accounts of reality (Letter II being broadly physiocratic, Letter III broadly progressive, for example), and under
pressure from exigent events they come into irreconcilable
rhetorical conflict in the final Letter.[18]

The *Letters from an American Farmer* begins to develop
an emotional register and a form of verbal expession for
the experience of being 'an American, this new man', as
Crèvecœur famously puts it in the Third Letter. It is a question which glints through all the subsequent refractions of
nineteenth-century American writing. America itself is a
tabula rasa on which Europe can imprint its dreams, and
its nightmares. The most interesting and significant attempt
to unite the book's argument against the degeneratists of
Europe with its advocacy of physiocratic ideals as a realistic
possibility in America is made by the minister in the Intro-
ductory Letter: 'If our soil is not remarkable as yet for the
excellence of its fruits, this exuberance is, however, a strong
proof of fertility, which wants nothing but the progressive
knowledge acquired by time to amend and to correct.' Crucially for the subsequent development of an American literary

---

[18] Crèvecœur's celebration of plenitude and possibility through enu-
meration stands in an already-established tradition in American writing that
includes Captain John Smith's *General History of Virginia, New England,
and the Summer Isles* (1624) and Robert Beverley's *History and Present
State of Virginia* (1705), and later Jefferson's *Notes on the State of Virginia*,
Melville's *Moby-Dick* (with which it shares more than the catalogue of
whale types in the Nantucket Letters), and Whitman's *Leaves of Grass*.
On the controversy over degeneration of species see, for example, Mark
Hulling, *The Autocritique of Enlightenment: Rousseau and the Philosophes*
(Cambridge, Mass., 1994), ch. 5, 'Generation, Degeneration, Regeneration'.

voice, he associates these qualities with the natural expression of Farmer James: 'You will appear to [an English reader] something like one of our wild American plants, irregularly luxuriant in its various branches.' Untamed spontaneity and multiplicity, rather than correctness and fixity, characterize both the land and the style of the American farmer. Crèvecœur had received a good and thorough classical education with the Jesuits. But this classicism comes over in strikingly practical and rather innovative ways in the American Farmer's prose. Allusion is minimal: scarcely any poetry, for example, beyond a couple of references to Pope; no Shakespeare or Milton, despite Crèvecœur's avowed passion for English culture; no Racine or Corneille; no Cervantes. Crèvecœur's language and ideas were influenced by his neighbour, the German Huguenot minister Jean-Pierre Têtard, who during the 1780s also oversaw Noah Webster's education in the writings of the French: Montesquieu, Rousseau, and the Abbé Raynal; as well as the English radical writer Thomas Paine, one of whose more striking stylistic claims was 'I scarcely ever quote; the reason is, I always think'.[19] From the beginning the text suggests that there may be a fundamental connection between ploughing the virgin soil and writing the virgin land:

the people of America, in particular the English descendants, speak the most *pure English* now known in the world. There is hardly a foreign idiom in their language . . . Let Englishmen take notice that when I speak of the American yeomanry, the latter are not to be compared to the illiterate peasantry of their own country. The yeomanry of this country consist of substantial independent freeholders, masters of their own persons and lords of their own soil. These men have considerable education. They not only learn to read, write, and keep accounts; but a vast proportion of them read newspapers every week, and besides the Bible, which is found in all families, they read the best English sermons and treatises upon

---

[19] 'The Forester's Letters', no. 3 (1776), in *The Complete Writings of Thomas Paine*, ed. Philip S. Foner (New York, 1945), ii. 78.

religion, ethics, geography and history; such as the works of Watts, Addison, Atterbury, Salmon, &c . . . in the extent of twelve hundred miles in America, there are very few, I question whether a hundred words, except such as are used in employments, wholly local, which are not universally intelligible.[20]

This passage affirms its literary models and denies them in the same breath; like Franklin in the *Autobiography*, it claims both to be self-authorized, recognizing no authority outside the self, and advertises its conformity to the best stylistic models. Crèvecœur's Farmer James is the consummate embodiment of Webster's linguistic nationalism.

Even this rhetorical ideal (endorsed by its continuities with the Puritan 'plain style') is questioned by a complicating artistry which compromises the authority of unadorned observation. Beyond the literal and empirical evidence lies the figurative possibility of a new life. The newly arrived immigrant begins immediately 'to feel the effects of a sort of resurrection' (Letter III). Scholars have traced literary sources for many of the episodes apparently described from nature by Farmer James: the fable of the hummingbird comes almost directly from Raynal's *Histoire philosophique*; variants of the story of the king-birds and the bees are found in several earlier works, and (as D. H. Lawrence suggested) it becomes here a parable of the 'American resurrection': 'true Yanks escaped from the craw of the king-bird of Europe'; the snake-fangs stuck in the farmer's boots is familiar in the realm of folklore, and the industrious hive obviously refers the reader back to Bernard de Mandeville and his *Fable of the Bees* (1714).[21] In this sense, we may see Crèvecœur as putting together an early mythology of America by translating European motifs to an American context, much as

[20] Noah Webster, *Dissertations on the English Language*, IV (1789; rpt. Gainesville, Fla., 1951), 288–9.

[21] For discussion of these sources, see Thomas Philbrick, *St. John de Crèvecœur* (New York, 1970), 95–6. Lawrence's remark is in *Studies in Classic American Literature*, 33.

Washington Irving would later do when he naturalized the
European folk-tale of Peter Klaus as the story of 'Rip Van
Winkle'.

The animals on James's farm behave themselves as beasts
in his fable of American Enlightened order, but even this
most ordered allegory seems to be predicated on violence
and depredation. The spectre of anarchy inheres in Letter
II's image of harmonious farmyard governance; to a perhaps
surprising extent, cruelty and ferocity structure the narrative
even in its earlier, more optimistic phases. As the book pro-
gresses, James is confronted by sights and events which disturb his equanimity and force fundamental and unwanted
changes upon his settled way of life. In fact, fear is a recurrent note in the farmer's descriptions of the landscape after
the first three Letters. Here is the violent unpredictability of
something larger than and alien to the human nature which
observes it. The awful wildness of American nature seemed
to bring out an answering echo of brute savagery in human
beings, and James's narrative shows a preoccupation—even
a fascination—with violence, even as it asserts order and natural governance. At the end of the Letter (IX) describing the
moral decadence of Charles-Town, James describes his horrific
encounter with the slave in the cage, the direct consequence
of the violence done by one person to another. The birds
and insects which are in the act of devouring the helpless
man are dark shadows or echoes of the king-bird and the
bees in the parable-like account of Letter II. One of the most
agonizing aspects of this awful scene is the farmer-narrator's
impotence to end the poor man's sufferings. Unlike the
earlier episode, in which James represents himself as inter-
vening decisively to rescue the bees from the craw of the bird,
and to restore order and law to the natural economy over
which he rules, here (faced with horror beyond conception)
he can, like the reader of his account, only look on appalled.
It is a grim anticipation of the terrors of the final Letter, which
reduce James to an even more abject passivity. Regeneration

itself involves destruction of an existing state. Newness, and therefore change, are at the heart of the issue.[22]

Human nature itself is threatened by this overwhelming environment. Those who live on the frontier, removed from the civilizing forces of government and trade, are merely 'carnivorous animals of a superior rank, living on the flesh of wild animals'.[23] The repetition is suggestive. Where ploughing calms the mind to regularity and routine, hunting awakens wild feelings in those who pursue it. Crèvecœur's Americans, unlike, for example, the 'Ben Franklin' of the *Autobiography*, are not self-made more or less in despite of circumstances; on the contrary, they are made *by* the opportunities of their surroundings: the 'American' is made by being in America. James himself—then Andrew the Hebridean, the Nantucket whalers, John Bartram the peaceable naturalist—all become the products of their environments. At one level, then, the answer to the question 'What is the American?' is to be found by observing the way the various American landscapes work on the characters of the people who settle there. Again, an idea deriving from the French *philosophes* (this time Montesquieu's *De l'Esprit des Lois* (1748)), comes to have menacing implications in the working out of the fictional logic of the *Letters*. Determinism stalks the pages of the book: 'our opinions, vices, and virtues are altogether local: we are machines fashioned by every circumstance around us'; men are 'like plants', nurtured by their physical surroundings. Here is the land of endless possibilities for the emigrant with 'moderate' talents or inclinations; it is a 'continent for men of middle stations'. 'Moderation', 'decency', and 'competence' are the defining terms of this section of the book. This allows

---

[22] See David Robinson, 'Crèvecœur's James: The Education of an American Farmer', *Journal of English and Germanic Philology*, 80: 4 (Oct. 1981), 558.

[23] On the *Letters* as a text of the frontier, see Richard Slotkin, *Regeneration through Violence: The Mythology of the American Frontier, 1600–1860* (Middletown, Conn., 1973), 259–67.

fairly ordinary men like Andrew the Hebridean (or indeed
James himself) to flourish—but it also introduces a potentially menacing element into the high-day freedoms of the
American climate. Even in the apparently exemplary life
of Nantucket, there is a sign that wants exceeding decent
competence may creep into human existence: 'It is hard to
conceive how a people always happy and healthy . . . never
oppressed with the vapours of idleness, yet should want the
fictitious effects of opium to preserve that cheerfulness to
which their temperance, their climate, their happy situation,
so justly entitle them' (Letter VIII).

The pleasures available to the inhabitants of Nantucket
are defined by their modestness in accordance with the
limited opportunities of their surroundings: 'the pleasure of
going and returning together, of chatting and walking about,
of throwing the bar, heaving stones, etc., are the only entertainments they are acquainted with.' No wonder they take
opium. This small but clearly significant detail in James's
description of the Nantucketers' life tells us something
sobering about the larger framework of the book's paean
to moderation and industrious virtue. For one thing, the
seascapes of Nantucket and Martha's Vineyard are, as Robert
Lawson-Peebles has finely put it, 'horrifically mutable'; the
life of even this most settled of communities is potentially
threatened by an untrustworthy environment.[24] Not reaching for too much is a way of propitiating treacherous natural forces. But it has, inevitably, its emotional backlash in
the people who so restrain themselves. Progress means
change, and change threatens the harmonious stability on
which Farmer James's security and happiness are founded.
No wonder, then, for someone so aware of the individual's

---

[24] *Landscape and Written Expression in Revolutionary America: The
World Turned Upside Down* (Cambridge, 1988), 267. This instability may
have been in the mind of Edgar Allan Poe when he located Edgartown,
on Martha's Vineyard—a town discussed by Crèvecœur—as the place from
which Arthur Gordon Pym sets off on his fabulous and deadly voyage to
the ice-floes of the South Pole.

vulnerability to change and contingency, that the events of
the Revolution create the note of sheer terror sounded in
the final Letter of the book. Crèvecœur's farmer is in no
sense in charge of his destiny.

Many of the changes demanded of the self seem, if not un-
acceptable, almost impossibly difficult. James's final decision,
to leave the settlement and pursue life among the Indians,
is the product only, of desperation and the instinct for self-
preservation. 'I wish for a change of place', he says at the
beginning of the last Letter, expressing the desperate nature
of his situation in this counteraction of every impulse of the
early Letters. He makes a forlorn attempt, by shifting the
myth of the savage from demon to that of untaught child of
nature, to turn back the personal and Revolutionary clock;
but the change, once begun, cannot be halted, just as the
voyage (in myth if not in reality) cannot be reversed or the
conversion undone. 'Distresses of a Frontier Man' dramat-
izes the disintegration of the rational, enlightened society of
Republican America into a nightmare of confusion, incom-
prehension, and premonitions of unspeakable evil. The ideological and rhetorical confusions unite and become manifest
in the near-unseating of James's reason. His removal to the
Indian camp at the end is a journey back in time, to man's
prehistoric origins; perhaps there the natural state will be
peaceable rather than warlike. At this point the American
farmer is driven by self-preservation rather than idealism or
principle. But idealization quickly creeps in, as James imagines his haven; the Indian village becomes, as Richard Slotkin
has put it, 'simply a more extreme form of the New World
society into which he symbolically inducted Andrew the
Hebridean. Freedom, ease of living, easy admission to the
full rights of the citizen, the advantage of a society that has
been freely and rationally chosen and not thrust on one at
birth—all await the "immigrant" to the Indian world.'[25] Or
so, one must add, the theory goes.

[25] *Regeneration through Violence*, 266.

Caught up in the violence of events, the peaceable man tries desperately to preserve his models and his mores when they have, manifestly, become quite inappropriate to the circumstances. Violent times call for violent measures; the Farmer is paralysed by the possibility that these may be the only kind of workable responses. James's programmatic pacifism and horror of violence of all kinds makes him—and his rhetorical model of America—a casualty of the times. James's account creates him as a victim, but in fact the reader must see the chaos as also self-created, the image of the narrator's own moral disintegration, and a kind of Fall presaged in his submission to the seductions of the snakes in Letter II. Both are emblems of the inevitable yielding of human nature to the structural flaw which conditions reality. Models, orders, ideas themselves prove only temporary and illusive dikes shored against the mutability of time. It is hardly surprising that James has difficulty keeping his poised Montesquieuvian philosophy of human nature in focus; under pressure from his terrorized imagination, he retreats to idealism. The Indians whose life he imagines now are quite different from the Indians of the earlier chapters; the contrast reveals both to be essentially creations of desire and fear. And so the cycle of elevation and disillusionment begins once more. Idealization is always dangerous, and carries within itself the inevitability of disenchantment and alienation. At this moment near the end of the book James is at his most 'American', and Crèvecœur's fable touches something at the heart of the self-definition of America. However grim, the experience of the past does not un-write a future story of hope. Sometimes against all the evidence, better times still seem just around the corner.

Is Crèvecœur's Farmer James trapped at the end within a myth of his own designing? Or a European myth, designed by Montesquieu, Buffon, and Raynal? At this point the fables of Enlightenment intersect with another, older model of what was involved in 'becoming American'. The ocean-crossing of the emigrant, it has often been remarked, was a kind of *rite de passage*, a progress from a world of constraints to a boundless land where the figuratively reborn immigrant could become a 'new man'. As such, it was an image of the conversion experience. The story told by the narrative of a sea-change into a new life was traditionally guaranteed by God, the divine authorial presence who presided over the painful renewal and sanctioned its meaning. Remove that authority, and the shaped narrative with its ending in a new beginning is transformed into amorphous at-sea-ness which is able to promise neither resurrection nor significance to suffering in the present. There may well be a biographical parallel here to earlier events in Crèvecœur's life: educated by Jesuits, with their powerful sense of mission and authority, he found a new, apparently human substitute in Enlightenment, only to have its rational explanations pulled from under him by a revolution which seemed to undo all promise of system and order, a chaos which was readily symbolized by its disruptive, destructive effect on the farming environment, and mirrored in the anarchy of soul suffered by the farmer.

At this point the frontier becomes an apt image of the unshaped terror which lies beyond the cultivated landscape. Crèvecœur's language in the early chapters draws on a myth of harmony and unity which is timeless; it cuts increasingly against the time-bound trajectory of the equally powerful myth of progress and personal advancement, which itself has to contend with the spectral shadow of degeneration and death. When the Revolution comes, he cannot ignore the evidence of divisiveness which would later be speedily and effectively elided again by post-Revolutionary American writers seeking to reassert the rhetoric of unity. The final chapter of the *Letters* provides an important indicator to an aspect of the Revolution which was subsequently written out of the record for ideological reasons. Where the early chapters project on to America through Farmer James's voice an essentially 'European' grammar of Americanism based on

French Enlightenment ideology, the idiom of the final chapter succumbs to the disordering skirmishings of the Indians
on the frontier. The frontier remains, as it had always been
for the American Puritans, a demonic world on the fringes
of consciousness, a moral wilderness (like that, at the opposite extreme, of the decadent city Charles-Town), constantly
on the point of encroaching on the realm of virtue. In these
nightmare images the reader glimpses the abandoned or even
murdered 'selves' which remain the negative shadow of the
American Farmer's chosen candid identity. Crèvecœur's discourse of Enlightenment fragments into a sentimental diction
of violated sensibilities. The change of register is a measure
of the magnitude of the disruption: this is indeed a 'world
turned upside down'—but perhaps the most sigificant thing to
note is that James's revised 'grammar of America' is actually
no more adequate to the circumstances than his previous
idiom had been. In fact, it is equally 'European' in a different way. Derived from another phase of Enlightenment
thinking and a different literary realm, it belongs with the
Richardsonian novel of outraged natural virtue.

   William Hazlitt recorded the observation, in his *Conversations of Northcote*, that: 'The fault of American literature
(when not a mere vapid imitation of ours) was, that it ran
too much into dry, minute, literal description; or if it made
an effort to rise above this ground of matter-of-fact, it was
forced and exaggerated, "horrors accumulating on horror's
head".'[26]

   The quotation points to two idiomatic extremes, two rhetorical identities, both borrowed and applied to circumstances
in which they proved inadequately expressive of reality. At
this point in American literature there appears to be neither
any mediating between them, nor any going beyond or outside
their terms. What taxes James almost more than anything

---

[26] William Hazlitt, *Conversations of James Northcote, Esq., R.A.* (1830;
rpt. London, 1952), 88. The allusion is to Shakespeare's *Othello*, III. iii.
370: 'On horror's head horrors accumulate.'

else in this final Letter is that his terror may simply not be accessible to anyone who has not similarly suffered the radical disillusionment of the ideal in the actual. It may, literally, be an incommunicable experience. At first sight, Crèvecœur's *Letters* might seem to be a prime example of just the sort of thing recorded by Hazlitt; the issue bears on the mutually contradictory identities noted above. Taking part in the Indian Wars of the 1750s, Crèvecœur saw himself as a Frenchman in Canada; subsequently he tried to write himself (as J. Hector St John) into an Englishman in the American colonies, then again metamorphosed into an 'American'. These multiple voices became too much for the idiom of his book to bear, and its diction fragments under the burden of multiplicity. In fact, everything in the book has two, quite discontinuous, emotional registers. 'Hector St John, you are an emotional liar', accused Lawrence.[27] But if there is a problem, it is that Crèvecœur's art is not duplicitous enough to smooth over the theoretical contradictions which conditioned and then splintered his experience. The book is the richer for it.[28]

The changes brought by the Revolution to colonial farming life were, then, so catastrophic as to bring about the creation almost of a new self: in 1787, once more in French, Crèvecœur described himself as no longer 'l'ancien *moi*, que vous avez connu dans le tems [*sic*] de mon bonheur et de ma liberté' (the old self that you knew in the days of my happiness and liberty).[29] Under pressure of circumstances, he too, like Andrew the Hebridean, had become (and not

[27] *Studies in Classic American Literature*, 30.

[28] As he revised and translated the *Letters* for a French audience, Crèvecœur jettisoned Farmer James and his attractively feisty wife entirely; the persona and complex point of view fragmented into a much-expanded compilation of documents of miscellaneous provenance, neutrally edited. If the French *Lettres d'un cultivateur américain* has greater documentary interest as information about life in colonial America, its artistic integrity has been fatally compromised.

[29] *Lettres* (1787), i. 475; cited by Chevignard, 'Crèvecœur in the Looking Glass', 178.

for the first time) a 'new man', in his own disastrous attempt to return to France to secure the European inheritance of his children. Unsympathetically viewed, 'Crèvecœur was off to France in high-heeled shoes and embroidered waistcoat, to pose as a literary man, and to prosper in the world'.[30] Crèvecœur, probably like most of the emigrants of whom Andrew is the representative, did not choose to be 'reborn', he had it thrust upon him, much against his will, by circumstances. 'Je devins un nouvel homme', as he put it in a letter of 1780; 'Je trouvai dans la solitude des jouissances que je ne connaissais pas auparavant.'[31] Becoming a real American is a baptism by fire indeed, and it was one which he sought to avoid for himself. In a sense, his fiction had more integrity than he did. All theory to the contrary, the 'new man' he created in Farmer James did not grow easily and organically out of the old like a butterfly emerging from a chrysalis; he was born of struggle and violence: 'Pardon my repetitions, my wild, my trifling reflections, they proceed from the agitations of my mind, and the fulness of my heart; the action of thus retracing them seems to lighten the burthen, and to exhilarate my spirits' (Letter XII).

Questions multiply; from the earlier philosophical inquiry 'Who is an American?', the narrative advances to more general, more helpless existential cries: 'What then is man?' 'Where shall man be happy?' 'Is there then no superintending power . . . ?' When the disorientation becomes overwhelming, even the existential plea is drowned in the cry of protest with which, the world over, humanity meets the mystery of pain: 'Why has he been created to suffer?' 'Why has the Master of the world permitted so much indiscriminate evil throughout every part of this poor planet, at all times and among all kinds of people?' The spectacle of unassimilable chaos outside

---

[30] *Studies in Classic American Literature*, 35.

[31] 'I became a new man . . . I found in solitude pleasures which I did not know about previously.' Letter quoted by Chevignard, 'Crèvecœur in the Looking Glass', 180.

produces inner fragmentation: 'I fly from one erratic thought to another, and my mind, irritated by these acrimonious reflections, is ready sometimes to lead me to dangerous extremes of violence.' The orderly, rule-governed world of the early chapters has disintegrated into fragments of horror. In the midst of crisis, the providential plan is not visible; it is one of the strengths of Crèvecœur's prose that it can convey the experience of living in history, without the comfort of perspective on its outcome. Harmony and unity, progress and providential purposes, are revealed as abstract principles hopelessly compromised by the manifest contradictions of experience. Like all the best American literature, the *Letters* encounters both poles and refuses to settle for either. So it seems entirely right that at the end, and in the face of everything which suggests its futility, the American farmer should still be making plans for a future idyll.

James's final Letter is written from the heart of the volcano. In the slaying of identity lies the mystery and the agony of rebirth: the tragedy of the immigrant—and, it turns out, the American farmer—is that he must, without guarantees, lose his old life and hope to find a new one. The book brings us within range of that strange closeness, in experience, of death to birth. Both are moments of metamorphosis: James's story, like America's, is an unfinished and uncertain one; it takes shape at a moment when the theory is known and admirable in the abstract, but the reality presents only a horror of uncertainty. He is like the kind of sleepwalker who inhabits the novels of Charles Brockden Brown, helplessly approaching the point of catastrophe, a violent end from which he is powerless to save himself: 'Whichever way I look, nothing but the most frightful precipices present themselves to my view, in which hundreds of my friends and acquaintances have already perished; of all animals that live on the surface of this planet, what is man when no longer connected with society, or when he finds himself surrounded by a convulsed and half-dissolved one?' (Letter XII).

James's solution to the intolerableness of his present position would become a familiar one in American literature and culture: move out and on, begin something new when the old goes sour and the going gets tough. His final decision to join the Indians is a secession like that of the United States themselves from Britain; in it lies symbolically Natty Bumppo's progressive movement west ahead of the eastern settlers in Fenimore Cooper's Leatherstocking novels, Huck Finn's resolve to 'light out for the territory', and countless modern American road-movies. Among them all, Crèvecœur is perhaps unique in dramatizing the *agony* of the decision to leave the known for the unfathomable—which must also have been the pre-emigrant moment of every hard-pressed Scottish or Irish crofter failing to make the intolerable co-ordinates of the present existence add up to a life, and weighing against these the unknown terrors and possibilities of the New World.

With hindsight, we may see the *Letters'* concern with 'process' rather than outcome as typically American: its structure reflects the open-ended experience of becoming, not the meditated accomplishment of being. In the early Letters it is clear that Farmer James is content now; he has no wish for progress or for change. 'I have never possessed or wished to possess anything more than what could be earned or produced by the united industry of my family. I wanted nothing more than to live at home independent and tranquil and to teach my children how to provide the means of a future ample subsistence, founded on labour, like that of their father.' But America demands it. And, as I have suggested, the working out of European ideas in an American context creates a kind of inherent instability in Crèvecœur's text which means that the larger argument of the *Letters* moves backwards from the idea of an American to the process of becoming one. Farmer James is making plans about what he will do next; the reader has no way of knowing whether he managed to accomplish them. His story, like an Emily

Dickinson poem with its characteristically arrested ending in a dash, is an unfinished and unfinishable one. The book closes, then, on a historical and personal pivot; both America and its Farmer stand poised on the brink of a new identity. At the end of the final Letter, James (like Benjamin Franklin's narrator) identifies his fate with that of his country. But his optative mode is an intrinsically qualified one. The future is deeply uncertain, but there can be no turning back from the precipice.

Crèvecœur's *Letters from an American Farmer* suggests an American myth with true tragic potential nowhere encompassed in the 'American Dream' of progress towards an ever-brighter future. Many great American books chart the disillusionment, criticism, sometimes cynicism which accompanies the perhaps inevitable failure of the American Dream. None is more able than Crèvecœur's narrative to suggest the tragedy which lurks in the repeated enactment of the Dream itself, in which the loss of the present becomes the price paid for the ever-receding promise of the future. John Berryman's translation 'Mr Heartbreak' suggests that, in the sea-change from the dreams of the Old World to the realities of the New, the 'new man' suffers a shattering which may involve more than that of his abstract ideals.

NOTE ON THE TEXT

The *Letters from an American Farmer* were first published in London by Davies and Davis (the publishers of Samuel Johnson) in 1782. It was not obviously a potential best-seller, and the publishers made a cautious bargain with the author, giving him 30 guineas for his manuscript essays in May 1781, with a promise of an unspecified 'present' if the public were to like the book. The *Letters* were instantly popular in England, for a variety of reasons. Reformers like William Godwin and Thomas Paine approved its radical anti-government implications; Romantic writers like William Hazlitt, P. B. Shelley, and Samuel Tayler Coleridge admired its lyrical descriptions of a virtuous life close to nature; and there was a general demand for documentary detail about America as the Revolutionary War of Independence drew towards its end. Despite the publishers' initial caution, individual essays began to be reprinted in journals and magazines almost immediately, and a second edition was called for a year later, in 1783. For the next fifty years the *Letters* had only moderate fame in America, but there were rapid Dutch and German translations, and constant European demand resulted in editions appearing in Dublin, Belfast, Leipzig, Leiden, Paris, and Maastricht. The book's timely evocations of the turmoil of civil strife of the American Revolutionary War caught public attention in France, and influential French literati (amongst whom Crèvecœur was by this stage living) called, on both patriotic and philosophic grounds, for the work to be translated into French. Crèvecœur had virtually to re-learn his native language in order to produce the further revised and much expanded *Lettres d'un cultivateur américain* for publication in 1784.

This edition is based on the revised 1783 text, which includes an 'Accurate Index' and a new 'Advertisement' in which the author pulls back from his original announcement of an imminent second volume of the work. The present edition restricts editorial changes to the 1783 text to minimal corrections of what are probably typesetter's errors. Crèvecœur's occasionally archaic spelling is unobtrusive and does not cause confusion; I have not altered it or regularized spellings of place-names. Orthography, particularly of Indian appellations, was notably unstable throughout the eighteenth century; more specifically, American spelling was beginning to distinguish itself from English just as Crèvecœur was writing, and it has therefore seemed important not to remove the minor inconsistencies (e.g. 'cruize' / 'cruise') which may be an indicator of the small but significant part which the *Letters* played in this process.

The following list indicates the emendations to the 1783 text made for the current edition:

p. 15, l. 24	out-lines/outlines
p. 52, l. 12	affect/effect
p. 55, l. 4	destinctions/distinctions
p. 57, l. 14	distnace/distance
p. 85, l. 3	posterity/prosperity [erratum indicated at the end of the 1783 text]
p. 91, l. 7	there/their [erratum indicated at the end of the 1783 text]
p. 91, l. 33	import/export
p. 93, l. 12	*these*/these
p. 103, l. 14	*Eartham/Eastham*
p. 105, l. 26	pegeantry/pageantry
p. 146, l. 24	predeliction/predilection
p. 152, l. 32	Masaical/Mosaical
p. 164, l. 11	full stop changed to comma
p. 169, l. 21	screems/screams
p. 177, l. 5	desert/dessert
p. 213, l. 34	Maniton/Manitou

Crèvecœur's text contains one or two brief explanatory notes, which are reproduced at the foot of the relevant page, and indicated in the text by a superscript numeral. The editor's explanatory notes are indicated in the text by an asterisk and appear at the end of the book.

SELECT BIBLIOGRAPHY

Works by Crèvecœur

Voyage dans la Haute Pennsylvanie et dans l'état de New-York. 'Par un Membre Adoptif de la Nation Onéida' (Paris, 1801).

Letters from an American farmer, reprinted from the original edition: with preface by W. P. Trent and Introduction by Ludwig Lewisohn (London, 1908).

Sketches of Eighteenth-Century America: More Letters from an American Farmer, ed. H. L. Bourdin, R. H. Gabriel, and S. T. Williams (New Haven, Conn., 1925).

Crèvecœur's Eighteenth-Century Travels in Pennsylvania and New York, selections from the 'Voyage' . . . , trans. Percy G. Adams (Lexington, Ky., 1961).

Journey into Northern Pennsylvania and the State of New York, trans. Clarissa S. Bostelmann (Ann Arbor, Mich., 1964).

The Divided Loyalist: Crèvecœur's America, selected from his Letters and Sketches, introd. Marcus Cunliffe (London, 1978).

Letters from an American Farmer and Sketches of Eighteenth-Century America, ed. Albert Stone (New York, 1981).

Bibliography

CUTTING, ROSE MARIE, *John & William Bartram, William Byrd II, and St. John de Crèvecœur: A Reference Guide* (Boston, 1976).

RICE, HOWARD C., 'The American Farmer's Letters, With a Checklist of the Different Editions', *The Colophon*, 18 (1933).

Biography

ALLEN, GAY WILSON, and ROGER ASSELINEAU, *St. John de Crèvecœur* (New York, 1987).

DE CRÈVECŒUR, ROBERT, *Saint John de Crèvecœur: sa vie et ses œuvres* (Paris, 1883).

MITCHELL, JULIA POST, *St. Jean de Crèvecœur* (New York, 1916).

Critical and Historical Studies

BEIDLER, PHILIP, 'Franklin and Crèvecœur's "Literary" Americans', *Early American Literature*, 13 (Spring 1978).

BERANGER, JEAN F., 'The Desire for Communication: Narrator and Narratee in *Letters from an American Farmer*', *Early American Literature*, 12: 1 (Spring 1977).

BEWLEY, MARIUS, *The Eccentric Design* (London, 1959).

CHEVIGNARD, BERNARD, 'St. John de Crèvecœur in the Looking Glass: *Letters from an American Farmer* and the Making of a Man of Letters', *Early American Literature*, 19: 2 (Fall 1984).

CUNLIFFE, MARCUS, 'St. John de Crèvecœur Revisited', *Journal of American Studies*, 9 (August 1975).

FLIEGELMAN, JAY, *Prodigals and Pilgrims* (Cambridge, 1982).

FRANKLIN, WAYNE, *Discoverers, Explorers, Settlers: The Diligent Writers of Early America* (Chicago and London, 1969).

JEHLEN, MYRA, 'J. Hector St. Crèvecœur: A Monarcho-Anarchist in Revolutionary America', *American Quarterly*, 31 (Summer 1979), 204–22.

LAWRENCE, D. H., *Studies in Classic American Literature* (London, 1924; rpt. Harmondsworth, 1971).

LAWSON-PEEBLES, ROBERT, *Landscape and Written Expression in Early America: The World Turned Upside Down* (Cambridge, 1988).

MARX, LEO, *The Machine in the Garden: Technology and the Pastoral Idea in America* (New York, 1968).

MINTER, DAVID, *The Interpreted Design* (New Haven, Conn., 1969).

MOIIR, JAMES C., 'Calculated Disillusionment; Crèvecœur's *Letters* Reconsidered', *South Atlantic Quarterly*, 69 (Summer 1970), 354–63.

PHILBRICK, THOMAS, *St. John de Crèvecœur* (New York, 1970).

PLUMSTEAD, A. W., 'Hector St. John de Crèvecœur,' in *American Literature 1764 –1789, The Revolutionary Years*, ed. E. Emerson (Madison, Wis., 1977).

RABAN, JONATHAN, *Hunting Mr. Heartbreak* (London, 1990).

RAPPING, ELAYNE ANTLER, 'Theory and Expression in Crèvecœur's America', *American Quarterly*, 19 (Winter 1967).

RICE, HOWARD C., *Le Cultivateur américain: étude sur l'œuvre de Saint John de Crèvecœur* (Paris, 1932).

ROBINSON, DAVID, 'Crèvecœur's James: The Education of an American Farmer', *Journal of English and Germanic Philology*, 80: 4 (Oct. 1981).

RUCKER, MARY E., 'Crèvecœur's *Letters* and Enlightenment Doctrine', *Early American Literature*, 13 (Fall 1978), 193–212.

SLOTKIN, RICHARD, *Regeneration through Violence: The Mythology of the American Frontier, 1600–1860* (Middletown, Conn., 1973).

TYLER, MOSES COIT, *The Literary History of the American Revolution, 1763–1783*, 2 vols. (New York, 1897).

ZIFF, LARZAR, *Writing in the New Nation: Prose, Print, and Politics in the Early United States* (New Haven and London, 1991).

CHRONOLOGY OF
J. HECTOR ST JOHN DE CRÈVECŒUR

1735   Michel-Guillaume-Jean de Crèvecœur born 31 January in Caen, France, to family of minor Norman nobility. Classical education at the Jesuit Collège Royal de Bourbon, where he studies Latin, rhetoric, mathematics, and theology.

1754   Pays extended visit to distant British relatives in Salisbury; engagement to a merchant's daughter ends suddenly with her premature death.

1755   Travels to Canada (New France), where he signs up as a cadet for four years in a French regiment based in the St Lawrence Valley; at the outbreak of the French and Indian War holds the rank of lieutenant.

1759   Wounded in action on the Plains of Abraham, 13 September, in the battle in which his French commander Montcalm loses Canada to the English. That autumn surrenders commission for £240 in mysterious circumstances. Travels widely in Pennsylvania and New York State, arriving in New York 16 December.

1765   Becomes official resident of New York and is naturalized as British subject, changing name to J. Hector St John. Begins new career as travelling merchant and surveyor, covering territory from Vermont to Virginia.

1766–7 Adopted as an honorary member of the Oneida tribe, whom he visits in Connecticut.

1767   Joins exploring and surveying party in spring and summer, travelling over Appalachians, down the Ohio River to St Louis, up Mississippi to Great Lakes, and returning to New York via Niagara, Mohawk Valley, and Albany.

1769   Marries Mehitabel Tippett of an established Westchester family. Purchases farm-land in Orange County. Spends following seven years domestically at Pine Hill, cultivating his farm and friendship with Hudson River neighbours, who include Cadwallader Colden, William Seton, and the Huguenot pastor Jean Pierre Têtard. Writes *Letters from an American Farmer* during these years.

1776   Revolutionary War hostilities escalate locally; Crèvecœur unable to take sides.

1778   Travels to New York City as first step to returning to France to safeguard his children's rights of inheritance. Suspected of spying, he is detained and his MSS confiscated by British authorities occupying New York; suffers nervous collapse.

1780   Authorities release him to travel in September, but his ship to England blockaded by French fleet supporting American struggles for independence. Finally lands in Ireland, and travels to London.

1781   Sells MS of *Letters* to Davies & Davis for 30 guineas. Subsequently continues to France on family business, recuperating at Caen for the rest of the year before settling temporarily in Paris. Joins circle of intellectuals including Turgot, Buffon, and Benjamin Franklin, becoming a favourite of Rousseau's friend Madame d'Houdetot.

1782   *Letters* published in London; immediately popular in England with reformers like Godwin and Paine, and Romantic radicals such as Hazlitt, Shelley, and Coleridge. The work receives moderate welcome in America, but constant European demand results in new editions in Dublin, Belfast, Leipzig, Leiden, Paris, and Maastricht. Re-learns French to produce expanded translation of *Letters* (published 1784). Writes comprehensive report for French government on American colonies' struggle for independence; becomes consular appointee, and chooses placement in New York.

1783   Received in New York as Louis XVI's official counsel; returns home to find Pine Hill burned by Indians, wife dead, and children gone. Traces children to custody of Gustavus Fellowes, Bostonian neighbour of five seamen succoured by Crèvecœur in 1781.

1784   Reunited with children in Boston. French translation of *Letters* published.

1783–9 Immerses himself in business in New York. Establishes packet line running from Lorient to New York for ten years; encourages importation of French luxury goods. Publishes newspaper articles on practical aspects of farming under pseudonym 'Agricola'. Sponsors agricultural improvements in France and America. Helps to found botanical gardens in New Jersey and New Haven; given freedom of latter city in gratitude. Distributes French medical journals to American doctors, seeds to Harvard College, and copies of Washington's speeches to French newspapers. Supplies information on new Republic of America for French *Encyclopédie*.

1785–7 Returns to France on sick leave.

1789   Elected to Société Royale d'Agriculture and the American Philosophical Society.

1790   Worsening health prompts second return to Paris, where he avoids entanglement in French Revolution.

1792   Allowed to resign from diplomatic service, he retires to Normandy. Apart from brief visits to Hamburg and Munich, spends remainder of his life in provincial obscurity.

1794   Unsuccessful attempt to return to America when Reign of Terror overtakes France.

1796   Elected to the Institute (as the Académie Française is renamed following the Revolution).

1800   Begins writing *Voyage dans la Haute Pennsylvanie et dans l'État de New York* (published 1801).

1813   Dies aged 78, with other literary materials unpublished.

1925   *Sketches of Eighteenth-Century America* published after discovery of MS in Normandy by Henri L. Bourdin.

LETTERS

FROM AN

AMERICAN FARMER:

DESCRIBING
CERTAIN PROVINCIAL SITUATIONS,
MANNERS, AND CUSTOMS,

NOT GENERALLY KNOWN;

AND CONVEYING
SOME IDEA OF THE LATE AND PRESENT
INTERIOR CIRCUMSTANCES

OF THE

BRITISH COLONIES

IN

NORTH AMERICA.

———

WRITTEN, FOR THE INFORMATION OF A FRIEND
IN ENGLAND,

By J. HECTOR ST. JOHN,
A FARMER IN PENNSYLVANIA.

A NEW EDITION, WITH AN ACCURATE INDEX.

LONDON:
PRINTED FOR THOMAS DAVIES, IN RUSSELL-STREET, COVENT-
GARDEN; AND LOCKYER DAVIS, IN HOLBORN.
M.DCC.LXXXIII.

ADVERTISEMENT

THE following Letters are the genuine production of the American Farmer whose name they bear. They were privately written, to gratify the curiosity of a friend;* and are made public, because they contain much authentic information, little known on this side the Atlantic. They cannot, therefore, fail of being highly interesting, to the people of England, at a time when every body's attention is directed toward the affairs of America.

That these Letters are the actual result of a private correspondence may fairly be inferred (exclusive of other evidence) from the style and manner in which they are conceived; for, though plain and familiar, and sometimes animated, they are by no means exempt from such inaccuracies as must unavoidably occur in the rapid effusions of a confessedly-inexperienced writer.

Our Farmer had long been an eye-witness of the transactions which have deformed the face of America. He is one of those who dreaded, and has severely felt, the desolating consequences of a rupture between the parent-state and her colonies: for he has been driven from a situation, the enjoyment of which the reader will find pathetically described in the early letters of this volume. The unhappy contest is, at length, however, drawing toward a period; and it is now only left us to hope, that the obvious interests, and mutual wants, of both countries, may, in due time, and in spite of all obstacles, happily re-unite them.

Should our Farmer's letters be found to afford matter of useful entertainment to an intelligent and candid public, a second volume, equally interesting with those now published, may soon be expected. *

ADVERTISEMENT

To the Second Edition

SINCE the publication of this volume; we hear that Mr. St. John has accepted a public employment at New York.* It is therefore, perhaps, doubtful, whether he will soon be at leisure to revise his papers, and give the world a second collection of the American Farmer's Letters.

ABBÉ RAYNAL, F.R.S.

BEHOLD, sir, an humble American planter, a simple cultivator of the earth, addressing you from the farther side of the Atlantic, and presuming to fix your name at the head of his trifling lucubrations. I wish they were worthy of so great an honour. Yet why should not I be permitted to disclose those sentiments which I have so often felt from my heart? A few years since, I met, accidentally, with your Political and Philosophical History, and perused it with infinite pleasure.* For the first time in my life, I reflected on the relative state of nations; I traced the extended ramifications of a commerce which ought to unite, but now convulses, the world; I admired that universal benevolence, that diffusive goodwill, which is not confined to the narrow limits of your own country, but, on the contrary, extends to the whole human race. As an eloquent and powerful advocate, you have pleaded the cause of humanity, in espousing that of the poor Africans. You viewed these provinces of North America in their true light: as the asylum of freedom; as the cradle of future nations, and the refuge of distressed Europeans. Why, then, should I refrain from loving and respecting a man whose writings I so much admire? These two sentiments are inseparable, at least in my breast. I conceived your genius to be present at the head of my study: under its invisible, but powerful, guidance, I prosecuted my small labours; and now, permit me to sanctify them under the auspices of your name. Let the sincerity of the motives which urge me prevent you from thinking, that this well-meant address contains aught but the purest tribute of reverence and affection. There is, no doubt, a secret communion among good men throughout the world; a mental affinity, connecting them by a similitude of sentiments. Then why, though an American, should not I be permitted to share in that extensive intellectual consanguity? Yes, I do: and, though the name of a man, who possesses neither titles nor places, who never rose above the humble rank of a farmer, may appear insignificant: yet, as the sentiments I have expressed are also the echo of those of my countrymen, on their behalf, as well as on my own, give me leave to subscribe myself,

                             Sir,
                             Your very sincere admirer,
Carlisle, in Pennsylvania   J. HECTOR ST. JOHN

TABLE OF CONTENTS

LETTER IX

LETTER X

LETTER XI

LETTER XII

LETTER I

INTRODUCTION

WHO would have thought, that, because I received you with hospitality and kindness, you should imagine me capable of writing with propriety and perspicuity? Your gratitude misleads your judgement. The knowledge, which I acquired from your conversation, has amply repaid me for your five weeks entertainment. I gave you nothing more than what common hospitality dictated; but could any other guest have instructed me as you did? You conducted me, on the map, from one European country to another; told me many extraordinary things of our famed mother-country, of which I knew very little; of its internal navigation, agriculture, arts, manufactures, and trade: you guided me through an extensive maze, and I abundantly profited by the journey; the contrast therefore proves the debt of gratitude to be on my side. The treatment you received at my house proceeded from the warmth of my heart, and from the corresponding sensibility of my wife; what you now desire must flow from a very limited power of mind. The task requires recollection, and a variety of talents which I do not possess. It is true I can describe our American modes of farming, our manners, and peculiar customs, with some degree of propriety, because I have ever attentively studied them; but my knowledge extends no farther. And is this local and unadorned information sufficient to answer all your expectations and to satisfy your curiosity? I am surprised that, in the course of your American travels, you should not have found out persons more enlightened and better educated than I am. Your predilection excites my wonder much more than my vanity; my share of the latter being confined merely to the neatness of my rural operations.

My father left me a few musty books, which *his* father brought from England with him. But what help can I draw from a library consisting mostly of Scotch divinity, the Navigation of Sir Francis Drake, the History of Queen Elizabeth,* and a few miscellaneous volumes? Our minister often comes to see me, though he lives upwards of twenty miles distant. I have shewn him your letter, asked his advice, and solicited his assistance; he tells me that he hath no time to spare, for that, like the rest of us, he must till his farm, and is moreover to study what he is to say on the sabbath. My wife (and I never do any thing without consulting her) laughs, and tells me that you cannot be in earnest. What! says she, James, wouldst thee pretend to send epistles to a great European man, who hath lived abundance of time in that big house called Cambridge;* where, they say, that worldly learning is so abundant, that people get it only by breathing the air of the place? Wouldst not thee be ashamed to write unto a man who has never in his life done a single day's work, no, not even felled a tree? who hath expended the Lord knows how many years in studying stars, geometry, stones, and flies, and in reading folio books? Who hath travelled, as he told us, to the city of Rome itself! Only think of a London man going to Rome! Where is it that these English folks won't go? One who hath seen the factory of brimstone at Suvius, and town of Pompey under ground!* Wouldst thou pretend to letter it with a person who hath been to Paris, to the Alps, to Petersburgh, and who hath seen so many fine things up and down the old countries; who hath come over the great sea unto us, and hath journeyed from our New Hampshire in the East to our Charles Town in the South; who hath visited all our great cities, knows most of our famous lawyers and cunning folks; who hath conversed with very many king's men, governors, and counsellors, and yet pitches upon thee for his correspondent, as thee calls it? Surely he means to jeer thee! I am sure he does: he cannot be in a real fair earnest. James, thee must read this letter over again, paragraph by paragraph, and warily observe whether thee can'st perceive some words of jesting; something that hath more than one meaning. And now I think on it, husband, I wish thee wouldst let me see his letter. Though I am but a woman, as thee mayest say, yet I understand the purport of words in good measure; for, when I was a girl, father sent us to the very best master in the precinct.*——She then read it herself very attentively. Our minister was present. We listened to and weighed every syllable. We all unanimously concluded that you must have been in a sober earnest intention, as my wife calls it, and your request appeared to be candid and sincere. Then, again, on recollecting the difference between your sphere of life and mine, a new fit of astonishment seized us all!

Our minister took the letter from my wife, and read it to himself. He made us observe the two last phrases, and we weighed the contents to the best of our abilities. The conclusion we all drew, made me resolve at last to write.—— You say you want nothing of me but what lies within the reach of my experience and knowledge: this I understand very well; the difficulty is, how to collect, digest, and arrange, what I know. Next you assert, that writing letters is nothing more than talking on paper; which, I must confess, appeared to me quite a new thought.—Well then, observed our minister, neighbour James, as you can talk well, I am sure you must write tolerably well also; imagine, then, that Mr. F. B. is still here, and simply write down what you would say to him. Suppose the questions he will put to you in his future letters to be asked by him *viva voce*,* as we used to call it at the college; then let your answers be conceived and expressed exactly in the same language as if he was present. This is all that he requires from you, and I am sure the task is not difficult. He is your friend. Who would be ashamed to write to such a person? Although he is a man of learning and taste, yet I am sure he will read your letters with pleasure. If they be not elegant, they will smell of the woods, and be a little wild. I know your turn; they will contain some

matters which he never knew before. Some people are so
fond of novelty, that they will overlook many errors of language for the sake of information. We are all apt to love and
admire exotics, though they may be often inferior to what
we possess; and that is the reason, I imagine, why so many
persons are continually going to visit Italy.——That country
is the daily resort of modern travellers.

James. I should like to know what is there to be seen so
goodly and profitable, that so many should wish to visit no
other country?

Minister. I do not very well know. I fancy their object is
to trace the vestiges of a once-flourishing people now extinct.
There they amuse themselves in viewing the ruins of temples
and other buildings which have very little affinity with those
of the present age, and must therefore impart a knowledge
which appears useless and trifling. I have often wondered that
no skilful botanists or learned men should come over here.
Methinks there would be much more real satisfaction in
observing among us, the humble rudiments and embryos of
societies spreading every where, the recent foundation of our
towns, and the settlements of so many rural districts. I am
sure that the rapidity of their growth would be more pleasing
to behold than the ruins of old towers, useless aqueducts, or
impending battlements.

James. What you say, minister, seems very true. Do go
on. I always love to hear you talk.

Minister. Do not you think, neighbour James, that the
mind of a good and enlightened Englishman would be more
improved in remarking, throughout these provinces, the
causes which render so many people happy? In delineating
the unnoticed means by which we daily increase the extent
of our settlements? How we convert huge forests into pleasing fields, and exhibit, through these thirteen provinces, so
singular a display of easy subsistence and political felicity?

In Italy, all the objects of contemplation, all the reveries
of the traveller, must have a reference to ancient generations,

and to very distant periods, clouded with the mist of ages.—
Here, on the contrary, every thing is modern, peaceful, and
benign. Here we have had no war to desolate our fields.[1] Our
religion does not oppress the cultivators. We are strangers to
those feudal institutions which have enslaved so many. Here
nature opens her broad lap to receive the perpetual accession
of new comers, and to supply them with food. I am sure
I cannot be called a partial American when I say, that the
spectacle, afforded by these pleasing scenes, must be more
entertaining, and more philosophical, than that which arises
from beholding the musty ruins of Rome. Here every thing
would inspire the reflecting traveller with the most philanthropic ideas. His imagination, instead of submitting to the
painful and useless retrospect of revolutions, desolations, and
plagues, would, on the contrary, wisely spring forward to the
anticipated fields of future cultivation and improvement, to
the future extent of those generations which are to replenish
and embellish this boundless continent. There the half-ruined
amphitheatres, and the putrid fevers of the Campania,* must
fill the mind with the most melancholy reflections, whilst he
is seeking for the origin and the intention of those structures
with which he is surrounded, and for the cause of so great
a decay. Here he might contemplate the very beginnings and
outlines of human society, which can be traced no where
now but in this part of the world. The rest of the earth, I am
told, is in some places too full, in others, half depopulated.
Misguided religion, tyranny, and absurd laws, every where
depress and afflict mankind. Here we have, in some measure,
regained the ancient dignity of our species; our laws are
simple and just; we are a race of cultivators; our cultivation
is unrestrained, and therefore every thing is prosperous and
flourishing. For my part, I had rather admire the ample barn
of one of our opulent farmers, who himself felled the first

---

[1] The troubles, that lately convulsed the American colonies, had not
broke out when this and some of the following letters were written.

tree in his plantation, and was the first founder of his settlement, than study the dimensions of the temple of Ceres.*
I had rather record the progressive steps of this industrious
farmer, throughout all the stages of his labours and other
operations, than examine how modern Italian convents can be
supported without doing any thing but singing and praying.

However confined the field of speculation might be here,
the time of English travellers would not be wholly lost. The
new and unexpected aspect of our extensive settlements, of
our fine rivers, that great field of action every where visible, that ease, that peace, with which so many people live
together, would greatly interest the observer: for, whatever
difficulties there might happen in the object of their re-
searches, that hospitality, which prevails from one end of the
continent to the other, would in all parts facilitate their excursions. As it is from the surface of the ground, which we till,
that we have gathered the wealth we possess, the surface of
that ground is therefore the only thing that has hitherto been
known. It will require the industry of subsequent ages, the
energy of future generations, ere mankind here will have
leisure and abilities to penetrate deep, and, in the bowels of
this continent, search for the subterranean riches it no doubt
contains.——Neighbour James, we want much the assistance
of men of leisure and knowledge, we want eminent chemists
to inform our iron masters; to teach us how to make and prepare most of the colours we use. Here we have none equal
to this task. If any useful discoveries are therefore made among
us, they are the effects of chance, or else arise from that
restless industry which is the principal characteristic of these
colonies.

James. Oh! could I express myself as you do, my friend, I
should not balance a single instant; I should rather be anxious
to commence a correspondence which would do me credit.

Minister. You can write full as well as you need, and would
improve very fast. Trust to my prophecy: your letters, at least,
will have the merit of coming from the edge of the great

wilderness, three hundred miles from the sea, and three thousand miles over that sea: this will be no detriment to them, take my word for it. You intend one of your children for the gown,* who knows but Mr. F. B. may give you some assistance when the lad comes to have concerns with the bishop. It is good for American farmers to have friends even in England. What he requires of you is but simple.—What we speak out among ourselves we call conversation, and a letter is only conversation put down in black and white.

James. You quite persuade me. If he laughs at my auk-wardness, surely he will be pleased with my ready compliance. On my part it will be well meant, be the execution what it may. I will write enough, and so let him have the trouble of sifting the good from the bad, the useful from the trifling: let him select what he may want, and reject what may not answer his purpose. After all, it is but treating Mr. F. B. now that he is in London, as I treated him when he was in America under this roof; that is, with the best things I had, given with a good intention, and the best manner I was able. Very different, James, very different indeed, said my wife; I like not thy comparison. Our small house and cellar, our orchard and garden, afforded what he wanted: one half of his time Mr. F. B. poor man, lived upon nothing but fruit-pies, or peaches and milk. Now these things were such as God had given us; myself and wench did the rest. We were not the creators of these victuals, we only cooked them as well and as neat as we could. The first thing, James, is to know what sort of materials thee hast within thy own self, and then, whether thee canst dish them up.—Well, well, wife, thee art wrong for once. If I was filled with worldly vanity, thy rebuke would be timely, but thee knowest that I have but little of that. How shall I know what I am cap-able of till I try? Hadst thee never employed thyself in thy father's house to learn and to practise the many branches of house-keeping that thy parents were famous for, thee wouldst have made but a sorry wife for an American farmer;

thee never shouldst have been mine. I married thee not for
what thee hadst, but for what thee knewest. Doest thee not
observe what Mr. F. B. says beside? He tells me, that the
art of writing is just like unto every other art of man; that
it is acquired by habit and by perseverance. That is singularly true, said our minister. He, that shall write a letter every
day of the week, will, on Saturday, perceive the sixth flowing
from his pen much more readily than the first. I observed,
when I first entered into the ministry and began to preach
the word, I felt perplexed and dry; my mind was like unto
a parched soil, which produced nothing, not even weeds. By
the blessing of heaven, and my perseverance in study, I grew
richer in thoughts, phrases, and words; I felt copious, and
now I can abundantly preach from any text that occurs to
my mind. So will it be with you, neighbour James; begin
therefore without delay; and Mr. F. B.'s letters may be of
great service to you: he will, no doubt, inform you of many
things: correspondence consists in reciprocal letters. Leave
off your diffidence, and I will do my best to help you whenever I have any leisure. Well then, I am resolved, I said, to
follow your counsel: my letters shall not be sent, nor will
I receive any, without reading them to you and my wife.
Women are curious: they love to know their husband's secrets. It will not be the first thing which I have submitted to
your joint opinions. Whenever you come to dine with us,
these shall be the last dish on the table. Nor will they be
the most unpalatable, answered the good man. Nature has
given you a tolerable share of sense, and that is one of her
best gifts, let me tell you. She has given you besides some
perspicuity, which qualifies you to distinguish interesting
objects, a warmth of imagination which enables you to think
with quickness. You often extract useful reflections from
objects which present none to my mind. You have a tender
and a well-meaning heart, you love description, and your
pencil, assure yourself, is not a bad one for the pencil of a
farmer: it seems to be held without any labour. Your mind

is what we called, at Yale college, a *tabula rasa*,* where spontaneous and strong impressions are delineated with facility. Ah, neighbour, had you received but half the education of Mr. F. B. you had been a worthy correspondent indeed. But, perhaps, you will be a more entertaining one, dressed in your simple American garb, than if you were clad in all the gowns of Cambridge. You will appear to him something like one of our wild American plants, irregularly luxuriant in its various branches, which an European scholar may probably think ill placed and useless. If our soil is not remarkable as yet for the excellence of its fruits, this exuberance is however a strong proof of fertility, which wants nothing but the progressive knowledge acquired by time to amend and to correct. It is easier to retrench than it is to add. I do not mean to flatter you, neighbour James; adulation would ill become my character; you may therefore believe what your pastor says. Were I in Europe, I should be tired with perpetually seeing espaliers, plashed hedges, and trees dwarfed into pigmies. Do let Mr. F. B. see on paper a few American wild cherry-trees, such as nature forms them here, in all her unconfined vigour, in all the amplitude of their extended limbs and spreading ramifications,—let him see that we are possessed with strong vegetative embryos. After all, why should not a farmer be allowed to make use of his mental faculties as well as others. Because a man works is he not to think? and, if he thinks usefully, why should not he, in his leisure hours, set down his thoughts? I have composed many a good sermon as I followed my plough. The eyes, not being then engaged on any particular object, leaves the mind free for the introduction of many useful ideas. It is not in the noisy shop of a blacksmith or of a carpenter that these studious moments can be enjoyed. It is as we silently till the ground, and muse along the odoriferous furrows of our low lands, uninterrupted either by stones or stumps. It is there that the salubrious effluvia of the earth animate our spirits, and serve to inspire us. Every other avocation of our farms are severe labours compared to this pleasing occupation. Of all the tasks, which mine imposes upon me, ploughing is the most agreeable, because I can think as I work; my mind is at leisure; my labour flows from instinct as well as that of my horses; there is no kind of difference between us in our different shares of that operation; one of them keeps the furrow; the other avoids it: at the end of my field they turn either to the right or left as they are bid, whilst I thoughtlessly hold and guide the plough, to which they are harnessed. Do therefore, neighbour, begin this correspondence, and persevere. Difficulties will vanish in proportion as you draw near them. You will be surprised at yourself by and by. When you come to look back, you will say as I often said to myself, had I been diffident I had never proceeded thus far. Would you painfully till your stony up-land and neglect the fine rich bottom which lies before your door? Had you never tried, you had never learned how to mend and make your ploughs. It will be no small pleasure to your children to tell hereafter, that their father was not only one of the most industrious farmers in the country, but one of the best writers. When you have once begun, do as when you begin breaking up your summer fallow; you never consider what remains to be done; you view only what you have ploughed. Therefore, neighbour James, take my advice: it will go well with you, I am sure it will.——And do you really think so, Sir? Your counsel, which I have long followed, weighs much with me. I verily believe that I must write to Mr. F. B. by the first vessel.——If thee persistest in being such a fool-hardy man, said my wife, for God's sake let it be kept a profound secret among us. If it were once known abroad that thee writest to a great and rich man over at London, there would be no end of the talk of the people. Some would vow that thee art going to turn author; others would pretend to foresee some great alterations in the welfare of thy family. Some would say this, some would say that. Who would wish to become the subject of public talk? Weigh this matter well before thee beginnest, James:—consider that a

great deal of thy time and of thy reputation is at stake, as I
may say. Wert thee to write as well as friend Edmund,* whose
speeches I often see in our papers, it would be the very self
same thing: thee wouldst be equally accused of idleness, and
vain notions not befitting thy condition. Our colonel would
be often coming here to know what it is that thee canst write
so much about. Some would imagine that thee wantest to
become either an assembly-man* or a magistrate, which God
forbid, and that thee art telling the king's men abundance
of things. Instead of being well looked upon, as now, and
living in peace with all the world, our neighbours would be
making strange surmises: I had rather be as we are, neither
better nor worse than the rest of our country folks. Thee
knowest what I mean, though I should be sorry to deprive
thee of any honest recreation. Therefore, as I have said before,
let it be as great a secret as if it was some heinous crime.
The minister, I am sure, will not divulge it: as for my part,
though I am a woman, yet I know what it is to be a wife.—
I would not have thee, James, pass for what the world calleth
a writer; no, not for a peck of gold, as the saying is. Thy
father, before thee, was a plain-dealing honest man; punctual
in all things. He was one of yea and nay, of few words; all he
minded was his farm and his work. I wonder from whence
thee hast got this love of the pen? Had he spent his time
in sending epistles to and fro, he never would have left thee
this goodly plantation free from debt. All I say is in good meaning. Great people over sea may write to our town's folks,
because they have nothing else to do. These Englishmen are
strange people; because they can live upon what they call
bank notes, without working, they think that all the world
can do the same. This goodly country never would have
been tilled and cleared with these notes. I am sure, when Mr.
F. B. was here, he saw thee sweat and take abundance of
pains. He often told me how the Americans worked a great
deal harder than the home Englishmen: for there, he told us,
that they have no trees to cut down, no fences to make, no

negroes to buy and to clothe. And, now I think on it, when wilt thee send him those trees he bespoke? But, if they have no trees to cut down, they have gold in abundance, they say; for they rake it and scrape it from all parts far and near. I have often heard my grandfather tell how they live there by writing. By writing, they send this cargo unto us, that to the West, and the other to the East, Indies. But, James, thee knowest that it is not by writing that we shall pay the blacksmith, the minister, the weaver, the tailor, and the English shop. But, as thee art an early man, follow thine own inclinations. Thee wantest some rest, I am sure, and why shouldst thee not employ it as it may seem meet unto thee? However, let it be a great secret. How wouldst thee bear to be called, at our country meetings, the man of the pen? If this scheme of thine was once known, travellers, as they go along, would point out to our house, saying, Here liveth the scribbling farmer. Better hear them, as usual, observe, Here liveth the warm substantial family that never begrudgeth a meal of victuals or a mess of oats to any one that steps in. Look how fat and well clad their negroes are.

Thus, Sir, have I given you an unaffected and candid detail of the conversation which determined me to accept of your invitation. I thought it necessary thus to begin, and to let you into these primary secrets, to the end that you may not hereafter reproach me with any degree of presumption. You'll plainly see the motives which have induced me to begin, the fears which I have entertained, and the principles on which my diffidence hath been founded. I have now nothing to do but to prosecute my task.—Remember, you are to give me my subjects, and on no other shall I write, lest you should blame me for an injudicious choice.—However incorrect my style, however inexpert my methods, however trifling my observations may hereafter appear to you, assure yourself they will all be the genuine dictates of my mind, and I hope will prove acceptable on that account. Remember that you have laid the foundation of this correspondence. You well know that I am neither a philosopher, politician, divine, or naturalist, but a simple farmer. I flatter myself, therefore, that you'll receive my letters as conceived, not according to scientific rules, to which I am a perfect stranger, but agreeable to the spontaneous impressions which each subject may inspire. This is the only line I am able to follow: the line which nature has herself traced for me. This was the covenant which I made with you, and with which you seemed to be well pleased. Had you wanted the style of the learned, the reflections of the patriot, the discussions of the politician, the curious observations of the naturalist, the pleasing garb of the man of taste, surely you would have applied to some of those men of letters with which our cities abound. But since, on the contrary, and for what reason I know not, you wish to correspond with a cultivator of the earth, with a simple citizen, you must receive my letters for better or worse.

LETTER II

ON THE SITUATION, FEELINGS, AND
PLEASURES, OF AN AMERICAN FARMER

As you are the first enlightened European I had ever the
pleasure of being acquainted with, you will not be surprised that I should, according to your earnest desire and
my promise, appear anxious of preserving your friendship
and correspondence. By your accounts, I observe a material
difference subsists between your husbandry, modes, and
customs, and ours. Every thing is local. Could we enjoy the
advantages of the English farmer, we should be much happier, indeed; but this wish, like many others, implies a contradiction; and, could the English farmer have some of those
privileges we possess, they would be the first of their class
in the world. Good and evil, I see, are to be found in all
societies, and it is in vain to seek for any spot where those
ingredients are not mixed. I therefore rest satisfied, and thank
God that my lot is to be an American farmer, instead of a
Russian boor or a Hungarian peasant. I thank you kindly for
the idea, however dreadful, which you have given me of their
lot and condition. Your observations have confirmed me in the
justness of my ideas, and I am happier now than I thought
myself before. It is strange that misery, when viewed in
others, should become to us a sort of real good; though I am
far from rejoicing to hear that there are in the world men
so thoroughly wretched. They are no doubt as harmless,
industrious, and willing to work, as we are. Hard is their fate
to be thus condemned to a slavery worse than that of our
negroes. Yet, when young, I entertained some thoughts of
selling my farm. I thought it afforded but a dull repetition of
the same labours and pleasures. I thought the former tedious
and heavy: the latter few and insipid. But, when I came to

consider myself as divested of my farm, I then found the world so wide, and every place so full, that I began to fear lest there would be no room for me. My farm, my house, my barn, presented, to my imagination, objects from which I adduced quite new ideas: they were more forcible than before. Why should not I find myself happy, said I, where my father was before? He left me no good books it is true; he gave me no other education than the art of reading and writing: but he left me a good farm and his experience: he left me free from debts, and no kind of difficulties to struggle with.—I married; and this perfectly reconciled me to my situation. My wife rendered my house all at once cheerful and pleasing: it no longer appeared gloomy and solitary as before. When I went to work in my fields, I worked with more alacrity and sprightliness. I felt that I did not work for myself alone, and this encouraged me much. My wife would often come with her knitting in her hand, and sit under the shady tree, praising the straightness of my furrows and the docility of my horses. This swelled my heart and made every thing light and pleasant, and I regretted that I had not married before. I felt myself happy in my new situation, and where is that station which can confer a more substantial system of felicity than that of an American farmer, possessing freedom of action, freedom of thoughts, ruled by a mode of government which requires but little from us? I owe nothing but a pepper-corn to my country, a small tribute to my king, with loyalty and due respect. I know no other landlord than the Lord of all land, to whom I owe the most sincere gratitude. My father left me three hundred and seventy-one acres of land, forty-seven of which are good timothy meadow,* an excellent orchard, a good house, and a substantial barn. It is my duty to think how happy I am that he lived to build and to pay for all these improvements. What are the labours which I have to undergo? What are my fatigues when compared to his, who had every thing to do, from the first tree he felled to the finishing of his house? Every year I kill from 1500 to 2000 weight of pork, 1200 of beef, half a dozen of good wethers in harvest; of fowls my wife has always a great stock: what can I wish more? My negroes are tolerably faithful and healthy. By a long series of industry and honest dealings, my father left behind him the name of a good man. I have but to tread his paths to be happy and a good man like him. I know enough of the law to regulate my little concerns with propriety, nor do I dread its power. These are the grand outlines of my situation; but as I can feel much more than I am able to express, I hardly know how to proceed. When my first son was born, the whole train of my ideas was suddenly altered. Never was there a charm that acted so quickly and powerfully. I ceased to ramble in imagination through the wide world. My excursions, since, have not exceeded the bounds of my farm; and all my principal pleasures are now centered within its scanty limits: but, at the same time, there is not an operation belonging to it in which I do not find some food for useful reflections. This is the reason, I suppose, that, when you were here, you used, in your refined style, to denominate me the farmer of feelings. How rude must those feelings be in him who daily holds the ax or the plough! How much more refined, on the contrary, those of the European, whose mind is improved by education, example, books, and by every acquired advantage! Those feelings, however, I will delineate as well as I can, agreeably to your earnest request. When I contemplate my wife, by my fire-side, while she either spins, knits, darns, or suckles our child, I cannot describe the various emotions of love, of gratitude, of conscious pride, which thrill in my heart, and often overflow in involuntary tears. I feel the necessity, the sweet pleasure, of acting my part, the part of a husband and father, with an attention and propriety which may entitle me to my good fortune. It is true these pleasing images vanish with the smoke of my pipe, but, though they disappear from my mind, the impression they have made on my heart is indelible. When I play with the infant, my warm imagination runs forward, and eagerly anticipates his future temper

and constitution. I would willingly open the book of fate, and
know in which page his destiny is delineated. Alas! where is
the father, who, in those moments of paternal extacy, can
delineate one half of the thoughts which dilate his heart? I
am sure I cannot. Then again I fear for the health of those
who are become so dear to me; and, in their sicknesses, I
severely pay for the joys I experienced while they were well.
Whenever I go abroad it is always involuntary. I never return
home without feeling some pleasing emotion, which I often
suppress as useless and foolish. The instant I enter on my
own land, the bright idea of property, of exclusive right, of
independence, exalt my mind. Precious soil, I say to myself,
by what singular custom of law is it that thou wast made
to constitute the riches of the freeholder? What should we
American farmers be without the distinct possession of that
soil? It feeds, it clothes, us: from it we draw even a great
exuberancy, our best meat, our richest drink; the very honey
of our bees comes from this privileged spot. No wonder we
should thus cherish its possession: no wonder that so many
Europeans, who have never been able to say that such portion
of land was theirs, cross the Atlantic to realize that happiness!
This formerly rude soil has been converted by my father into
a pleasant farm, and, in return, it has established all our rights.
On it is founded our rank, our freedom, our power, as citizens; our importance, as inhabitants of such a district. These
images, I must confess, I always behold with pleasure, and
extend them as far as my imagination can reach; for this is
what may be called the true and the only philosophy of an
American farmer. Pray do not laugh in thus seeing an artless
countryman tracing himself through the simple modifications
of his life. Remember that you have required it, therefore,
with candour, though with diffidence, I endeavour to follow
the thread of my feelings, but I cannot tell you all. Often,
when I plough my low ground, I place my little boy on a chair
which screws to the beam of the plow. Its motion and that
of the horses please him: he is perfectly happy, and begins

to chat. As I lean over the handle, various are the thoughts which croud into my mind. I am now doing for him, I say, what my father formerly did for me: may God enable him to live that he may perform the same operations for the same purposes when I am worn out and old! I relieve his mother of some trouble while I have him with me; the odoriferous furrow exhilarates his spirits, and seems to do the child a great deal of good, for he looks more blooming since I have adopted that practice. Can more pleasure, more dignity, be added to that primary occupation? The father, thus ploughing with his child, and to feed his family, is inferior only to the emperor of China ploughing as an example to his kingdom.* In the evening, when I return home through my low grounds, I am astonished at the myriads of insects which I perceive dancing in the beams of the setting sun. I was before scarcely acquainted with their existence; they are so small that it is difficult to distinguish them: they are carefully improving this short evening space, not daring to expose themselves to the blaze of our meridian sun. I never see an egg brought on my table but I feel penetrated with the wonderful change it would have undergone but for my gluttony. It might have been a gentle useful hen leading her chicken with a care and vigilance which speaks shame to many women. A cock, perhaps, arrayed with the most majestic plumes, tender to its mate, bold, courageous, endowed with an astonishing instinct, with thoughts, with memory, and every distinguishing characteristic of the reason of man! I never see my trees drop their leaves and their fruit in the autumn, and bud again in the spring, without wonder. The sagacity of those animals, which have long been the tenants of my farm, astonish me: some of them seem to surpass even men in memory and sagacity. I could tell you singular instances of that kind. What then is this instinct which we so debase, and of which we are taught to entertain so diminutive an idea? My bees, above any other tenants of my farm, attract my attention and respect. I am astonished to see that nothing exists but what has its enemy; one species pursues and lives upon the other. Unfortunately our kingbirds* are the destroyers of those industrious insects; but, on the other hand, these birds preserve our fields from the depredation of crows which they pursue on the wing with great vigilance and astonishing dexterity. Thus divided by two interested motives, I have long resisted the desire I had to kill them, until last year, when I thought they increased too much, and my indulgence had been carried too far. It was at the time of swarming, when they all came and fixed themselves on the neighbouring trees, whence they caught those that returned loaded from the fields. This made me resolve to kill as many as I could, and was just ready to fire, when a bunch of bees, as big as my fist, issued from one of the hives, rushed on one of these birds, and probably stung him, for he instantly screamed, and flew, not as before in an irregular manner, but in a direct line. He was followed by the same bold phalanx, at a considerable distance, which unfortunately becoming too sure of victory, quitted their military array and disbanded themselves. By this inconsiderate step they lost all that aggregate of force which had made the bird fly off. Perceiving their disorder, he immediately returned, and snapped as many as he wanted; nay, he had even the impudence to alight on the very twig from which the bees had driven him. I killed him, and immediately opened his craw, from which I took 171 bees. I laid them all on a blanket, in the sun, and, to my great surprise, 54 returned to life, licked themselves clean, and joyfully went back to the hive; where they probably informed their companions of such an adventure and escape, as I believe had never happened before to American bees? I draw a great fund of pleasure from the quails which inhabit my farm: they abundantly repay me, by their various notes and peculiar tameness, for the inviolable hospitality I constantly shew them in the winter. Instead of perfidiously taking advantage of their great and affecting distress, when nature offers nothing but a barren universal bed of snow, when irresistible necessity forces them to my barn doors, I permit them to feed unmolested; and it is not the least agreeable spectacle which that dreary season presents, when I see those beautiful birds, tamed by hunger, intermingling with all my cattle and sheep, seeking, in security, for the poor scanty grain, which, but for them, would be useless and lost. Often in the angles of the fences, where the motion of the wind prevents the snow from settling, I carry them both chaff and grain; the one to feed them, the other to prevent their tender feet from freezing fast to the earth, as I have frequently observed them to do. I do not know an instance in which the singular barbarity of man is so strongly delineated, as in the catching and murthering those harmless birds at that cruel season of the year. Mr. ****, one of the most famous and extraordinary farmers that has ever done honour to the province of Connecticut, by his timely and humane assistance in a hard winter, saved this species from being entirely destroyed. They perished all over the country; none of their delightful whistlings were heard the next spring, but upon this gentleman's farm; and to his humanity we owe the continuation of their music. When the severities of that season have dispirited all my cattle, no farmer ever attends them with more pleasure than I do: it is one of those duties which is sweetened with the most rational satisfaction. I amuse myself in beholding their different tempers, actions, and the various effects of their instinct, now powerfully impelled by the force of hunger. I trace their various inclinations, and the different effects of their passions, which are exactly the same as among men. The law is to us precisely what I am in my barn yard, a bridle and check to prevent the strong and greedy from oppressing the timid and weak. Conscious of superiority, they always strive to encroach on their neighbours. Unsatisfied with their portion, they eagerly swallow it in order to have an opportunity of taking what is given to others, except they are prevented. Some I chide; others, unmindful of my admonitions, receive some blows. Could victuals thus be given to men, without the assistance of any language, I am sure they would not behave better to one another, nor more philosophically, than my cattle do. The same spirit prevails in the stable; but there I have to do with more generous animals; there my well-known voice has immediate influence; and soon restores peace and tranquillity. Thus, by superior knowledge, I govern all my cattle as wise men are obliged to govern fools and the ignorant. A variety of other thoughts croud on my mind at that peculiar instant, but they all vanish by the time I return home. If, in a cold night, I swiftly travel in my sledge, carried along at the rate of twelve miles an hour, many are the reflections excited by surrounding circumstances. I ask myself what sort of an agent is that which we call frost? Our minister compares it to needles, the points of which enter our pores. What is become of the heat of the summer? In what part of the world is it that the N.W.* keeps these grand magazines of nitre? When I see, in the morning, a river over which I can travel, that, in the evening before, was liquid, I am astonished indeed! What is become of those millions of insects which played in our summer fields and in our evening meadows? They were so puny and so delicate, the period of their existence was so short, that one cannot help wondering how they could learn, in that short space, the sublime art to hide themselves and their offspring in so perfect a manner as to baffle the rigour of the season, and preserve that precious embryo of life, that small portion of ethereal heat, which, if once destroyed, would destroy the species! Whence that irresistible propensity to sleep, so common in all those who are severely attacked by the frost! Dreary as this season appears, yet it has, like all others, its miracles. It presents to man a variety of problems which he can never resolve. Among the rest, we have here a set of small birds which never appear until the snow falls. Contrary to all others, they dwell and appear to delight in that element.

It is my bees, however, which afford me the most pleasing and extensive themes. Let me look at them when I will, their government, their industry, their quarrels, their passions, always present me with something new; for which reason, when weary with labour, my common place of rest is under my locust trees, close by my bee-house. By their movements I can predict the weather, and can tell the day of their swarming; but the most difficult point is, when on the wing, to know whether they want to go to the woods or not. If they have previously pitched in some hollow trees, it is not the allurements of salt and water, of fennel, hickory leaves, &c. nor the finest box, that can induce them to stay. They will prefer those rude, rough, habitations, to the best polished mahogany hive. When that is the case with mine, I seldom thwart their inclinations. It is in freedom that they work. Were I to confine them, they would dwindle away and quit their labour. In such excursions we only part for a while. I am generally sure to find them again the following fall. This elopement of theirs only adds to my recreations. I know how to deceive even their superlative instinct. Nor do I fear losing them, though eighteen miles from my house, and lodged in the most lofty trees in the most impervious of our forests. I once took you along with me in one of these rambles, and yet you insist on my repeating the detail of our operations. It brings back into my mind many of the useful and entertaining reflections with which you so happily beguiled our tedious hours.

After I have done sowing, by way of recreation, I prepare for a week's jaunt in the woods, not to hunt either the deer or the bears, as my neighbours do, but to catch the more harmless bees. I cannot boast that this chace is so noble or so famous among men, but I find it less fatiguing, and full as profitable; and the last consideration is the only one that moves me. I take with me my dog, as a companion, for he is useless as to this game. My gun, for no man you know ought to enter the woods without one, my blanket, some provisions, some wax, vermilion, honey, and a small pocket-compass. With these implements I proceed to such woods as are at a considerable distance from any settlements. I carefully examine whether they abound with large trees; if so, I make a small fire, on some flat stones, in a convenient place. On the fire I put some wax: close by this fire, on another stone, I drop honey in distinct drops, which I surround with small quantities of vermilion, laid on the stone; and then I retire carefully to watch whether any bees appear. If there are any in that neighbourhood, I rest assured that the smell of the burnt wax will unavoidably attract them. They will soon find out the honey, for they are fond of preying on that which is not their own; and, in their approach, they will necessarily tinge themselves with some particles of vermilion, which will adhere long to their bodies. I next fix my compass, to find out their course, which they keep invariably strait, when they are returning home loaded. By the assistance of my watch, I observe how long those are returning which are marked with vermilion. Thus, possessed of the course, and, in some measure, of the distance, which I can easily guess at, I follow the first, and seldom fail of coming to the tree where those republics are lodged. I then mark it; and thus, with patience, I have found out sometimes eleven swarms in a season; and it is inconceivable what a quantity of honey these trees will sometimes afford. It entirely depends on the size of the hollow, as the bees never rest nor swarm till it is all replenished; for, like men, it is only the want of room that induces them to quit the maternal hive. Next I proceed to some of the nearest settlements, where I procure proper assistance to cut down the trees, get all my prey secured, and then return home with my prize. The first bees I ever procured were thus found in the woods by mere accident; for, at that time, I had no kind of skill in this method of tracing them. The body of the tree being perfectly sound, they had lodged themselves in the hollow of one of its principal limbs, which I carefully sawed off, and, with a good deal of labour and industry, brought it home, where I fixed it up in the same position in which I found it growing. This was in April. I had five swarms that year, and they have been ever since very prosperous. This business generally takes up a week of my time every fall, and to me it is a week of solitary ease and relaxation.

The seed is by that time committed to the ground. There is nothing very material to do at home, and this additional quantity of honey enables me to be more generous to my home bees, and my wife to make a due quantity of mead. The reason, Sir, that you found mine better than that of others, is, that she puts two gallons of brandy in each barrel, which ripens it, and takes off that sweet, luscious, taste, which it is apt to retain a long time. If we find any where in the woods, no matter on whose land, what is called a bee-tree, we must mark it. In the fall of the year, when we propose to cut it down, our duty is to inform the proprietor of the land, who is entitled to half the contents. If this is not complied with, we are exposed to an action of trespass, as well as he who should go and cut down a bee-tree which he had neither found out nor marked.

We have twice a year the pleasure of catching pigeons, whose numbers are sometimes so astonishing as to obscure the sun in their flight. Where is it that they hatch? for such multitudes must require an immense quantity of food. I fancy they breed toward the plains of Ohio, and those about lake Michigan, which abound in wild oats; though I have never killed any that had that grain in their craws. In one of them, last year, I found some undigested rice. Now the nearest rice fields, from where I live, must be at least 560 miles; and either their digestion must be suspended while they are flying, or else they must fly with the celerity of the wind. We catch them with a net extended on the ground, to which they are allured by what we call *tame wild pigeons*, made blind, and fastened to a long string. His short flights, and his repeated calls, never fail to bring them down. The greatest number I ever caught was fourteen dozen, though much larger quantities have often been trapped. I have frequently seen them at the market so cheap, that, for a penny, you might have as many as you could carry away; and yet, from the extreme cheapness, you must not conclude that they are but any ordinary food; on the contrary, I think they are excellent. Every farmer has a tame wild pigeon in a cage, at his door, all the year round, in order to be ready whenever the season comes for catching them.

The pleasure I receive from the warblings of the birds in the spring is superior to my poor description, as the continual succession of their tuneful notes is for ever new to me. I generally rise from bed about that indistinct interval, which, properly speaking, is neither night nor day; for this is the moment of the most universal vocal choir. Who can listen, unmoved, to the sweet love-tales of our robins, told from tree to tree? or to the shrill cat-birds?* The sublime accents of the thrush, from on high, always retard my steps, that I may listen to the delicious music. The variegated appearances of the dew-drops, as they hang to the different objects, must present, even to a clownish imagination, the most voluptuous ideas. The astonishing art which all birds display in the construction of their nests, ill-provided as we may suppose them with proper tools, their neatness, their convenience, always make me ashamed of the slovenliness of our houses. Their love to their dame, their incessant careful attention, and the peculiar songs they address to her while she tediously incubates their eggs, remind me of my duty, could I ever forget it. Their affection, to their helpless little ones, is a lively precept; and, in short, the whole œconomy, of what we proudly call the brute creation, is admirable in every circumstance; and vain man, though adorned with the additional gift of reason, might learn, from the perfection of instinct, how to regulate the follies, and how to temper the errors, which this second gift often makes him commit. This is a subject on which I have often bestowed the most serious thoughts. I have often blushed within myself, and been greatly astonished, when I have compared the unerring path they all follow, all just, all proper, all wise, up to the necessary degree of perfection, with the coarse, the imperfect, systems of men, not merely as governors and kings, but as masters, as husbands, as fathers, as citizens. But this is a sanctuary in which an ignorant farmer must not presume to enter. If ever man was permitted to receive and enjoy some blessings that might alleviate the many sorrows to which he is exposed, it is certainly in the country, when he attentively considers those ravishing scenes with which he is every where surrounded. This is the only time of the year in which I am avaricious of every moment: I therefore lose none that can add to this simple and inoffensive happiness. I roam early throughout all my fields. Not the least operation do I perform which is not accompanied with the most pleasing observations. Were I to extend them as far as I have carried them, I should become tedious. You would think me guilty of affectation, and perhaps I should represent many things as pleasurable, from which you might not perhaps receive the least agreeable emotions. But, believe me, what I write is all true and real.

Some time ago, as I sat smoking a contemplative pipe in my piazza, I saw, with amazement, a remarkable instance of selfishness displayed in a very small bird, which I had hitherto respected for its inoffensiveness. Three nests were placed almost contiguous to each other in my piazza. That of a swallow was affixed in the corner next to the house, that of a phebe* in the other; a wren possessed a little box, which I had made on purpose, and hung between. Be not surprised at their tameness. All my family had long been taught to respect them as well as myself. The wren had shewn before signs of dislike to the box which I had given it, but I knew not on what account. At last it resolved, small as it was, to drive the swallow from its own habitation, and, to my very great surprise, it succeeded. Impudence often gets the better of modesty, and this exploit was no sooner performed than it removed every material to its own box with the most admirable dexterity. The signs of triumph appeared very visible; it fluttered its wings with uncommon velocity; an universal joy was perceivable in all its movements. Where did this little bird learn that spirit of injustice? It was not endowed with what we term reason! Here then is a proof that both those gifts border very near on one another, for we see the perfection of the one mixing with the errors of the other! The peaceable swallow, like the passive Quaker, meekly sat at a small distance, and never offered the least resistance. But, no sooner was the plunder carried away, than the injured bird went to work with unabated ardour, and, in a few days, the depredations were repaired. To prevent, however, a repetition of the same violence, I removed the wren's box to another part of the house.

In the middle of my parlour I have, you may remember, a curious republic of industrious hornets. Their nest hangs to the cieling by the same twig on which it was so admirably built and contrived in the woods. Its removal did not displease them, for they find, in my house, plenty of food; and I have left a hole open, in one of the panes of the window, which answers all their purposes. By this kind usage they are become quite harmless. They live on the flies, which are very troublesome to us throughout the summer. They are constantly busy in catching them, even on the eyelids of my children. It is surprising how quickly they smear them with a sort of glue, lest they might escape; and, when thus prepared, they carry them to their nests as food for their young ones. These globular nests are most ingeniously divided into many stories, all provided with cells and proper communications. The materials, with which this fabric is built, they procure from the cottony furze, with which our oak-rails are covered. This substance, tempered with glue, produces a sort of pasteboard, which is very strong, and resists all the inclemencies of the weather. By their assistance I am but little troubled with flies. All my family are so accustomed to their strong buzzing, that no one takes any notice of them; and, though they are fierce and vindictive, yet kindness and hospitality have made them useful and harmless.

We have a great variety of wasps. Most of them build their nests in mud, which they fix against the shingles of our roofs, as nigh the pitch as they can. These aggregates represent nothing, at first view, but coarse and irregular lumps, but, if you break them, you will observe that the inside of them contains a great number of oblong cells, in which they deposit their eggs, and in which they bury themselves in the fall of the year. Thus immured, they securely pass through the severity of that season, and, on the return of the sun, are enabled to perforate their cells, and to open themselves a passage from these recesses into the sunshine. The yellow wasps, which build under ground, in our meadows, are much more to be dreaded; for, when the mower unwittingly passes his scythe over their holes, they immediately sally forth with a fury and velocity superior even to the strength of man. They make the boldest fly, and the only remedy is to lie down and cover our heads with hay, for it is only at the head they aim their blows; nor is there any possibility of finishing that part of the work, until, by means of fire and brimstone, they are all silenced. But, though I have been obliged to execute this dreadful sentence in my own defence, I have often thought it a great pity, for the sake of a little hay, to lay waste so ingenious a subterranean town, furnished with every conveniency, and built with a most surprising mechanism.

I never should have done, were I to recount the many objects which voluntarily strike my imagination in the midst of my work, and spontaneously afforded me the most pleasing relief. These may appear insignificant trifles to a person who has travelled through Europe and America, and is acquainted with books and with many sciences. But such simple objects of contemplation suffice me, who have no time to bestow on more extensive observations. Happily these require no study: they are obvious: they gild the moments I dedicate to them, and enliven the severe labours which I perform. At home my happiness springs from very different objects. The gradual unfolding of my children's reason, the study of their dawning tempers, attract all my paternal attention. I have to contrive little punishments for their little faults, small encouragements for their good actions, and a variety of other expedients dictated by various occasions. But these are themes unworthy your perusal, and which ought not to be carried beyond the walls of my house, being domestic mysteries, adapted only to the locality of the small sanctuary wherein my family resides. Sometimes I delight in inventing and executing machines, which simplify my wife's labour. I have been tolerably successful that way. And these, Sir, are the narrow circles within which I constantly revolve; and what can I wish for beyond them? I bless God for all the good he has given me. I envy no man's prosperity, and wish no other portion of happiness than that I may live to teach the same philosophy to my children, and give each of them a farm, shew them how to cultivate it, and be, like their father, good substantial independent American farmers.—An appellation which will be the most fortunate one a man of my class can possess, so long as our civil government continues to shed blessings on our husbandry. Adieu.

LETTER III

WHAT IS AN AMERICAN?

I WISH I could be acquainted with the feelings and thoughts which must agitate the heart and present themselves to the mind of an enlightened Englishman, when he first lands on this continent. He must greatly rejoice that he lived at a time to see this fair country discovered and settled. He must necessarily feel a share of national pride when he views the chain of settlements which embellish these extended shores. When he says to himself, this is the work of my countrymen, who, when convulsed by factions, afflicted by a variety of miseries and wants, restless and impatient, took refuge here. They brought along with them their national genius, to which they principally owe what liberty they enjoy and what substance they possess. Here he sees the industry of his native country displayed in a new manner, and traces, in their works, the embryos of all the arts, sciences, and ingenuity, which flourish in Europe. Here he beholds fair cities, substantial villages, extensive fields, an immense country filled with decent houses, good roads, orchards, meadows, and bridges, where, a hundred years ago, all was wild, woody, and uncultivated! What a train of pleasing ideas this fair spectacle must suggest! It is a prospect which must inspire a good citizen with the most heartfelt pleasure! The difficulty consists in the manner of viewing so extensive a scene. He is arrived on a new continent: a modern society offers itself to his contemplation, different from what he had hitherto seen. It is not composed, as in Europe, of great lords who possess every thing, and of a herd of people who have nothing. Here are no aristocratical families, no courts, no kings, no bishops, no ecclesiastical dominion, no invisible power giving to a few a very visible one, no great manufactures employing thousands, no great refinements of luxury. The rich and the poor are not so far removed from each other as they are in Europe. Some few towns excepted, we are all tillers of the earth, from Nova Scotia to West Florida. We are a people of cultivators, scattered over an immense territory, communicating with each other by means of good roads and navigable rivers, united by the silken bands of mild government, all respecting the laws, without dreading their power, because they are equitable. We are all animated with the spirit of an industry which is unfettered and unrestrained, because each person works for himself. If he travels through our rural districts, he views not the hostile castle and the haughty mansion contrasted with the clay-built hut and miserable cabin, where cattle and men help to keep each other warm, and dwell in meanness, smoke, and indigence. A pleasing uniformity of decent competence appears throughout our habitations. The meanest of our log-houses is a dry and comfortable habitation. Lawyer or merchant are the fairest titles our towns afford: that of a farmer is the only appellation of the rural inhabitants of our country. It must take some time ere he can reconcile himself to our dictionary, which is but short in words of dignity and names of honour. There, on a Sunday, he sees a congregation of respectable farmers and their wives, all clad in neat homespun, well mounted, or riding in their own humble waggons. There is not among them an esquire, saving the unlettered magistrate. There he sees a parson as simple as his flock, a farmer who does not riot on the labour of others. We have no princes, for whom we toil, starve, and bleed. We are the most perfect society now existing in the world. Here man is free as he ought to be; nor is this pleasing equality so transitory as many others are. Many ages will not see the shores of our great lakes replenished with inland nations, nor the unknown bounds of North America entirely peopled. Who can tell how far it extends? Who can tell the millions of men whom it will feed and contain? for no European foot has, as yet, travelled half the extent of this mighty continent.

The next wish of this traveller will be, to know whence came all these people? They are a mixture of English, Scotch, Irish, French, Dutch, Germans, and Swedes. From this promiscuous breed, that race, now called Americans, have arisen. The Eastern provinces must indeed be excepted, as being the unmixed descendents of Englishmen. I have heard many wish that they had been more intermixed also: for my part, I am no wisher, and think it much better as it has happened. They exhibit a most conspicuous figure in this great and variegated picture. They too enter for a great share in the pleasing perspective displayed in these thirteen provinces. I know it is fashionable to reflect on them, but I respect them for what they have done; for the accuracy and wisdom with which they have settled their territory; for the decency of their manners; for their early love of letters; their antient college,* the first in this hemisphere; for their industry; which to me, who am but a farmer, is the criterion of every thing. There never was a people, situated as they are, who, with so ungrateful a soil, have done more in so short a time. Do you think that the monarchical ingredients, which are more prevalent in other governments, have purged them from all foul stains? Their histories assert the contrary.

In this great American asylum, the poor of Europe have by some means met together, and in consequence of various causes. To what purpose should they ask one another what countrymen they are? Alas, two thirds of them had no country. Can a wretch, who wanders about, who works and starves, whose life is a continual scene of sore affliction or pinching penury; can that man call England or any other kingdom his country? A country that had no bread for him; whose fields procured him no harvest; who met with nothing but the frowns of the rich, the severity of the laws, with jails and punishments; who owned not a single foot of the extensive surface of this planet. No! Urged by a variety of motives here they came. Every thing has tended to regenerate them. New laws, a new mode of living, a new social system. Here

they are become men. In Europe they were as so many useless plants, wanting vegetative mould and refreshing showers.
They withered; and were mowed down by want, hunger, and
war; but now, by the power of transplantation, like all other
plants, they have taken root and flourished! Formerly they
were not numbered in any civil lists of their country, except
in those of the poor: here they rank as citizens. By what
invisible power hath this surprising metamorphosis been performed? By that of the laws and that of their industry. The
laws, the indulgent laws, protect them as they arrive, stamping
on them the symbol of adoption: they receive ample rewards
for their labours: these accumulated rewards procure them
lands: those lands confer on them the title of freemen, and
to that title every benefit is affixed which men can possibly
require. This is the great operation daily performed by our
laws. Whence proceed these laws? From our government.
Whence that government? It is derived from the original
genius and strong desire of the people ratified and confirmed
by the crown. This is the great chain which links us all; this
is the picture which every province exhibits, Nova Scotia excepted. There the crown has done all. Either there were
no people who had genius, or it was not much attended to.
The consequence is, that the province is very thinly inhabited
indeed. The power of the crown, in conjunction with the
musketoes,* has prevented men from settling there. Yet some
parts of it flourished once, and it contained a mild harmless
set of people. But, for the fault of a few leaders, the whole
was banished. The greatest political error, the crown ever
committed in America, was, to cut off men from a country
which wanted nothing but men.

What attachment can a poor European emigrant have for
a country where he had nothing? The knowledge of the language, the love of a few kindred as poor as himself, were
the only cords that tied him. His country is now that which
gives him his land, bread, protection, and consequence. *Ubi
panis ibi patria** is the motto of all emigrants. What then is

the American, this new man? He is neither an European, nor the descendent of an European: hence that strange mixture of blood, which you will find in no other country. I could point out to you a family, whose grandfather was an Englishman, whose wife was Dutch, whose son married a French woman, and whose present four sons have now four wives of different nations. He is an American, who, leaving behind him all his antient prejudices and manners, receives new ones from the new mode of life he has embraced, the new government he obeys, and the new rank he holds. He becomes an American by being received in the broad lap of our great *alma mater*. Here individuals of all nations are melted into a new race of men, whose labours and posterity will one day cause great changes in the world. Americans are the western pilgrims, who are carrying along with them that great mass of arts, sciences, vigour, and industry, which began long since in the east. They will finish the great circle. The Americans were once scattered all over Europe. Here they are incorporated into one of the finest systems of population which has ever appeared, and which will hereafter become distinct by the power of the different climates they inhabit. The American ought therefore to love this country much better than that wherein either he or his forefathers were born. Here the rewards of his industry follow, with equal steps, the progress of his labour. His labour is founded on the basis of nature, *self-interest:* can it want a stronger allurement? Wives and children, who before in vain demanded of him a morsel of bread, now, fat and frolicksome, gladly help their father to clear those fields whence exuberant crops are to arise, to feed and to clothe them all, without any part being claimed, either by a despotic prince, a rich abbot, or a mighty lord. Here religion demands but little of him; a small voluntary salary to the minister, and gratitude to God: can he refuse these? The American is a new man, who acts upon new principles; he must therefore entertain new ideas and form new opinions. From involuntary idleness, servile dependence, penury, and useless labour, he has passed to toils of a very different nature, rewarded by ample subsistence.—This is an American.

British America is divided into many provinces, forming a large association, scattered along a coast of 1500 miles extent and about 200 wide. This society I would fain examine, at least such as it appears in the middle provinces; if it does not afford that variety of tinges and gradations which may be observed in Europe, we have colours peculiar to ourselves. For instance, it is natural to conceive that those who live near the sea must be very different from those who live in the woods: the intermediate space will afford a separate and distinct class.

Men are like plants. The goodness and flavour of the fruit proceeds from the peculiar soil and exposition in which they grow. We are nothing but what we derive from the air we breathe, the climate we inhabit, the government we obey, the system of religion we profess, and the nature of our employment. Here you will find but few crimes; these have acquired as yet no root among us. I wish I were able to trace all my ideas. If my ignorance prevents me from describing them properly, I hope I shall be able to delineate a few of the outlines, which is all I propose.

Those, who live near the sea, feed more on fish than on flesh, and often encounter that boisterous element. This renders them more bold and enterprising: this leads them to neglect the confined occupations of the land. They see and converse with a variety of people. Their intercourse with mankind becomes extensive. The sea inspires them with a love of traffic, a desire of transporting produce from one place to another; and leads them to a variety of resources, which supply the place of labour. Those who inhabit the middle settlements, by far the most numerous, must be very different. The simple cultivation of the earth purifies them; but the indulgences of the government, the soft remonstrances of religion, the rank of independent freeholders, must necessarily inspire them with sentiments very little known in Europe among a people of the same class. What do I say? Europe has no such class of men. The early knowledge they acquire, the early bargains they make, give them a great degree of sagacity. As freemen they will be litigious. Pride and obstinacy are often the cause of law-suits; the nature of our laws and governments may be another. As citizens, it is easy to imagine that they will carefully read the newspapers, enter into every political disquisition, freely blame, or censure, governors and others. As farmers, they will be careful and anxious to get as much as they can, because what they get is their own. As northern men, they will love the cheerful cup. As Christians, religion curbs them not in their opinions: the general indulgence leaves every one to think for themselves in spiritual matters. The law inspects our actions; our thoughts are left to God. Industry, good living, selfishness, litigiousness, country politics, the pride of freemen, religious indifference, are their characteristics. If you recede still farther from the sea, you will come into more modern settlements: they exhibit the same strong lineaments in a ruder appearance. Religion seems to have still less influence, and their manners are less improved.

Now we arrive near the great woods, near the last inhabited districts. There men seem to be placed still farther beyond the reach of government, which, in some measure, leaves them to themselves. How can it pervade every corner, as they were driven there by misfortunes, necessity of beginnings, desire of acquiring large tracks of land, idleness, frequent want of œconomy, antient debts. The re-union of such people does not afford a very pleasing spectacle. When discord, want of unity and friendship, when either drunkenness or idleness, prevail in such remote districts, contention, inactivity, and wretchedness, must ensue. There are not the same remedies to these evils as in a long-established community. The few magistrates they have are, in general, little better than the rest. They are often in a perfect state of war; that of man against man; sometimes decided by blows, sometimes by means of the law: that of man against every wild inhabitant of these venerable woods, of which they are come to dispossess them. There men appear to be no better than carnivorous animals, of a superior rank, living on the flesh of wild animals when they can catch them, and, when they are not able, they subsist on grain. He, who would wish to see America in its proper light, and to have a true idea of its feeble beginnings and barbarous rudiments, must visit our extended line of frontiers, where the last settlers dwell, and where he may see the first labours of settlement, the mode of clearing the earth, in all their different appearances. Where men are wholly left dependent on their native tempers and on the spur of uncertain industry, which often fails when not sanctified by the efficacy of a few moral rules. There, remote from the power of example and check of shame, many families exhibit the most hideous parts of our society. They are a kind of forlorn hope, preceding, by ten or twelve years, the most respectable army of veterans which come after them. In that space, prosperity will polish some, vice and the law will drive off the rest, who, uniting again with others like themselves, will recede still farther, making room for more industrious people, who will finish their improvements, convert the log-house into a convenient habitation, and, rejoicing that the first heavy labours are finished, will change, in a few years, that hitherto-barbarous country into a fine, fertile, well-regulated, district. Such is our progress, such is the march of the Europeans toward the interior parts of this continent. In all societies there are off-casts. This impure part serves as our precursors or pioneers. My father himself was one of that class; but he came upon honest principles, and was therefore one of the few who held fast. By good conduct and temperance he transmitted to me his fair inheritance, when not above one in fourteen of his contemporaries had the same good fortune.

Forty years ago this smiling country was thus inhabited. It is now purged. A general decency of manners prevails throughout, and such has been the fate of our best countries.

Exclusive of those general characteristics, each province has its own, founded on the government, climate, mode of husbandry, customs, and peculiarity of circumstances. Europeans submit insensibly to these great powers, and become, in the course of a few generations, not only Americans in general, but either Pennsylvanians, Virginians, or provincials, under some other name. Whoever traverses the continent must easily observe those strong differences which will grow more evident in time. The inhabitants of Canada, Massachuset, the middle provinces, the southern ones, will be as different as their climates. Their only points of unity will be those of religion and language.

As I have endeavoured to shew you how Europeans became Americans, it may not be disagreeable to shew you likewise how the various Christian sects introduced wear out, and how religious indifference becomes prevalent. When any considerable number of a particular sect happen to dwell contiguous to each other, they immediately erect a temple, and there worship the Divinity agreeably to their own peculiar ideas. Nobody disturbs them. If any new sect springs up in Europe, it may happen that many of its professors will come and settle in America. As they bring their zeal with them, they are at liberty to make proselytes if they can, and to build a meeting, and to follow the dictates of their consciences; for neither the government nor any other power interferes. If they are peaceable subjects, and are industrious, what is it to their neighbours how and in what manner they think fit to address their prayers to the Supreme Being? But, if the sectaries are not settled close together, if they are mixed with other denominations, their zeal will cool for want of fuel, and will be extinguished in a little time. Then the Americans become, as to religion what they are as to country, allied to all. In them the name of Englishman, Frenchman, and European, is lost, and, in like manner, the strict modes of Christianity, as practised in Europe, are lost also. This effect will extend itself still farther hereafter, and, though this may appear to you as a strange idea, yet it is a very true one. I shall be able perhaps hereafter to explain myself better; in the mean while, let the following example serve as my first justification.

Let us suppose you and I to be travelling. We observe that in this house, to the right, lives a Catholic, who prays to God as he has been taught, and believes in transubstantiation. He works and raises wheat, he has a large family of children, all hale and robust. His belief, his prayers, offend nobody. About one mile farther, on the same road, his next neighbour may be a good honest plodding German Lutheran,* who addresses himself to the same God, the God of all, agreeably to the modes he has been educated in, and believes in consubstantiation; by so doing he scandalizes nobody. He also works in his fields, embellishes the earth, clears swamps, &c. What has the world to do with his Lutheran principles? He persecutes nobody, and nobody persecutes him; he visits his neighbours, and his neighbours visit him. Next to him lives a Seceder,* the most enthusiastic of all sectaries; his zeal is hot and fiery; but, separated as he is from others of the same complexion, he has no congregation of his own to resort to, where he might cabal and mingle religious pride with worldly obstinacy. He likewise raises good crops, his house is handsomely painted, his orchard is one of the fairest in the neighbourhood. How does it concern the welfare of the country, or of the province at large, what this man's religious sentiments are, or really whether he has any at all? He is a good farmer, he is a sober, peaceable, good, citizen. William Penn* himself would not wish for more. This is the visible character; the invisible one is only guessed at, and is nobody's business. Next again lives a Low Dutchman, who implicitly believes the rules laid down by the synod of Dort.* He conceives no other idea of a clergyman than that of a hired man. If he does his work well he will pay him the stipulated sum; if not, he will dismiss him, and do without his sermons, and let his church be shut up for years. But, notwithstanding this coarse idea,

you will find his house and farm to be the neatest in all the
country; and you will judge, by his waggon and fat horses,
that he thinks more of the affairs of this world than of those
of the next. He is sober and laborious, therefore he is all he
ought to be as to the affairs of this life; as for those of the
next, he must trust to the great Creator. Each of these
people instruct their children as well as they can, but these
instructions are feeble compared to those which are given to
the youth of the poorest class in Europe. Their children
will therefore grow up less zealous and more indifferent in
matters of religion than their parents. The foolish vanity, or
rather the fury of making proselytes, is unknown here: they
have no time: the seasons call for all their attention; and thus,
in a few years, this mixed neighbourhood will exhibit a strange
religious medley, that will be neither pure Catholicism nor
pure Calvinism. A very perceptible indifference, even in the
first generation, will become apparent; and it may happen that
the daughter of the Catholic will marry the son of the Seceder,
and settle by themselves at a distance from their parents.
What religious education will they give their children? A very
imperfect one. If there happens to be in the neighbourhood
any place of worship, we will suppose a Quaker's meeting,
rather than not shew their fine clothes, they will go to it, and
some of them may perhaps attach themselves to that society.
Others will remain in a perfect state of indifference. The
children of these zealous parents will not be able to tell what
their religious principles are, and their grandchildren still less.
The neighbourhood of a place of worship generally leads
them to it, and the action of going thither is the strongest
evidence they can give of their attachment to any sect. The
Quakers are the only people who retain a fondness for their
own mode of worship; for, be they ever so far separated from
each other, they hold a sort of communion with the society,
and seldom depart from its rules, at least in this country.
Thus all sects are mixed as well as all nations. Thus religious
indifference is imperceptibly disseminated from one end of

the continent to the other, which is at present one of the strongest characteristics of the Americans. Where this will reach no one can tell: perhaps it may leave a vacuum fit to receive other systems. Persecution, religious pride, the love of contradiction, are the food of what the world commonly calls religion. These motives have ceased here: zeal, in Europe, is confined: here, it evaporates in the great distance it has to travel; there, it is a grain of powder inclosed; here, it burns away in the open air, and consumes without effect.

But to return to our back settlers. I must tell you, that there is something in the proximity of the woods which is very singular. It is with men as it is with the plants and animals that grow and live in the forests. They are entirely different from those that live in the plains. I will candidly tell you all my thoughts, but you are not to expect that I shall advance any reasons. By living in or near the woods, their actions are regulated by the wildness of the neighbourhood. The deer often come to eat their grain, the wolves to destroy their sheep, the bears to kill their hogs, the foxes to catch their poultry. This surrounding hostility immediately puts the gun into their hands: they watch these animals; they kill some; and thus, by defending their property, they soon be- come professed hunters. This is the progress. Once hunters, farewel to the plough. The chase renders them ferocious, gloomy, and unsocial. A hunter wants no neighbour; he rather hates them, because he dreads the competition. In a little time their success in the woods makes them neglect their tillage. They trust to the natural fecundity of the earth, and therefore do little. Carelessness in fencing often exposes what little they sow to destruction: they are not at home to watch: in order therefore to make up the deficiency, they go oftener to the woods. That new mode of life brings along with it a new set of manners, which I cannot easily describe. These new manners, being grafted on the old stock, produce a strange sort of lawless profligacy, the impressions of which are in-delible. The manners of the Indian natives are respectable

compared with this European medley. Their wives and
children live in sloth and inactivity, and, having no proper
pursuits, you may judge what education the latter receive.
Their tender minds have nothing else to contemplate but the
example of their parents; like them they grow up a mongrel
breed, half civilized, half savage, except nature stamps on
them some constitutional propensities. That rich, that voluptuous, sentiment is gone, which struck them so forcibly. The
possession of their freeholds no longer conveys to their minds
the same pleasure and pride. To all these reasons you must
add their lonely situation, and you cannot imagine what an
effect on manners the great distances they live from each other
has! Consider one of the last settlements in its first view: of
what is it composed? Europeans, who have not that sufficient
share of knowledge they ought to have, in order to prosper:
people, who have suddenly passed from oppression, dread of
government, and fear of laws, into the unlimited freedom of
the woods. This sudden change must have a very great effect
on most men, and on that class particularly. Eating of wild
meat, whatever you may think, tends to alter their temper,
though all the proof I can adduce is, that I have seen it; and,
having no place of worship to resort to, what little society
this might afford is denied them. The Sunday meetings,
exclusive of religious benefits, were the only social bonds
that might have inspired them with some degree of emulation
in neatness. Is it then surprising to see men, thus situated,
immersed in great and heavy labours, degenerate a little? It
is rather a wonder the effect is not more diffusive. The
Moravians* and the Quakers are the only instances in excep-
tion to what I have advanced. The first never settle singly;
it is a colony of the society which emigrates: they carry with
them their forms, worship, rules, and decency. The others never
begin so hard; they are always able to buy improvements in
which there is a great advantage, for, by that time, the country is recovered from its first barbarity. Thus our bad people
are those who are half cultivators and half hunters; and the

worst of them are those who have degenerated altogether into the hunting state. As old ploughmen and new men of the woods, as Europeans and new-made Indians, they contract the vices of both. They adopt the moroseness and ferocity of a native, without his mildness, or even his industry at home. If manners are not refined, at least they are rendered simple and inoffensive by tilling the earth: all our wants are supplied by it: our time is divided between labour and rest, and leaves none for the commission of great misdeeds. As hunters, it is divided between the toil of the chase, the idleness of repose, or the indulgence of inebriation. Hunting is but a licentious idle life, and, if it does not alway pervert good dispositions, yet, when it is united with bad luck, it leads to want: want stimulates that propensity to rapacity and injustice, too natural to needy men, which is the fatal gradation. After this explanation of the effects which follow by living in the woods, shall we yet vainly flatter ourselves with the hope of converting the Indians? We should rather begin with converting our back-settlers; and now, if I dare mention the name of religion, its sweet accents would be lost in the immensity of these woods. Men, thus placed, are not fit either to receive or remember its mild instructions; they want temples and ministers; but, as soon as men cease to remain at home and begin to lead an erratic life, let them be either tawny or white, they cease to be its disciples.

Thus have I faintly and imperfectly endeavoured to trace our society from the sea to our woods; yet you must not imagine that every person, who moves back, acts upon the same principles, or falls into the same degeneracy. Many families carry with them all their decency of conduct, purity of morals, and respect of religion; but these are scarce, the power of example is sometimes irresistible. Even among these back-settlers, their depravity is greater or less, according to what nation or province they belong. Were I to adduce proofs of this, I might be accused of partiality. If there happens to be some rich intervals, some fertile bottoms, in those remote

districts, the people will there prefer tilling the land to hunting, and will attach themselves to it; but, even on these fertile
spots, you may plainly perceive the inhabitants to acquire a
great degree of rusticity and selfishness.

It is in consequence of this straggling situation, and the
astonishing power it has on manners, that the back-settlers
of both the Carolinas, Virginia, and many other parts, have
been long a set of lawless people; it has been even dangerous to travel among them. Government can do nothing in so
extensive a country; better it should wink at these irregularities than that it should use means inconsistent with its usual
mildness. Time will efface those stains: in proportion as the
great body of population approaches them, they will reform,
and become polished and subordinate. Whatever has been
said of the four New-England provinces, no such degeneracy
of manners has ever tarnished their annals: their back-settlers
have been kept within the bounds of decency and government, by means of wise laws, and by the influence of religion. What a detestable idea such people must have given
to the natives of the Europeans! They trade with them; the
worst of people are permitted to do that which none but
persons of the best characters should be employed in. They
get drunk with them, and often defraud the Indians. Their
avarice, removed from the eyes of their superiors, knows
no bounds; and, aided by a little superiority of knowledge,
these traders deceive them, and even sometimes shed blood.
Hence those shocking violations, those sudden devastations
which have so often stained our frontiers, when hundreds of
innocent people have been sacrificed for the crimes of a few.
It was in consequence of such behaviour that the Indians took
the hatchet against the Virginians in 1774.* Thus are our
first steps trodden, thus are our first trees felled, in general,
by the most vicious of our people; and thus the path is
opened for the arrival of a second and better class, the true
American freeholders; the most respectable set of people in
this part of the world: respectable for their industry, their

happy independence, the great share of freedom they possess, the good regulation of their families, and for extending the trade and the dominion of our mother-country.

Europe contains hardly any other distinctions but lords and tenants; this fair country alone is settled by freeholders, the possessors of the soil they cultivate, members of the government they obey, and the framers of their own laws, by means of their representatives. This is a thought which you have taught me to cherish; our distance from Europe, far from diminishing, rather adds to, our usefulness and consequence as men and subjects. Had our forefathers remained there, they would only have crouded it, and perhaps prolonged those convulsions which had shaken it so long. Every industrious European, who transports himself here, may be compared to a sprout growing at the foot of a great tree; it enjoys and draws but a little portion of sap; wrench it from the parent roots, transplant it, and it will become a tree bearing fruit also. Colonists are therefore intitled to the consideration due to the most useful subjects; a hundred families, barely existing in some parts of Scotland, will here, in six years, cause an annual exportation of 10,000 bushels of wheat: 100 bushels being but a common quantity for an industrious family to fell, if they cultivate good land. It is here then that the idle may be employed, the useless become useful, and the poor become rich; but by riches I do not mean gold and silver, we have but little of those metals: I mean a better sort of wealth; cleared lands, cattle, good houses, good clothes, and an increase of people to enjoy them.

There is no wonder that this country has so many charms, and presents to Europeans so many temptations to remain in it. A traveller in Europe becomes a stranger as soon as he quits his own kingdom; but it is otherwise here. We know, properly speaking, no strangers; this is every person's country; the variety of our soils, situations, climates, governments, and produce, hath something which must please every body. No sooner does an European arrive, no matter of what condition, than his eyes are opened upon the fair prospect; he hears his language spoken, he retraces many of his own country manners, he perpetually hears the names of families and towns with which he is acquainted; he sees happiness and prosperity in all places disseminated; he meets with hospitality, kindness, and plenty, every where: he beholds hardly any poor, he seldom hears of punishments and executions; and he wonders at the elegance of our towns, those miracles of industry and freedom. He cannot admire enough our rural districts, our convenient roads, good taverns, and our many accommodations; he involuntarily loves a country where every thing is so lovely. When in England, he was a mere Englishman; here he stands on a larger portion of the globe, not less than its fourth part, and may see the productions of the north, in iron and naval stores; the provisions of Ireland, the grain of Egypt, the indigo, the rice, of China. He does not find, as in Europe, a crouded society, where every place is over-stocked; he does not feel that perpetual collision of parties, that difficulty of beginning, that contention which oversets so many. There is room for every body in America; has he any particular talent or industry? he exerts it in order to procure a livelihood, and it succeeds. Is he a merchant? the avenues of trade are infinite. Is he eminent in any respect? he will be employed and respected. Does he love a country life? pleasant farms present themselves; he may purchase what he wants, and thereby become an American farmer. Is he a labourer, sober and industrious? he need not go many miles, nor receive many informations before he will be hired, well fed at the table of his employer, and paid four or five times more than he can get in Europe. Does he want uncultivated lands? thousands of acres present themselves, which he may purchase cheap. Whatever be his talents or inclinations, if they are moderate, he may satisfy them. I do not mean that every one who comes will grow rich in a little time; no, but he may procure an easy decent maintenance by his industry. Instead of starving he will be fed, instead of being idle he will have employment;

and these are riches enough for such men as come over here. The rich stay in Europe; it is only the middling and poor that emigrate. Would you wish to travel in independent idleness, from north to south, you will find easy access, and the most cheerful reception, at every house; society without ostentation, good cheer without pride, and every decent diversion which the country affords, with little expence. It is no wonder that the European, who has lived here a few years, is desirous to remain; Europe, with all its pomp, is not to be compared to this continent, for men of middle stations or labourers.

An European, when he first arrives, seems limited in his intentions as well as in his views; but he very suddenly alters his scale; two hundred miles formerly appeared a very great distance, it is now but a trifle; he no sooner breathes our air than he forms schemes, and embarks in designs, he never would have thought of in his own country. There the plenitude of society confines many useful ideas, and often extinguishes the most laudable schemes which here ripen into maturity. Thus Europeans become Americans.

But how is this accomplished in that croud of low indigent people, who flock here every year from all parts of Europe? I will tell you; they no sooner arrive than they immediately feel the good effects of that plenty of provisions we possess: they fare on our best food, and are kindly entertained; their talents, character, and peculiar industry, are immediately inquired into; they find countrymen every where disseminated, let them come from whatever part of Europe. Let me select one as an epitome of the rest; he is hired, he goes to work, and works moderately; instead of being employed by a haughty person, he finds himself with his equal, placed at the substantial table of the farmer, or else at an inferior one as good; his wages are high, his bed is not like that bed of sorrow on which he used to lie: if he behaves with propriety, and is faithful, he is caressed, and becomes as it were a member of the family. He begins to feel the effects of a sort of resurrection; hitherto he had not lived, but simply vegetated; he now

feels himself a man, because he is treated as such; the laws
of his own country had overlooked him in his insignificancy;
the laws of this cover him with their mantle. Judge what an
alteration there must arise in the mind and the thoughts of
this man; he begins to forget his former servitude and dependence, his heart involuntarily swells and glows; this first swell
inspires him with those new thoughts which constitute an
American. What love can he entertain for a country where
his existence was a burthen to him? if he is a generous good
man, the love of this new adoptive parent will sink deep into
his heart. He looks around, and sees many a prosperous person, who, but a few years before, was as poor as himself. This
encourages him much; he begins to form some little scheme,
the first, alas! he ever formed in his life. If he is wise, he
thus spends two or three years, in which time he acquires
knowledge, the use of tools, the modes of working the lands,
felling trees, &c. This prepares the foundation of a good name,
the most useful acquisition he can make. He is encouraged,
he has gained friends; he is advised and directed, he feels
bold, he purchases some land; he gives all the money he has
brought over, as well as what he has earned, and trusts to
the God of harvests for the discharge of the rest. His good
name procures him credit; he is now possessed of the deed,
conveying to him and his posterity the fee simple and absolute property of two hundred acres of land, situated on such
a river. What an epocha in this man's life! He is become a
freeholder, from perhaps a German boor; he is now an American, a Pennsylvanian, an English subject. He is naturalized,
his name is enrolled with those of the other citizens of the
province. Instead of being a vagrant, he has a place of residence; he is called the inhabitant of such a country, or of such
a district, and, for the first time in his life, counts for something; for hitherto he had been a cipher. I only repeat what
I have heard many say; and no wonder their hearts should
glow, and be agitated with a multitude of feelings, not easy to
describe. From nothing, to start into being; from a servant, to

the rank of a master; from being the slave of some despotic prince, to become a free man, invested with lands, to which every municipal blessing is annexed! What a change indeed! It is in consequence of that change that he becomes an American. This great metamorphosis has a double effect; it extinguishes all his European prejudices, he forgets that mechanism of subordination, that servility of disposition, which poverty had taught him; and sometimes he is apt to forget it too much, often passing from one extreme to the other. If he is a good man, he forms schemes of future prosperity, he proposes to educate his children better than he has been educated himself; he thinks of future modes of conduct, feels an ardour to labour he never felt before. Pride steps in, and leads him to every thing that the laws do not forbid: he respects them; with a heart-felt gratitude he looks toward the east, toward that insular government from whose wisdom all his new felicity is derived, and under whose wings and protection he now lives. These reflections constitute him the good man and the good subject. Ye poor Europeans, ye, who sweat, and work for the great; ye, who are obliged to give so many sheaves to the church, so many to your lords, so many to your government, and have hardly any left for yourselves;* ye, who are held in less estimation than favourite hunters or useless lap-dogs; ye, who only breathe the air of nature, because it cannot be withholden from you; it is here that ye can conceive the possibility of those feelings I have been describing; it is here the laws of naturalization invite every one to partake of our great labours and felicity, to till unrented, untaxed, lands! Many, corrupted beyond the power of amendment, have brought with them all their vices, and, disregarding the advantages held to them, have gone on in their former career of iniquity, until they have been overtaken and punished by our laws. It is not every emigrant who succeeds; no, it is only the sober, the honest, and industrious: happy those to whom this transition has served as a powerful spur to labour, to prosperity, and to the good establishment of

children, born in the days of their poverty! and who had no
other portion to expect but the rags of their parents, had it
not been for their happy emigration. Others, again, have been
led astray by this enchanting scene; their new pride, instead
of leading them to the fields, has kept them in idleness;
the idea of possessing lands is all that satisfies them; though
surrounded with fertility, they have mouldered away their
time in inactivity, misinformed husbandry, and ineffectual
endeavours. How much wiser, in general, the honest Germans
than almost all other Europeans; they hire themselves to some
of their wealthy landsmen, and, in that apprenticeship, learn
every thing that is necessary. They attentively consider the
prosperous industry of others, which imprints in their minds
a strong desire of possessing the same advantages. This forcible
idea never quits them; they launch forth, and, by dint of
sobriety, rigid parsimony, and the most persevering industry,
they commonly succeed. Their astonishment at their first
arrival from Germany is very great; it is to them a dream;
the contrast must be very powerful indeed; they observe their
countrymen flourishing in every place; they travel through
whole counties where not a word of English is spoken; and,
in the names and the language of the people, they retrace
Germany. They have been an useful acquisition to this continent, and to Pennsylvania in particular; to them it owes
some share of its prosperity: to their mechanical knowledge
and patience it owes the finest mills in all America, the best
teams of horses, and many other advantages. The recollection
of their former poverty and slavery never quits them as long
as they live.

The Scotch and the Irish might have lived in their own
country perhaps as poor; but, enjoying more civil advantages,
the effects of their new situation do not strike them so forcibly, nor has it so lasting an effect. Whence the difference
arises I know not; but, out of twelve families of emigrants
of each country, generally seven Scotch will succeed, nine
German, and four Irish. The Scotch are frugal and laborious,

but their wives cannot work so hard as German women, who on the contrary vie with their husbands, and often share with them the most severe toils of the field, which they understand better. They have therefore nothing to struggle against but the common casualties of nature. The Irish do not prosper so well; they love to drink and to quarrel; they are litigious, and soon take to the gun, which is the ruin of every thing; they seem beside to labour under a greater degree of ignorance in husbandry than the others; perhaps it is that their industry had less scope, and was less exercised at home. I have heard many relate how the land was parcelled out in that kingdom; their ancient conquest has been a great detriment to them, by oversetting their landed property. The lands, possessed by a few, are leased down *ad infinitum*, and the occupiers often pay five guineas an acre. The poor are worse lodged there than any where else in Europe; their potatoes, which are easily raised, are perhaps an inducement to laziness: their wages are too low and their whisky too cheap.

There is no tracing observations of this kind without making at the same time very great allowances, as there are every where to be found a great many exceptions. The Irish themselves, from different parts of that kingdom, are very different. It is difficult to account for this surprising locality; one would think, on so small an island, an Irishman must be an Irishman: yet it is not so; they are different in their aptitude to, and in their love of, labour.

The Scotch, on the contrary, are all industrious and saving; they want nothing more than a field to exert themselves in, and they are commonly sure of succeeding. The only difficulty they labour under is, that technical American knowledge which requires some time to obtain; it is not easy for those who seldom saw a tree, to conceive how it is to be felled, cut up, and split into rails and posts.*

As I am fond of seeing and talking of prosperous families, I intend to finish this letter by relating to you the history of an honest Scotch Hebridean, who came here in 1774, which will shew you, in epitome, what the Scotch can do, wherever they have room for the exertion of their industry. Whenever I hear of any new settlement, I pay it a visit once or twice a year, on purpose to observe the different steps each settler takes, the gradual improvements, the different tempers of each family, on which their prosperity in a great measure depends; their different modifications of industry, their ingenuity, and contrivance; for, being all poor, their life requires sagacity and prudence. In an evening I love to hear them tell their stories, they furnish me with new ideas; I sit still and listen to their ancient misfortunes, observing in many of them a strong degree of gratitude to God and the government. Many a well-meant sermon have I preached to some of them. When I found laziness and inattention prevail, who could refrain from wishing well to these new countrymen, after having undergone so many fatigues. Who could withhold good advice? What a happy change it must be, to descend from the high, sterile, bleak, lands of Scotland, where every thing is barren and cold, and to rest on some fertile farms in these middle provinces! Such a transition must have afforded the most pleasing satisfaction.

The following dialogue passed at an out-settlement, where I lately paid a visit:

Well, friend, how do you do now? I am come fifty odd miles on purpose to see you; how do you go on with your new cutting and slashing? Very well, good Sir, we learn the use of the axe bravely, we shall make it out; we have a belly full of victuals every day, our cows run about, and come home full of milk, our hogs get fat of themselves in the woods: Oh, this is a good country! God bless the king and William Penn; we shall do very well by and by, if we keep our healths. Your log-house looks neat and light, where did you get these shingles? One of our neighbours is a New-England man, and he shewed us how to split them out of chesnut-trees. Now for a barn; but all in good time, here are fine trees to build it with. Who is to frame it, sure you do not understand that work yet? A countryman of ours, who has been in America these ten years, offers to wait for his money until the second crop is lodged in it. What did you give for your land? Thirty-five shillings per acre, payable in seven years. How many acres have you got? A hundred and fifty. That is enough to begin with. Is not your land pretty hard to clear? Yes, Sir, hard enough, but it would be harder still if it was ready cleared, for then we should have no timber, and I love the woods much; the land is nothing without them. Have not you found out any bees yet? No, Sir, and if we had we should not know what to do with them. I will tell you by and by. You are very kind. Farewel, honest man, God prosper you; whenever you travel toward**, enquire for J. S. he will entertain you kindly, provided you bring him good tidings from your family and farm. In this manner I often visit them, and carefully examine their houses, their modes of ingenuity, their different ways; and make them relate all they know, and describe all they feel. These are scenes which I believe you would willingly share with me. I well remember your philanthropic turn of mind. Is it not better to contemplate, under these humble roofs, the rudiments of future wealth and population, than to behold the accumulated bundles of litigious papers in the office of a lawyer? To examine how the world is gradually settled, how the howling swamp is converted into a pleasing meadow, the rough ridge into a fine field; and to hear the cheerful whistling, the rural song, where there was no sound heard before, save the yell of the savage, the screech of the owl, or the hissing of the snake? Here an European, fatigued with luxury, riches, and pleasures, may find a sweet relaxation in a series of interesting scenes, as affecting as they are new. England, which now contains so many domes, so many castles, was once like this, a place woody and marshy; its inhabitants, now the favourite nation for arts and commerce, were once painted like our neighbours. This country will flourish in its turn, and the same observations will be made which I have just delineated.

Posterity will look back, with avidity and pleasure, to trace, if possible, the æra of this or that particular settlement.

Pray, what is the reason that the Scots are in general more religious, more faithful, more honest, and industrious, than the Irish? I do not mean to insinuate national reflections, God forbid! It ill becomes any man, and much less an American; but, as I know men are nothing of themselves, and that they owe all their different modifications either to government or other local circumstances, there must be some powerful causes which constitute this great national difference.

Agreeable to the account which several Scotchmen have given me of the north of Britain, of the Orkneys, and the Hebride Islands, they seem, on many accounts, to be unfit for the habitation of men; they appear to be calculated only for great sheep pastures. Who then can blame the inhabitants of these countries for transporting themselves hither? This great continent must in time absorb the poorest part of Europe; and this will happen in proportion as it becomes better known; and as war, taxation, oppression, and misery, increase there. The Hebrides appear to be fit only for the residence of malefactors, and it would be much better to send felons there than either to Virginia or Maryland. What a strange compliment has our mother-country paid to two of the finest provinces in America! England has entertained in that respect very mistaken ideas; what was intended as a punishment is become the good fortune of several; many of those, who have been transported as felons, are now rich, and strangers to the stings of those wants that urged them to violations of the laws: they are become industrious, exemplary, and useful, citizens. The English government should purchase the most northern and barren of those islands; it should send over to us the honest primitive Hebrideans, settle them here on good lands, as a reward for their virtue and ancient poverty, and replace them with a colony of her wicked sons. The severity of the climate, the inclemency of the seasons, the sterility of the soil, the tempestuousness of the sea, would afflict and punish enough. Could there be found a spot better adapted to retaliate the injury it had received by their crimes? Some of those islands might be considered as the hell of Great Britain, where all evil spirits should be sent. Two essential ends would be answered by this simple operation. The good people, by emigration, would be rendered happier; the bad ones would be placed where they ought to be. In a few years the dread of being sent to that wintery region would have a much stronger effect than that of transportation.—This is no place of punishment; were I a poor hopeless, breadless, Englishman, and not restrained by the power of shame, I should be very thankful for the passage. It is of very little importance how and in what manner an indigent man arrives; for, if he is but sober, honest, and industrious, he has nothing more to ask of heaven. Let him go to work, he will have opportunities enough to earn a comfortable support, and even the means of procuring some land; which ought to be the utmost wish of every person who has health and hands to work. I knew a man, who came to this country, in the literal sense of the expression, stark naked; I think he was a Frenchman, and a sailor on-board an English man of war. Being discontented, he had stripped himself and swam on-shore; where, finding clothes and friends, he settled afterwards at Maraneck, in the county of Chester, in the province of New-York: he married and left a good farm to each of his sons. I knew another person, who was but twelve years old when he was taken on the frontiers of Canada by the Indians; at his arrival at Albany he was purchased by a gentleman, who generously bound him apprentice to a tailor. He lived to the age of ninety, and left behind him a fine estate and a numerous family, all well settled; many of them I am acquainted with.—Where is then the industrious European who ought to despair?

After a foreigner from any part of Europe is arrived, and become a citizen, let him devoutly listen to the voice of our great parent, which says to him, "Welcome to my shores, distressed European; bless the hour in which thou didst see my verdant fields, my fair navigable rivers, and my green mountains!—If thou wilt work, I have bread for thee; if thou wilt be honest, sober, and industrious, I have greater rewards to confer on thee—ease and independence. I will give thee fields to feed and clothe thee; a comfortable fire-side to sit by, and tell thy children by what means thou hast prospered; and a decent bed to repose on. I shall endow thee beside with the immunities of a freeman, if thou wilt carefully educate thy children, teach them gratitude to God, and reverence to that government, that philanthropic government, which has collected here so many men and made them happy. I will also provide for thy progeny; and to every good man this ought to be the most holy, the most powerful, the most earnest, wish we can possibly form, as well as the most consolatory prospect when he dies. Go thou, and work, and till; thou shalt prosper, provided thou be just, grateful, and industrious."

HISTORY OF ANDREW, THE HEBRIDEAN

LET historians give the detail of our charters, the succession of our several governors, and of their administrations; of our political struggles, and of the foundation of our towns: let annalists amuse themselves with collecting anecdotes of the establishment of our modern provinces: eagles soar high— I, a feebler bird, cheerfully content myself with skipping from bush to bush, and living on insignificant insects. I am so habituated to draw all my food and pleasure from the surface of the earth which I till, that I cannot nor indeed am I able to quit it.—I therefore present you with the short history of a simple Scotchman; though it contain not a single remarkable event to amaze the reader; no tragical scene to convulse the heart, or pathetic narrative to draw tears from sympathetic eyes. All I wish to delineate is, the progressive steps of a poor man, advancing from indigence to ease; from oppression to freedom; from obscurity and contumely to some degree of consequence—not by virtue of any freaks of fortune, but by the gradual operation of sobriety, honesty, and emigration. These are the limited fields through which I love to wander; sure to find in some parts the smile of new-born happiness, the glad heart inspiring the cheerful song, the glow of manly pride excited by vivid hopes and rising independence. I always return from my neighbourly excursions extremely happy, because there I see good living almost under every roof, and prosperous endeavours almost in every field. But you may say, why don't you describe some of the more ancient opulent settlements of our country, where even the eye of an European has something to admire? It is true, our American fields are in general pleasing to behold, adorned and intermixed as they are with so many substantial houses, flourishing orchards, and coppices of woodlands; the pride of our farms, the source of every good we possess. But what I might observe there is but natural and common; for to draw comfortable subsistence from well-fenced cultivated fields is easy to conceive. A father dies and leaves a decent house and rich farm to his son; the son modernizes the one, and carefully tills the other; he marries the daughter of a friend and neighbour: this is the common prospect; but, though it is rich and pleasant, yet it is far from being so entertaining and instructive as the one now in my view.

I had rather attend on the shore to welcome the poor European when he arrives; I observe him in his first moments of embarrassment, trace him throughout his primary difficulties, follow him step by step, until he pitches his tent on some piece of land, and realizes that energetic wish which has made him quit his native land, his kindred, and induced him to traverse a boisterous ocean. It is there I want to observe his first thoughts and feelings, the first essays of an industry, which hitherto has been suppressed. I wish to see men cut down the first trees, erect their new buildings, till their first fields, reap their first crops, and say, for the first time in their lives, "This is our own grain, raised from American soil—on it we shall feed and grow fat, and convert the rest into gold and silver." I want to see how the happy effects of their sobriety, honesty, and industry, are first displayed: and who would not take a pleasure in seeing these strangers settling as new countrymen, struggling with arduous difficulties, overcoming them, and becoming happy?

Landing on this great continent is like going to sea, they must have a compass, some friendly directing needle; or else they will uselessly err and wander for a long time, even with a fair wind: yet these are the struggles through which our forefathers have waded; and they have left us no other records of them, but the possession of our farms. The reflections I make on these new settlers recal to my mind what my grandfather did in his days; they fill me with gratitude to his memory as well as to that government which invited him to come, and helped him when he arrived, as well as many others. Can I pass over these reflections without remembering thy name, O Penn! thou best of legislators; who, by the wisdom of thy laws, hast endowed human nature, within the bounds of thy province, with every dignity it can possibly enjoy in a civilized state; and shewed, by this singular establishment, what all men might be if they would follow thy example!

In the year 1770, I purchased some lands in the county of ——, which I intended for one of my sons; and was obliged to go there in order to see them properly surveyed and marked out: the soil is good, but the country has a very wild aspect. However, I observed, with pleasure, that land sells very fast; and I am in hopes, when the lad gets a wife, it will be a well-settled, decent, country. Agreeable to our customs, which indeed are those of nature, it is our duty to provide for our eldest children while we live, in order that our homesteads may be left to the youngest, who are the most helpless. Some people are apt to regard the portions given to daughters as so much loss to the family; but this is selfish, and is not agreeable to my way of thinking; they cannot work

as men do; they marry young: I have given an honest European a farm to till for himself, rent free, provided he clears
an acre of swamp every year, and that he quits it whenever
my daughter shall marry. It will procure her a substantial
husband, a good farmer—and that is all my ambition.

Whilst I was in the woods I met with a party of Indians;
I shook hands with them, and I perceived they had killed a
cub; I had a little peach brandy, they perceived it also, we
therefore joined company, kindled a large fire, and ate a
hearty supper. I made their hearts glad, and we all reposed on
good beds of leaves. Soon after dark, I was surprised to hear
a prodigious hooting through the woods; the Indians laughed
heartily. One of them, more skilful than the rest, mimicked
the owls so exactly, that a very large one perched on a high
tree over our fire. We soon brought him down; he measured
five feet seven inches from one extremity of the wings to
the other. By Captain ——— I have sent you the talons, on
which I have had the heads of small candlesticks fixed. Pray
keep them on the table of your study for my sake.

Contrary to my expectation, I found myself under the necessity of going to Philadelphia, in order to pay the purchase-
money, and to have the deeds properly recorded. I thought
little of the journey, though it was above two hundred miles,
because I was well acquainted with many friends, at whose
houses I intended to stop. The third night after I left the
woods, I put up at Mr. ———'s, the most worthy citizen I know;
he happened to lodge at my house when you were there.
—He kindly enquired after your welfare, and desired I
would make a friendly mention of him to you. The neatness
of these good people is no phænomenon, yet I think this
excellent family surpasses every thing I know. No sooner did
I lie down to rest than I thought myself in a most odoriferous
arbour, so sweet and fragrant were the sheets. Next morning
I found my host in his orchard destroying caterpillars. I think,
friend B. said I, that thee art greatly departed from the good
rules of the society; thee seemeth to have quitted that happy

simplicity for which it hath hitherto been so remarkable. Thy
rebuke, friend James, is a pretty heavy one; what motive
canst thee have for thus accusing us? Thy kind wife made
a mistake last evening, I said; she put me on a bed of roses
instead of a common one; I am not used to such delicacies.
And is that all, friend James, that thee hast to reproach us
with?—Thee wilt not call it luxury I hope? thee canst but
know that it is the produce of our garden; and friend Pope
sayeth, that "to enjoy is to obey."* This is a most learned
excuse indeed, friend B. and must be valued because it is
founded upon truth. James, my wife hath done nothing more
to thy bed than what is done all the year round to all the
beds in the family; she sprinkles her linen with rose-water
before she puts it under the press; it is her fancy, and I have
nought to say. But thee shalt not escape so, verily I will send
for her; thee and she must settle the matter, whilst I proceed on my work, before the sun gets too high.—Tom, go
thou and call thy mistress Philadelphia. What, said I, is thy
wife called by that name? I did not know that before. I'll tell
thee, James, how it came to pass: her grandmother was the
first female child born after William Penn landed with the
rest of our brethren; and, in compliment to the city he intended
to build, she was called after the name he intended to give
it; and so there is always one of the daughters of her family
known by the name of Philadelphia. She soon came; and,
after a most friendly altercation, I gave up the point; break-
fasted, departed, and in four days reached the city.

A week after, news came that a vessel was arrived with
Scotch emigrants. Mr. C. and I went to the dock to see them
disembark. It was a scene which inspired me with a variety
of thoughts: here are, said I to my friend, a number of people,
driven by poverty, and other adverse causes, to a foreign land,
in which they know nobody. The name of a stranger, instead
of implying relief, assistance, and kindness, on the contrary
conveys very different ideas. They are now distressed; their
minds are racked by a variety of apprehensions, fears, and

hopes. It was this last powerful sentiment which has brought them here. If they are good people, I pray that heaven may realize them. Whoever were to see them, thus gathered again, in five or six years, would behold a more pleasing sight, to which this would serve as a very powerful contrast. By their honesty, the vigour of their arms, and the benignity of government, their condition will be greatly improved; they will be well clad, fat, possessed of that manly confidence which property confers; they will become useful citizens. Some of their posterity may act conspicuous parts in our future American transactions. Most of them appeared pale and emaciated, from the length of the passage, and the indifferent provision on which they had lived. The number of children seemed as great as that of the people; they had all paid for being conveyed here. The captain told us they were a quiet, peaceable, and harmless, people, who had never dwelt in cities. This was a valuable cargo; they seemed, a few excepted, to be in the full vigour of their lives. Several citizens, impelled either by spontaneous attachments or motives of humanity, took many of them to their houses; the city, agreeable to its usual wisdom and humanity, ordered them all to be lodged in the barracks, and plenty of provisions to be given them. My friend pitched upon one also and led him to his house, with his wife, and a son about fourteen years of age. The majority of them had contracted for land the year before, by means of an agent; the rest depended entirely upon chance; and the one who followed us was of this last class. Poor man, he smiled on receiving the invitation, and gladly accepted it, bidding his wife and son do the same, in a language which I did not understand. He gazed with uninterrupted attention on every thing he saw; the houses, the inhabitants, the negroes, and carriages: every thing appeared equally new to him; and we went slow, in order to give him time to feed on this pleasing variety. Good God! said he, is this Philadelphia, that blessed city of bread and provisions, of which we have heard so much? I am told it was founded the same year in which my father was born; why it is finer than Greenock and Glasgow, which are ten times as old. It is so, said my friend to him, and, when thee hast been here a month, thee will soon see that it is the capital of a fine province, of which thee art going to be a citizen: Greenock enjoys neither such a climate nor such a soil. Thus we slowly proceeded along, when we met several large Lancaster six-horse waggons,* just arrived from the country. At this stupendous sight he stopped short, and with great diffidence asked us what was the use of these great moving houses, and where those big horses came from? Have you none such at home, I asked him? Oh no; these huge animals would eat all the grass of our island! We at last reached my friend's house, who, in the glow of well-meant hospitality, made them all three sit down to a good dinner, and gave them as much cider as they could drink. God bless the country, and the good people it contains, said he; this is the best meal's victuals I have made a long time.—I thank you kindly.

What part of Scotland dost thee come from, friend Andrew? said Mr. C. Some of us come from the Main, some from the island of Barra, he answered, I myself am a Barra man. I looked on the map, and, by its latitude, easily guessed that it must be an inhospitable climate. What sort of land have you got there? I asked him. Bad enough, said he; we have no such trees as I see here, no wheat, no kine, no apples. Then, I observed, that it must be hard for the poor to live. We have no poor, he answered, we are all alike, except our laird; but he cannot help every body. Pray what is the name of your laird? Mr. Neiel, said Andrew; the like of him is not to be found in any of the isles; his forefathers have lived there thirty generations ago, as we are told. Now, gentlemen, you may judge what an ancient family-estate it must be. But it is cold, the land is thin, and there were too many of us, which are the reasons that some are come to seek their fortunes here. Well, Andrew, what step do you intend to take in order to become rich? I do not know, Sir; I am but an ignorant

man, a stranger besides:—I must rely on the advice of good
Christians, they would not deceive me, I am sure. I have
brought with me a character from our Barra minister, can it
do me any good here? Oh, yes; but your future success will
depend entirely on your own conduct; if you are a sober man,
as the certificate says, laborious and honest, there is no fear
but that you will do well. Have you brought any money with
you, Andrew? Yes, Sir, eleven guineas and a half. Upon my
word it is a considerable sum for a Barra man! how came
you by so much money? Why seven years ago I received a
legacy of thirty-seven pounds from an uncle, who loved me
much; my wife brought me two guineas, when the laird gave
her to me for a wife, which I have saved ever since. I have
sold all I had; I worked in Glasgow for some time. I am glad
to hear you are so saving and prudent; be so still: you must
go and hire yourself with some good people; what can you do?
I can thresh a little, and handle the spade. Can you plough?
Yes, Sir, with the little breast-plough I have brought with me.
These won't do here, Andrew; you are an able man; if you
are willing you will soon learn. I'll tell you what I intend to
do; I'll send you to my house, where you shall stay two or
three weeks, there you must exercise yourself with the axe,
that is the principal tool the Americans want, and particularly
the back-settlers. Can your wife spin? Yes, she can. Well
then, as soon as you are able to handle the axe, you shall go
and live with Mr. P. R. a particular friend of mine, who will
give you four dollars per month for the first six, and the
usual price of five as long as you remain with him. I shall
place your wife in another house, where she shall receive
half a dollar a week for spinning; and your son a dollar a month
to drive the team. You shall have besides good victuals to eat,
and good beds to lie on; will all this satisfy you, Andrew? He
hardly understood what I said; the honest tears of gratitude
fell from his eyes as he looked at me, and its expressions
seemed to quiver on his lips.—Though silent, this was saying
a great deal; there was besides something extremely moving

to see a man six feet high thus shed tears; and they did not lessen the good opinion I had entertained of him. At last he told me, that my offers were more than he deserved, and that he would first begin to work for his victuals. No, no, said I, if you are careful and sober, and do what you can, you shall receive what I told you, after you have served a short apprenticeship at my house. May God repay you for all your kindnesses! said Andrew; as long as I live I shall thank you, and do what I can for you! A few days after, I sent them all three to ——, by the return of some waggons, that he might have an opportunity of viewing and convincing himself of the utility of those machines, which he had at first so much admired.

The farther descriptions he gave us of the Hebrides in general, and of his native island in particular; of the customs and modes of living of the inhabitants; greatly entertained me. Pray is the sterility of the soil the cause that there are no trees, or is it because there are none planted? What are the modern families of all the kings of the earth, compared to the date of that of Mr. Neiel? Admitting that each generation should last but forty years, this makes a period of 1200; an extraordinary duration for the uninterrupted descent of any family! Agreeably to the description he gave us of those countries, they seem to live according to the rules of nature, which gives them but bare subsistence; their constitutions are uncontaminated by any excess or effeminacy, which their soil refuses. If their allowance of food is not too scanty, they must all be healthy, by perpetual temperance and exercise; if so, they are amply rewarded for their poverty. Could they have obtained but necessary food, they would not have left it; for it was not in consequence of oppression, either from their patriarch or the government, that they had emigrated. I wish we had a colony of these honest people settled in some parts of this province; their morals, their religion, seem to be as simple as their manners. This society would present an interesting spectacle, could they be transported on a richer soil. But perhaps that soil would soon alter every thing; for our opinions, vices, and virtues, are altogether local: we are machines fashioned by every circumstance around us.

Andrew arrived at my house a week before I did, and I found my wife, agreeably to my instructions, had placed the axe in his hands as his first task. For some time he was very aukward, but he was so docile, so willing, and grateful, as well as his wife, that I foresaw he would succeed. Agreeably to my promise, I put them all with different families, where they were well liked, and all parties were pleased. Andrew worked hard, lived well, grew fat, and every Sunday came to pay me a visit on a good horse, which Mr. P. R. lent him. Poor man, it took him a long time ere he could sit on the saddle and hold the bridle properly. I believe he had never before mounted such a beast, though I did not choose to ask him that question, for fear it might suggest some mortifying ideas. After having been twelve months at Mr. P. R.'s, and having received his own and his family's wages, which amounted to eighty-four dollars, he came to see me on a week-day, and told me, that he was a man of middle age, and would willingly have land of his own, in order to procure him a home, as a shelter against old age: that, whenever this period should come, his son, to whom he would give his land, would then maintain him, and thus live all together; he therefore required my advice and assistance. I thought his desire very natural and praise-worthy, and told him that I should think of it, but that he must remain one month longer with Mr. P. R. who had 3000 rails to split.* He immediately consented. The spring was not far advanced enough yet for Andrew to begin clearing any land, even supposing that he had made a purchase; as it is always necessary that the leaves should be out, in order that this additional combustible may serve to burn the heaps of brush more readily.

A few days after, it happened that the whole family of Mr. P. R. went to meeting, and left Andrew to take care of the house. While he was at the door, attentively reading the

Bible, nine Indians, just come from the mountains, suddenly made their appearance, and unloaded their packs of furs on the floor of the piazza. Conceive, if you can, what was Andrew's consternation at this extraordinary sight! From the singular appearance of these people, the honest Hebridean took them for a lawless band come to rob his master's house. He therefore, like a faithful guardian, precipitately withdrew, and shut the doors; but, as most of our houses are without locks, he was reduced to the necessity of fixing his knife over the latch, and then flew up stairs in quest of a broad sword he had brought from Scotland. The Indians, who were Mr. P. R.'s particular friends, guessed at his suspicions and fears; they forcibly lifted the door, and suddenly took possession of the house, got all the bread and meat they wanted, and sat themselves down by the fire. At this instant Andrew, with his broad sword in his hand, entered the room; the Indians earnestly looking at him, and attentively watching his motions. After a very few reflections, Andrew found that his weapon was useless, when opposed to nine tomahawks. But this did not diminish his anger; on the contrary, it grew greater, on observing the calm impudence with which they were devouring the family-provisions. Unable to resist, he called them names in broad Scotch, and ordered them to desist and be gone; to which the Indians (as they told me afterwards) replied in their equally broad idiom. It must have been a most unintelligible altercation between this honest Barra man and nine Indians who did not much care for any thing he could say. At last he ventured to lay his hands on one of them, in order to turn him out of the house. Here Andrew's fidelity got the better of his prudence; for the Indian, by his motions, threatened to scalp him, while the rest gave the war-hoop. This horrid noise so effectually frightened poor Andrew, that, unmindful of his courage, of his broad sword, and his intentions, he rushed out, left them masters of the house, and disappeared. I have heard one of the Indians say since, that he never laughed so heartily in his life. Andrew, at a distance,

soon recovered from the fears which had been inspired by
this infernal yell, and thought of no other remedy than to
go to the meeting-house, which was about two miles distant. In the eagerness of his honest intentions, with looks of
affright still marked on his countenance, he called Mr. P. R.
out, and told him with great vehemence of style, that nine
monsters were come to his house—some blue, some red, and
some black; that they had little axes in their hands, out of
which they smoked; and that, like highlanders, they had no
breeches; that they were devouring all his victuals; and that
God only knew what they would do more. Pacify yourself, said
Mr. P. R. my house is as safe with these people as if I was
there myself. As for the victuals, they are heartily welcome,
honest Andrew; they are not people of much ceremony; they
help themselves thus whenever they are among their friends;
I do so too in their whigwhams, whenever I go to their village: you had better therefore step in and hear the remainder
of the sermon, and when the meeting is over we will all go
back in the waggon together.

At their return, Mr. P. R. who speaks the Indian language
very well, explained the whole matter; the Indians renewed
their laugh, and shook hands with honest Andrew, whom
they made to smoke out of their pipes; and thus peace was
made, and ratified, according to the Indian custom, by the
calumet.*

Soon after this adventure, the time approached when I
had promised Andrew my best assistance to settle him; for
that purpose I went to Mr. A. V. in the county of ——, who,
I was informed, had purchased a track of land contiguous to
—— settlement. I gave him a faithful detail of the progress
Andrew had made in the rural arts; of his honesty, sobriety,
and gratitude; and pressed him to sell him a hundred acres.
This I cannot comply with, said Mr. A. V. but at the same
time I will do better; I love to encourage honest Europeans
as much as you do, and to see them prosper: you tell me he
has but one son; I will lease them a hundred acres for any

term of years you please, and make it more valuable to your
Scotchman than if he was possessed of the fee simple. By
that means he may, with that little money he has, buy a
plough, a team, and some stock; he will not be incumbered
with debts and mortgages; what he raises will be his own;
had he two or three sons as able as himself, then I should
think it more eligible for him to purchase the fee simple. I
join with you in opinion, and will bring Andrew along with
me in a few days.

Well, honest Andrew, said Mr. A. V. in consideration of
your good name, I will let you have a hundred acres of good
arable land, that shall be laid out along a new road; there is
a bridge already erected on the creek that passes through
the land, and a fine swamp of about twenty acres. These are
my terms; I cannot sell, but I will lease you the quantity that
Mr. James, your friend, has asked; the first seven years you
shall pay no rent, whatever you sow and reap, and plant and
gather, shall be entirely your own; neither the king, government, nor church, will have any claim on your future property: the remaining part of the time you must give me twelve
dollars and a half a year; and that is all you will have to pay
me. Within the three first years you must plant fifty apple
trees, and clear seven acres of swamp within the first part
of the lease; it will be your own advantage: whatever you do
more, within that time, I will pay you for it, at the common
rate of the country. The term of the lease shall be thirty years;
how do you like it, Andrew? Oh, Sir, it is very good; but I
am afraid, that the king, or his ministers, or the governor,
or some of our great men, will come and take the land from
me; your son may say to me, by and by, this is my father's
land, Andrew, you must quit it. No, no, said Mr. A. V. there
is no such danger; the king and his ministers are too just to
take the labour of a poor settler; here we have no great men,
but what are subordinate to our laws; but, to calm all your
fears, I will give you a lease, so that none can make you afraid.
If ever you are dissatisfied with the land, a jury of your own

neighbourhood shall value all your improvements, and you shall be paid agreeably to their verdict. You may sell the lease; or, if you die, you may previously dispose of it as if the land was your own. Expressive, yet inarticulate, joy was mixed in his countenance, which seemed impressed with astonishment and confusion. Do you understand me well? said Mr. A. V. No, Sir, replied Andrew, I know nothing of what you mean about lease, improvement, will, jury, &c. That is honest, we will explain these things to you by and by. It must be confessed that those were hard words, which he had never heard in his life; for, by his own account, the ideas they convey would be totally useless in the island of Barra. No wonder, therefore, that he was embarrassed; for how could the man, who had hardly a will of his own since he was born, imagine he could have one after his death? How could the person, who never possessed any thing, conceive that he could extend his new dominion over this land, even after he should be laid in his grave? For my part, I think Andrew's amazement did not imply any extraordinary degree of ignorance; he was an actor introduced upon a new scene, it required some time ere he could reconcile himself to the part he was to perform. However, he was soon enlightened, and introduced into those mysteries with which we native Americans are but too well acquainted.

Here then is honest Andrew, invested with every municipal advantage they confer; become a freeholder, possessed of a vote, of a place of residence, a citizen of the province of Pennsylvania. Andrew's original hopes and the distant prospects he had formed in the island of Barra, were at the eve of being realized; we therefore can easily forgive him a few spontaneous ejaculations, which would be useless to repeat. This short tale is easily told; few words are sufficient to describe this sudden change of situation; but in his mind it was gradual, and took him above a week before he could be sure, that, without disbursing any money, he could possess lands. Soon after he prepared himself; I lent him a barrel of

pork, and 200 lb. weight of meal, and made him purchase
what was necessary besides.

He set out, and hired a room in the house of a settler, who
lived the most contiguous to his own land. His first work was
to clear some acres of swamp, that he might have a supply
of hay the following year for his two horses and cows. From
the first day he began to work he was indefatigable; his honesty procured him friends, and his industry the esteem of his
new neighbours. One of them offered him two acres of cleared
land, whereon he might plant corn, pompions,* squashes, and
a few potatoes, that very season. It is astonishing how quick
men will learn when they work for themselves. I saw with
pleasure, two months after, Andrew holding a two-horse
plough, and tracing his furrows quite straight: thus the spade-
man of the island of Barra was become the tiller of American
soil. Well done, said I, Andrew, well done; I see that God
speeds and directs your works; I see prosperity delineated in
all your furrows and head-lands. Raise this crop of corn with
attention and care, and then you will be master of the art.

As he had neither mowing nor reaping to do that year,
I told him that the time was come to build his house; and
that, for the purpose, I would myself invite the neighbourhood to a frolic;* that thus he would have a large dwelling
erected, and some upland cleared, in one day. Mr. P. R. his
old friend, came at the time appointed, with all his hands, and
brought victuals in plenty: I did the same. About forty people
repaired to the spot; the songs and merry stories went round
the woods from cluster to cluster, as the people had gathered
to their different works; trees fell on all sides; bushes were
cut up and heaped; and, while many were thus employed,
others with their teams hauled the big logs to the spot which
Andrew had pitched upon for the erection of his new dwelling. We all dined in the woods; in the afternoon the logs were
placed with skids and the usual contrivances. Thus the rude
house was raised, and above two acres of land cut up, cleared,
and heaped.

Whilst all these different operations were performing, Andrew was absolutely incapable of working; it was to him the most solemn holiday he had ever seen; it would have been sacrilegious in him to have defiled it with menial labour. Poor man, he sanctified it with joy and thanksgiving, and honest libations!—he went from one to the other with the bottle in his hand, pressing every body to drink, and drinking himself to shew the example. He spent the whole day in smiling, laughing, and uttering monosyllables. His wife and son were there also; but, as they could not understand the language, their pleasure must have been altogether that of the imagination. The powerful lord, the wealthy merchant, on seeing the superb mansion finished, never can feel half the joy and real happiness which was felt and enjoyed on that day by this honest Hebridean, though this new dwelling, erected in the midst of the woods, was nothing more than a square inclosure, composed of twenty-four large clumsy logs, let in at the ends. When the work was finished, the company made the woods resound with the noise of their three cheers, and the honest wishes they formed for Andrew's prosperity. He could say nothing; but, with thankful tears, he shook hands with them all. Thus, from the first day he had landed, Andrew marched towards this important event: this memorable day made the sun shine on that land on which he was to sow wheat and other grain. What swamp he had cleared lay before his door; the essence of future bread, milk, and meat, were scattered all round him. Soon after he hired a carpenter, who put on a roof and laid the floors; in a week more the house was properly plastered and the chimney finished. He moved into it, and purchased two cows, which found plenty of food in the woods; his hogs had the same advantage. That very year, he and his son sowed three bushels of wheat, from which he reaped ninety-one and a half; for I had ordered him to keep an exact account of all he should raise. His first crop of other corn would have been as good, had it not been for the squirrels, which were enemies not to be dispersed by the broad sword. The fourth year I took an inventory of the wheat this man possessed, which I send you. Soon after, farther settlements were made on that road, and Andrew, instead of being the last man towards the wilderness, found himself, in a few years, in the middle of a numerous society. He helped others as generously as others had helped him; and I have dined many times at his table with several of his neighbours. The second year he was made overseer of the road, and served on two petty juries, performing as a citizen all the duties required of him. The historiographer of some great prince or general does not bring his hero victorious, to the end of a successful campaign, with one half of the heart-felt pleasure with which I have conducted Andrew to the situation he now enjoys: he is independent and easy. Triumph and military honours do not always imply those two blessings. He is unincumbered with debts, services, rents, or any other dues: the successes of a campaign, the laurels of war, must be purchased at the dearest rate, which makes every cool, reflecting, citizen to tremble and shudder. By the literal account, hereunto annexed, you will easily be made acquainted with the happy effects which constantly flow, in this country, from sobriety and industry, when united with good land and freedom.

The account of the property he acquired with his own hands and those of his son, in four years, is as under:

	Dollars.
The value of his improvements and lease	225
Six cows, at 13 dollars	78
Two breeding mares	50
The rest of the stock	100
Seventy-three bushels of wheat	66
Money due to him on notes	43
Pork and beef in his cellar	28
Wool and flax	19
Ploughs and other utensils of husbandry	31
240l. Pennsylvania currency.—Dollars	640

LETTER IV

DESCRIPTION OF THE ISLAND OF
NANTUCKET, WITH THE MANNERS, CUSTOMS,
POLICY, AND TRADE, OF THE INHABITANTS

THE greatest compliment that can be paid to the best of
kings, to the wisest ministers, or the most patriotic rulers, is
to think, that the reformation of political abuses, and the
happiness of their people, are the primary objects of their
attention. But, alas! how disagreeable must the work of reformation be! how dreaded the operation! for we hear of no
amendment: on the contrary, the great number of European
emigrants, yearly coming over here, informs us, that the severity of taxes, the injustice of laws, the tyranny of the rich, and
the oppressive avarice of the church, are as intolerable as ever.
Will these calamities have no end? Are not the great rulers
of the earth afraid of losing, by degrees, their most useful
subjects? This country, providentially intended for the general
asylum of the world, will flourish by the oppression of other
people; they will every day become better acquainted with the
happiness we enjoy, and seek for the means of transporting
themselves here, in spite of all obstacles and laws. To what
purpose then have so many useful books and divine maxims
been transmitted to us from preceding ages?—Are they all
vain, all useless? Must human nature ever be the sport of the
few, and its many wounds remain unhealed? How happy are
we here, in having fortunately escaped the miseries which
attended our fathers! how thankful ought we to be, that they
reared us in a land, where sobriety and industry never fail
to meet with the most ample rewards! You have, no doubt,
read several histories of this continent; yet there are a thousand facts, a thousand explanations, overlooked. Authors will
certainly convey to you a geographical knowledge of this

country; they will acquaint you with the æras of the several
settlements, the foundations of our towns, the spirit of our
different charters, &c. yet they do not sufficiently disclose
the genius of the people, their various customs, their modes
of agriculture, the innumerable resources which the industrious have of raising themselves to a comfortable and easy
situation. Few of these writers have resided here; and those
who have had not pervaded every part of the country, nor
carefully examined the nature and principles of our association. It would be a task worthy a speculative genius, to enter
intimately into the situation and characters of the people from
Nova Scotia to West Florida; and surely history cannot possibly present any subject more pleasing to behold. Sensible
how unable I am to lead you through so vast a maze, let us
look attentively for some small unnoticed corner; but where
shall we go in quest of such an one? Numberless settlements,
each distinguished by some peculiarities, present themselves
on every side; all seem to realize the most sanguine wishes
that a good man could form for the happiness of his race.
Here they live by fishing on the most plentiful coasts in the
world; there they fell trees, by the sides of large rivers, for
masts and lumber; here others convert innumerable logs into
the best boards; there again others cultivate the land, rear
cattle, and clear large fields. Yet I have a spot in my view,
where none of these occupations are performed, which will,
I hope, reward us for the trouble of inspection; but, though
it is barren in its soil, insignificant in its extent, inconvenient
in its situation, deprived of materials for building, it seems to
have been inhabited merely to prove what mankind can do
when happily governed! Here I can point out to you exertions
of the most successful industry; instances of native sagacity
unassisted by science; the happy fruits of a well-directed
perseverance. It is always a refreshing spectacle to me, when,
in my review of the various component parts of this immense
whole, I observe the labours of its inhabitants singularly
rewarded by nature; when I see them emerged out of their

first difficulties, living with decency and ease, and conveying to their posterity that plentiful subsistence, which their fathers have so deservedly earned. But, when their prosperity arises from the goodness of the climate, and fertility of the soil, I partake of their happiness it is true, yet stay but a little while with them, as they exhibit nothing but what is natural and common. On the contrary, when I meet with barren spots fertilized, grass growing where none grew before; grain gathered from fields which had hitherto produced nothing better than brambles; dwellings raised where no building materials were to be found; wealth acquired by the most uncommon means: there I pause, to dwell on the favourite object of my speculative inquiries. Willingly do I leave the former to enjoy the odoriferous furrow or their rich vallies, with anxiety repairing to the spot, where so many difficulties have been overcome; where extraordinary exertions have produced extraordinary effects, and where every natural obstacle has been removed by a vigorous industry.

I want not to record the annals of the island of Nantucket; —its inhabitants have no annals, for they are not a race of warriors. My simple wish is, to trace them throughout their progressive steps, from their arrival here to this present hour; to enquire by what means they have raised themselves, from the most humble, the most insignificant, beginnings, to the ease and the wealth they now possess; and to give you some idea of their customs, religion, manners, policy, and mode of living.

This happy settlement was not founded on intrusion, forcible entries, or blood, as so many others have been; it drew its origin from necessity on the one side, and from good will on the other; and, ever since, all has been a scene of uninterrupted harmony.—Neither political nor religious broils, neither disputes with the natives, nor any other contentions, have in the least agitated or disturbed its detached society. Yet the first founders knew nothing either of Lycurgus or Solon;* for this settlement has not been the work of eminent men or powerful legislators, forcing nature by the accumulated labours of art. This singular establishment has been effected by means of that native industry and perseverance, common to all men, when they are protected by a government which demands but little for its protection; when they are permitted to enjoy a system of rational laws founded on perfect freedom. The mildness and humanity of such a government necessarily implies that confidence which is the source of the most arduous undertakings and permanent success. Would you believe that a sandy spot, of about twenty-three thousand acres, affording neither stones nor timber, meadows nor arable, yet can boast of a handsome town consisting of more than 500 houses, should possess above 200 sail of vessels, constantly employ upwards of 2000 seamen, feed more than 15,000 sheep, 500 cows, 200 horses, and has several citizens worth 20,000l. sterling? Yet all these facts are uncontroverted. Who would have imagined that any people should have abandoned a fruitful and extensive continent, filled with the riches which the most ample vegetation affords, replete with good soil, enamelled meadows, rich pastures, every kind of timber, and with all other materials necessary to render life happy and comfortable, to come and inhabit a little sand-bank, to which nature had refused those advantages; to dwell on a spot where there scarcely grew a shrub to announce, by the budding of its leaves, the arrival of the spring, and to warn, by their fall, the proximity of winter? Had this island been contiguous to the shores of some ancient monarchy, it would only have been occupied by a few wretched fishermen, who, oppressed by poverty, would hardly have been able to purchase or build little fishing barks; always dreading the weight of taxes, or the servitude of men of war. Instead of that boldness of speculation for which the inhabitants of this island are so remarkable, they would fearfully have confined themselves within the narrow limits of the most trifling attempts; timid in their excursions, they never could have extricated themselves from their first difficulties. This island, on the contrary, contains 5000 hardy people, who boldly derive their riches from the element that surrounds them, and have been compelled, by the sterility of the soil, to seek abroad for the means of subsistence. You must not imagine, from the recital of these facts, that they enjoyed any exclusive privileges or royal charters, or that they were nursed by particular immunities, in the infancy of their settlement. No; their freedom, their skill, their probity, and perseverance, have accomplished every thing, and brought them by degrees to the rank they now hold.

From this first sketch, I hope that my partiality to this island will be justified. Perhaps you hardly know that such an one exists in the neighbourhood of Cape Cod. What has happened here has and will happen every where else. Give mankind the full rewards of their industry, allow them to enjoy the fruit of their labour under the peaceable shade of their vines and fig-trees, leave their native activity unshackled and free, like a fair stream without dams or other obstacles; the first will fertilize the very sand on which they tread, the other exhibit a navigable river, spreading plenty and cheerfulness wherever the declivity of the ground leads it. If these people are not famous for tracing the fragrant furrow on the plain, they plough the rougher ocean, they gather from its surface, at an immense distance and with Herculean labours, the riches it affords; they go to hunt and catch that huge fish, which, by its strength and velocity, one would imagine ought to be beyond the reach of man. This island has nothing deserving of notice but its inhabitants; here you meet with neither ancient monuments, spacious halls, solemn temples, nor elegant dwellings; not a citadel nor any kind of fortification, not even a battery to rend the air with its loud peals on any solemn occasion. As for their rural improvements, they are many, but all of the most simple and useful kind.

The island of Nantucket, a map of which, drawn by Dr. James Tupper, son of the sheriff of the island, I send you inclosed, lies in latitude 41° 10′. 100 miles N.E. from Cape Cod. 27 N. from Hyanes or Barnstable, a town on the most

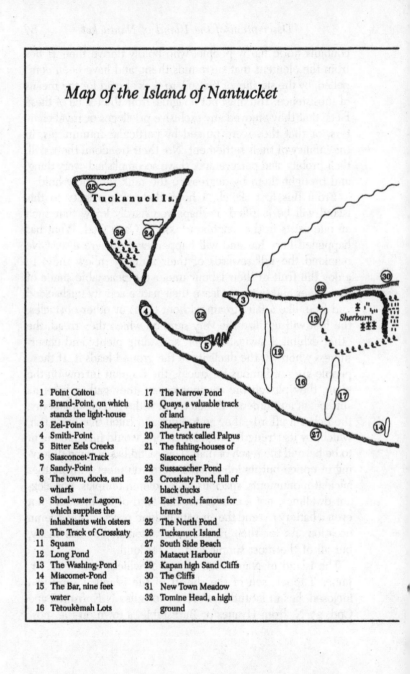

Map of the Island of Nantucket

Tuckanuck Is.

Sherburn

1 Point Coitou
2 Brand-Point, on which stands the light-house
3 Eel-Point
4 Smith-Point
5 Bitter Eels Creeks
6 Siasconcet-Track
7 Sandy-Point
8 The town, docks, and wharfs
9 Shoal-water Lagoon, which supplies the inhabitants with oisters
10 The Track of Crosskaty
11 Squam
12 Long Pond
13 The Washing-Pond
14 Miacomet-Pond
15 The Bar, nine feet water
16 Tètoukèmah Lots
17 The Narrow Pond
18 Quays, a valuable track of land
19 Sheep-Pasture
20 The track called Palpus
21 The fishing-houses of Siasconcet
22 Sussacacher Pond
23 Crosskaty Pond, full of black ducks
24 East Pond, famous for brants
25 The North Pond
26 Tuckanuck Island
27 South Side Beach
28 Matacut Harbour
29 Kapan high Sand Cliffs
30 The Cliffs
31 New Town Meadow
32 Tomine Head, a high ground

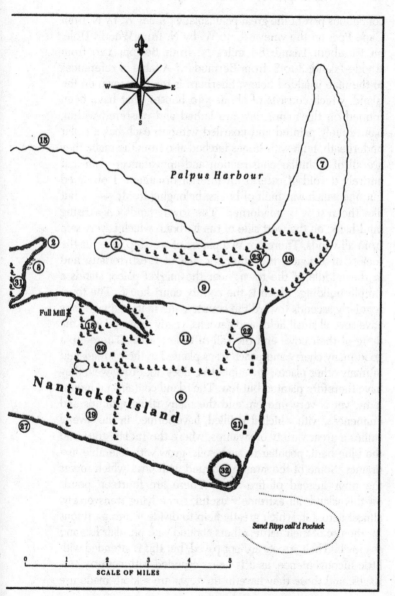

Palpus Harbour

Nantucket Island

Full Mill

Sand Ripp call'd Pochick

0   1   2   3   4   5
SCALE OF MILES

contiguous part of the great peninsula; 21 miles W. by N. from
Cape Pog, on the vineyard; 50 W. by N. from Wood's Hole,
on Elizabeth Island; 80 miles N. from Boston; 120 from
Rhode-Island; 800 S. from Bermudas.* A table of references
to the map is added below. Sherborn is the only town on the
island, which consists of about 530 houses, that have been
framed on the main; they are lathed and plastered within,
handsomely painted and boarded without; each has a cellar
underneath, built with stones fetched also from the main: they
are all of a similar construction and appearance; plain and
entirely devoid of exterior or interior ornament. I observed
but one which was built of bricks, belonging to Mr. ——, but
like the rest it is unadorned. The town stands on a rising
sand-bank, on the west side of the harbour, which is very safe
from all winds. There are two places of worship, one for the
society of Friends, the other for that of Presbyterians; and
in the middle of the town, near the market-place, stands a
simple building, which is the county court-house. The town
regularly ascends toward the country, and in its vicinage they
have several small fields and gardens, yearly manured with the
dung of their cows and the soil of their streets. There are a
good many cherry and peach trees planted in their streets and
in many other places; the apple-tree does not thrive well, they
have therefore planted but few. The island contains no mountains, yet is very uneven; and the many rising grounds and
eminences, with which it is filled, have formed in the several
vallies a great variety of swamps, where the Indian grass and
the blue bent, peculiar to such soils, grow with tolerable lux-
uriancy. Some of the swamps abound with peat, which serves
the poor instead of fire-wood. There are fourteen ponds
on this island, all extremely useful, some lying transversely,
almost across it, which greatly help to divide it into partitions
for the use of their cattle; others abound with peculiar fish and
sea fowls. Their streets are not paved, but this is attended with
little inconvenience, as it is never crouded with country carriages; and those they have in the town are seldom made use

of but in the time of coming in and before the sailing of
their fleets. At my first landing I was much surprized at the
disagreeable smell which struck me in many parts of the town;
it is caused by the whale-oil, and is unavoidable; the neatness
peculiar to these people can neither remove or prevent it.
There are near the wharfs a great many storehouses, where
their staple commodity is deposited, as well as the innumerable materials which are always wanted to repair and fit out
so many whale-men. They have three docks, each three hundred feet long, and extremely convenient; at the head of which
there are ten feet of water. These docks are built like those
in Boston, of logs fetched from the continent, filled with
stones, and covered with sand. Between these docks and the
town there is room sufficient for the landing of goods and
for the passage of their numerous carts; for almost every
man here has one: the wharfs, to the north and south of the
docks, are built of the same materials, and give a stranger,
at his first landing, a high idea of the prosperity of these
people; and there is room around these three docks for 300
sail of vessels. When their fleets have been successful, the
bustle and hurry of business on this spot, for some days after
their arrival, would make you imagine, that Sherborn is the
capital of a very opulent and large province. On that point
of land, which forms the west side of the harbour, stands a
very neat light-house; the opposite peninsula, called Coitou,
secures it from the most dangerous winds. There are but few
gardens and arable fields in the neighbourhood of the town,
for nothing can be more sterile and sandy than this part of the
island; they have however with unwearied perseverance, by
bringing a variety of manure, and by cow-penning, enriched
several spots where they raise Indian corn, potatoes, pompions,
turnips, &c. On the highest part of this sandy eminence, four
windmills grind the grain they raise to export; and contiguous
to them their rope-walk is to be seen, where full half of their
cordage is manufactured. Between the shores of the harbour,
the docks, and the town, there is a most excellent piece of

meadow, inclosed and manured with such cost and pains
as shew how necessary and precious grass is at Nantucket.
Towards the point of Shemah the island is more level and the
soil better; and there they have considerable lots well fenced
and richly manured, where they diligently raise their yearly
crops. There are but very few farms on this island, because
there are but very few spots that will admit of cultivation without the assistance of dung and other manure; which is very
expensive to fetch from the main. This island was patented,
in the year 1671, by twenty-seven proprietors, under the
province of New-York; which then claimed all the islands from
the Neway Sink to Cape Cod. They found it so universally
barren, and so unfit for cultivation, that they mutually agreed
not to divide it, as each could neither live on, nor improve,
that lot which might fall to his share. They then cast their
eyes on the sea, and, finding themselves obliged to become
fishermen, they looked for a harbour; and, having found one,
they determined to build a town in its neighbourhood and
to dwell together. For that purpose they surveyed as much
ground as would afford to each what is generally called here
a home-lot. Forty acres were thought sufficient to answer this
double purpose; for, to what end should they covet more land
than they could improve, or even inclose? not being possessed
of a single tree in the whole extent of their new dominion.
This was all the territorial property they allotted; the rest
they agreed to hold in common; and, seeing that the scanty
grass of the island might feed sheep, they agreed that each
proprietor should be entitled to feed on it, if he pleased, 560
sheep. By this agreement, the national flock was to consist
of 15,120; that is, the undivided part of the Island was, by
such means, ideally divisible into as many parts or shares; to
which nevertheless no certain determinate quantity of land
was affixed: for they knew not how much the island contained,
nor could the most judicious surveyor fix this small quota as
to quality and quantity. Farther they agreed, in case the grass
should grow better by feeding, that then four sheep should

represent a cow, and two cows a horse: such was the method this wise people took to enjoy in common their new settlement; such was the mode of their first establishment, which may be truly and literally called a pastoral one. Several hundred of sheep-pasture titles have since been divided on those different tracks, which are now cultivated; the rest by inheritance and intermarriages have been so subdivided, that it is very common for a girl to have no other portion but her outset and four sheep-pastures, or the privilege of feeding a cow. But, as this privilege is founded on an ideal though real title to some unknown piece of land, which one day or another may be ascertained, these *sheep-pasture titles* should convey to your imagination something more valuable and of greater credit than the mere advantage arising from the benefit of a cow, which in that case would be no more than a right of commonage. Whereas here, as labour grows cheaper, as misfortunes from their sea-adventures may happen, each person, possessed of a sufficient number of these sheep-pasture titles, may one day realize them on some peculiar spot, such as shall be adjudged, by the council of the proprietors, to be adequate to their value; and this is the reason that these people very unwillingly sell those small rights, and esteem them more than you would imagine. They are the representation of a future freehold, they cherish in the mind of the possessor a latent, though distant, hope, that, by his success in his next whale season, he may be able to pitch on some predilected spot, and there build himself a home, to which he may retire, and spend the latter end of his days in peace. A council of proprietors always exists in this island, who decide their territorial differences; their titles are recorded in the books of the county, which this town represents, as well as every conveyance of lands and other sales.

This island furnishes the naturalist with few or no objects worthy observation: it appears to be the uneven summit of a sandy submarine mountain, covered here and there with sorrel, grass, a few cedar-bushes, and scrubby oaks; their swamps are much more valuable for the peat they contain than for the trifling pasture of their surface; those declining grounds which lead to the sea-shores abound with *beach grass*, a light fodder when cut and cured, but very good when fed green. On the east side of the island they have several tracks of salt grasses, which, being carefully fenced, yield a considerable quantity of that wholesome fodder. Among the many ponds, or lakes, with which this island abounds, there are some which have been made by the intrusion of the sea, such as Wiwidiah, the Long, the Narrow, and several others; consequently those are salt and the others fresh. The former answer two considerable purposes; first, by enabling them to fence the island with greater facility; at peculiar high tides a great number of fish enter into them, where they feed and grow large, and, at some known seasons of the year, the inhabitants assemble and cut down the small bars which the waves always throw up. By these easy means the waters of the pond are let out, and, as the fish follow their native element, the inhabitants with proper nets catch as many as they want, in their way out, without any other trouble. Those which are most common are the streaked bass, the blue fish, the tom-cod, the mackarel, the tew-tag, the herring, the flounder, eel, &c. Fishing is one of the greatest diversions the island affords. At the west end lies the harbour of Mardiket, formed by Smith Point on the south-west, by Eel Point on the north, and *Tuckanut Island* on the north-west; but it is neither so safe, nor has it so good anchoring ground, as that near which the towns stands. Three small creeks run into it, which yield the bitterest eels I have ever tasted. Between the lots of Palpus on the east, Barry's Vally and Miacomet pond on the south, and the narrow pond on the west, not far from Shèmà Point, they have a considerable track of even ground, being the least sandy and the best on the island. It is divided into seven fields, one of which is planted by that part of the community which are entitled to it. This is called the common plantation, a simple but useful expedient; for, were each holder of this track to fence his property, it would require a prodigious quantity of posts and rails, which you must remember are to be purchased and fetched from the main. Instead of those private subdivisions, each man's allotment of land is thrown into the general field, which is fenced at the expence of the parties; within it every one does, with his own portion of the ground, whatever he pleases. This apparent community saves a very material expence, a great deal of labour, and perhaps raises a sort of emulation among them, which urges every one to fertilize his share with the greatest care and attention. Thus, every seven years, the whole of this track is under cultivation, and, enriched by manure and ploughing, yields afterwards excellent pasture; to which the town-cows, amounting to 500, are daily led by the town-shepherd, and as regularly driven back in the evening. There each animal easily finds the house to which it belongs, where they are sure to be well rewarded, for the milk they give, by a present of bran, grain, or some farinaceous preparation; their œconomy being very great in that respect. These are commonly called Tètoukèmah lots. You must not imagine that every person on the island is either a land-holder, or concerned in rural operations; no, the greater part are at sea, busily employed in their different fisheries; others are mere strangers, who come to settle as handicrafts, mechanics, &c. and, even among the natives, few are possessed of determinate shares of land; for, engaged in sea affairs or trade, they are satisfied with possessing a few sheep-pastures, by means of which they may have perhaps one or two cows. Many have but one; for, the great number of children they have has caused such subdivisions of the original proprietorship as is sometimes puzzling to trace; and several of the most fortunate at sea have purchased and realized a great number of these original pasture titles. The best land on the island is at Palpus, remarkable for nothing but a house of entertainment. Quayes is a small but valuable track, long since purchased by Mr. Coffin, where he has erected the best house on the island. By long attention, proximity of the sea, &c.

this fertile spot has been well manured and is now the garden of Nantucket. Adjoining to it, on the west side, there is a small stream, on which they have erected a fulling-mill;* on the east side is the lot, known by the name of Squam, watered likewise by a small rivulet, on which stands another fulling-mill. Here is a fine loomy* soil, producing excellent clover, which is mowed twice a year. These mills prepare all the cloth which is made here: you may easily suppose that, having so large a flock of sheep, they abound in wool; part of this they export, and the rest is spun by their industrious wives, and converted into substantial garments. To the south-east is a great division of the island, fenced by itself, known by the name of Siasconcèt lot. It is a very uneven track of ground, abounding with swamps; here they turn in their fat cattle, or such as they intend to stall-feed for their winter's provisions. It is on the shores of this part of the island, near Pochick Rip, where they catch their best fish, such as sea bass, tewtag, or black fish, cod, smelt, perch, shadine, pike, &c. They have erected a few fishing-houses on this shore, as well as at Sankate's Head, and Suffakatchè Beach, where the fishermen dwell in the fishing season. Many red cedar bushes and beach grass grow on the peninsula of Coitou; the soil is light and sandy, and serves as a receptacle for rabbits. It is here that their sheep find shelter in the snow-storms of the winter. At the north end of Nantucket, there is a long point of land, projecting far into the sea, called Sandy Point; nothing grows on it but plain grass; and this is the place whence they often catch porpoises and sharks, by a very ingenious method. On this point they commonly drive their horses in the spring of the year, in order to feed on the grass it bears, which is useless when arrived at maturity. Between that point and the main island they have a valuable salt meadow, called Croskaty, with a pond of the same name, famous for black ducks. Hence we must return to Squam, which abounds in clover and herdsgrass; those who possess it follow no maritime occupation, and therefore neglect nothing that can render it fertile and

profitable. The rest of the undescribed part of the island is
open, and serves as a common pasture for their sheep. To
the west of the island is that of Tackanuck, where, in the
spring, their young cattle are driven to feed; it has a few oak
bushes, and two fresh-water ponds, abounding with teals,
brandts, and many other sea fowls, brought to this island by
the proximity of their sand-banks and shallows; where thousands are seen feeding at low water. Here they have neither
wolves nor foxes; those inhabitants therefore, who live out
of town, raise with all security as much poultry as they want;
their turkeys are very large and excellent. In summer this
climate is extremely pleasant; they are not exposed to the
scorching sun of the continent, the heats being tempered by
the sea breezes, with which they are perpetually refreshed.
In the winter, however, they pay severely for those advantages; it is extremely cold; the north-west wind, the tyrant of
this country, after having escaped from our mountains and
forests, free from all impediment in its short passage, blows
with redoubled force, and renders this island bleak and uncom-
fortable. On the other hand, the goodness of their houses,
the social hospitality of their fire-sides, and their good cheer,
make them ample amends for the severity of the season; nor
are the snows so deep as on the main. The necessary and
unavoidable inactivity of that season, combined with the
vegetative rest of nature, force mankind to suspend their toils:
often, at this season, more than half the inhabitants of the
island are at sea, fishing in milder latitudes.

This island, as has been already hinted, appears to be the
summit of some huge sandy mountain, affording some acres
of dry land for the habitation of man; other submarine ones
lie to the southward of this, at different depths and different
distances. This dangerous region is well known to the mariners
by the name of Nantucket Shoals: these are the bulwarks
which so powerfully defend this island from the impulse of
the mighty ocean, and repel the force of its waves; which, but
for the accumulated barriers, would ere now have dissolved

its foundations, and torn it in pieces. These are the banks which afforded to the first inhabitants of Nantucket their daily subsistence, as it was from these shoals that they drew the origin of that wealth which they now possess; and it was the school where they first learned how to venture farther, as the fish of their coast receded. The shores of this island abound with the soft-shelled, the hard-shelled, and the great, sea-clams, a most nutricious shellfish. Their sands, their shallows, are covered with them; they multiply so fast, that they are a never-failing resource. These, and the great variety of fish they catch, constitute the principal food of the inhabitants. It was likewise that of the aborigines, whom the first settlers found here; the posterity of whom still live together in decent houses along the shores of Miacomet pond, on the south side of the island. They are an industrious, harmless, race, as expert and as fond of a seafaring life as their fellow inhabitants, the whites. Long before their arrival they had been engaged in petty wars against one another; the latter brought them peace, for it was in quest of peace that they abandoned the main. This island was then supposed to be under the jurisdiction of New York, as well as the islands of the Vineyard, Elizabeth's, &c. but have been since adjudged to be a part of the province of Massachuset's Bay. This change of jurisdiction procured them that peace they wanted, and which their brethren had so long refused them in the days of their religious phrensy: thus have enthusiasm and persecution, both in Europe as well as here, been the cause of the most arduous undertakings, and the means of those rapid settlements which have been made along these extended seashores. This island, having been since incorporated with the neighbouring province, is become one of its counties, known by the name of Nantucket, as well as the island of the Vineyard by that of Duke's County. They enjoy here the same municipal establishment in common with the rest; and therefore every requisite officer, such as sheriff, justice of the peace, supervisors, assessors, constables, overseers of the poor, &c.

Their taxes are proportioned to those of the metropolis; they are levied, as with us, by valuations, agreed on and fixed according to the laws of the province; and by assessments formed by the assessors, who are yearly chosen by the people, and whose office obliges them to take either an oath or an affirmation. Two-thirds of the magistrates they have here are of the society of Friends.

Before I enter into the farther detail of this people's government, industry, mode of living, &c. I think it necessary to give you a short sketch of the political state the natives had been in a few years preceding the arrival of the whites among them. They are hastening towards a total annihilation, and this may be, perhaps, the last compliment that will ever be paid them by any traveller. They were not extirpated by fraud, violence, or injustice, as hath been the case in so many provinces; on the contrary, they have been treated by these people as brethren; the peculiar genius of their sect inspiring them with the same spirit of moderation which was exhibited at Pennsylvania. Before the arrival of the Europeans, they lived on the fish of their shores; and it was from the same resources the first settlers were compelled to draw their first subsistence. It is uncertain whether the original right of the Earl of Sterling,* or that of the Duke of York,* was founded on a fair purchase of the soil or not; whatever injustice might have been committed in that respect cannot be charged to the account of those Friends, who purchased from others, who, no doubt, founded their right on Indian grants; and, if their numbers are now so decreased, it must not be attributed either to tyranny or violence, but to some of those causes, which have uninterruptedly produced the same effects from one end of the continent to the other, wherever both nations have been mixed. This insignificant spot, like the sea-shores of the great peninsula, was filled with these people; the great plenty of clams, oisters, and other fish, on which they lived, and which they easily caught, had prodigiously increased their num-bers. History does not inform us what particular nation the

aborigines of Nantucket were of; it is however very probable
that they anciently emigrated from the opposite coast, perhaps from the Hyanneès, which is but twenty-seven miles
distant. As they then spoke and still speak the Nattick, it is reasonable to suppose that they must have had some affinity with
that nation; or else that the Nattick, like the Huron, in the
north-western parts of this continent, must have been the most
prevailing one in this region. Mr. Elliot,* an eminent New
England divine, and one of the first founders of that great
colony, translated the Bible into this language in the year 1666,
which was printed soon after at Cambridge, near Boston; he
translated also the catechism, and many other useful books,
which are still very common on this island, and are daily made
use of by those Indians who are taught to read. The young
Europeans learn it with the same facility as their own tongues;
and ever after speak it both with ease and fluency. Whether
the present Indians are the descendants of the ancient natives
of the island, or whether they are the remains of the many
different nations which once inhabited the regions of Mashpè
and Nobscusset, in the peninsula now known by the name
of Cape Cod, no one can positively tell, not even themselves.
The last opinion seems to be that of the most sensible people
of the island. So prevailing is the disposition of man to quarrel, and to shed blood; so prone is he to divisions and parties;
that even the ancient natives of this little spot were separated
into two communities, inveterately waging war against each
other, like the more powerful tribes of the continent. What
do you imagine was the cause of this national quarrel? All the
coast of their island equally abounded with the same quantity
of fish and clams; in that instance there could be no jealousy,
no motives to anger; the country afforded them no game: one
would think this ought to have been the country of harmony
and peace. But behold the singular destiny of the human kind,
ever inferior, in many instances, to the more certain instinct
of animals; among which the individuals of the same species
are always friends, though reared in different climates: they

understand the same language, they shed not each other's blood, they eat not each other's flesh. That part of these rude people, who lived on the eastern shores of the island, had from time immemorial tried to destroy those who lived on the west; those latter, inspired with the same evil genius, had not been behind hand in retaliating: thus was a perpetual war subsisting between these people, founded on no other reason but the adventitious place of their nativity and residence. In process of time both parties became so thin and depopulated, that the few who remained, fearing lest their race should become totally extinct, fortunately thought of an expedient which prevented their entire annihilation. Some years before the Europeans came, they mutually agreed to settle a partition line, which should divide the island from north to south; the people of the west agreed not to kill those of the east, except they were found transgressing over the western part of the line; those of the last entered into a reciprocal agreement. By these simple means peace was established among them, and this is the only record which seems to entitle them to the denomination of men. This happy settlement put a stop to their sanguinary depredations; none fell afterward but a few rash imprudent individuals; on the contrary, they multiplied greatly. But another misfortune awaited them; when the Europeans came, they caught the small-pox, and their improper treatment of that disorder swept away great numbers: this calamity was succeeded by the use of rum; and these are the two principal causes which so much diminished their numbers, not only here but all over the continent. In some places whole nations have disappeared. Some years ago, three Indian canoes, on their return to Detroit from the falls of Niagara, unluckily got the small-pox from the Europeans with whom they had traded. It broke out near the long point on lake Erie; there they all perished; their canoes, and their goods, were afterwards found by some travellers journeying the same way; their dogs were yet alive. Besides the small-pox, and the use of spirituous liquors, the two greatest curses they have received from us, there is a sort of physical antipathy, which is equally powerful from one end of the continent to the other. Wherever they happen to be mixed, or even to live in the neighbourhood of the Europeans, they became exposed to a variety of accidents and misfortunes to which they always fall victims: such are particular fevers, to which they were strangers before, and sinking into a singular sort of indolence and sloth. This has been invariably the case wherever the same association has taken place; as at Nattick, Mashpè, Soccanoket in the bounds of Falmouth, Nobscusset, Houratonick, Monhauset, and the Vineyard. Even the Mohawks themselves, who were once so populous and such renowned warriors, are now reduced to less than 200 since the European settlements have circumscribed the territories which their ancestors had reserved. Three years before the arrival of the Europeans at Cape Cod, a frightful distemper had swept away a great many along its coasts, which made the landing and intrusion of our forefathers much easier than it otherwise might have been. In the year 1763, above half of the Indians of this island perished by a strange fever, which the Europeans who nursed them never caught; they appear to be a race doomed to recede and disappear before the superior genius of the Europeans. The only antient custom of these people that is remembered is, that, in their mutual exchanges, forty sun-dried clams, strung on a string, passed for the value of what might be called a copper. They were strangers to the use and value of wampum,* so well known to those of the main. The few families now remaining are meek and harmless; their antient ferocity is gone: they were early christianized by the New-England missionaries, as well as those of the Vineyard, and of several other parts of the Massachusets; and to this day they remain strict observers of the laws and customs of that religion, being carefully taught while young. Their sedentary life has led them to this degree of civilization much more effectually than if they had still remained hunters. They are fond of the sea, and expert mariners.

They have learned from the Quakers the art of catching both the cod and whale; in consequence of which, five of them always make part of the complement of men requisite to fit out a whale-boat. Many have removed hither from the Vineyard, on which account they are more numerous in Nantucket than any where else.

It is strange what revolution has happened among them in less than two hundred years! What is become of those numerous tribes which formerly inhabited the extensive shores of the great Bay of Massachusets? even from Numkeag, *(Salem,)* Saugus, *(Lynn,)* Shawmut, *(Boston,)* Pataxet, Napouset, *(Milton,)* Matapan, *(Dorchester,)* Winèsimèt, *(Chelsea,)* Poïasset, Pokànoket, *(New Plymouth,)* Suecanosset, *(Falmouth,)* Titicut, *(Chatham,)* Nobscusset, *(Yarmouth,)* Naussit, *(Eastham,)* Hyanneès, *(Barnstaple,)* &c. and many others who lived on seashores of above three hundred miles in length; without mentioning those powerful tribes which once dwelt between the rivers Hudson, Connecticut, Piskàtàquà, and Kènnebèck, the Mèhikaudret, Mohiguine, Pèquods, Narragansets, Nianticks, Massachusets, Wamponougs, Nipnets, Tarranteens, &c.—They are gone, and every memorial of them is lost; no vestiges whatever are left of those swarms which once inhabited this country, and replenished both sides of the great peninsula of Cape Cod: not even one of the posterity of the famous Masconomèo is left, (the sachem* of Cape Ann); not one of the descendants of Massasoit, father of Mètacomèt, *(Philip,)* and Wamsutta, *(Alexander,)* he who first conveyed some lands to the Plymouth Company. They have all disappeared either in the wars which the Europeans carried on against them, or else they have mouldered away, gathered in some of their ancient towns, in contempt and oblivion: nothing remains of them all, but one extraordinary monument, and even this they owe to the industry and religious zeal of the Europeans, I mean the Bible, translated into the Nattick tongue. Many of these tribes, giving way to the superior power of the whites, retired to their ancient villages, collecting the scattered remains of nations once populous; and, in their grant of lands, reserved to themselves and posterity certain portions, which lay contiguous to them. There, forgetting their ancient manners, they dwelt in peace; in a few years their territories were surrounded by the improvements of the Europeans; in consequence of which they grew lazy, inactive, unwilling, and unapt, to imitate or to follow any of our trades, and, in a few generations, either totally perished or else came over to the Vineyard, or to this island, to reunite themselves with such societies of their countrymen as would receive them. Such has been the fate of many nations, once warlike and independent; what we see now on the main, or on those islands, may be justly considered as the only remains of those ancient tribes: might I be permitted to pay, perhaps, a very useless compliment to *those* at least who inhabit the great peninsula of Namset, now Cape Cod, with whose names and ancient situation I am well acquainted. This peninsula was divided into two great regions; that on the side of the bay was known by the name of Nobscusset, from one of its towns; the capital was called Nausit, *(now Eastham)*; hence the Indians of that region were called Nausit Indians, though they dwelt in the villages of Pamet, Nosset, Pashèe, Potomaket, Soktoowoket, Nobscusset, *(Yarmouth)*.

The region on the Atlantic side was called Mashpèe, and contained the tribes of Hyannèes, Costowet, Waquoit, Scootin, Saconasset, Mashpèe, and Namset. Several of these Indian towns have been since converted into flourishing European settlements, known by different names; for, as the natives were excellent judges of land, which they had fertilized besides with the shells of their fish, &c. the latter could not make a better choice; though in general this great peninsula is but a sandy pine track, a few good spots excepted. It is divided into seven townships, viz. Barnstable, Yarmouth, Harwich, Chatham, Eastham, Pamet, Namset, or Province-town, at the extremity of the Cape. Yet these are very populous, though I am at a loss to conceive on what the inhabitants live, besides clams,

oisters, and fish; their piny lands being the most ungrateful
soil in the world. The minister of Namset, or Province-town,
receives from the government of Massachuset a salary of fifty
pounds per annum; and, such is the poverty of the inhabitants of that place, that, unable to pay him any money, each
master of a family is obliged to allow him two hundred horse
feet, (*sea spin,*)* with which this primitive priest fertilizes the
land of his glebe, which he tills himself: for nothing will grow
on these hungry soils without the assistance of this extraordinary manure, fourteen bushels of Indian corn being looked
upon as a good crop. But it is time to return from a digres-
sion, which I hope you will pardon. Nantucket is a great
nursery of seamen, pilots, coasters, and bank-fishermen; as
a country belonging to the province of Massachusets, it has
yearly the benefit of a court of Common Pleas, and their
appeal lies to the supreme court at Boston. I observed before,
that the Friends compose two-thirds of the magistracy of this
island; thus they are the proprietors of its territory, and the
principal rulers of its inhabitants; but, with all this apparatus
of law, its coercive powers are seldom wanted or required.
Seldom is it that any individual is amerced or punished; their
jail conveys no terror; no man has lost his life here judicially
since the foundation of this town, which is upwards of a hundred years. Solemn tribunals, public executions, humiliating
punishments, are altogether unknown. I saw neither governors,
nor any pageantry of state; neither ostentatious magistrates,
nor any individuals clothed with useless dignity: no artificial
phantoms subsist here, either civil or religious; no gibbets
loaded with guilty citizens offer themselves to your view; no
soldiers are appointed to bayonet their compatriots into servile
compliance. But how is a society composed of 5000 individuals preserved in the bonds of peace and tranquillity?
How are the weak protected from the strong? I will tell you.
Idleness and poverty, the causes of so many crimes, are
unknown here; each seeks, in the prosecution of his lawful
business, that honest gain which supports them; every period

of their time is full, either on shore or at sea. A probable expectation of reasonable profits, or of kindly assistance, if they fail of success, renders them strangers to licentious expedients. The simplicity of their manners shortens the catalogue of their wants; the law at a distance is ever ready to exert itself in the protection of those who stand in need of its assistance. The greatest part of them are always at sea, pursuing the whale, or raising the cod from the surface of the banks; some cultivate their little farms with the utmost diligence; some are employed in exercising various trades; others again in providing every necessary resource in order to refit their vessels or repair what misfortunes may happen, looking out for future markets, &c. Such is the rotation of those different scenes of business which fill the measure of their days, of that part of their lives, at least, which is enlivened by health, spirits, and vigour. It is but seldom that vice grows on a barren sand like this, which produces nothing without extreme labour. How could the common follies of society take root in so despicable a soil? they generally thrive on its exuberant juices: here there are none but those which administer to the useful, to the necessary, and to the indispensable, comforts of life. This land must necessarily either produce health, temperance, and a great equality of conditions, or the most abject misery. Could the manners of luxurious countries be imported here, like an epidemical disorder they would destroy every thing; the majority of them could not exist a month, they would be obliged to emigrate. As in all societies, except that of the natives, some difference must necessarily exist between individual and individual, (for there must be some more exalted than the rest either by their riches or their talents,) so in *this*, there are what you might call the high, the middling, and the low; and this difference will always be more remarkable among people who live by sea-excursions than among those who live by the cultivation of their land. The first run greater hazard, and adventure more: the profits and the misfortunes attending this mode of life must necessarily introduce a greater disparity than among the latter, where the equal division of the land offers no short road to superior riches. The only difference that may arise among them is that of industry, and perhaps of superior goodness of soil: the gradations, I observed here, are founded on nothing more than the good or ill success of their maritime enterprises, and do not proceed from education; that is the same throughout every class; simple, useful, and unadorned, like their dress and their houses. This necessary difference in their fortunes does not however cause those heart-burnings, which in other societies generate crimes. The sea, which surrounds them, is equally open to all, and presents to all an equal title to the chance of good fortune. A collector from Boston is the only king's officer who appears on these shores to receive the trifling duties which this community owe to those who protect them, and under the shadow of whose wings they navigate to all parts of the world.

LETTER V

CUSTOMARY EDUCATION AND EMPLOYMENT
OF THE INHABITANTS OF NANTUCKET

THE easiest way of becoming acquainted with the modes of
thinking, the rules of conduct, and the prevailing manners
of any people, is to examine what sort of education they give
their children; how they treat them at home, and what they
are taught in their places of public worship. At home their
tender minds must be early struck with the gravity, the serious though cheerful deportment, of their parents; they are
inured to a principle of subordination, arising neither from
sudden passions nor inconsiderate pleasure; they are gently
holden by an uniform silk cord, which unites softness and
strength. A perfect equanimity prevails in most of their families, and bad example hardly ever sows in their hearts the
seeds of future and similar faults. They are corrected with
tenderness, nursed with the most affectionate care, clad with
that decent plainness, from which they observe their parents
never to depart: in short, by the force of example, which is
superior even to the strongest instinct of nature, more than
by precepts, they learn to follow the steps of their parents, to
despise ostentatiousness as being sinful. They acquire a taste
for that neatness for which their fathers are so conspicuous;
they learn to be prudent and saving; the very tone of voice,
with which they are always addressed, establishes in them that
softness of diction, which ever after becomes habitual. Frugal,
sober, orderly, parents, attached to their business, constantly
following some useful occupation, never guilty of riot, dissipation, or other irregularities, cannot fail of training up children
to the same uniformity of life and manners. If they are left
with fortunes, they are taught how to save them, and how to
enjoy them with moderation and decency; if they have none,

they know how to venture, how to work, and toil, as their fathers have done before them. If they fail of success, there are always in this island (and wherever this society prevails) established resources, founded on the most benevolent principles. At their meetings they are taught the few, the simple, tenets of their sect; tenets, as fit to render men sober, industrious, just, and merciful, as those delivered in the most magnificent churches and cathedrals: they are instructed in the most essential duties of Christianity, so as not to offend the Divinity by the commission of evil deeds; to dread his wrath, and the punishments he has denounced; they are taught at the same time to have a proper confidence in his mercy, while they deprecate his justice. As every sect, from their different modes of worship, and their different interpretations of some parts of the Scriptures, necessarily have various opinions and prejudices, which contribute something in forming their characteristics in society, so those of the Friends are well known: obedience to the laws, even to non-resistance, justice, good-will to all, benevolence at home, sobriety, meekness, neatness, love of order, fondness and appetite for commerce. They are as remarkable here for those virtues as at Philadelphia, which is their American cradle, and the boast of that society. At school they learn to read, and write a good hand, until they are twelve years old; they are then in general put apprentices to the cooper's trade, which is the second essential branch of business followed here; at fourteen they are sent to sea, where in their leisure hours their companions teach them the art of navigation, which they have an opportunity of practising on the spot. They learn the great and useful art of working a ship in all the different situations which the sea and wind so often require; and surely there cannot be a better or a more useful school of that kind in the world. They then go gradually through every station of rowers, steersmen, and harpooners; thus they learn to attack, to pursue, to overtake, to cut, to dress, their huge game: and, after having performed several such voyages, and perfected themselves

in this business, they are fit either for the counting-house
or the chase.

The first proprietors of this island, or rather the first
founders of this town, began their career of industry with a
single whale-boat, with which they went to fish for cod; the
small distance from their shores, at which they caught it,
enabled them soon to increase their business, and those early
successes first led them to conceive that they might likewise catch the whales, which hitherto sported undisturbed
on their banks. After many trials, and several miscarriages,
they succeeded; thus they proceeded, step by step; the profits
of one successful enterprize helped them to purchase and
prepare better materials for a more extensive one: as these
were attended with little costs, their profits grew greater. The
south sides of the island, from east to west, were divided into
four equal parts, and each part was assigned to a company of
six, which, though thus separated, still carried on their business in common. In the middle of this distance they erected
a mast, provided with a sufficient number of rounds, and near
it they built a temporary hut, where five of the associates
lived, whilst the sixth from his high station carefully looked
toward the sea, in order to observe the spouting of the whales.
As soon as any were discovered, the centinel descended, the
whale-boat was launched, and the company went forth in
quest of their game. It may appear strange to you, that so
slender a vessel as an *American whale-boat*, containing six
diminutive beings, should dare to pursue and to attack, in its
native element, the largest and strongest fish that nature has
created. Yet, by the exertions of an admirable dexterity, improved by a long practice, in which these people are become
superior to any other whale-men, by knowing the temper
of the whale after her first movement, and by many other
useful observations, they seldom failed to harpoon it, and to
bring the huge leviathan on the shores. Thus they went on,
until the profits they made enabled them to purchase larger
vessels, and to pursue them farther, when the whales quitted

their coasts; those, who failed in their enterprizes, returned to the cod-fisheries, which had been their first school, and their first resources; they even began to visit the banks of Cape Breton, the isle of Sable, and all the other fishing-places, with which this coast of America abounds. By degrees they went a whaling to Newfoundland, to the Gulph of St. Laurence, to the Straits of Belleisle, the coast of Labrador, Davis's Straits, even to Cape Desolation, in 70° of latitude; where the Danes carry on some fisheries in spite of the perpetual severities of that inhospitable climate. In process of time they visited the western islands, the latitude of 34°, famous for that fish, the Brazils, the coast of Guinea. Would you believe that they have already gone to the Falkland Islands, and that I have heard several of them talk of going to the South Sea! Their confidence is so great, and their knowledge of this branch of business so superior to that of any other people, that they have acquired a monopoly of this commodity. Such were their feeble beginnings, such the infancy and the progress of their maritime schemes; such is now the degree of boldness and activity to which they are arrived in their manhood. After their examples several companies have been formed in many of our capitals, where every necessary article of provisions, implements, and timber, are to be found. But the industry, exerted by the people of Nantucket, hath hitherto enabled them to rival all their competitors; consequently this is the greatest mart for oil, whale-bone, and sperma-ceti,* on the continent. It does not follow however that they are always successful; this would be an extraordinary field indeed, where the crops should never fail; many voyages do not repay the original cost of fitting out: they bear such misfortunes like true merchants, and, as they never venture their all like gamesters, they try their fortunes again; the latter hope to win by chance alone, the former by industry, well-judged speculation, and some hazard. I was there when Mr. —— had missed one of his vessels; she had been given over for lost by every body, but happily arrived, before I came away, after an absence of thirteen months. She had met with a variety of disappointments on the station she was ordered to, and, rather than return empty, the people steered for the coast of Guinea, where they fortunately fell in with several whales, and brought home upward of 600 barrels of oil, beside bone. Those returns are sometimes disposed of in the towns of the continent, where they are exchanged for such commodities as are wanted; but they are most commonly sent to England, where they always sell for cash. When this is intended, a vessel larger than the rest is fitted out to be filled with oil on the spot where it is found and made, and thence she sails immediately for London. This expedient saves time, freight, and expense; and from that capital they bring back whatever they want. They employ also several vessels in transporting lumber to the West-Indian Islands, from whence they procure in return the various productions of the country, which they afterwards exchange wherever they can hear of an advantageous market. Being extremely acute, they well know how to improve all the advantages which the combination of so many branches of business constantly affords; the spirit of commerce, which is the simple art of a reciprocal supply of wants, is well understood here by every body. They possess, like the generality of the Americans, a large share of native penetration, activity, and good sense, which leads them to a variety of other secondary schemes too tedious to mention: they are well acquainted with the cheapest method of procuring lumber from Kennebeck River, Penobscot, &c. pitch and tar, from North Carolina; flour and biscuit, from Philadelphia; beef and pork, from Connecticut. They know how to exchange their cod-fish, and West-Indian produce, for those articles which they are continually either bringing to their island, or sending off to other places where they are wanted. By means of all these commercial negotiations, they have greatly cheapened the fitting out of their whaling fleets, and therefore much improved their fisheries. They are indebted for all these advantages, not only to their national genius but to the poverty of their soil; and, as a proof of what I have so often advanced, look at the Vineyard,* (their neighbouring island,) which is inhabited by a set of people as keen and as sagacious as themselves. Their soil being in general extremely fertile, they have fewer navigators; though they are equally well situated for the fishing-business. As, in my way back to Falmouth on the Main, I visited this sister island, permit me to give you, as concisely as I can, a short but true description of it; I am not so limited in the principal object of this journey as to wish to confine myself to the single spot of Nantucket.

LETTER VI

DESCRIPTION OF THE ISLAND OF MARTHA'S VINEYARD; AND OF THE WHALE-FISHERY

THIS island is twenty miles in length, and from seven to eight miles in breadth, as you may see by the annexed map. It lies nine miles from the continent, and, with the Elizabeth Islands, forms one of the counties of Massachuset's Bay, known by the name of Duke's County. Those latter, which are six in number, are about nine miles distant from the Vineyard, and are all famous for excellent dairies. A good ferry is established between Edgar Town and Falmouth on the main, the distance being nine miles. Martha's Vineyard is divided into three townships, viz. Edgar, Chilmark, and Tisbury; the number of inhabitants is computed at about 4000, 300 of which are Indians. Edgar is the best sea-port, and the shire-town, and, as its soil is light and sandy, many of its inhabitants follow the example of the people of Nantucket. The town of Chilmark has no good harbour, but the land is excellent and no way inferior to any on the continent: it contains excellent pastures, convenient brooks for mills, stone for fencing, &c. The town of Tisbury is remarkable for the excellence of its timber, and has a harbour where the water is deep enough for ships of the line. The stock of the island is 20000 sheep, 2000 neat cattle, besides horses and goats; they have also some deer, and abundance of sea-fowls. This has been from the beginning, and is to this day, the principal seminary of the Indians; they live on that part of the island which is called Chapoquidick, and were very early christianised by the respectable family of the Mahews, the first proprietors of it. The first settler of that name conveyed by will to a favourite daughter a certain part of it, on which there grew many wild vines; thence it was called Martha's Vineyard, after her name, which, in process of time, extended to the whole island. The posterity of the ancient aborigines remain here, to this day, on lands which their forefathers reserved for themselves, and which are religiously kept from any incroachments. The New-England people are remarkable for the honesty with which they have fulfilled, all over that province, those antient covenants which in many others have been disregarded, to the scandal of those governments. The Indians there appeared, by the decency of their manners, their industry, and neatness, to be wholly Europeans, and no way inferior to many of the inhabitants. Like them they are sober, laborious, and religious, which are the principal characteristics of the four New-England provinces. They often go, like the young men of the Vineyard, to Nantucket, and hire themselves for whalemen or fishermen; and indeed their skill and dexterity in all sea affairs is nothing inferior to that of the whites. The latter are divided into two classes; the first occupy the land, which they till with admirable care and knowledge; the second, who are possessed of none, apply themselves to the sea, the general resource of mankind in this part of the world. This island therefore, like Nantucket, is become a great nursery, which supplies with pilots and seamen the numerous coasters with which this extended part of America abounds. Go where you will, from Nova Scotia to the Missisippi, you will find almost every where some natives of these two islands, employed in seafaring occupations. Their climate is so favourable to population, that marriage is the object of every man's earliest wish; and it is a blessing so easily obtained, that great numbers are obliged to quit their native land and go to some other countries in quest of subsistence. The inhabitants are all Presbyterians, which is the established religion of Massachusets; and here let me remember, with gratitude, the hospitable treatment I received from B. Norton, Esq. the colonel of the island, as well as from Dr. Mahew, the lineal descendant of the first proprietor. Here are to be found the most expert pilots, either for the great day, their sound, Nantucket shoals,

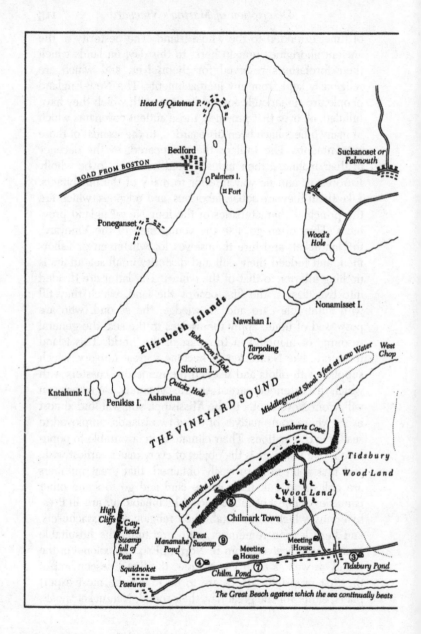

Head of Quisinut P.

Bedford

ROAD FROM BOSTON

Palmers I.

Fort

Poneganset

Suckanoset or
Falmouth

Wood's
Hole

Nonamisset I.

Nawshan I.

Elizabeth Islands

Roberston's Hole

Tarpoling
Cove

Slocum I.

West
Chop

Kntahunk I.

Penikiss I.

Ashawina

Quicks Hole

THE VINEYARD SOUND

Middleground Shoal 3 feet at Low Water

Lumberts Cove

Tidsbury
Wood Land

Manamshe Bite

Wood Land

⑤

High
Cliffs

Gay-
head
Swamp
full of
Peat

Manamshe
Pond

Peat
Swamp

⑨

Chilmark Town

Meeting
House

Meeting
House

③

Squidnoket
Pastures

④

⑦

Chilm. Pond

Tidsbury Pond

The Great Beach against which the sea continually beats

Map of the Island of Martha's Vineyard
with its Dependencies

1. Starbuck Point
2. Beniah Norton's house, the colonel of the island
3. The house of James Athearn, Esq
4. Dr. Mahew's house
5. Iron-mine, the ore of which is carried to the forges at Taunton
6. Lagoon, famous for catching bass under the ice
7. The best mowing grounds in the island, yielding four tons of black grass per acre
8. Excellent planting ground
9. A mine of good pipe-clay

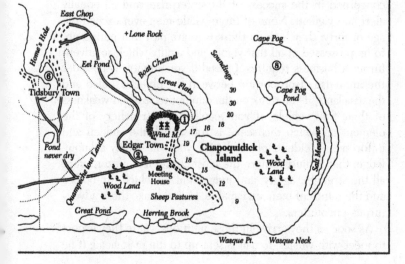

SCALE OF ENGLISH MILES

0 1 2 3 4 5 6 7 8

or the different ports in their neighbourhood. In stormy weather they are always at sea, looking out for vessels, which they board with singular dexterity, and hardly ever fail to bring safe to their intended harbour. Gay-Head, the western point of this island, abounds with a variety of ochres of different colours, with which the inhabitants paint their houses.

The vessels most proper for whale fishing are brigs of about 150 tons burthen, particularly when they are intended for distant latitudes; they always man them with thirteen hands, in order that they may row two whale-boats; the crews of which must necessarily consist of six, four at the oars, one standing on the bows with the harpoon, and the other at the helm. It is also necessary that there should be two of these boats, that, if one should be destroyed in attacking the whale, the other, which is never engaged at the same time, may be ready to save the hands. Five of the thirteen are always Indians; the last of the complement remains on-board to steer the vessel during the action. They have no wages; each draws a certain established share in partnership with the proprietor of the vessel; by which œconomy they are all proportionably concerned in the success of the enterprise, and all equally alert and vigilant. None of these whale-men ever exceed the age of forty: they look on those who are past that period not to be possessed of all that vigour and agility which so adventurous a business requires. Indeed if you attentively consider the immense disproportion between the object assailed and the assailants; if you think on the diminutive size and weakness of their frail vehicle; if you recollect the treachery of the element on which this scene is transacted; the sudden and unforeseen accidents of winds, &c. you will readily acknowledge, that it must require the most consummate exertion of all the strength, agility, and judgement, of which the bodies and the minds of men are capable, to undertake these adventurous encounters.

As soon as they arrive in those latitudes where they expect to meet with whales, a man is sent up to the mast-head; if he sees one, he immediately cries out AWAITE PAWANA, *here is a whale*; they all remain still and silent until he repeats PAWANA, *a whale*, when in less than six minutes the two boats are launched, filled with every implement necessary for the attack. They row toward the whale with astonishing velocity; and, as the Indians early became their fellow-labourers in this new warfare, you can easily conceive how the Nattick expressions became familiar on-board the whale-boats. Formerly it often happened that whale-vessels were manned with none but Indians and the master; recollect also that the Nantucket people understand the Nattick, and that there are always five of these people on-board. There are various ways of approaching the whale, according to their peculiar species; and this previous knowledge is of the utmost consequence. When these boats are arrived at a reasonable distance, one of them rests on its oars and stands off, as a witness of the approaching engagement; near the bows of the other the harpooner stands up, and on him principally depends the success of the enterprise. He wears a jacket closely buttoned, and round his head a handkerchief tightly bound: in his hands he holds the dreadful weapon, made of the best steel, marked sometimes with the name of their town, and sometimes with that of their vessel; to the shaft of which the end of a cord of due strength, coiled up with the utmost care in the middle of the boat, is firmly tied; the other end is fastened to the bottom of the boat. Thus prepared, they row in profound silence, leaving the whole conduct of the enterprise to the harpooner and to the steersman, attentively following their directions. When the former judges himself to be near enough to the whale, that is, at the distance of about fifteen feet, he bids them stop: perhaps she has a calf, whose safety attracts all the attention of the dam, which is a favourable circumstance; perhaps she is of a dangerous species, and it is safest to retire, though their ardour will seldom permit them; perhaps she is asleep, in that case he balances high the harpoon, trying in this important moment to collect all the energy of which he is capable. He launches it forth—she is struck: from her first movement they judge of her temper as well as of their future success. Sometimes, in the immediate impulse of rage, she will attack the boat, and demolish it with one stroke of her tail: in an instant the frail vehicle disappears, and the assailants are immersed in the dreadful element. Were the whale armed with the jaws of the shark, and as voracious, they never would return home to amuse their listening wives with the interesting tale of the adventure. At other times she will dive and disappear from human sight; and every thing must then give way to her velocity, or else all is lost. Sometimes she will swim away as if untouched, and draw the cord with such swiftness that it will set the edge of the boat on fire by the friction. If she rises before she has run out the whole length, she is looked upon as a sure prey. The blood she has lost in her flight weakens her so much, that, if she sinks again, it is but for a short time; the boat follows her course with an almost equal speed. She soon re-appears; tired at last with convulsing the element, which she tinges with her blood, she dies, and floats on the surface. At other times it may happen that she is not dangerously wounded, though she carries the harpoon fast in her body; when she will alternately dive and rise, and swim on with unabated vigour. She then soon reaches beyond the length of the cord, and carries the boat along with amazing velocity: this sudden impediment sometimes will retard her speed, at other times it only serves to rouse her anger and to accelerate her progress. The harpooner, with the axe in his hands, stands ready. When he observes that the bows of the boat are greatly pulled down by the diving whale, and that it begins to sink deep and to take much water, he brings the axe almost in contact with the cord; he pauses, still flattering himself that she will relax; but the moment grows critical, unavoidable danger approaches: sometimes men, more intent on gain than on the preservation of their lives, will run great risks; and it is wonderful how far these people have carried their daring courage at this awful moment! But it is vain to hope, their lives must be saved, the cord is cut, the boat rises again. If, after thus getting loose, she re-appears, they will attack and wound her a second time. She soon dies, and, when dead, she is towed along-side of their vessel, where she is fastened.

The next operation is to cut, with axes and spades, every part of her body which yields oil; the kettles are set a boiling, they fill their barrels as fast as it is made; but, as this operation is much slower than that of *cutting-up*, they fill the hold of their ship with those fragments, lest a storm should arise and oblige them to abandon their prize. It is astonishing what a quantity of oil some of these fish will yield, and what profit it affords to those who are fortunate enough to overtake them! The river St. Laurence whale, which is the only one I am well acquainted with, is seventy-five feet long, sixteen deep, twelve in the length of its bone, which commonly weighs 3000 lb. twenty in the breadth of their tails, and produces 180 barrels of oil: I once saw 16 boiled out of the tongue only. After having once vanquished this leviathan, there are two enemies to be dreaded beside the wind; the first of which is the shark: that fierce voracious fish, to which nature has given such dreadful offensive weapons, often comes alongside, and, in spite of the people's endeavours, will share with them in their prey; at night particularly. They are very mischievious, but the second enemy is much more terrible and irresistible; it is the killer, sometimes called the thrasher, a species of whales about thirty feet long. They are possessed of such a degree of agility and fierceness as often to attack the largest spermaceti whales, and not seldom to rob the fishermen of their prey; nor are there any means of defence against so potent an adversary. When all their barrels are full, (for every thing is done at sea,) or when their limited time is expired and their stores almost expended, they return home, freighted with their valuable cargo; unless they have put it on-board a vessel for the European market. Such are, as briefly as I can relate them, the different branches of the œconomy practised by these bold navigators, and the method with which they go such distances from their island to catch this huge game.

The following are the names and principal characteristics of the various species of whales known to these people:

The river St. Laurence whale just described.

The disko, or Greenland ditto.

The right whale, or seven feet bone, common on the coasts of this country, about sixty feet long.

The spermaceti-whale, found all over the world, and of all sizes; the longest are sixty feet, and yield about 100 barrels of oil.

The hump-backs, on the coast of Newfoundland, from forty to seventy feet in length.

The fin-back, an American whale, never killed, as being too swift.

The sulphur-bottom, river St. Laurence, ninety feet long; they are but seldom killed, as being extremely swift.

The grampus, thirty feet long, never killed on the same account.

The killer or thrasher, about thirty feet, they often kill the other whales with which they are at perpetual war.

The black-fish whale, twenty feet, yields from 8 to 10 barrels.

The porpoise, weighing about 160 lb.

In 1769 they fitted out 125 whalemen; the first 50 that returned brought with them 11000 barrels of oil. In 1770 they fitted out 135 vessels for the fisheries, at thirteen hands each; 4 West-Indiamen, twelve hands; 25 wood vessels, four hands; 18 coasters, five hands; 15 London traders, eleven hands. All these amount to 2158 hands, employed in 197 vessels. Trace their progressive steps between the possession of a few whale-boats and that of such a fleet!

The moral conduct, prejudices, and customs, of a people, who live two-thirds of their time at sea, must naturally be very different from those of their neighbours, who live by cultivating the earth. That long abstemiousness to which the former are exposed, the breathing of saline air, the frequent repetitions of danger, the boldness acquired in surmounting them, the very impulse of the winds, to which they are exposed; all these, one would imagine, must lead them, when on shore, to no small desire of inebriation, and a more eager pursuit of those pleasures, of which they have been so long deprived, and which they must soon forego. There are many appetites that may be gratified on shore, even by the poorest man, but which must remain unsatisfied at sea. Yet, notwithstanding the powerful effects of all these causes, I observe here, at the return of their fleets, no material irregularities; no tumultuous drinking assemblies: whereas, in our continental towns, the thoughtless seaman indulges himself in the coarsest pleasures; and, vainly thinking that a week of debauchery can compensate for months of abstinence, foolishly lavishes, in a few days of intoxication, the fruits of half a year's labour. On the contrary, all was peace here, and a general decency prevailed throughout; the reason, I believe, is, that almost every body here is married, for they get wives very young; and the pleasure of returning to their families absorbs every other desire. The motives, that lead them to the sea, are very different from those of most other sea-faring men; it is neither idleness nor profligacy that sends them to that element; it is a settled plan of life, a well-founded hope of earning a livelihood; it is because their soil is bad that they are early initiated to this profession, and, were they to stay at home, what could they do? The sea therefore becomes to them a kind of patrimony; they go to whaling with as much pleasure and tranquil indifference, with as strong an expectation of success, as a landman undertakes to clear a piece of swamp. The first is obliged to advance his time and labour to procure oil on the surface of the sea; the second advances the same to procure himself grass from grounds that produced nothing before but hassocks and bogs. Among those who do not use the sea, I observed the same calm appearance as among the inhabitants on the continent; here I found, without gloom, a decorum and reserve, so natural to them, that I thought myself in Philadelphia. At my landing I was cordially received by those to whom I was recommended, and treated with unaffected hospitality by such others with whom I became acquainted; and I can tell you, that it is impossible for any traveller to dwell here one month without knowing the heads of the principal families. Wherever I went I found simplicity of diction and manners, rather more primitive and rigid than I expected; and I soon perceived that it proceeded from their secluded situation, which has prevented them from mixing with others. It is therefore easy to conceive how they have retained every degree of peculiarity for which this sect was formerly distinguished. Never was a bee-hive more faithfully employed in gathering wax, bee-bread, and honey, from all the neighbouring fields, than are the members of this society; every one in the town follows some particular occupation with great diligence, but without that servility of labour which I am informed prevails in Europe. The mechanic seemed to be descended from as good parentage, was as well dressed and fed, and held in as much estimation, as those who employed him; they were once nearly related; their different degrees of prosperity is what has caused the various shades of their community. But this accidental difference has introduced, as yet, neither arrogance nor pride on the one part, nor meanness and servility on the other. All their houses are neat, convenient, and comfortable: some of them are filled with two families; for, when the husbands are at sea, the wives require less house-room. They all abound with the most substantial furniture more valuable from its usefulness than from any ornamental appearance. Wherever I went, I found good cheer, a welcome reception; and after the second visit I felt myself as much at my ease as if I had been an old acquaintance of the family. They had as great plenty of every thing as if their island had been part of the golden quarter of Virginia, (a valuable track of land on Cape Charles): I could hardly persuade myself that I had quitted the adjacent

continent, where every thing abounds, and that I was on a
barren sand-bank, fertilized with whale-oil only. As their rural
improvements are but trifling, and only of the useful kind,
and as the best of them are at a considerable distance from
the town, I amused myself for several days in conversing
with the most intelligent of the inhabitants of both sexes,
and making myself acquainted with the various branches of
their industry, the different objects of their trade, the nature
of that sagacity, which, deprived as they are of every necessary material, produce, &c. yet enables them to flourish, to
live well, and sometimes to make considerable fortunes. The
whole is an enigma to be solved only by coming to the spot
and observing the national genius which the original founders
brought with them, as well as their unwearied patience and
perseverance. They have all, from the highest to the lowest,
a singular keenness of judgement, unassisted by any aca-
demical light; they all possess a large share of good sense,
improved upon the experience of their fathers; and this is
the surest and best guide to lead us through the path of life,
because it approaches nearest to the infallibility of instinct.
Shining talents and University knowledge would be entirely
useless here, nay, would be dangerous; it would pervert
their plain judgement, it would lead them out of that useful
path which is so well adapted to their situation: it would
make them more adventurous, more presumptuous, much
less cautious, and therefore less successful. It is pleasing to
hear some of them tracing a father's progress and their own
through the different vicissitudes of good and adverse fortune. I have often, by their fire-sides, travelled with them
the whole length of their career, from their earliest steps,
from their first commercial adventure, from the possession
of a single whale-boat, up to that of a dozen large vessels!
This does not imply, however, that every one, who began
with a whale-boat, has ascended to a like pitch of fortune;
by no means; the same casualty, the same combination of
good and evil which attends human affairs in every other

part of the globe, prevails here: great prosperity is not the lot of every man, but there are many and various gradations; if they all do not attain riches, they all attain an easy subsistence. After all, is it not better to be possessed of a single whale-boat, or a few sheep-pastures; to live free and independent under the mildest government, in a healthy climate, in a land of charity and benevolence; than to be wretched, as so many are in Europe, possessing nothing but their industry; tossed from one rough wave to another; engaged either in the most servile labours for the smallest pittance, or fettered with the links of the most irksome dependence, even without the hopes of rising?

The majority of those inferior hands which are employed in this fishery, many of the mechanics, such as coopers, smiths, caulkers, carpenters, &c. who do not belong to the society of Friends, are Presbyterians, and originally came from the main. Those who are possessed of the greatest fortunes at present belong to the former; but they all began as simple whalemen: it is even looked upon as honourable and necessary for the son of the wealthiest man to serve an apprenticeship to the same bold, adventurous, business which has enriched his father; they go several voyages, and these early excursions never fail to harden their constitutions, and introduce them to the knowledge of their future means of subsistence.

LETTER VII

MANNERS AND CUSTOMS AT NANTUCKET

As I observed before, every man takes a wife as soon as
he chooses, and that is generally very early; no portion is
required, none is expected; no marriage-articles are drawn up
among us, by skilful lawyers, to puzzle and lead posterity to
the bar, or to satisfy the pride of the parties. We give nothing
with our daughters; their education, their health, and the customary out-set, are all that the fathers of numerous families
can afford: as the wife's fortune consists principally in her
future œconomy, modesty, and skilful management, so the
husband's is founded on his abilities to labour, on his health,
and the knowledge of some trade or business. Their mutual
endeavours, after a few years of constant application, seldom
fail of success, and of bringing them the means to rear and
support the new race which accompanies the nuptial bed.
Those children, born by the sea-side, hear the roaring of its
waves as soon as they are able to listen; it is the first noise
with which they become acquainted, and by early plunging
in it they acquire that boldness, that presence of mind, and
dexterity, which make them ever after such expert seamen.
They often hear their fathers recount the adventures of their
youth, their combats with the whales; and these recitals imprint on their opening minds an early curiosity and taste for
the same life. They often cross the sea to go to the main,
and learn, even in those short voyages, how to qualify themselves for longer and more dangerous ones; they are therefore
deservedly conspicuous for their maritime knowledge and
experience all over the continent. A man born here is distin-
guishable by his gait from among a hundred other men, so
remarkable are they for a pliability of sinews, and a peculiar
agility, which attends them even to old age. I have heard some

persons attribute this to the effects of the whale oil, with
which they are so copiously anointed in the various operations it must undergo ere it is fit either for the European
market or the candle-manufactory.

But you may perhaps be solicitous to ask, what becomes of
that exuberancy of population which must arise from so much
temperance, from healthiness of climate, and from early marriage? You may justly conclude that their native island and
town can contain but a limited number. Emigration is both
natural and easy to a maritime people, and that is the very
reason why they are always populous, problematical as it may
appear. They yearly go to different parts of this continent, constantly engaged in sea affairs; as our internal riches increase,
so does our external trade, which consequently requires more
ships and more men: sometimes they have emigrated like
bees, in regular and connected swarms. Some of the Friends,
(by which word I always mean the people called Quakers,)
fond of a contemplative life, yearly visit the several congregations which this society has formed throughout the continent. By their means a sort of correspondence is kept up
among them all; they are generally good preachers, friendly
censors, checking vice wherever they find it predominating;
preventing relaxations in any parts of the ancient customs
and worship. They every where carry admonition and useful
advice; and, by thus travelling, they unavoidably gather the
most necessary observations concerning the various situations
of particular districts, their soils, their produce, their distance
from navigable rivers, the price of the land, &c. In consequence of informations of this kind, received at Nantucket
in the year 1766, a considerable number of them purchased
a large track of land in the county of Orange, in North Carolina,
situated on the several spring-heads of *Deep-River*, which
is the western branch of Cape Fear, or North West River.
The advantage of being able to convey themselves by sea to
within forty miles of the spot, the richness of the soil, &c. made
them cheerfully quit an island on which there was no longer

any room for them. There they have founded a beautiful settlement, known by the name of *New-Garden*, contiguous to the famous one which the Moravians have at Bethabara, Bethamia, and Salem, on Yadkin River. No spot of earth can be more beautiful; it is composed of gentle hills, of easy declivities, excellent low lands, accompanied by different brooks which traverse this settlement. I never saw a soil that rewards men so early for their labours and disbursements; such in general, with very few exceptions, are the lands which adjoin the innumerable heads of all the large rivers which fall into the Chesapeak, or flow through the provinces of North and South Carolina, Georgia, &c. It is perhaps the most pleasing, the most bewitching, country which the continent affords: because, while it preserves an easy communication with the sea-port towns at some seasons of the year, it is perfectly free from the contagious air often breathed in those flat countries, which are more contiguous to the Atlantic. These lands are as rich as those over the Alligany; the people of New-Garden are situated at the distance of between 200 and 300 miles from Cape Fear; Cape Fear is at least 450 from Nantucket: you may judge therefore that they have but little correspondence with this their little metropolis, except it is by means of the itinerant Friends. Others have settled on the famous river Kennebeck, in that territory of the province of Massachusets, which is known by the name of Sagadahock. Here they have softened the labours of clearing the heaviest timbered land in America, by means of several branches of trade, which their fair river and proximity to the sea afford them. Instead of entirely consuming the timber, as we are obliged to do, some parts of it are converted into useful articles for exportation, such as staves, scantlings,* boards, hoops, poles, &c. For that purpose they keep a correspondence with their native island, and I know many of the principal inhabitants of Sherburn, who, though merchants and living at Nantucket, yet possess valuable farms on that river; from whence they draw great part of their subsistence, meat, grain, fire-wood, &c. The title of these lands is vested in the antient Plymouth Company, under the powers of which the Massachusets was settled; and that company which resides in Boston are still the granters of all the vacant lands within their limits.

Although this part of the province is so fruitful, and so happily situated, yet it has been singularly overlooked and neglected: it is surprising that the excellence of that soil, which lies on the river, should not have caused it to be filled before now with inhabitants; for the settlements, from thence to Penobscot, are as yet but in their infancy. It is true that immense labour is required to make room for the plough, but the peculiar strength and quality of the soil never fails most amply to reward the industrious possessor; I know of no soil in this country more rich or more fertile. I do not mean that sort of transitory fertility which evaporates with the sun, and disappears in a few years; here, on the contrary, even their highest grounds are covered with a rich, moist, swamp, mould, which bears the most luxuriant grass, and never-failing crops of grain.

If New-Garden exceeds this settlement by the softness of its climate, the fecundity of its soil, and a greater variety of produce from less labour, it does not breed men equally hardy, nor capable to encounter dangers and fatigues. It leads too much to idleness and effeminacy; for great is the luxuriance of that part of America and the ease with which the earth is cultivated. Were I to begin life again, I would prefer the country of Kennebeck to the other, however bewitching; the navigation of the river for above 200 miles, the great abundance of fish it contains, the constant healthiness of the climate, the happy severities of the winters always sheltering the earth with a voluminous coat of snow, the equally happy necessity of labour: all these reasons would greatly preponderate against the softer situations of Carolina; where mankind reap too much, do not toil enough, and are liable to enjoy too fast the benefits of life. There are many, I know, who would despise my opinion, and think me a bad judge; let those go and settle at the Ohio, the Monogahela, Red-Stone Creek, &c. let them go and inhabit the extended shores of that superlative river; I with equal cheerfulness would pitch my tent on the rougher shores of Kennebeck; this will always be a country of health, labour, and strong activity, and those are characteristics of society which I value more than greater opulence and voluptuous ease.

Thus, though this fruitful hive constantly sends out swarms as industrious as themselves, yet it always remains full without having any useless drones: on the contrary, it exhibits constant scenes of business and new schemes; the richer an individual grows, the more extensive his field of action becomes; he that is near ending his career, drudges on as well as he who has just begun it; nobody stands still. But is it not strange, that, after having accumulated riches, they should never wish to exchange their barren situation for a more sheltered, more pleasant, one on the main? Is it not strange, that, after having spent the morning and the meridian of their days amidst the jarring waves, weary with the toils of a laborious life, they should not wish to enjoy the evenings of those days of industry, in a larger society, on some spots of terra firma, where the severity of the winters is balanced by a variety of more pleasing scenes, not to be found here? But the same magical power of habit and custom, which makes the Laplander, the Siberian, the Hottentot, prefer their climates, their occupations, and their soil, to more beneficial situations, leads these good people to think, that no other spot on the globe is so analogous to their inclinations as Nantucket. Here their connections are formed; what would they do at a distance removed from them? Live sumptuously, you will say, procure themselves new friends, new acquaintances, by their splendid tables, by their ostentatious generosity, and by affected hospitality. These are thoughts that have never entered into their heads; they would be filled with horror at the thought of forming wishes and plans so different from that

simplicity, which is their general standard in affluence as well
as in poverty. They abhor the very idea of expending, in useless waste and vain luxuries, the fruits of prosperous labour;
they are employed in establishing their sons, and in many
other useful purposes: strangers to the honours of monarchy,
they do not aspire to the possession of affluent fortunes, with
which to purchase founding titles, and frivolous names!

Yet there are not at Nantucket so many wealthy people as
one would imagine, after having considered their great successes, their industry, and their knowledge. Many die poor,
though hardly able to reproach fortune with a frown; others
leave not behind them that affluence which the circle of their
business and of their prosperity naturally promised. The
reason of this is, I believe, the peculiar expence necessarily
attending their tables; for, as their island supplies the town
with little or nothing, (a few families excepted,) every one
must procure what they want from the main. The very hay
their horses consume, and every other article necessary to support a family, though cheap in a country of so great abundance
as Massachusets; yet the necessary waste and expences, attending their transport, render these commodities dear. A vast
number of little vessels from the main, and from the Vineyard,
are constantly resorting here, as to a market. Sherburn is
extremely well supplied with every thing, but this very con-
stancy of supply necessarily drains off a great deal of money.
The first use they make of their oil and bone is to exchange
it for bread and meat, and whatever else they want; the
necessities of a large family are very great and numerous let
its œconomy be what it will; they are so often repeated, that
they perpetually draw off a considerable branch of the profits.
If by any accidents those profits are interrupted, the capital
must suffer; and it very often happens that the greatest part
of their property is floating on the sea.

There are but two congregations in this town. They assemble every Sunday in meeting-houses, as simple as the dwelling of the people; and there is but one priest on the whole

island. What! (would a good Portuguese observe)—but one single priest to instruct a whole island, and to direct their consciences! It is even so; each individual knows how to guide his own, and is content to do it, as well as he can. This lonely clergyman is a Presbyterian minister, who has a very large and respectable congregation; the other is composed of Quakers, who, you know, admit of no particular person, who, in consequence of being ordained, becomes exclusively entitled to preach, to catechise, and to receive certain salaries for his trouble. Among them, every one may expound the Scriptures, who thinks he is called so to do; beside, as they admit of neither sacrament, baptism, nor any other outward forms whatever, such a man would be useless. Most of these people are continually at sea, and have often the most urgent reasons to worship the Parent of Nature in the midst of the storms which they encounter. These two sects live in perfect peace and harmony with each other; those ancient times of religious discords are now gone, (I hope never to return,) when each thought it meretorious, not only to damn the other, which would have been nothing, but to persecute and murther one another, for the glory of that Being, who requires no more of us than that we should love one another and live! Every one goes to that place of worship which he likes best, and thinks not that his neighbour does wrong by not following him; each, busily employed in their temporal affairs, is less vehement about spiritual ones, and fortunately you will find, at Nantucket, neither idle drones, voluptuous devotees, ranting enthusiasts, nor sour demagogues. I wish I had it in my power to send the most persecuting bigot I could find in —— to the whale-fisheries; in lest than three or four years you would find him a much more tractable man, and therefore a better Christian.

Singular as it may appear to you, there are but two medical professors on the island; for of what service can physic be in a primitive society, where the excesses of inebriation are so rare? What need of galenical medicines,* where fevers, and stomachs loaded by the loss of the digestive powers, are so few? Temperance, the calm of passions, frugality, and continual exercise, keep them healthy, and preserve unimpaired that constitution which they have received from parents as healthy as themselves; who, in the unpolluted embraces of the earliest and chastest love, conveyed to them the soundest bodily frame which nature could give. But, as no habitable part of this globe is exempt from some diseases, proceeding either from climate or modes of living, here they are sometimes subject to consumptions and to fevers. Since the foundation of that town no epidemical distempers have appeared, which, at times, cause such depopulations in other countries; many of them are extremely well acquainted with the Indian methods of curing simple diseases, and practise them with success. You will hardly find, any where, a community, composed of the same number of individuals, possessing such uninterrupted health, and exhibiting so many green old men, who shew their advanced age by the maturity of their wisdom rather than by the wrinkles of their faces; and this is indeed one of the principal blessings of the island, which richly compensates their want of the richer soils of the south; where iliac complaints and bilious fevers grow by the side of the sugar-cane, the ambrosial ananas,* &c. The situation of this island, the purity of the air, the nature of their marine occupations, their virtue and moderation, are the causes of that vigour and health which they possess. The poverty of their soil has placed them, I hope, beyond the danger of conquest or the wanton desire of extirpation. Were they to be driven from this spot, the only acquisition of the conquerors would be a few acres of land, inclosed and cultivated; a few houses, and some moveables. The genius, the industry, of the inhabitants would accompany them; and it is those alone which constitute the sole wealth of their island. Its present fame would perish, and, in a few years, it would return to its pristine state of barrenness and poverty: they might, perhaps, be allowed to transport themselves, in their own vessels, to

some other spot or island, which they would soon fertilise
by the same means with which they have fertilised this.

One single lawyer has, of late years, found means to live
here, but his best fortune proceeds more from having married one of the wealthiest heiresses of the island than from
the emoluments of his practice: however he is sometimes
employed in recovering money lent on the main, or in preventing those accidents to which the contentious propensity
of its inhabitants may sometimes expose them. He is seldom
employed as the means of self-defence, and much seldomer
as the channel of attack; to which they are strangers, except
the fraud is manifest, and the danger imminent. Lawyers are
so numerous in all our populous towns, that I am surprised
they never thought before of establishing themselves here:
they are plants that will grow in any soil that is cultivated
by the hands of others; and, when once they have taken root,
they will extinguish every other vegetable that grows around
them. The fortunes they daily acquire, in every province, from
the misfortunes of their fellow citizens, are surprising! The
most ignorant, the most bungling, member of that profession,
will, if placed in the most obscure part of the country, pro-
mote litigiousness, and amass more wealth, without labour,
than the most opulent farmer with all his toils. They have
so dexterously interwoven their doctrines and quirks with the
laws of the land, or rather they are become so necessary an
evil in our present constitutions that it seems unavoidable
and past all remedy. What a pity that our forefathers, who
happily extinguished so many fatal customs, and expunged
from their new government so many errors and abuses, both
religious and civil, did not also prevent the introduction of
a set of men so dangerous! In some provinces, where every
inhabitant is constantly employed in tilling and cultivating
the earth, they are the only members of society who have
any knowledge; let these provinces attest what iniquitous use
they have made of that knowledge. They are here what the
clergy were in past centuries with you; the reformation, which

clipped the clerical wings, is the boast of that age, and the happiest event that could possibly happen; a reformation equally useful is now wanted, to relieve us from the shameful shackles and the oppressive burthen under which we groan: this perhaps is impossible; but, if mankind would not become too happy, it were an event most devoutly to be wished.

Here, happily, unoppressed with any civil bondage, this society of fishermen and merchants live, without any military establishments, without governors, or any masters but the laws; and their civil code is so light, that it is never felt. A man may pass (as many have done whom I am acquainted with) through the various scenes of a long life, may struggle against a variety of adverse fortune, peaceably enjoy the good when it comes, and never, in that long interval, apply to the law either for redress or assistance. The principal benefits it confers is the general protection of individuals, and this protection is purchased by the most moderate taxes, which are cheerfully paid, and by the trifling duties incident in the course of their lawful trade (for they despise contraband). Nothing can be more simple than their municipal regulations, though similar to those of the other counties of the same province; because they are more detached from the rest, more distinct in their manners as well as in the nature of the business they pursue, and more unconnected with the populous province to which they belong. The same simplicity attends the worship they pay to the Divinity; their elders are the only teachers of their congregations, the instructors of their youth, and often the example of their flock. They visit and comfort the sick; after death, the society bury them, with their fathers, without pomp, prayers, or ceremonies; not a stone or monument is erected, to tell where any person was buried; their memory is preserved by tradition. The only essential memorial, that is left of them, is their former industry, their kindness, their charity, or else their most conspicuous faults.

The Presbyterians live in great charity with them, and with one another; their minister, as a true pastor of the gospel, inculcates to them the doctrines it contains, the rewards it promises, the punishments it holds out to those who shall commit injustice. Nothing can be more disencumbered likewise from useless ceremonies and trifling forms than their mode of worship; it might with great propriety have been called a truly primitive one, had that of the Quakers never appeared. As fellow Christians, obeying the same legislator, they love and mutually assist each other in all their wants; as fellow-labourers they unite with cordiality, and without the least rancour, in all their temporal schemes: no other emulation appears among them but in their sea-excursions, in the art of fitting out their vessels, in that of sailing, in harpooning the whale, and in bringing home the greatest harvest. As fellow-subjects, they cheerfully obey the same laws and pay the same duties: but let me not forget another peculiar characteristic of this community: there is not a slave, I believe, on the whole island, at least among the Friends; whilst slavery prevails all around them, this society alone, lamenting that shocking insult offered to humanity, have given the world a singular example of moderation, disinterestedness, and Christian charity, in emancipating their negroes. I shall explain to you farther the singular virtue and merit to which it is so justly entitled by having set, before the rest of their fellow-subjects, so pleasing, so edifying, a reformation. Happy the people who are subject to so mild a government! happy the government which has to rule over such harmless and such industrious subjects!

While we are clearing forests, making the face of nature smile, draining marshes, cultivating wheat, and converting it into flour, they yearly skim, from the surface of the sea, riches equally necessary. Thus, had I leisure and abilities to lead you through this continent, I could shew you an astonishing prospect very little known in Europe; one diffusive scene of happiness, reaching from the sea-shores to the last settlements on the borders of the wilderness: a happiness, interrupted only by the folly of individuals, by our spirit of litigiousness, and by those unforeseen calamities, from which no human society can possibly be exempted. May the citizens of Nantucket dwell long here in uninterrupted peace, undisturbed either by the waves of the surrounding element, or the political commotions which sometimes agitate our continent!

LETTER VIII

PECULIAR CUSTOMS AT NANTUCKET

THE manners of *the Friends* are entirely founded on that simplicity which is their boast, and their most distinguished characteristic; and those manners have acquired the authority of laws. Here they are strongly attached to plainness of dress as well as to that of language; insomuch that, though some part of it may be ungrammatical, yet, should any person, who was born and brought up here, attempt to speak more correctly, he would be looked upon as a fop or an innovator. On the other hand, should a stranger come here and adopt their idiom in all its purity, (as they deem it,) this accomplishment would immediately procure him the most cordial reception; and they would cherish him like an antient member of their society. So many impositions have they suffered on this account, that they begin now indeed to grow more cautious. They are so tenacious of their antient habits of industry and frugality, that, if any of them were to be seen with a long coat, made of English cloth, on any other than the *first-day*, (Sunday,) he would be greatly ridiculed and censured; he would be looked upon as a careless spendthrift, whom it would be unsafe to trust and in vain to relieve. A few years ago two *single-horse chairs* were imported from Boston, to the great offence of these prudent citizens; nothing appeared to them more culpable than the use of such gaudy painted vehicles, in contempt of the more useful and more simple *single-horse carts* of their fathers. This piece of extravagant and unknown luxury almost caused a schism, and set every tongue a-going; some predicted the approaching ruin of those families that had imported them; others feared the dangers of example: never, since the foundation of the town, had there happened any thing which so much alarmed this primitive community. One of the possessors of these profane chairs, filled with repentance, wisely sent it back to the continent; the other, more obstinate and perverse, in defiance of all re- monstrances, persisted in the use of his chair until by degrees they became more reconciled to it; though I observed that the wealthiest and the most respectable people still go to meeting or to their farms in a *single-horse cart*, with a decent awning fixed over it: indeed, if you consider their sandy soil, and the badness of their roads, these appear to be the best- contrived vehicles for this island.

Idleness is the most heinous sin that can be committed in Nantucket: an idle man would soon be pointed out as an object of compassion; for idleness is considered as another word for want and hunger. This principle is so thoroughly well understood, and is become so universal, so prevailing, a prejudice, that, literally speaking, they are never idle. Even if they go to the market-place, which is (if I may be allowed the expression) the coffee-house of the town, either to transact business, or to converse with their friends, they always have a piece of cedar in their hands, and, while they are talking, they will, as it were instinctively, employ themselves in con- verting it into something useful, either in making bungs or spoyls* for their oil-casks, or other useful articles. I must confess that I have never seen more ingenuity in the use of the knife: thus the most idle moments of their lives become usefully employed. In the many hours of leisure, which their long cruises afford them, they cut and carve a variety of boxes and pretty toys, in wood, adapted to different uses; which they bring home, as testimonies of remembrance, to their wives and sweethearts. They have shewn me a variety of little bowls and other implements, executed cooper-wise, with the greatest neatness and elegance. You will be pleased to remember they are all brought up to the trade of coopers be their future intentions or fortunes what they may: therefore almost every man in this island has always two knives in his pocket, one much larger than the other; and, though they hold every

thing that is called *fashion* in the utmost contempt, yet they
are as difficult to please, and as extravagant in the choice and
price of their knives, as any young buck in Boston would be
about his hat, buckles, or coat. As soon as a knife is injured,
or superseded by a more convenient one, it is carefully laid
up in some corner of their desk. I once saw upwards of fifty
thus preserved at Mr. ——'s, one of the worthiest men on
this island; and, among the whole, there was not one that
perfectly resembled another. As the sea-excursions are often
very long, their wives, in their absence, are necessarily obliged
to transact business, to settle accounts, and, in short, to rule
and provide for their families. These circumstances being
often repeated give women the abilities as well as a taste for
that kind of superintendency, to which, by their prudence and
good management, they seem to be, in general, very equal.
This employment ripens their judgement, and justly entitles
them to a rank superior to that of other wives; and this is
the principle reason why those of Nantucket as well as those
of Montreal[1] are so fond of society, so affable, and so con-
versant with the affairs of the world. The men at their return,
weary with the fatigues of the sea, full of confidence and love,
cheerfully give their consent to every transaction that has
happened during their absence, and all is joy and peace. "Wife,
thee hast done well" is the general approbation they receive
for their application and industry. What would the men do
without the agency of these faithful mates? The absence of
so many of them, at particular seasons, leaves the town quite
desolate; and this mournful situation disposes the women to
go to each other's house much oftener than when their husbands are at home: hence the custom of incessant visiting
has infected every one, and even those whose husbands do
not go abroad. The house is always cleaned before they set

---

[1] Most of the merchants and young men of Montreal spend the greatest part of their time in trading with the Indians, at an amazing distance
from Canada; and it often happens that they are three years together absent
from home.

out, and with peculiar alacrity they pursue their intended visit, which consists of a social chat, a dish of tea, and a hearty supper. When the good man of the house returns from his labour, he peaceably goes after his wife and brings her home; mean while the young fellows, equally vigilant, easily find out which is the most convenient house, and there they assemble with the girls of the neighbourhood. Instead of cards, musical instruments, or songs, they relate stories of their whaling voyages, their various sea-adventures, and talk of the different coasts and people they have visited. "The island of Catharine in the Brazils, says one, is a very droll island; it is inhabited by none but men; women are not permitted to come in sight of it; not a woman is there on the whole island. Who among us is not glad it is not so here? The Nantucket girls and boys beat the world!" At this innocent sally the titter goes round, they whisper to one another their spontaneous reflexions: puddings, pies, and custards, never fail to be produced on such occasions; for I believe there never were any people, in their circumstances, who lived so well, even to super-abundance. As inebriation is unknown, and music, singing, and dancing, are holden in equal detestation, they never could fill all the vacant hours of their lives without the repast of the table. Thus these young people sit and talk, and divert themselves as well as they can; if any one has lately returned from a cruize, he is generally the speaker of the night; they often all laugh and talk together; but they are happy, and would not exchange their pleasures for those of the most brilliant assemblies in Europe. This lasts until the father and mother return; when all retire to their respective homes, the men re-conducting the partners of their affections.

Thus they spend many of the youthful evenings of their lives; no wonder, therefore, that they marry so early. But no sooner have they undergone this ceremony than they cease to appear so cheerful and gay; the new rank they hold in the society impresses them with more serious ideas than were entertained before. The title of master of a family necessarily requires more solid behaviour and deportment; the new wife follows in the trammels of custom, which are as powerful as the tyranny of fashion; she gradually advises and directs; the new husband soon goes to sea, he leaves her to learn and exercise the new government in which she is entered. Those who stay at home are full as passive in general, at least with regard to the inferior departments of the family. But you must not imagine from this account that the Nantucket wives are turbulent, of high temper, and difficult to be ruled; on the contrary, the wives of Sherburn, in so doing, comply only with the prevailing custom of the island: the husbands, equally submissive to the ancient and respectable manners of their country, submit, without ever suspecting that there can be any impropriety. Were they to behave otherwise, they would be afraid of subverting the principles of their society by altering its ancient rules: thus both parties are perfectly satisfied, and all is peace and concord. The richest person now in the island owes all his present prosperity and success to the ingenuity of his wife: this is a known fact which is well recorded; for, while he was performing his first cruises, she traded with pins and needles, and kept a school. Afterward she purchased more considerable articles, which she sold with so much judgement, that she laid the foundation of a system of business that she has ever since prosecuted with equal dexterity and success. She wrote to London, formed connections, and, in short, became the only ostensible instrument of that house, both at home and abroad. Who is he in this country, and who is a citizen of Nantucket or Boston, who does not know *Aunt Kesiah?* I must tell you that she is the wife of Mr. C——n, a very respectable man, who, well pleased with all her schemes, trusts to her judgement, and relies on her sagacity, with so entire a confidence, as to be altogether passive to the concerns of his family. They have the best country-seat on the island, at Quayes, where they live with hospitality, and in perfect union: He seems to be altogether the contemplative man.

To this dexterity, in managing the husband's business whilst he is absent, the Nantucket wives unite a great deal of industry. They spin, or cause to be spun, in their houses, abundance of wool and flax; and would be for ever disgraced and looked upon as idlers if all the family were not clad in good, neat, and sufficient, homespun cloth. *First Days* are the only seasons when it is lawful for both sexes to exhibit some garments of English manufacture; even *these* are of the most moderate price, and of the gravest colours: there is no kind of difference in their dress, they are all clad alike, and resemble in that respect the members of one family.

A singular custom prevails here among the women, at which I was greatly surprized; and am really at a loss how to account for the original cause that has introduced in this primitive society so remarkable a fashion, or rather so extraordinary a want. They have adopted, these many years, the Asiatic custom of taking a dose of opium every morning; and, so deeply rooted is it, that they would be at a loss how to live without this indulgence; they would rather be deprived of any necessary than forego their favourite luxury. This is much more prevailing among the women than the men, few of the latter having caught the contagion; though the sheriff, whom I may call the first person in the island, who is an eminent physician beside, and whom I had the pleasure of being well acquainted with, has for many years submitted to this custom. He takes three grains of it every day after breakfast, without the effects of which, he often told me, he was not able to transact any business.

It is hard to conceive how a people, always happy and healthy, in consequence of the exercise and labour they undergo, never oppressed with the vapours of idleness, yet should want the fictitious effects of opium to preserve that cheerfulness, to which their temperance, their climate, their happy situation, so justly entitle them. But where is the society perfectly free from error or folly? the least imperfect is undoubtedly that where the greatest good preponderates;

and, agreeable to this rule, I can truly say, that I never was acquainted with a less vicious or more harmless one.

The majority of the present inhabitants are the descendants of the twenty-seven first proprietors, who patenteed* the island; of the rest, many others have since come over amongst them, chiefly from the Massachusets: here are neither Scotch, Irish, nor French, as is the case in most other settlements; they are an unmixed English breed. The consequence of this extended connexion is, that they are all in some degree related to each other: you must not be surprized, therefore, when I tell you, that they always call each other cousin, uncle, or aunt; which are become such common appellations, that no other are made use of in their daily intercourse: you would be deemed stiff and affected were you to refuse conforming yourself to this ancient custom, which truly depicts the image of a large family. The many who reside here, that have not the least claim of relationship with any one in the town, yet by the power of custom make use of no other address in their conversation. Were you here yourself but a few days, you would be obliged to adopt the same phraseology, which is far from being disagreeable, as it implies a general acquaintance, and friendship, which connects them all in unity and peace.

Their taste for fishing has been so prevailing, that it has engrossed all their attention, and even prevented them from introducing some higher degree of perfection in their agriculture. There are many useful improvements which might have meliorated their soil; there are many trees which if transplanted here would have thriven extremely well, and would have served to shelter as well as decorate the favourite spots they have so carefully manured. The red cedar, the locust,[1] the button-wood, I am persuaded would have grown here rapidly and to a great size, with many others; but their thoughts are turned altogether toward the sea. The Indian corn begins to

---

[1] A species of what we call here the two-thorn acacia: it yields the most valuable timber we have, and its shade is very beneficial to the growth and goodness of the grass.

yield them considerable crops, and the wheat sown on its stocks is become a very profitable grain; rye will grow with little care; they might raise, if they would, an immense quantity of buck-wheat.

Such an island, inhabited as I have described, is not the place where gay travellers should resort, in order to enjoy that variety of pleasures the more splendid towns of this continent afford. Not that they are wholly deprived of what we might call recreations and innocent pastimes; but opulence, instead of luxuries and extravagancies, produces nothing more here than an increase of business, an additional degree of hospitality, greater neatness in the preparation of dishes, and better wines. They often walk and converse with each other, as I have observed before; and, upon extraordinary occasions, will take a ride to Palpus, where there is a house of entertainment; but these rural amusements are conducted upon the same plan of moderation as those in town. They are so simple as hardly to be described; the pleasure of going and returning together, of chatting and walking about, of throwing the bar, heaving stones, &c. are the only entertainments they are acquainted with. This is all they practise, and all they seem to desire. The house at Palpus is the general resort of those who possess the luxury of a horse and chaise, as well as those who still retain, as the majority do, a predilection for their primitive vehicle. By resorting to that place they enjoy a change of air, they taste the pleasures of exercise; perhaps an exhilarating bowl, not at all improper in this climate, affords the chief indulgence known to these people on the days of their greatest festivity. The mounting a horse must afford a most pleasing exercise to those men who are so much at sea. I was once invited to that house, and had the satisfaction of conducting thither one of the many beauties of that island, (for it abounds with handsome women,) dressed in all the bewitching attire of the most charming simplicity: like the rest of the company, she was cheerful without loud laughs, and smiling without affectation. They all appeared gay without levity. I had never before in my life seen so much unaffected mirth mixed with so much modesty. The pleasures of the day were enjoyed with the greatest liveliness and the most innocent freedom; no disgusting pruderies, no coquetish airs tarnished this enlivening assembly: they behaved according to their native dispositions, the only rules of decorum with which they were acquainted. What would an European visitor have done here without a fiddle, without a dance, without cards? He would have called it an insipid assembly, and ranked this among the dullest days he had ever spent. This rural excursion had a very great affinity to those practised in our province, with this difference only, that we have no objection to the sportive dance, though conducted by the rough accents of some self-taught African fidler. We returned as happy as we went; and the brightness of the moon kindly lengthened a day which had past, like other agreeable ones, with singular rapidity.

In order to view the island in its longest direction from the town, I took a ride to the easternmost parts of it, remarkable only for the Pochick Rip, where their best fish are caught. I past by the Tetoukèmah lots, which are the fields of the community; the fences were made of cedar posts and rails, and looked perfectly straight and neat; the various crops they enclosed were flourishing: thence I descended into Barrey's Valley, where the *blue* and the *spear* grass looked more abundant than I had seen on any other part of the island; thence to Gib's Pond; and arrived at last at Siàsconcèt. Several dwellings had been erected on this wild shore, for the purpose of sheltering the fishermen in the season of fishing; I found them all empty, except that particular one to which I had been directed. It was like the others, built on the highest part of the shore, in the face of the great ocean; the soil appeared to be composed of no other stratum but sand, covered with a thinly-scattered herbage. What rendered this house still more worthy of notice, in my eyes, was, that it had been built on the ruins of one of the antient huts, erected by the first settlers for observing the appearance of the whales. Here lived a single family without a neighbour; I had never before seen a spot better calculated to cherish contemplative ideas; perfectly unconnected with the great world, and far removed from its perturbations. The ever-raging ocean was all that presented itself to the view of this family; it irresistibly attracted my whole attention; my eyes were involuntarily directed to the horizontal line of that watery surface, which is ever in motion, and ever threatening destruction to these shores. My ears were stunned with the roar of its waves, rolling one over the other, as if impelled by a superior force to overwhelm the spot on which I stood. My nostrils involuntarily inhaled the saline vapours which arose from the dispersed particles of the foaming billows, or from the weeds scattered on the shores. My mind suggested a thousand vague reflections, pleasing in the hour of their spontaneous birth, but now half forgotten, and all indistinct. And who is the landman that can behold, without affright, so singular an element, which, by its impetuosity, seems to be the destroyer of this poor planet, yet, at particular times, accumulates the scattered fragments, and produces islands and continents fit for men to dwell on! Who can observe the regular vicissitudes of its waters without astonishment? Now, swelling themselves in order to penetrate through every river and opening, and thereby facilitate navigation; at other times, retiring from the shores, to permit man to collect that variety of shell-fish which is the support of the poor! Who can see the storms of wind, blowing sometimes with an impetuosity sufficiently strong even to move the earth, without feeling himself affected beyond the sphere of common ideas? Can this wind, which but a few days ago refreshed our American fields and cooled us in the shade, be the same element which now and then so powerfully convulses the waters of the sea, dismasts vessels, causes so many shipwrecks, and such extensive desolations? How diminutive does a man appear to himself when filled with these thoughts, and standing, as I did, on the verge of the ocean! This family lived entirely by fishing, for the plough has not dared yet to

disturb the parched surface of the neighbouring plain; and
to what purpose could this operation be performed? Where
is it that mankind will not find safety, peace, and abundance,
with freedom and civil happiness? Nothing was wanting here
to make this a most philosophic retreat, but a few ancient
trees, to shelter contemplation in its beloved solitude. There
I saw a numerous family of children of various ages,—the
blessings of an early marriage; they were ruddy as the cherry,
healthy as the fish they lived on, hardy as the pine-knots: the
eldest were already able to encounter the boisterous waves,
and shuddered not at their approach; early initiating themselves
in the mysteries of that sea-faring career, for which they were
all intended: the younger, timid as yet, on the edge of a less-
agitated pool, were teaching themselves with nut-shells and
pieces of wood, in imitation of boats, how to navigate, in
a future day, the larger vessels of their father through a
rougher and deeper ocean. I staid two days there on purpose to become acquainted with the different branches of
their œconomy and their manner of living in this singular
retreat. The clams, the oisters, of the shores, with the addition of Indian dumplings,[1] constituted their daily and most
substantial food. Larger fish were often caught on the neighbouring rip; these afforded them their greatest dainties: they
had likewise plenty of smoked bacon. The noise of the wheels
announced the industry of the mother and daughters; one
of them had been bred a weaver; and, having a loom in the
house, found means of clothing the whole family; they were
perfectly at ease, and seemed to want for nothing. I found
very few books among these people, who have very little time
for reading; the Bible and a few school tracts, both in the
Nattick and English languages, constituted their most numerous libraries. I saw indeed several copies of Hudibras and
Josephus;* but no one knows who first imported them. It is

---

[1] Indian dumplings are a peculiar preparation of Indian meal boiled in
large lumps.

something extraordinary to see this people, professedly so grave, and strangers to every branch of literature, reading with pleasure the former work, which should seem to require some degree of taste and antecedent historical knowledge. They all read it much, and can, by memory, repeat many passages; which, yet, I could not discover that they understood the beauties of. Is it not a little singular to see these books in the hands of fishermen, who are perfect strangers almost to any other? Josephus's history is indeed intelligible, and much fitter for their modes of education and taste, as it describes the history of a people, from whom we have received the prophecies which we believe, and the religious laws which we follow.

Learned travellers, returned from seeing the paintings and antiquities of Rome and Italy, still filled with the admiration and reverence they inspire, would hardly be persuaded that so contemptible a spot, which contains nothing remarkable but the genius and the industry of its inhabitants, could ever be an object worthy attention. But I, having never seen the beauties which Europe contains, cheerfully satisfy myself with attentively examining what my native country exhibits: if we have neither ancient amphitheatres, gilded palaces, nor elevated spires, we enjoy in our woods a substantial happiness which the wonders of art cannot communicate. None among us suffer oppression either from government or religion; there are very few poor except the idle, and, fortunately, the force of example and the most ample encouragement soon create a new principle of activity, which had been extinguished, perhaps, in their native country, for want of those opportunities which so often compel honest Europeans to seek shelter among us. The means of procuring subsistence in Europe are limited; the army may be full, the navy may abound with seamen, the land perhaps wants no additional labourers, the manufacturer is overcharged with supernumerary hands;—what then must become of the unemployed? Here, on the contrary, human industry has acquired a boundless field to exert itself in;— a field which will not be fully cultivated in many ages!

LETTER IX

DESCRIPTION OF CHARLES-TOWN;
THOUGHTS ON SLAVERY; ON PHYSICAL EVIL;
A MELANCHOLY SCENE

CHARLES-TOWN is in the north what Lima is in the south; both are capitals of the richest provinces of their respective hemispheres; you may therefore conjecture, that both cities must exhibit the appearances necessarily resulting from riches. Peru abounding in gold, Lima is filled with inhabitants, who enjoy all those gradations of pleasure, refinement, and luxury, which proceed from wealth. Carolina produces commodities, more valuable perhaps than gold, because they are gained by greater industry; it exhibits also on our northern stage a display of riches and luxury, inferior indeed to the former, but far superior to what are to be seen in our northern towns. Its situation is admirable; being built at the confluence of two large rivers, which receive, in their course, a great number of inferior streams; all navigable, in the spring, for flat boats. Here the produce of this extensive territory concentres; here, therefore, is the seat of the most valuable exportation; their wharfs, their docks, their magazines, are extremely convenient to facilitate this great commercial business. The inhabitants are the gayest in America; it is called the center of our beau monde, and is always filled with the richest planters in the province, who resort hither in quest of health and pleasure. Here is always to be seen a great number of valetudinarians from the West-Indies, seeking for the renovation of health, exhausted by the debilitating nature of their sun, air, and modes of living. Many of these West-Indians have I seen, at thirty, loaded with the infirmities of old age; for, nothing is more common, in those countries of wealth, than for persons to lose the abilities of enjoying the

comforts of life at a time when we northern men just begin
to taste the fruits of our labour and prudence. The round of
pleasure, and the expences of those citizens tables, are much
superior to what you would imagine: indeed the growth of this
town and province have been astonishingly rapid. It is pity
that the narrowness of the neck, on which it stands, prevents
it from increasing, and which is the reason why houses are
so dear. The heat of the climate, which is sometimes very
great in the interior parts of the country, is always temperate
in Charles-Town, though, sometimes, when they have no sea
breezes, the sun is too powerful. The climate renders excesses
of all kinds very dangerous, particularly those of the table; and
yet, insensible or fearless of danger, they live on, and enjoy
a short and a merry life: the rays of their sun seem to urge
them irresistibly to dissipation and pleasure: on the contrary,
the women, from being abstemious, reach to a longer period
of life, and seldom die without having had several husbands.
An European at his first arrival must be greatly surprised
when he sees the elegance of their houses, their sumptuous
furniture, as well as the magnificence of their tables; can he
imagine himself in a country, the establishment of which is
so recent?

The three principal classes of inhabitants are, lawyers,
planters, and merchants; this is the province which has
afforded to the first the richest spoils; for nothing can exceed
their wealth, their power, and their influence. They have
reached the *ne-plus-ultra** of worldly felicity; no plantation
is secured, no title is good, no will is valid, but what they
dictate, regulate, and approve. The whole mass of provincial
property is become tributary to this society; which, far above
priests and bishops, disdain to be satisfied with the poor
Mosaical portion of the tenth.* I appeal to the many inhabitants, who, while contending perhaps for their right to a few
hundred acres, have lost by the mazes of the law their whole
patrimony. These men are more properly law-givers than
interpreters of the law, and have united here, as well as in

most other provinces, the skill and dexterity of the scribe with the power and ambition of the prince: who can tell where this may lead in a future day? The nature of our laws, and the spirit of freedom which often tends to make us litigious, must necessarily throw the greatest part of the property of the colonies into the hands of these gentlemen. In another century, the law will possess in the north what now the church possesses in Peru and Mexico.

While all is joy, festivity, and happiness, in Charles-Town, would you imagine that scenes of misery overspread in the country? Their ears, by habit, are become deaf, their hearts are hardened; they neither see, hear, nor feel for, the woes of their poor slaves, from whose painful labours all their wealth proceeds. Here the horrors of slavery, the hardship of incessant toils, are unseen; and no one thinks with compassion of those showers of sweat and of tears which from the bodies of Africans daily drop, and moisten the ground they till. The cracks of the whip, urging these miserable beings to excessive labour, are far too distant from the gay capital to be heard. The chosen race eat, drink, and live happy, while the unfortunate one grubs up the ground, raises indigo, or husks the rice: exposed to a sun full as scorching as their native one without the support of good food, without the cordials of any cheering liquor. This great contrast has often afforded me subjects of the most afflicting meditations. On the one side, behold a people enjoying all that life affords most bewitching and pleasurable, without labour, without fatigue, hardly subjected to the trouble of wishing. With gold, dug from Peruvian mountains, they order vessels to the coasts of Guinea; by virtue of that gold, wars, murders, and devastations, are committed in some harmless, peaceable, African neighbourhood, where dwelt innocent people, who even knew not but that all men were black. The daughter torn from her weeping mother, the child from the wretched parents, the wife from the loving husband; whole families swept away, and brought, through storms and tempests, to this rich metropolis! There, arranged like horses at a fair, they are branded like cattle, and then driven to toil, to starve, and to languish, for a few years, on the different plantations of these citizens. And for whom must they work? For persons they know not, and who have no other power over them than that of violence; no other right than what this accursed metal has given them! Strange order of things! O Nature, where art thou?—Are not these blacks thy children as well as we? On the other side, nothing is to be seen but the most diffusive misery and wretchedness, unrelieved even in thought or wish! Day after day they drudge on without any prospect of ever reaping for themselves; they are obliged to devote their lives, their limbs, their will, and every vital exertion, to swell the wealth of masters, who look not upon them with half the kindness and affection with which they consider their dogs and horses. Kindness and affection are not the portion of those who till the earth, who carry burdens, who convert the logs into useful boards. This reward, simple and natural as one would conceive it, would border on humanity; and planters must have none of it!

If negroes are permitted to become fathers, this fatal indulgence only tends to increase their misery: the poor companions of their scanty pleasures are likewise the companions of their labours; and when, at some critical seasons, they could wish to see them relieved, with tears in their eyes they behold them perhaps doubly oppressed, obliged to bear the burden of nature—a fatal present!—as well as that of unabated tasks. How many have I seen cursing the irresistible propensity, and regretting that, by having tasted of those harmless joys, they had become the authors of double misery to their wives. Like their masters, they are not permitted to partake of those ineffable sensations with which nature inspires the hearts of fathers and mothers; they must repel them all, and become callous and passive. This unnatural state often occasions the most acute, the most pungent, of their afflictions; they have no time, like us, tenderly to rear their helpless offspring, to nurse them on their knees, to enjoy the delight of being parents. Their paternal fondness is imbittered by considering, that, if their children live, they must live to be slaves like themselves; no time is allowed them to exercise their pious office, the mothers must fasten them on their backs, and, with this double load, follow their husbands in the fields, where they too often hear no other sound than that of the voice or whip of the task-master, and the cries of their infants broiling in the sun. These unfortunate creatures cry and weep, like their parents, without a possibility of relief; the very instinct of the brute, so laudable, so irresistible, runs counter here to their master's interest; and, to that god, all the laws of nature must give way. Thus planters get rich; so raw, so inexperienced, am I in this mode of life, that, were I to be possessed of a plantation, and my slaves treated as in general they are here, never could I rest in peace; my sleep would be perpetually disturbed by a retrospect of the frauds committed in Africa in order to entrap them; frauds, surpassing in enormity every thing which a common mind can possibly conceive. I should be thinking of the barbarous treatment they meet with on ship-board; of their anguish, of the despair necessarily inspired by their situation; when torn from their friends and relations; when delivered into the hands of a people, differently coloured, whom they cannot understand; carried in a strange machine over an ever-agitated element, which they had never seen before; and finally delivered over to the severities of the whippers and the excessive labours of the field. Can it be possible that the force of custom should ever make me deaf to all these reflections, and as insensible to the injustice of that trade, and to their miseries, as the rich inhabitants of this town seem to be? What then is man? this being who boasts so much of the excellence and dignity of his nature, among that variety of inscrutable mysteries, of unsolvable problems, with which he is surrounded? The reason why man has been thus created is not the least astonishing. It is said, I know, that they are much happier here than in the

West-Indies; because, land being cheaper upon this continent than in those islands, the fields, allowed them to raise
their subsistence from, are in general more extensive. The only
possible chance of any alleviation depends on the humour of
the planters, who, bred in the midst of slaves, learn, from the
example of their parents, to despise them; and seldom conceive, either from religion or philosophy, any ideas that tend
to make their fate less calamitous; except some strong native
tenderness of heart, some rays of philanthropy, overcome
the obduracy contracted by habit.

I have not resided here long enough to become insensible
of pain for the objects which I every day behold. In the choice
of my friends and acquaintance, I always endeavour to find
out those whose dispositions are somewhat congenial with my
own. We have slaves likewise in our northern provinces; I hope
the time draws near when they will be all emancipated: but
how different their lot, how different their situation, in every
possible respect! They enjoy as much liberty as their masters,
they are as well clad and as well fed; in health and sickness
they are tenderly taken care of; they live under the same roof,
and are, truly speaking, a part of our families. Many of them
are taught to read and write, and are well instructed in the
principles of religion; they are the companions of our labours,
and treated as such; they enjoy many perquisites, many established holidays, and are not obliged to work more than white
people. They marry where inclination leads them; visit their
wives every week; are as decently clad as the common people;
they are indulged in educating, cherishing, and chastising,
their children, who are taught subordination to them as to
their lawful parents: in short, they participate in many of the
benefits of our society, without being obliged to bear any of
its burthens. They are fat, healthy, and hearty, and far from
repining at their fate; they think themselves happier than many
of the lower class of whites: they share with their masters the
wheat and meat provision they help to raise; many of those,
whom the good Quakers have emancipated, have received

that great benefit with tears of regret, and have never quitted, though free, their former masters and benefactors.

But is it really true, as I have heard it asserted here, that those blacks are incapable of feeling the spurs of emulation and the cheerful sound of encouragement? By no means; there are a thousand proofs existing of their gratitude and fidelity: those hearts, in which such noble dispositions can grow, are then like ours, they are susceptible of every generous sentiment, of every useful motive of action; they are capable of receiving lights, of imbibing ideas, that would greatly alleviate the weight of their miseries. But what methods have in general been made use of to obtain so desirable an end? None; the day, in which they arrive and are sold, is the first of their labours; labours, which from that hour admit of no respite; for, though indulged by law with relaxation on Sundays, they are obliged to employ that time, which is intended for rest, to till their little plantations. What can be expected from wretches in such circumstances? Forced from their native country, cruelly treated when on-board, and not less so on the plantations to which they are driven; is there any thing in this treatment but what must kindle all the passions, sow the seeds of inveterate resentment, and nourish a wish of perpetual revenge? They are left to the irresistible effects of those strong and natural propensities; the blows they receive, are they conducive to extinguish them or to win their affections? they are neither soothed by the hopes that their slavery will ever terminate but with their lives, nor yet encouraged by the goodness of their food or the mildness of their treatment. The very hopes held out to mankind by religion, that consolatory system, so useful to the miserable, are never presented to them; neither moral nor physical means are made use of to soften their chains; they are left in their original and untutored state; that very state, wherein the natural propensities of revenge and warm passions are so soon kindled. Cheered by no one single motive that can impel the will or excite their efforts, nothing but terrors and punishments are presented

to them; death is denounced if they run away; horrid dilaceration* if they speak with their native freedom; perpetually
awed by the terrible cracks of whips, or by the fear of capital
punishments, while even those punishments often fail of their
purpose!

A clergyman settled a few years ago at George-Town; and,
feeling as I do now, warmly recommended to the planters,
from the pulpit, a relaxation of severity; he introduced the
benignity of Christianity, and pathetically made use of the
admirable precepts of that system to melt the hearts of his
congregation into a greater degree of compassion toward
their slaves than had been hitherto customary. "Sir, (said one
of his hearers,) we pay you a genteel salary to read to us
the prayers of the liturgy, and to explain to us such parts of
the Gospel as the rule of the church directs; but we do not
want you to teach us what we are to do with our blacks." The
clergyman found it prudent to with-hold any farther admonition. Whence this astonishing right, or rather this barbarous
custom? for, most certainly, we have no kind of right beyond
that of force. We are told, it is true, that slavery cannot be
so repugnant to human nature as we at first imagine, because
it has been practised in all ages and in all nations: the Lacede-
monians themselves, those great assertors of liberty, conquered the Helotes* with the design of making them their
slaves. The Romans, whom we consider as our masters in civil
and military policy, lived in the exercise of the most horrid
oppression: they conquered to plunder and to enslave. What
a hideous aspect the face of the earth must then have exhibited! Provinces, towns, districts, often depopulated: their
inhabitants driven to Rome, the greatest market in the world,
and there sold by thousands! The Roman dominions were
tilled by the hands of unfortunate people, who had once been,
like their victors, free, rich, and possessed of every benefit
society can confer, until they became subject to the cruel right
of war and to lawless force. Is there then no superintending
power who conducts the moral operations of the world as well

as the physical? The same sublime hand, which guides the planets round the sun with so much exactness, which preserves the arrangement of the whole with such exalted wisdom and paternal care, and prevents the vast system from falling into confusion, doth it abandon mankind to all the errors, the follies, and the miseries, which their most frantic rage, and their most dangerous vices and passions can produce?

The history of the earth! doth it present any thing but crimes of the most heinous nature, committed from one end of the world to the other? We observe avarice, rapine, and murder, equally prevailing in all parts. History perpetually tells us of millions of people abandoned to the caprice of the maddest princes, and of whole nations devoted to the blind fury of tyrants; countries destroyed; nations alternately buried in ruins by other nations; some parts of the world, beautifully cultivated, returned again into their pristine state; the fruits of ages of industry, the toil of thousands, in a short time destroyed by few! If one corner breathes in peace for a few years, it is, in turn, subjected, torn, and levelled. One would almost believe the principles of action in man, considered as the first agent of this planet, to be poisoned in their most essential parts. We certainly are not that class of beings which we vainly think ourselves to be. Man, an animal of prey, seems to have rapine and the love of bloodshed implanted in his heart; nay, to hold it the most honourable occupation in society. We never speak of a hero of mathematics, a hero of knowledge or humanity: no! this illustrious appellation is reserved for the most successful butchers of the world. If Nature has given us a fruitful soil to inhabit, she has refused us such inclinations and propensities as would afford us the full enjoyment of it: extensive as the surface of this planet is, not one half of it is yet cultivated, not half replenished: she created man, and placed him either in the woods or plains, and provided him with passions which must for ever oppose his happiness. Every thing is submitted to the power of the strongest. Men, like the elements, are always at war: the weakest yield to the most potent; force, subtilty, and malice, always triumph over unguarded honesty and simplicity. Benignity, moderation, and justice, are virtues adapted only to the humble paths of life. We love to talk of virtue, and to admire its beauty, while in the shade of solitude and retirement; but, when we step forth into active life, if it happen to be in competition with any passion or desire, do we observe it to prevail? Hence so many religious impostors have triumphed over the credulity of mankind, and have rendered their frauds the creeds of succeeding generations, during the course of many ages, until, worn away by time, they have been replaced by new ones. Hence the most unjust war, if supported by the greatest force, always succeeds: hence the most just ones, when supported only by their justice, as often fail. Such is the ascendancy of power, the supreme arbiter of all the revolutions which we observe in this planet: so irresistible is power, that it often thwarts the tendency of the most forcible causes, and prevents their subsequent salutary effects, though ordained for the good of man by the Governor of the universe. Such is the perverseness of human nature! who can describe it in all its latitude?

In the moments of our philanthropy we often talk of an indulgent Nature, a kind Parent, who, for the benefit of man-kind, has taken singular pains to vary the genera of plants, fruits, grain, and the different productions of the earth, and has spread peculiar blessings in each climate. This is un-doubtedly an object of contemplation which calls forth our warmest gratitude; for, so singularly benevolent have those paternal intentions been, that, where barrenness of soil or severity of climate prevail, there she has implanted, in the heart of man, sentiments which over-balance every misery, and supply the place of every want. She has given to the inhabitants of these regions an attachment to their savage rocks and wild shores, unknown to those who inhabit the fertile fields of the temperate zone. Yet, if we attentively view this globe, will it not appear rather a place of punishment than of delight? And, what misfortune! that those punishments should fall on the innocent, and its few delights be enjoyed by the most unworthy. Famine, diseases, elementary convulsions, human feuds, dissentions, &c. are the produce of every climate; each climate produces, besides, vices and miseries peculiar to its latitude. View the frigid sterility of the north, whose famished inhabitants, hardly acquainted with the sun, live and fare worse than the bears they hunt; and to which they are superior only in the faculty of speaking. View the arctic and antarctic regions, those huge voids, where nothing lives; regions of eternal snow; where Winter in all his horrors has established his throne, and arrested every creative power of nature. Will you call the miserable stragglers in these countries by the name of men? Now contrast this frigid power of the north and south with that of the sun; examine the parched lands of the torrid zone, replete with sulphureous exhalations; view those countries of Asia subject to pestilential infections which lay nature waste; view this globe often convulsed both from within and without; pouring forth, from several mouths, rivers of boiling matter, which are imperceptibly leaving immense subterranean graves, wherein millions will one day perish! Look at the poisonous soil of the equator, at those putrid slimy tracks, teeming with horrid monsters, the enemies of the human race; look next at the sandy continent, scorched perhaps by the fatal approach of some ancient comet, now the abode of desolation. Examine the rains, the convulsive storms of those climates, where masses of sulphur, bitumen, and electrical fire, combining their dreadful powers, are incessantly hovering and bursting over a globe threatened with dissolution. On this little shell, how very few are the spots where man can live and flourish! even under those mild climates, which seem to breathe peace and happiness, the poison of slavery, the fury of despotism, and the rage of superstition, are all combined against man. There only the few live and rule, while the many starve and utter ineffectual complaints: there, human nature appears more debased, perhaps, than in the less-favoured climates. The fertile plains of Asia, the rich low lands of Egypt and of Diarbeck,* the fruitful fields bordering on the Tigris and the Euphrates, the extensive country of the East-Indies in all its separate districts; all these must, to the geographical eye, seem as if intended for terrestrial paradises: but, though surrounded with the spontaneous riches of nature, though her kindest favours seem to be shed on those beautiful regions with the most profuse hand, yet there, in general, we find the most wretched people in the world. Almost every where, liberty, so natural to mankind, is refused, or rather enjoyed but by their tyrants; the word *slave* is the appellation of every rank, who adore, as a divinity, a being worse than themselves; subject to every caprice, and to every lawless rage which unrestrained power can give. Tears are shed, perpetual groans are heard, where only the accents of peace, alacrity, and gratitude, should resound. There the very delirium of tyranny tramples on the best gifts of nature, and sports with the fate, the happiness, the lives, of millions: there the extreme fertility of the ground always indicates the extreme misery of the inhabitants.

Every where one part of the human species is taught the art of shedding the blood of the other: of setting fire to their dwellings; of levelling the works of their industry: half of the existence of nations regularly employed in destroying other nations. What little political felicity is to be met with here and there has cost oceans of blood to purchase; as if good was never to be the portion of unhappy man. Republics, kingdoms, monarchies, founded either on fraud or successful violence, increase by pursuing the steps of the same policy, until they are destroyed, in their turn, either by the influence of their own crimes or by more successful but equally criminal enemies.

If, from this general review of human nature, we descend to the examination of what is called civilized society; there the combination of every natural and artificial want makes us pay very dear for what little share of political felicity we enjoy. It is a strange heterogeneous assemblage of vices and virtues, and of a variety of other principles, for ever at war, for ever jarring, for ever producing some dangerous, some distressing, extreme. Where do you conceive, then, that nature intended we should be happy? Would you prefer the state of men in the woods to that of men in a more improved situation? Evil preponderates in both; in the first they often eat each other for want of food, and in the other they often starve each other for want of room. For my part, I think the vices and miseries to be found in the latter exceed those of the former, in which real evil is more scarce, more supportable, and less enormous. Yet we wish to see the earth peopled, to accomplish the happiness of kingdoms, which is said to consist in numbers. Gracious God! to what end is the introduction of so many beings into a mode of existence, in which they must grope amidst as many errors, commit as many crimes, and meet with as many diseases, wants, and sufferings!

The following scene will, I hope, account for these melancholy reflections, and apologize for the gloomy thoughts with which I have filled this letter: my mind is, and always has been, oppressed since I became a witness to it. I was not long since invited to dine with a planter who lived three miles from ——, where he then resided. In order to avoid the heat of the sun, I resolved to go on foot, sheltered in a small path, leading through a pleasant wood. I was leisurely travelling along, attentively examining some peculiar plants which I had collected, when all at once I felt the air strongly agitated, though the day was perfectly calm and sultry. I immediately cast my eyes toward the cleared ground, from which I was but a small distance, in order to see whether it was not occasioned by a sudden shower; when at that instant a sound, resembling a deep rough voice, uttered, as I thought, a few inarticulate monosyllables. Alarmed and surprized, I precipitately looked all round, when I perceived, at about six rods distance, something resembling a cage, suspended to the limbs of a tree, all the branches of which appeared covered with large birds of prey, fluttering about, and anxiously endeavouring to perch on the cage. Actuated by an involuntary motion of my hands, more than by any design of my mind, I fired at them; they all flew to a short distance, with a most hideous noise: when, horrid to think and painful to repeat, I perceived a negro, suspended in the cage, and left there to expire! I shudder when I recollect that the birds had already picked out his eyes; his cheek bones were bare; his arms had been attacked in several places, and his body seemed covered with a multitude of wounds. From the edges of the hollow sockets, and from the lacerations with which he was disfigured, the blood slowly dropped, and tinged the ground beneath. No sooner were the birds flown, than swarms of insects covered the whole body of this unfortunate wretch, eager to feed on his mangled flesh and to drink his blood. I found myself suddenly arrested by the power of affright and terror; my nerves were convulsed; I trembled, I stood motionless, involuntarily contemplating the fate of this negro in all its dismal latitude. The living spectre, though deprived of his eyes, could still distinctly hear, and, in his uncouth dialect, begged me to give him some water to allay his thirst. Humanity herself would have recoiled back with horror; she would have balanced whether to lessen such reliefless distress, or mercifully with one blow to end this dreadful scene of agonizing torture. Had I had a ball in my gun, I certainly should have dispatched him; but, finding myself unable to perform so kind an office, I sought, though trembling, to relieve him as well as I could. A shell ready fixed to a pole, which had been used by some negroes, presented itself to me; I filled it with water, and with trembling hands I guided it to the quivering lips of the wretched sufferer. Urged by the irresistible power of thirst, he endeavoured to meet it, as he instinctively guessed its approach by the noise it made in passing through the bars of the cage. "Tankè you, whitè man, tankè you, putè somè poison and givè me." How long have you been hanging there? I asked him. "Two days, and me no die; the birds, the birds; aaah me!" Oppressed with

the reflections which this shocking spectacle afforded me, I
mustered strength enough to walk away, and soon reached
the house at which I intended to dine. There I heard that the
reason for this slave's being thus punished was on account
of his having killed the overseer of the plantation. They told me
that the laws of self-preservation rendered such executions
necessary; and supported the doctrine of slavery with the
arguments generally made use of to justify the practice; with
the repetition of which I shall not trouble you at present.

Adieu.

LETTER X

ON SNAKES; AND ON THE HUMMING-BIRD

WHY would you prescribe this task? you know that what we take up ourselves seems always lighter than what is imposed on us by others. You insist on my saying something about our snakes; and, in relating what I know concerning them, were it not for two singularities, the one of which I saw, and the other I received from an eye-witness, I should have but very little to observe. The southern provinces are the countries where nature has formed the greatest variety of alligators, snakes, serpents, and scorpions, from the smallest size, up to the *pine barren*, the largest species known here. We have but two, whose stings are mortal, which deserve to be mentioned; as for the black one, it is remarkable for nothing but its industry, agility, beauty, and the art of inticing birds by the power of its eyes. I admire it much, and never kill it, though its formidable length and appearance often get the better of the philosophy of some people, particularly Europeans. The most dangerous one is the *pilot* or *copperhead*; for the poison of which no remedy has yet been discovered. It bears the first name because it always precedes the rattle-snake; that is, quits its state of torpidity in the spring a week before the other. It bears the second name on account of its head being adorned with many copper-coloured spots. It lurks in rocks near the water, and is extremely active and dangerous. Let man beware of it. I have heard only of one person who was stung by a copperhead in this country. The poor wretch instantly swelled in a most dreadful manner; a multitude of spots of different hues alternately appeared and vanished on different parts of his body: his eyes were filled with madness and rage; he cast them on all present with the most vindictive looks; he thrust out his tongue as the snakes do; he hissed through his teeth with inconceivable strength, and became an object of terror to all by-standers. To the lividness of a corpse he united the desperate force of a maniac. They hardly were able to fasten him, so as to guard themselves from his attacks; when, in the space of two hours, death relieved the poor wretch from his struggles, and the spectators from their apprehensions. The poison of the rattle-snake is not mortal in so short a space, and hence there is more time to procure relief: we are acquainted with several antidotes with which almost every family is provided. They are extremely inactive, and, if not touched, are perfectly inoffensive. I once saw, as I was travelling, a great cliff which was full of them: I handled several, and they appeared to be dead: they were all entwined together, and thus they remain until the return of the sun. I found them out by following the track of some wild hogs which had fed on them, and even the Indians often regale on them. When they find them asleep, they put a small forked stick over their necks, which they keep immovably fixed on the ground, giving the snake a piece of leather to bite; and this they pull back several times with great force, until they observe their two poisonous fangs torn out. Then they cut off the head, skin the body, and cook it as we do eels, and their flesh is extremely sweet and white. I once saw a *tamed one*, as gentle as you can possibly conceive a reptile to be: it took to the water and swam whenever it pleased; and, when the boys to whom it belonged called it back, their summons was readily obeyed. It had been deprived of its fangs by the preceding method; they often stroked it with a soft brush, and this friction seemed to cause the most pleasing sensations, for it would turn on its back to enjoy it, as a cat does before the fire. One of this species was the cause, some years ago, of a most deplorable accident, which I shall relate to you, as I had it from the widow and mother of the victims. A Dutch farmer of the Minisink went to mowing, with his negroes, in his boots, a precaution used to prevent being stung. Inadvertently he trod on a snake, which immediately flew at his legs, and, as it drew back in order to renew its blow, one of his negroes cut it in two with his scythe. They prosecuted their work and returned home: at night the farmer pulled off his boots and went to bed, and was soon after attacked with a strange sickness at his stomach; he swelled, and, before a physician could be sent for, died. The sudden death of this man did not cause much inquiry. The neighbourhood wondered, as is usual in such cases, and without any farther examination the corpse was buried. A few days after, the son put on his father's boots, and went to the meadow: at night he pulled them off, went to bed, and was attacked with the same symptoms, about the same time, and died in the morning. A little before he expired the doctor came, but was not able to assign what could be the cause of so singular a disorder; however, rather than appear wholly at a loss before the country people, he pronounced both father and son to have been bewitched. Some weeks after, the widow sold all the movables for the benefit of the younger children, and the farm was leased. One of the neighbours, who bought the boots, presently put them on, and was attacked in the same manner as the other two had been; but this man's wife, being alarmed by what had happened in the former family, dispatched one of her negroes for an eminent physician, who, fortunately having heard something of the dreadful affair, guessed at the cause, applied oil, &c. and recovered the man. The boots, which had been so fatal, were then carefully examined; and he found that the two fangs of the snake had been left in the leather, after being wrenched out of their sockets by the strength with which the snake had drawn back its head. The bladders, which contained the poison, and several of the small nerves, were still fresh, and adhered to the boot. The unfortunate father and son had been poisoned by pulling off these boots, in which action they imperceptibly scratched their legs with the points of the fangs, through the hollow of which some of this astonishing poison was conveyed. You have, no doubt, heard of their rattles, if you have not seen them. The only observation I wish to make is, that the rattling is loud and distinct when they are angry; and, on the contrary, when pleased, it sounds like a distant trepidation,* in which nothing distinct is heard. In the thick settlements they are now become very scarce; for, wherever they are met with, open war is declared against them, so that, in a few years, there will be none left but on our mountains. The black snake, on the contrary, always diverts me, because it excites no idea of danger. Their swiftness is astonishing; they will sometimes equal that of a horse; at other times they will climb up trees in quest of our tree toads, or glide on the ground at full length. On some occasions, they present themselves half in the reptile state,* half erect. Their eyes and their heads, in the erect posture, appear to great advantage: the former display a fire which I have often admired, and it is by these they are enabled to fascinate birds and squirrels. When they have fixed their eyes on an animal, they become immovable, only turning their head sometimes to the right and sometimes to the left, but still with their sight invariably directed to the object. The distracted victim, instead of flying its enemy, seems to be arrested by some invincible power; it screams; now approaches, and then recedes; and, after skipping about with unaccountable agitation, finally rushes into the jaws of the snake, and is swallowed, as soon as it is covered with a slime or glue to make it slide easily down the throat of the devourer.

One anecdote I must relate, the circumstances of which are as true as they are singular. One of my constant walks, when I am at leisure, is in my lowlands, where I have the pleasure of seeing my cattle, horses, and colts. Exuberant grass replenishes all my fields, the best representative of our wealth; in the middle of that track I have cut a ditch, eight feet wide, the banks of which nature adorns every spring with the wild salendine, and other flowering weeds, which on these luxuriant grounds shoot up to a great height. Over this ditch I have erected a bridge, capable of bearing a loaded waggon; on each side, I carefully sow every year some grains of hemp, which rise to the height of fifteen feet, so strong, and so full of limbs, as to resemble young trees; I once ascended one of them four feet above the ground. These produce natural arbours, rendered often still more compact by the assistance of an annual creeping plant, which we call a vine, that never fails to entwine itself among their branches, and always produces a very desirable shade. From this simple grove I have amused myself a hundred times in observing the great number of humming-birds with which our country abounds: the wild blossoms every where attract the attention of these birds, which, like bees, subsist by suction. From this retreat I distinctly watch them in all their various attitudes; but their flight is so rapid that you cannot distinguish the motion of their wings. On this little bird Nature has profusely lavished her most splendid colours; the most perfect azure, the most beautiful gold, the most dazzling red, are for ever in contrast, and help to embellish the plumes of his majestic head. The richest pallet of the most luxuriant painter could never invent any thing to be compared to the variegated tints with which this insect-bird is arrayed. Its bill is as long and as sharp as a coarse sewing-needle; like the bee, nature has taught it to find out the calix of flowers and blossoms, those mellifluous particles that serve it for sufficient food; and yet it seems to leave them untouched, undeprived of any thing that our eyes can possibly distinguish. When it feeds, it appears as if immovable, though continually on the wing; and, sometimes, from what motives I know not, it will tear and lacerate flowers into a hundred pieces; for, strange to tell, they are the most irascible of the feathered tribe.—Where do passions find room in so diminutive a body?—They often fight with the fury of lions, until one of the combatants falls a sacrifice and dies. When fatigued, it has often perched within a few feet of me, and, on such favourable opportunities, I have surveyed it with the most minute attention. Its little eyes appear like diamonds, reflecting light on every side: most elegantly finished in all parts, it is a miniature-work of our great Parent; who seems to have

formed it the smallest, and, at the same time, the most beautiful, of the winged species.

As I was one day sitting solitary and pensive in my primitive arbour, my attention was engaged by a strange sort of rustling noise at some paces distance. I looked all around without
distinguishing any thing, until I climbed one of my great hemp-
stalks; when, to my astonishment, I beheld two snakes of
considerable length, the one pursuing the other, with great
celerity, through a hemp-stubble field. The aggressor was of
the black kind, six feet long; the fugitive was a water-snake,
nearly of equal dimensions. They soon met, and, in the fury
of their first encounter, they appeared in an instant firmly
twisted together; and, whilst their united tails beat the ground,
they mutually tried with open jaws to lacerate each other.
What a fell aspect did they present! their heads were com-
pressed to a very small size, their eyes flashed fire; and, after
this conflict had lasted about five minutes, the second found
means to disengage itself from the first, and hurried toward
the ditch. Its antagonist instantly assumed a new posture; and,
half creeping and half erect, with a majestic mein, overtook
and attacked the other again, which placed itself in the same
attitude and prepared to resist. The scene was uncommon
and beautiful; for, thus opposed, they fought with their jaws,
biting each other with the utmost rage; but, notwithftanding
this appearance of mutual courage and fury, the water-snake
still seemed desirous of retreating toward the ditch, its natural
element. This was no sooner perceived by the keen-eyed black
one, than, twisting its tail twice round a stalk of hemp, and
seizing its adversary by the throat, not by means of its jaws,
but by twisting its own neck twice round that of the water-
snake, pulled it back from the ditch. To prevent a defeat, the
latter took hold likewise of a stalk on the bank, and, by the
acquisition of that point of resistance, became a match for its
fierce antagonist. Strange was this to behold; two great snakes
strongly adhering to the ground, mutually fastened together,
by means of the writhings, which lashed them to each other,

and, stretched at their full length, they pulled, but pulled in vain; and, in the moments of greatest exertion, that part of their bodies which was entwined seemed extremely small, while the rest appeared inflated, and, now and then, convulsed with strong undulations rapidly following each other. Their eyes seemed on fire and ready to start out of their heads; at one time the conflict seemed decided; the water-snake bent itself into two great folds, and, by that operation, rendered the other more than commonly outstretched; the next minute, the new struggles of the black one gained an unexpected superiority; it acquired two great folds likewise, which necessarily extended the body of its adversary in proportion as it had contracted its own. These efforts were alternate; victory seemed doubtful; inclining sometimes to the one side and sometimes to the other; until, at last, the stalk, to which the black snake fastened, suddenly gave way, and, in consequence of this accident, they both plunged into the ditch. The water did not extinguish their vindictive rage; for, by their agitations, I could trace, though not distinguish, their mutual attacks. They soon re-appeared on the surface twisted together as in their first onset; but the black snake seemed to retain its wonted superiority, for its head was exactly fixed above that of the other, which it incessantly pressed down under the water until it was stifled and sunk. The victor no sooner perceived its enemy incapable of farther resistance, than, abandoning it to the current, it returned on shore and disappeared.

LETTER XI

EXAMINE this flourishing province, in whatever light you will, the eyes, as well as the mind, of an European traveller are equally delighted, because a diffusive happiness appears in every part; happiness which is established on the broadest basis. The wisdom of Lycurgus and Solon never conferred on man one half of the blessings and uninterrupted prosperity which the Pennsylvanians now possess. The name of *Penn*, that simple but illustrious citizen, does more honour to the English nation than those of many of their kings!

In order to convince you that I have not bestowed undeserved praises in my former letters on this celebrated government, and that either nature or the climate seems to be more favourable here to the arts and sciences than to any other American province, let us together, agreeable to your desire, pay a visit to Mr. John Bertram, the first botanist in this new hemisphere; become such by a native impulse of disposition. It is to this simple man that America is indebted for several useful discoveries and the knowledge of many new plants. I had been greatly prepossessed in his favour by the extensive correspondence which I knew he held with the most eminent Scotch and French botanists: I knew also that he had been honoured with that of Queen Ulrica of Sweden.*

His house is small, but decent: there was something peculiar in its first appearance, which seemed to distinguish it from those of his neighbours: a small tower, in the middle of it, not only helped to strengthen it, but afforded convenient room for a staircase. Every disposition of the fields, fences, and trees, seemed to bear the marks of perfect order and regularity, which, in rural affairs, always indicate a prosperous industry.

I was received at the door by a woman dressed extremely neat and simple, who, without courtesying, or any other cere- monial, asked me, with an air of benignity, whom I wanted? I answered, I should be glad to see Mr. Bertram. If thee wilt step in, and take a chair, I will send for him. No, I said, I had rather have the pleasure of walking through his farm; I shall easily find him out, with your directions. After a little time I perceived the Schuylkill, winding through delightful meadows, and soon cast my eyes on a new-made bank, which seemed greatly to confine its stream. After having walked on its top a considerable way I at last reached the place where ten men were at work. I asked, if any of them could tell me where Mr. Bertram was? An elderly-looking man, with wide trowsers and a large leather apron on, looking at me, said, "My name is Bertram, dost thee want me?" Sir, I am come on purpose to converse with you, if you can be spared from your labour. "Very easily, (he answered,) I direct and advise more than I work." We walked toward the house, where he made me take a chair while he went to put on clean clothes, after which he returned and sat down by me. The fame of your knowledge, said I, in American botany, and your well- known hospitality, have induced me to pay you a visit, which I hope you will not think troublesome: I should be glad to spend a few hours in your garden. "The greatest advantage (replied he) which I receive, from what thee callest my botan- ical fame, is the pleasure which it often procureth me in receiving the visits of friends and foreigners: but our jaunt into the garden must be postponed for the present, as the bell is ringing for dinner." We entered into a large hall, where there was a long table full of victuals; at the lowest part sat his negroes, his hired men were next, then the family and myself; and, at the head, the venerable father and his wife presided. Each reclined his head and said his prayers, divested of the tedious cant of some, and of the ostentatious style of others. "After the luxuries of our cities, (observed he,) this plain fare must appear to thee a severe fast." By no means, Mr. Bertram, this honest country dinner convinces me that you receive me as a friend and an old acquaintance. "I am glad of it, for thee art heartily welcome. I never knew how to use ceremonies; they are insufficient proofs of sincerity; our society, besides, are utterly strangers to what the world calleth polite expressions. We treat others as we treat ourselves. I received yesterday a letter from Philadelphia, by which I understand thee art a Russian; what motives can possibly have induced thee to quit thy native country and to come so far in quest of knowledge or pleasure? Verily it is a great compliment thee payest to this our young province, to think that any thing it exhibiteth may be worthy thy attention." I have been most amply repaid for the trouble of the passage. I view the present Americans as the seed of future nations, which will replenish this boundless continent; the Russians may be in some respects compared to you; we likewise are a new people, new I mean in knowledge, arts, and improvements. Who knows what revolutions Russia and America may one day bring about: we are perhaps nearer neighbours than we imagine. I view, with peculiar attention, all your towns; I examine their situation, and the police, for which many are already famous. Though their foundations are now so recent, and so well remembered, yet their origin will puzzle posterity as much as we are now puzzled to ascertain the beginning of those which time has in some measure destroyed. Your new buildings, your streets, put me in mind of those of the city of *Pompeia*, where I was a few years ago. I attentively examined every thing there, particularly the foot-path which runs along the houses. They appeared to have been considerably worn by the great number of people which had once travelled over them. But now how distant: neither builder nor proprietors remain; nothing is known! "Why, thee hast been a great traveller for a man of thy years." Few years, sir, will enable any body to journey over a great track of country, but it requires a superior degree of knowledge to gather harvests as we go. Pray, Mr. Bertram, what banks are those which you are making? to what purpose is so much expence and so much labour bestowed? "Friend Iwan, no branch of industry was ever more profitable to any country as well as to the proprietors. The Schuylkill, in its many windings, once covered a great extent of ground, though its waters were but shallow even in our highest tides; and, though some parts were always dry, yet the whole of this great track presented to the eye nothing but a putrid swampy soil, useless either for the plough or the scythe. The proprietors of these grounds are now incorporated: we yearly pay to the treasurer of the company a certain sum, which makes an aggregate superior to the casualties that generally happen either by inundations or the musk squash.* It is owing to this happy contrivance that so many thousand acres of meadows have been rescued from the Schuylkill, which now both enricheth and embellisheth so much of the neighbourhood of our city. Our brethren of Salem, in New Jersey, have carried the art of banking to a still higher degree of perfection." It is really an admirable contrivance, which greatly redounds to the honour of the parties concerned, and shews a spirit of discernment and perseverance which is highly praiseworthy. If the Virginians would imitate your example, the state of their husbandry would greatly improve. I have not heard of any such association in any other parts of the continent. Pennsylvania, hitherto, seems to reign the unrivalled queen of these fair provinces. Pray, sir, what expences are you at ere these grounds be fit for the scythe? "The expences are very considerable, particularly when we have land, brooks, trees, and brush, to clear away. But, such is the excellence of these bottoms, and the goodness of the grass, for fattening of cattle, that the produce of three years pays all advances." Happy the country where nature has bestowed such rich treasures, treasures superior to mines! said I; if all this fair province is thus cultivated, no wonder it has acquired such reputation, for the prosperity and the industry of its inhabitants.

By this time the working part of the family had finished their dinner, and had retired with a decency and silence which pleased me much. Soon after I heard, as I thought, a distant concert of instruments.—However simple and pastoral your fare was, Mr. Bertram, this is the dessert of a prince; pray what is this I hear? "Thee must not be alarmed, it is of a piece with the rest of thy treatment, friend Iwan." Anxious I followed the sound; and, by ascending the stair-case, found that it was the effect of the wind through the strings of an Eolian harp; an instrument which I had never before seen. After dinner we quaffed an honest bottle of Madeira wine, without the irksome labour of toasts, healths, or sentiments; and then retired into his study.

I was no sooner entered, than I observed a coat of arms, in a gilt frame, with the name of *John Bertram*. The novelty of such a decoration, in such a place, struck me; I could not avoid asking, Does the Society of Friends take any pride in these armorial bearings, which, sometimes, serve as marks of distinction between families, and, much oftener, as food for pride and ostentation? "Thee must know (said he) that my father was a Frenchman, he brought this piece of paint-ing over with him; I keep it as a piece of family-furniture, and as a memorial of his removal hither." From his study we went into the garden, which contained a great variety of curious plants and shrubs; some grew in a green-house, over the door of which were written these lines;

> "Slave to no sect, who takes no private road,
> But looks, through nature, up to nature's God!"*

He informed me that he had often followed General Bouquet* to Pittsburgh, with the view of herbarizing;* that he had made useful collections in Virginia, and that he had been employed by the King of England to visit the two Floridas.

Our walks and botanical observations engrossed so much of our time, that the sun was almost down ere I thought of returning to Philadelphia. I regretted that the day had been so short, as I had not spent so rational an one for a long time before. I wanted to stay, yet was doubtful whether it would not appear improper, being an utter stranger. Knowing, however, that I was visiting the least ceremonious people in the world, I bluntly informed him of the pleasure I had enjoyed, and with the desire I had of staying a few days with him. "Thee art as welcome as if I was they father. Thee art no stranger. Thy desire of knowledge, thy being a foreigner besides, entitleth thee to consider my house as thine own as long as thee pleaseth: use thy time with the most perfect freedom; I too shall do so myself." I thankfully accepted the kind invitation.

We went to view his favourite bank; he shewed me the principles and method on which it was erected; and we walked over the grounds which had been already drained. The whole store of nature's kind luxuriance seemed to have been exhausted on these beautiful meadows; he made me count the amazing number of cattle and horses now feeding on solid bottoms, which but a few years before had been covered with water. Thence we rambled through his fields, where the right-angular fences, the heaps of pitched stones, the flourishing clover, announced the best husbandry as well as the most assiduous attention. His cows were then returning home, deep bellied, short legged, having udders ready to burst; seeking, with seeming toil, to be delivered from the great exuberance they contained; he next shewed me his orchard, formerly planted on a barren sandy soil, but long since converted into one of the richest spots in that vicinage.

"This, said he, is altogether the fruit of my own contrivance. I purchased, some years ago, the privilege of a small spring, about a mile and a half from hence, which, at a considerable expence, I have brought to this reservoir; therein I throw old lime, ashes, horsedung, &c. and, twice a week, I let it run, thus impregnated. I regularly spread on this ground, in the fall, old hay, straw, and whatever damaged fodder I have about my barn. By these simple means I mow, one year with another, fifty-three hundreds of excellent hay per acre, from a soil which scarcely produced *five-fingers* [*a small plant resembling strawberries*] some years before." This is, Sir, a miracle in husbandry; happy the country which is cultivated by a society of men, whose application and taste lead them to prosecute and accomplish useful works! "I am not the only person who do these things, (he said,) wherever water can be had it is always turned to that important use; wherever a farmer can water his meadows, the greatest crops of the best hay and excellent after-grass are the sure rewards of his labours. With the banks of my meadow-ditches I have greatly enriched my upland fields; those which I intend to rest for a few years I constantly sow with red clover, which is the greatest meliorator of our lands. For three years after, they yield abundant pasture. When I want to break up my clover-fields, I give them a good coat of mud, which hath been exposed to the severities of three or four of our winters. This is the reason that I commonly reap from twenty-eight to thirty-six bushels of wheat an acre; my flax, oats, and Indian corn, I raise in the same proportion. Wouldst thee inform me whether the inhabitants of thy country follow the same methods of husbandry?" No, Sir; in the neighbourhood of our towns there are indeed some intelligent farmers, who prosecute their rural schemes with attention; but we should be too numerous, too happy, too powerful, a people, if it were possible for the whole Russian Empire to be cultivated like the province of Pennsylvania. Our lands are so unequally divided, and so few of our farmers are possessors of the soil they till, that they cannot execute plans of husbandry with the same vigour as you do, who hold yours, as it were, from the Master of nature, unincumbered and free. O America! exclaimed I, thou knowest not as yet the whole extent of thy happiness: the foundation of thy civil polity must lead thee in a few years to a degree of population and power which Europe little thinks of! "Long before this happen (answered the good man) we shall rest beneath the turf; it is vain for mortals to be presumptuous in their conjectures: our country is, no doubt, the cradle of an extensive future population; the old world is growing

weary of its inhabitants, they must come here to flee from
the tyranny of the great. But doth not thee imagine, that the
great will, in the course of years, come over here also; for
it is the misfortune of all societies every where to hear of great
men, great rulers, and of great tyrants." My dear Sir, I replied,
tyranny never can take a strong hold in this country, the land
is too wisely distributed: it is poverty in Europe that makes
slaves. "Friend Iwan, as I make no doubt that thee under-
standest the Latin tongue, read this kind epistle which the
good Queen of Sweden, *Ulrica*, sent me a few years ago. Good
woman! that she should think, in her palace at Stockholm, of
poor John Bertram on the banks of the Schuylkill, appeareth
to me very strange." Not in the least, dear Sir, you are the first
man whose name, as a botanist, has done honour to America.
It is very natural, at the same time, to imagine that so extensive a continent must contain many curious plants and trees:
is it then surprising to see a princess, fond of useful knowledge, descend sometimes from the throne to walk in the
gardens of Linnæus?* " 'Tis to the directions of that learned
man (said Mr. Bertram) that I am indebted for the method
which has led me to the knowledge I now possess: the science
of botany is so diffusive, that a proper thread is absolutely
wanted to conduct the beginner." Pray, Mr. Bertram, when did
you imbibe the first wish to cultivate the science of botany?
were you regularly bred to it in Philadelphia? "I have never
received any other education than barely reading and writing. This small farm was all the patrimony my father left me:
certain debts, and the want of meadows, kept me rather low
in the beginning of my life. My wife brought me nothing in
money; all her riches consisted in her good temper and great
knowledge of housewifery. I scarcely know how to trace my
steps in the botanical career: they appear to me now like unto
a dream; but thee mayest rely on what I shall relate, though
I know that some of our friends have laughed at it." I am
not one of those people, Mr. Bertram, who aim at finding
out the ridiculous in what is sincerely and honestly averred.

"Well, then, I'll tell thee. One day I was very busy in holding my plough, (for thee seest I am but a ploughman,) and, being weary, I ran under the shade of a tree to repose myself. I cast my eyes on a *daisy*: I plucked it mechanically, and viewed it with more curiosity than common country farmers are wont to do, and observed therein very many distinct parts, some perpendicular, some horizontal. *What a shame, said my mind, or something that inspired my mind, that thee shouldst have employed so many years in tilling the earth and destroying so many flowers and plants, without being acquainted with their structures and their uses!* This seeming inspiration suddenly awakened my curiosity, for these were not thoughts to which I had been accustomed. I returned to my team, but this new desire did not quit my mind; I mentioned it to my wife, who greatly discouraged me from prosecuting my new scheme, as she called it. I was not opulent enough, she said, to dedicate much of my time to studies and labours which might rob me of that portion of it which is the only wealth of the American farmer. However, her prudent caution did not discourage me; I thought about it continually, at supper, in bed, and wherever I went. At last I could not resist the impulse; for, on the fourth day of the following week, I hired a man to plough for me, and went to Philadelphia. Though I knew not what book to call for, I ingenuously told the bookseller my errand, who provided me with such as he thought best, and a Latin grammar beside. Next I applied to a neighbouring schoolmaster, who in three months taught me Latin enough to understand Linnæus, which I purchased afterward. Then I began to botanize all over my farm; in a little time I became acquainted with every vegetable that grew in my neighbourhood; and next ventured into Maryland, living among the Friends: in proportion as I thought myself more learned I proceeded farther, and, by a steady application of several years, I have acquired a pretty general knowledge of every plant and tree to be found in our continent. In process of time I was applied to from the old countries, whither I every year

send many collections. Being now made easy in my circumstances, I have ceased to labour, and am never so happy as
when I see and converse with my friends. If, among the many
plants or shrubs I am acquainted with, there are any thee
wantest to send to thy native country, I will cheerfully procure them, and give thee moreover whatever directions thee
mayest want."

Thus I passed several days in ease, improvement, and pleasure; I observed, in all the operations of his farm as well as in
the mutual correspondence between the master and the inferior members of his family, the greatest ease and decorum;
not a word like command seemed to exceed the tone of a
simple wish. The very negroes themselves appeared to partake of such a decency of behaviour, and modesty of countenance, as I had never before observed. By what means, said
I, Mr. Bertram, do you rule your slaves so well, that they seem
to do their work with the cheerfulness of white men? "Though
our erroneous prejudices and opinions once induced us to
look upon them as fit only for slavery, though ancient custom
had very unfortunately taught us to keep them in bondage;
yet of late, in consequence of the remonstrances of several
Friends, and of the good books they have published on that
subject, our society treats them very differently. With us they
are now free. I give those, whom thee didst see at my table,
eighteen pounds a year, with victuals and clothes, and all other
privileges which the white men enjoy. Our society treats them
now as the companions of our labours; and, by this management as well as by means of the education we have given
them, they are in general become a new set of beings. Those,
whom I admit to my table, I have found to be good, trusty,
moral, men; when they do not what we think they should do,
we dismiss them, which is all the punishment we inflict. Other
societies of Christians keep them still as slaves, without teaching them any kind of religious principles. What motive beside
fear can they have to behave well? In the first settlement of
this province, we employed them as slaves, I acknowledge;

but, when we found that good example, gentle admonition, and religious principles, could lead them to subordination and sobriety, we relinquished a method so contrary to the profession of Christianity. We gave them freedom, and yet few have quitted their ancient masters. The women breed in our families; and we become attached to one another. I taught mine to read and to write; they love God, and fear his judgements. The oldest person among them transacts my business in Philadelphia with a punctuality from which he has never deviated. They constantly attend our meetings, they participate in health and sickness, infancy and old age, in the advantages our society affords. Such are the means we have made use of to relieve them from that bondage and ignorance in which they were kept before. Thee, perhaps, hast been surprised to see them at my table, but, by elevating them to the rank of freemen, they necessarily acquire that emulation, without which we ourselves should fall into debasement and profligate ways." Mr. Bertram, this is the most philosophical treatment of negroes that I have heard of; happy would it be for America would other denominations of Christians imbibe the same principles, and follow the same admirable rules! A great number of men would be relieved from those cruel shackles, under which they now groan; and, under this impression, I cannot endure to spend more time in the southern provinces. The method with which they are treated there, the meanness of their food, the severity of their talks, are spectacles I have not patience to behold. "I am glad to see that thee hast so much compassion; are there any slaves in thy country?" Yes, unfortunately; but they are more properly civil than domestic slaves; they are attached to the soil on which they live; it is the remains of ancient barbarous customs, established in the days of the greatest ignorance and savageness of manners, and preserved, notwithstanding the repeated tears of humanity, the loud calls of policy, and the commands of religion. The pride of great men, with the avarice of landholders, make them look on this class as necessary tools of husbandry, as if freemen could not cultivate the ground. "And is it really so, Friend Iwan? To be poor, to be wretched, to be a slave, is hard indeed; existence is not worth enjoying on these terms. I am afraid the country can never flourish under such impolitic government." I am very much of your opinion, Mr. Bertram; though I am in hopes that the present reign, illustrious by so many acts of the soundest policy, will not expire without this salutary, this necessary, emancipation, which would fill the Russian empire with tears of gratitude. "How long hast thee been in this country?" Four years, Sir. "Why thee speakest English almost like a native: what a toil a traveller must undergo to learn various languages, to divest himself of his native prejudices, and to accommodate himself to the customs of all those among whom he chooseth to reside!"

Thus I spent my time with this enlightened botanist—this worthy citizen; who united all the simplicity of rustic manners to the most useful learning. Various and extensive were the conversations that filled the measure of my visit. I accompanied him to his fields, to his barn, to his bank, to his garden, to his study, and at the last to the meeting of the society on the Sunday following. It was at the town of Chester, whither the whole family went in two waggons; Mr. Bertram and I on horseback. When I entered the house where the Friends were assembled, who might be about two hundred men and women, the involuntary impulse of ancient custom made me pull off my hat; but, soon recovering myself, I sat with it on at the end of a bench. The meeting-house was a square building, devoid of any ornament whatever; the whiteness of the walls, the conveniency of seats, that of a large stove, which in cold weather keeps the whole house warm, were the only essential things which I observed. Neither pulpit nor desk, fount nor altar, tabernacle nor organ, were there to be seen; it is merely a spacious room, in which these good people meet every Sunday. A profound silence ensued, which lasted about half an hour; every one had his head reclined, and seemed absorbed in profound meditation; when a female friend arose, and declared, with a most engaging modesty, that the spirit moved her to entertain them on the subject she had chosen. She treated it with great propriety, as a moral useful discourse, and delivered it without theological parade or the ostentation of learning. Either she must have been a great adept in public speaking, or had studiously prepared herself; a circumstance that cannot well be supposed, as it is a point, in their profession, to utter nothing but what arises from spontaneous impulse: or else, the great Spirit of the world, the patronage and influence of which they all came to invoke, must have inspired her with the soundest morality. Her discourse lasted three quarters of an hour. I did not observe one single face turned toward her; never before had I seen a congregation listening with so much attention to a public oration. I observed neither contortions of body, nor any kind of affectation in her face, style, or manner of utterance; every thing was natural, and therefore pleasing; and, shall I tell you more? she was very handsome, although upward of forty. As soon as she had finished, every one seemed to return to their former meditation for about a quarter of an hour; when they rose up by common consent, and, after some general conversation, departed.

How simple their precepts, how unadorned their religious system: how few the ceremonies through which they pass during the course of their lives! At their deaths they are interred by the fraternity, without pomp, without prayers; thinking it then too late to alter the course of God's eternal decrees: and, as you well know, without either monument or tomb-stone. Thus, after having lived under the mildest government, after having been guided by the mildest doctrine, they die just as peaceably as those who, being educated in more pompous religions, pass through a variety of sacraments, subscribe to complicated creeds, and enjoy the benefits of a church-establishment. These good people flatter themselves with following the doctrines of Jesus Christ in that simplicity with which they were delivered: a happier system could not have been devised for the use of mankind! It appears to be entirely free from those ornaments and political additions which each country, and each government, hath fashioned after its own manners.

At the door of this meeting-house I had been invited to spend some days at the houses of some respectable farmers in the neighbourhood. The reception I met with every where insensibly led me to spend two months among these good people; and I must say they were the golden days of my riper years. I never shall forget the gratitude I owe them for the innumerable kindnesses they heaped on me; it was to the letter you gave me that I am indebted for the extensive acquaintance I now have throughout Pennsylvania. I must defer thanking you, as I ought, until I see you again. Before that time comes, I may, perhaps, entertain you with more curious anecdotes than this letter affords. Farewel.

I——N AL——Z.

I WISH for a change of place; the hour is come at last that I must fly from my house and abandon my farm! But, what course shall I steer, inclosed as I am? The climate, best adapted to my present situation and humour, would be the polar regions, where six months day and six months night divide the dull year: nay, a simple Aurora Borealis would suffice me, and greatly refresh my eyes, fatigued now by so many disagreeable objects. The severity of those climates, that great gloom, where melancholy dwells, would be perfectly analagous to the turn of my mind. Oh! could I remove my plantation to the shores of the Oby, willingly would I dwell in the hut of a Samoyede; with cheerfulness would I go and bury myself in the cavern of a Laplander. Could I but carry my family along with me, I would winter at Pello or Tobolsky,* in order to enjoy the peace and innocence of that country. But, let me arrive under the pole, or reach the antipodes, I never can leave behind me the remembrance of the dreadful scenes to which I have been witness; therefore never can I be happy! Happy! why would I mention that sweet, that enchanting, word? Once happiness was our portion; now it is gone from us, and I am afraid not to be enjoyed again by the present generation. Which ever way I look, nothing but the most frightful precipices present themselves to my view, in which hundreds of my friends and acquaintances have already perished: of all animals, that live on the surface of this planet, what is man when no longer connected with society; or when he finds himself surrounded by a convulsed and a half-dissolved one? He cannot live in solitude, he must belong to some community, bound by some ties, however imperfect. Men mutually support and add to

the boldness and confidence of each other; the weakness of
each is strengthened by the force of the whole. I had never,
before these calamitous times, formed any such ideas; I lived
on, laboured, and prospered, without having ever studied on
what the security of my life and the foundation of my prosperity were established. I perceived them just as they left me.
Never was a situation so singularly terrible as mine, in every
possible respect; as a member of an extensive society, as a
citizen of an inferior division of the same society, as a husband, as a father, as a man who exquisitely feels for the miseries of others as well as for his own! But, alas! so much
is every thing now subverted among us, that the very word
misery, with which we were hardly acquainted before, no
longer conveys the same ideas; or rather, tired with feeling
for the miseries of others, every one feels now for himself
alone. When I consider myself as connected in all these characters, as bound by so many cords, all uniting in my heart, I
am seised with a fever of the mind, I am transported beyond
that degree of calmness which is necessary to delineate our
thoughts. I feel as if my reason wanted to leave me, as if it
would burst its poor weak tenement: again I try to compose
myself, I grow cool, and, preconceiving the dreadful loss, I
endeavour to retain the useful guest.

You know the position of our settlement; I need not therefore describe it. To the west it is inclosed by a chain of
mountains, reaching to——; to the east, the country is as
yet but thinly inhabited; we are almost insulated, and the
houses are at a considerable distance from each other. From
the mountains we have but too much reason to expect
our dreadful enemy; the wilderness is a harbour where it is
impossible to find them. It is a door through which they can
enter our country whenever they please; and, as they seem
determined to destroy the whole chain of frontiers, our fate
cannot be far distant: from Lake Champlain, almost all has
been conflagrated one after another. What renders these
incursions still more terrible is, that they most commonly

take place in the dead of the night. We never go to our fields but we are seised with an involuntary fear, which lessens our strength and weakens our labour. No other subject of conversation intervenes between the different accounts, which spread through the country, of successive acts of devastation; and these, told in chimney-corners, swell themselves, in our affrighted imaginations, into the most terrific ideas! We never sit down, either to dinner or supper, but the least noise immediately spreads a general alarm, and prevents us from enjoying the comfort of our meals. The very appetite, proceeding from labour and peace of mind, is gone: we eat just enough to keep us alive: our sleep is disturbed by the most frightful dreams: sometimes I start awake, as if the great hour of danger was come; at other times the howling of our dogs seems to announce the arrival of our enemy: we leap out of bed and run to arms: my poor wife, with panting bosom and silent tears, takes leave of me, as if we were to see each other no more; she snatches the youngest children from their beds, who, suddenly awakened, increase, by their innocent questions, the horror of the dreadful moment. She tries to hide them in the cellar, as if our cellar was inaccessible to the fire. I place all my servants at the windows and myself at the door, where I have determined to perish. Fear industriously increases every sound; we all listen; each communicates to the other his ideas and conjectures. We remain thus sometimes for whole hours, our hearts and our minds racked by the most anxious suspense: what a dreadful situation, a thousand times worse than that of a soldier engaged in the midst of the most severe conflict! Sometimes, feeling the spontaneous courage of a man, I seem to wish for the decisive minute; the next instant a message from my wife, sent by one of the children, puzzling me beside with their little questions, unmans me: away goes my courage, and I descend again into the deepest despondency. At last, finding that it was a false alarm, we return once more to our beds; but what good can the kind sleep of nature do to us when interrupted by such scenes! Securely placed as you are, you can have no idea of our agitations but by hear-say: no relation can be equal to what we suffer and to what we feel. Every morning my youngest children are sure to have frightful dreams to relate: in vain I exert my authority to keep them silent; it is not in my power; and these images of their disturbed imagination, instead of being frivolously looked upon as in the days of our happiness, are, on the contrary, considered as warnings and sure prognostics of our future fate. I am not a superstitious man, but, since our misfortunes, I am grown more timid, and less disposed to treat the doctrine of omens with contempt.

Though these evils have been gradual, yet they do not become habitual like other incidental evils. The nearer I view the end of this catastrophe, the more I shudder. But why should I trouble you with such unconnected accounts? Men, secure and out of danger, are soon fatigued with mournful details. Can you enter with me into fellowship with all these afflictive sensations? Have you a tear ready to shed over the approaching ruin of a once opulent and substantial family? Read this, I pray, with the eyes of sympathy; with a tender sorrow pity the lot of those whom you once called your friends; who were once surrounded with plenty, ease, and perfect security; but who now expect every night to be their last, and who are as wretched as criminals under an impending sentence of the law!

As a member of a large society, which extends to many parts of the world, my connection with it is too distant to be as strong as that which binds me to the inferior division, in the midst of which I live. I am told that the great nation, of which we are a part, is just, wise, and free, beyond any other on earth, within its own insular boundaries, but not always so to its distant conquests. I shall not repeat all I have heard, because I cannot believe half of it. As a citizen of a smaller society, I find that any kind of opposition to its now-prevailing sentiments immediately begets hatred. How easily

do men pass from loving to hating and cursing one another!
I am a lover of peace, what must I do? I am divided between
the respect I feel for the antient connection and the fear of
innovations, with the consequence of which I am not well
acquainted, as they are embraced by my own countrymen.
I am conscious that I was happy before this unfortunate
revolution. I feel that I am no longer so; therefore I regret
the change. This is the only mode of reasoning adapted to
persons in my situation. If I attach myself to the mother-
country, which is 3000 miles from me, I become what is called
an enemy to my own region; if I follow the rest of my countrymen I become opposed to our ancient masters: both extremes appear equally dangerous to a person of so little weight
and consequence as I am, whose energy and example are of
no avail. As to the argument, on which the dispute is founded,
I know little about it. Much has been said and written on both
sides, but who has a judgement capacious and clear enough
to decide? The great moving principles which actuate both
parties are much hidden from vulgar eyes like mine: nothing but the plausible and the probable are offered to our
contemplation. The innocent class are always the victims
of the few: they are, in all countries and at all times, the inferior agents, on which the popular phantom is erected; they
clamour, and must toil, and bleed, and are always sure of meeting with oppression and rebuke. It is for the sake of the great
leaders, on both sides, that so much blood must be spilt; that
of the people is counted as nothing. Great events are not
atchieved for us, though it is *by* us that they are principally
accomplished; by the arms, the sweat, the lives, of the people.
Books tell me so much that they inform me of nothing. Soph-
istry, the bane of freemen, launches forth in all her deceiving
attire! After all, most men reason from passions; and shall
such an ignorant individual as I am decide, and say this
side is right, that side is wrong? Sentiment and feeling are
the only guides I know. Alas, how should I unravel an argument in which reason herself has given way to brutality and

bloodshed! What then must I do? I ask the wisest lawyers,
the ablest casuists, the warmest patriots, for I mean honestly.
Great Source of wisdom! inspire me with light sufficient to
guide my benighted steps out of this intricate maze! Shall I
discard all my ancient principles, shall I renounce that name,
that nation, which I held once so respectable? I feel the powerful attraction. The sentiments they inspired grew with my
earliest knowledge, and were grafted upon the first rudiments
of my education. On the other hand, shall I arm myself against
that country where I first drew breath, against the play-mates
of my youth, my bosom-friends, my acquaintance?—the idea
makes me shudder! Must I be called a parricide, a traitor, a
villain; lose the esteem of all those whom I love to preserve
my own; be shunned like a rattle-snake, or be pointed at like
a bear? I have neither heroism nor magnanimity enough to
make so great a sacrifice. Here I am tied, I am fastened, by
numerous strings, nor do I repine at the pressure they cause.
Ignorant as I am, I can pervade* the utmost extent of the
calamities which have already overtaken our poor afflicted
country. I can see the great and accumulated ruin yet extending itself as far as the theatre of war has reached: I hear the
groans of thousands of families now ruined and desolated by
our aggressors. I cannot count the multitude of orphans this
war has made, nor ascertain the immensity of blood we have
lost. Some have asked whether it was a crime to resist, to repel,
some parts of this evil. Others have asserted, that a resistance
so general makes pardon unattainable and repentance useless,
and dividing the crime among so many renders it imperceptible. What one party calls meritorious, the other denominates
flagitious. These opinions vary, contract, or expand, like the
events of the war on which they are founded. What can an
insignificant man do in the midst of these jarring contradictory parties, equally hostile to persons situated as I am? And,
after all, who will be the really guilty?—Those most certainly
who fail of success. Our fate, the fate of thousands, is then
necessarily involved in the dark wheel of fortune. Why then

so many useless reasonings? we are the sport of fate. Farewel, education, principles, love of our country, farewel; all are become useless to the generality of us. He, who governs himself according to what he calls his principles, may be punished, either by one party or the other, for those very principles. He who proceeds without principle, as chance, timidity, or self-preservation, directs, will not perhaps fare better, but he will be less blamed. What are *we* in the great scale of events, we poor defenceless frontier-inhabitants? What is it to the gazing world whether we breathe or whether we die? whatever virtue, whatever merit and distinterestedness, we may exhibit in our secluded retreats, of what avail? We are like the pismires* destroyed by the plough, whose destruction prevents not the future crop. Self-preservation, therefore, the rule of nature, seems to be the best rule of conduct. What good can we do by vain resistance, by useless efforts? The cool, the distant, spectator, placed in safety, may arraign me for ingratitude, may bring forth the principles of Solon or Montesquieu;* he may look on me as wilfully guilty; he may call me by the most opprobrious names. Secure from personal danger, his warm imagination, undisturbed by the least agitation of the heart, will expatiate freely on this grand question, and will consider this extended field but as exhibiting the double scene of attack and defence. To him the object becomes abstracted; the intermediate glares, the perspective distance, and a variety of opinions unimpaired by affections, present to his mind but one set of ideas. Here he proclaims the high guilt of the one, and there the right of the other: but let him come and reside with us one single month; let him pass with us through all the successive hours of necessary toil, terror, and affright; let him watch with us, his musket in his hand, through tedious, sleepless, nights, his imagination furrowed by the keen chissel of every passion; let his wife and his children become exposed to the most dreadful hazards of death; let the existence of his property depend on a single spark, blown by the breath of an enemy; let him tremble with us in our fields, shudder at the rustling of every leaf; let his heart, the seat of the most affecting passions, be powerfully wrung by hearing the melancholy end of his relations and friends; let him trace on the map the progress of these desolations; let his alarmed imagination predict to him the night, the dreadful night, when it may be his turn to perish as so many have perished before! observe then, whether the man will not get the better of the citizen, whether his political maxims will not vanish! Yes, he will cease to glow so warmly with the glory of the metropolis; all his wishes will be turned toward the preservation of his family. Oh! were he situated where I am, were his house perpetually filled, as mine is, with miserable victims just escaped from the flames and the scalping-knife, telling of barbarities and murders, that make human nature tremble! his situation would suspend every political reflection, and expel every abstract idea. My heart is full, and involuntarily takes hold of any notion whence it can receive ideal ease or relief. I am informed that the king has the most numerous, as well as the fairest, progeny of children, of any potentate now in the world: he may be a great king, but he must feel as we common mortals do, in the good wishes he forms for their lives and prosperity. His mind, no doubt, often springs forward on the wings of anticipation, and contemplates us as happily settled in the world. If a poor frontier-inhabitant may be allowed to suppose this great personage, the first in our system, to be exposed, but for one hour, to the exquisite pangs we so often feel, would not the preservation of so numerous a family engross all his thoughts; would not the ideas of dominion, and other felicities attendant on royalty, all vanish in the hour of danger? The regal character, however sacred, would be superseded by the stronger, because more natural, one of man and father. Oh! did he but know the circumstances of this horrid war, I am sure he would put a stop to that long destruction of parents and children. I am sure that, while he turned his ears to state-policy, he would attentively listen also to the dictates of

Nature, that great parent; for, as a good king, he, no doubt, wishes to create, to spare, and to protect, as she does. Must I then, in order to be called a faithful subject, coolly and philosophically say, it is necessary, for the good of Britain, that my childrens brains should be dashed against the walls of the house in which they were reared; that my wife should be stabbed and scalped before my face; that I should be either murdered or captivated; or that, for greater expedition, we should all be locked up and burnt to ashes as the family of the B———n was? Must I with meekness wait for that last pitch of desolation, and receive, with perfect resignation, so hard a fate from ruffians, acting at such a distance from the eyes of any superior; monsters, left to the wild impulses of the wildest nature? Could the lions of Africa be transported here and let loose, they would, no doubt, kill us in order to prey upon our carcasses; but their appetites would not require so many victims. Shall I wait to be punished with death, or else to be stripped of all food and raiment, reduced to despair without redress and without hope? Shall those, who may escape, see every thing they hold dear destroyed and gone? Shall those few survivors, lurking in some obscure corner, deplore in vain the fate of their families, mourn over parents, either captivated, butchered, or burnt; roam among our wilds, and wait for death at the foot of some tree, without a murmur, or without a sigh, for the good of the cause? No, it is impossible! so astonishing a sacrifice is not to be expected from human nature; it must belong to beings of an inferior or superior order, actuated by less or by more refined principles. Even those great personages who are so far elevated above the common ranks of men, those, I mean, who wield and direct so many thunders; those who have let loose against us these demons of war; could they be transported here, and metamorphosed into simple planters as we are, they would, from being the arbiters of human destiny, sink into miserable victims; they would feel and exclaim as we do, and be as much at a loss what line of conduct to prosecute. Do you well comprehend the difficulties of our situation? If we stay, we are sure to perish at one time or another; no vigilance on our part can save us: if we retire, we know not where to go; every house is filled with refugees as wretched as ourselves: and, if we remove, we become beggars. The property of farmers is not like that of merchants; and absolute poverty is worse than death. If we take up arms, to defend ourselves; we are denominated rebels; should we not be rebels against nature, could we be shamefully passive? Shall we then, like martyrs, glory in an allegiance, now become useless, and voluntarily expose ourselves to a species of desolation, which, though it ruin us entirely, yet enriches not our ancient masters? By this inflexible and sullen attachment, we shall be despised by our countrymen, and destroyed by our ancient friends; whatever we may say, whatever merit we may claim, will not shelter us from those indiscriminate blows, given by hired banditti, animated by all those passions which urge men to shed the blood of others; how bitter the thought! On the contrary, blows, received by the hands of those from whom we expected protection, extinguish ancient respect and urge us to self-defence—perhaps to revenge; this is the path which Nature herself points out as well to the civilized as to the uncivilized. The Creator of hearts has himself stamped on them those propensities at their first formation; and must we then daily receive this treatment from a power once so loved? The fox flies or deceives the hounds that pursue him; the bear, when overtaken, boldly resists and attacks them; the hen, the very timid hen, fights for the preservation of her chicken, nor does she decline to attack, and to meet on the wing, even the swift kite. Shall man then, provided both with instinct and reason, unmoved, unconcerned, and passive, see his subsistence consumed, and his progeny either ravished from him or murdered? Shall fictitious reason extinguish the unerring impulse of instinct? No; my former respect, my former attachment, vanishes with my safety; that respect and attachment were purchased by protection, and it has ceased.

Could not the great nation we belong to have accomplished her designs by means of her numerous armies, by means of those fleets which cover the ocean? Must those who are masters of two-thirds of the trade of the world; who have in their hands the power which almighty gold can give; who possess a species of wealth that increases with their desires; must they establish their conquest with our insignificant innocent blood!

Must I then bid farewel to Britain, to that renowned country? Must I renounce a name so ancient and so venerable? Alas! she herself, that once-indulgent parent, forces me to take up arms against her. She herself first inspired the most unhappy citizens of our remote districts with the thoughts of shedding the blood of those whom they used to call by the name of friends and brethren. That great nation, which now convulses the world; which hardly knows the extent of her Indian kingdoms; which looks toward the universal monarchy of trade, of industry, of riches, of power: why must she strew our poor frontiers with the carcasses of her friends, with the wrecks of our insignificant villages, in which there is no gold? When, oppressed by painful recollection, I revolve all these scattered ideas in my mind; when I contemplate my situation, and the thousand streams of evil with which I am surrounded; when I descend into the particular tendency even of the remedy I have proposed, I am convulsed—convulsed sometimes to that degree as to be tempted to exclaim—Why has the Master of the world permitted so much indiscriminate evil throughout every part of this poor planet, at all times, and among all kinds of people? It ought surely to be the punishment of the wicked only. I bring that cup to my lips, of which I must soon taste, and shudder at its bitterness. What then is life, I ask myself, is it a gracious gift? No, it is too bitter; a gift means something valuable conferred, but life appears to be a mere accident, and of the worst kind: we are born to be victims of diseases and passions, of mischances and death: better not to be than to be miserable.—Thus impiously I roam, I fly from one erratic thought to another, and my mind, irritated by these acrimonious reflections, is ready sometimes to lead me to dangerous extremes of violence. When I recollect that I am a father and a husband, the return of these endearing ideas strikes deep into my heart. Alas! they once made it glow with pleasure and with every ravishing exultation; but now they fill it with sorrow. At other times, my wife industriously rouses me out of these dreadful meditations, and soothes me by all the reasoning she is mistress of; but her endeavours only serve to make me more miserable, by reflecting that she must share with me all these calamities, the bare apprehensions of which, I am afraid, will subvert her reason. Nor can I, with patience, think that a beloved wife, my faithful helpmate throughout all my rural schemes, the principal hand which has assisted me in rearing the prosperous fabric of ease and independence I lately possessed, as well as my children, those tenants of my heart, should daily and nightly be exposed to such a cruel fate. Self-preservation is above all political precepts and rules, and even superior to the dearest opinions of our minds; a reasonable accommodation of ourselves, to the various exigencies of the times in which we live, is the most irresistible precept. To this great evil I must seek some sort of remedy adapted to remove or to palliate it. Situated as I am, what steps should I take that will neither injure nor insult any of the parties, and at the same time save my family from that certain destruction which awaits it if I remain here much longer? Could I insure them bread, safety, and subsistence; not the bread of idleness, but that earned by proper labour as heretofore; could this be accomplished by the sacrifice of my life, I would willingly give it up. I attest before heaven, that it is only for these I would wish to live and toil; for these whom I have brought into this miserable existence. I resemble, methinks, one of the stones of a ruined arch, still retaining that pristine form which anciently fitted the place I occupied, but the centre is tumbled down; I can be nothing until I am replaced, either in the former circle, or in some stronger one. I see one on a smaller scale, and at a considerable distance, but it is within my power to reach it; and, since I have ceased to consider myself as a member of the ancient state, now convulsed, I willingly descend into an inferior one. I will revert into a state approaching nearer to that of nature, unincumbered either with voluminous laws or contradictory codes, often galling the very necks of those whom they protect, and, at the same time, sufficiently remote from the brutality of unconnected savage nature. Do you, my friend, perceive the path I have found out? it is that which leads to the tenants of the great —— village of ——, where, far removed from the accursed neighbourhood of Europeans, its inhabitants live with more ease, decency, and peace, than you imagine; who, though governed by no laws, yet find, in uncontaminated simple manners, all that laws can afford. Their system is sufficiently complete to answer all the primary wants of man, and to constitute him a social being, such as he ought to be in the great forest of nature. There it is that I have resolved at any rate to transport myself and family: an eccentric thought, you may say, thus to cut asunder all former connections, and to form new ones with a people whom nature has stamped with such different characteristics! But, as the happiness of my family is the only object of my wishes, I care very little where we are, or where we go, provided that we are safe and all united together. Our new calamities, being shared equally by all, will become lighter; our mutual affection for each other will, in this great transmutation, become the strongest link of our new society, will afford us every joy we can receive on a foreign soil, and preserve us in unity, as the gravity and coherency of matter prevent the world from dissolution. Blame me not; it would be cruel in you; it would beside be entirely useless; for, when you receive this, we shall be on the wing. When we think all hopes are gone, must we, like poor pusillanimous wretches, despair and die? No. I perceive before me a few resources, though through many dangers, which I will explain to you hereafter. It is not, believe me, a disappointed

ambition which leads me to take this step; it is the bitterness
of my situation, it is the impossibility of knowing what better
measure to adopt. My education fitted me for nothing more
than the most simple occupations of life: I am but a feller of
trees, a cultivator of lands, the most honourable title an American can have. I have no exploits, no discoveries, no inventions,
to boast of; I have cleared about 370 acres of land, some for
the plough, some for the scythe; and this has occupied many
years of my life. I have never possessed, or wish to possess,
any thing more than what could be earned or produced by
the united industry of my family. I wanted nothing more than
to live at home independent and tranquil, and to teach my
children how to provide the means of a future ample subsistence, founded on labour, like that of their father. This is
the career of life I have pursued, and that which I had marked
out for them, and for which they seemed to be so well calculated by their inclinations and by their constitutions. But,
now these pleasing expectations are gone, we must abandon
the accumulated industry of nineteen years, we must fly we
hardly know whither, through the most impervious paths, and
become members of a new and strange community. O virtue!
is this all the reward thou hast to confer on thy votaries?
Either thou art only a chimera, or thou art a timid useless
being; soon affrighted, when ambition, thy great adversary,
dictates, when war re-echoes the dreadful sounds, and poor
helpless individuals are mowed down by its cruel reapers like
useless grass. I have at all times generously relieved what few
distressed people I have met with; I have encouraged the
industrious; my house has always been opened to travellers;
I have not lost a month in illness since I have been a man;
I have caused upwards of a hundred and twenty families to
remove hither. Many of them I have led by the hand in the
days of their first trial; distant as I am from any places of
worship or school of education, I have been the pastor of
my family, and the teacher of many of my neighbours. I have
taught them, as well as I could, the gratitude they owe to God,

the Father of harvests; and their duties to man: I have been an useful subject; ever obedient to the laws, ever vigilant to see them respected and observed. My wife hath faithfully followed the same line within her province; no woman was ever a better œconomist, or spun or wove better linen; yet we must perish, perish like wild beasts, included within a ring of fire!

Yes, I will cheerfully embrace that resource, it is a holy inspiration: by night and by day it presents itself to my mind: I have carefully revolved the scheme; I have considered, in all its future effects and tendencies, the new mode of living we must pursue, without salt, without spices, without linen, and with little other clothing; the art of hunting we must acquire, the new manners we must adopt, the new language we must speak; the dangers attending the education of my children we must endure. These changes may appear more terrific at a distance, perhaps, than when grown familiar by practice: what is it to us, whether we eat well made pastry, or pounded àlagrichés;* well-roasted beef, or smoked venison; cabbages, or squashes? Whether we wear neat home-spun, or good beaver: whether we sleep on featherbeds, or on bear-skins? The difference is not worth attending to. The difficulty of the language, the fear of some great intoxication among the Indians; finally, the apprehension lest my younger children should be caught by that singular charm, so dangerous at their tender years, are the only considerations that startle me. By what power does it come to pass, that children, who have been adopted when young among these people, can never be prevailed on to re-adopt European manners? Many an anxious parent have I seen last war, who, at the return of the peace, went to the Indian villages where they knew their children had been carried in captivity; when, to their inexpressible sorrow, they found them so perfectly Indian-ised, that many knew them no longer; and those, whose more advanced ages permitted them to recollect their fathers and mothers, absolutely refused to follow them, and ran to their

adoptive parents for protection against the effusions of love
their unhappy real parents lavished on them. Incredible as this
may appear, I have heard it asserted in a thousand instances,
among persons of credit. In the village of ——, where I purpose to go, there lived, about fifteen years ago, an Englishman and a Swede, whose history would appear moving had
I time to relate it. They were grown to the age of men when
they were taken; they happily escaped the great punishment
of war-captives, and were obliged to marry the *Squaws* who
had saved their lives by adoption. By the force of habit, they
become at last thoroughly naturalised to this wild course of
life. While I was there, their friends sent them a considerable
sum of money to ransom themselves with. The Indians, their
old masters, gave them their choice, and, without requiring
any consideration, told them, that they had been long as free
as themselves. They chose to remain; and the reasons they
gave me would greatly surprise you: the most perfect freedom,
the ease of living, the absence of those cares and corroding
solicitudes which so often prevail with us; the peculiar goodness of the soil they cultivated, for they did not trust altogether to hunting; all these, and many more motives, which
I have forgot, made them prefer that life, of which we entertain such dreadful opinions. It cannot be, therefore, so bad
as we generally conceive it to be; there must be in their social
bond something singularly captivating, and far superior to
any thing to be boasted of among us; for thousands of Europeans are Indians, and we have no examples of even one of
those Aborigines having from choice become Europeans! There
must be something more congenial to our native dispositions
than the fictitious society in which we live; or else why should
children, and even grown persons, become in a short time
so invincibly attached to it? There must be something very
bewitching in their manners, something very indelible, and
marked by the very hands of nature. For, take a young Indian
lad, give him the best education you possibly can, load him
with your bounty, with presents, nay with riches; yet he will

secretly long for his native woods, which you would imagine he must have long since forgot; and, on the first opportunity he can possibly find, you will see him voluntarily leave behind all you have given him, and return with inexpressible joy to lie on the mats of his fathers. Mr. ——, some years ago, received from a good old Indian, who died in his house, a young lad of nine years of age, his grandson. He kindly educated him with his children, and bestowed on him the same care and attention in respect to the memory of his venerable grandfather, who was a worthy man. He intended to give him a genteel trade; but in the spring season, when all the family went to the woods to make their maple sugar, he suddenly disappeared; and it was not until seventeen months after that his benefactor heard he had reached the village of Bald-Eagle, where he still dwelt. Let us say what we will of them, of their inferior organs, of their want of bread, &c. they are as stout and well-made as the Europeans. Without temples, without priests, without kings, and without laws, they are in many instances superior to us; and the proofs of what I advance are, that they live without care, sleep without inquietude, take life as it comes, bearing all its asperities with unparalleled patience, and die without any kind of apprehension for what they have done or for what they expect to meet with hereafter. What system of philosophy can give us so many necessary qualifications for happiness? They most certainly are much more closely connected with nature than we are; they are her immediate children; the inhabitants of the woods are her undefiled offspring; those of the plains are her degenerated breed, far, very far, removed from her primitive laws, from her original design. It is therefore resolved on. I will either die in the attempt or succeed; better perish all together in one fatal hour than to suffer what we daily endure. I do not expect to enjoy, in the village of ——, an uninterrupted happiness; it cannot be our lot let us live where we will; I am not founding my future prosperity on golden dreams. Place mankind where you will, they must always have adverse circumstances to struggle with; from nature, accidents, constitution; from seasons; from that great combination of mischances which perpetually leads us to diseases, to poverty, &c. Who knows but I may meet, in this new situation, some accident, whence may spring up new sources of unexpected prosperity? Who can be presumptuous enough to predict all the good? Who can foresee all the evils which strew the paths of our lives? But, after all, I cannot but recollect what sacrifice I am going to make, what amputation I am going to suffer, what transition I am going to experience. Pardon my repetitions, my wild, my trifling, reflections, they proceed from the agitations of my mind and the fulness of my heart; the action of thus retracing them seems to lighten the burthen, and to exhilarate my spirits; this is, besides, the last letter you will receive from me; I would fain tell you all, though I hardly know how. Oh! in the hours, in the moments of my greatest anguish, could I intuitively represent to you that variety of thought which crouds on my mind, you would have reason to be surprized, and to doubt of their possibility. Shall we ever meet again? If we should, where will it be? On the wild shores of ———. If it be my doom to end my days there, I will greatly improve them; and perhaps make room for a few more families, who will choose to retire from the fury of a storm, the agitated billows of which will yet roar for many years on our extended shores. Perhaps I may repossess my house, if it be not burnt down; but how will my improvements look? why, half-defaced, bearing the strong marks of abandonment, and of the ravages of war. However, at present I give every thing over for lost; I will bid a long farewel to what I leave behind. If ever I repossess it, I shall receive it as a gift, as a reward for my conduct and fortitude. Do not imagine, however, that I am a stoic; by no means: I must, on the contrary, confess to you, that I feel the keenest regret at abandoning a house which I have in some measure reared with my own hands. Yes, perhaps I may never revisit those fields which I have cleared, those trees which I have planted, those meadows which, in my youth, were a hideous wilderness, now converted by my industry into rich pastures and pleasant lawns. If in Europe it is praise-worthy to be attached to paternal inheritances, how much more natural, how much more powerful, must the tie be with us, who, if I may be permitted the expression, are the founders, the creators, of our own farms. When I see my table surrounded with my blooming offspring, all united in the bonds of the strongest affection, it kindles in my paternal heart a variety of tumultuous sentiments, which none but a father and a husband in my situation can feel or describe. Perhaps I may see my wife, my children, often distressed, involuntarily recalling to their minds the ease and abundance which they enjoyed under the paternal roof. Perhaps I may see them want that bread which I now leave behind; overtaken by diseases and penury, rendered more bitter by the recollection of former days of opulence and plenty. Perhaps I may be assailed on every side by unforeseen accidents, which I shall not be able to prevent or to alleviate. Can I contemplate such images without the most unutterable emotions? My fate is determined; but I have not determined it, you may assure yourself, without having undergone the most painful conflicts of a variety of passions;— interest, love of ease, disappointed views, and pleasing expectations frustrated; —I shuddered at the review! Would to God I was master of the stoical tranquillity of that magnanimous sect; oh! that I were possessed of those sublime lessons which Apollonius of Chalcis gave to the emperor Antoninus!* I could then with much more propriety guide the helm of my little bark, which is soon to be freighted with all that I possess most dear on earth, through this stormy passage to a safe harbour; and, when there, become, to my fellow-passengers, a surer guide, a brighter example, a pattern more worthy of imitation, throughout all the new scenes they must pass and the new career they must traverse. I have observed, notwithstanding, the means hitherto made use of to arm the principal nations against our frontiers: Yet they have not, they will not

take up the hatchet against a people who have done them no
harm. The passions, necessary to urge these people to war,
cannot be roused, they cannot feel the stings of vengeance,
the thirst of which alone can impel them to shed blood: far
superior in their motives of action to the Europeans, who, for
sixpence per day, may be engaged to shed that of any people
on earth. They know nothing of the nature of our disputes,
they have no ideas of such revolutions as this; a civil division
of a village, or tribe, are events which have never been recorded in their traditions: many of them know very well that
they have too long been the dupes and the victims of both
parties; foolishly arming for our sakes, sometimes against each
other, sometimes against our white enemies. They consider us
as born on the same land, and, though they have no reasons
to love us, yet they seem carefully to avoid entering into
this quarrel, from whatever motives. I am speaking of those
nations with which I am best acquainted, a few hundreds of
the worst kind, mixed with whites worse than themselves, are
now hired, by Great-Britain, to perpetrate those dreadful
incursions. In my youth I traded with the ——, under the
conduct of my uncle, and always traded justly and equitably;
some of them remember it to this day. Happily their village
is far removed from the dangerous neighbourhood of the
whites. I sent a man, last spring, to it, who understands the
woods extremely well, and who speaks their language: he is
just returned, after several weeks absence, and has brought
me, as I had flattered myself, a string of thirty purple wampum,
as a token that their honest chief will spare us half of his
wigwham until we have time to erect one. He has sent me
word that they have land in plenty, of which they are not so
covetous as the whites; that we may plant for ourselves, and
that, in the mean time, he will procure us some corn and
meat; that fish is plenty in the waters of ——, and that the
village, to which he had laid open my proposals, have no
objection to our becoming dwellers with them. I have not
yet communicated these glad tidings to my wife, nor do I know

how to do it. I tremble lest she should refuse to follow me; lest the sudden idea of this removal, rushing on her mind, might be too powerful. I flatter myself I shall be able to accomplish it, and to prevail on her; I fear nothing but the effects of her strong attachment to her relations. I would willingly let you know how I purpose to remove my family to so great a distance, but it would become unintelligible to you, because you are not acquainted with the geographical situation of this part of the country. Suffice it for you to know, that, with about twenty-three miles land-carriage, I am enabled to perform the rest by water; and, when once afloat, I care not whether it be two or three hundred miles. I propose to send all our provisions, furniture, and clothes, to my wife's father, who approves of the scheme, and to reserve nothing but a few necessary articles of covering, trusting to the furs of the chace for our future apparel. Were we imprudently to incumber ourselves too much with baggage, we should never reach to the waters of ――――, which is the most dangerous, as well as the most difficult, part of our journey, and yet but a trifle in point of distance. I intend to say to my negroes,—In the name of God, be free, my honest lads; I thank you for your past services; go, from henceforth, and work for yourselves; look on me as your old friend and fellow-labourer; be sober, frugal, and industrious, and you need not fear earning a comfortable subsistence.—Lest my countrymen should think that I am gone to join the incendiaries of our frontiers, I intend to write a letter to Mr ――――, to inform him of our retreat, and of the reasons that have urged me to it. The man, whom I sent to ―――― village, is to accompany us also, and a very useful companion he will be on every account.

You may therefore, by means of anticipation, behold me under the wigwham; I am so well acquainted with the principal manners of these people that I entertain not the least apprehension from them. I rely more securely on their strong hospitality than on the witnessed compacts of many Europeans.

As soon as possible after my arrival, I design to build myself a wigwham, after the same manner and size with the
rest, in order to avoid being thought singular or giving occasion for any railleries; though these people are seldom guilty
of such European follies. I shall erect it hard by the lands
which they propose to allot me, and will endeavour that my
wife, my children, and myself, may be adopted soon after our
arrival. Thus, becoming truly inhabitants of their village, we
shall immediately occupy that rank, within the pale of their
society, which will afford us all the amends we can possibly
expect for the loss we have met with by the convulsions of
our own. According to their customs we shall likewise receive
names from them, by which we shall always be known. My
youngest children shall learn to swim, and to shoot with the
bow, that they may acquire such talents as will necessarily raise
them into some degree of esteem among the Indian lads of
their own age; the rest of us must hunt with the hunters. I
have been for several years an expert marksman; but I dread
lest the imperceptible charm of Indian education may seise
my younger children, and give them such a propensity to
that mode of life as may preclude their returning to the manners and customs of their parents. I have but one remedy
to prevent this great evil; and that is, to employ them in the
labour of the fields as much as I can; I have even resolved
to make their daily subsistence depend altogether on it. As
long as we keep ourselves busy in tilling the earth, there is no
fear of any of us becoming wild; it is the chase and the food
it procures that have this strange effect. Excuse a simile;—
those hogs which range in the woods, and to whom grain is
given once a week, preserve their former degree of tameness;
but if, on the contrary, they are reduced to live on ground-
nuts, and on what they can get, they soon become wild and
fierce. For my part, I can plough, sow, and hunt, as occasion
may require; but my wife, deprived of wool and flax, will have
no room for industry; what is she then to do? like the other
squaws, she must cook for us the nasaump, the ninchickè,

and such other preparations of corn as are customary among
these people. She must learn to bake squashes and pompions
under the ashes; to slice and smoke the meat of our own
killing, in order to preserve it; she must cheerfully adopt
the manners and customs of her neighbours, in their dress,
deportment, conduct, and internal œconomy, in all respects.
Surely, if we can have fortitude enough to quit all we have,
to remove so far, and to associate with people so different
from us, these necessary compliances are but subordinate parts
of the scheme. The change of garments, when those they
carry with them are worne out, will not be the least of my
wife's and daughter's concerns: though I am in hopes that
self-love will invent some sort of reparation. Perhaps you would
not believe that there are in the woods looking-glasses
and paint of every colour; and that the inhabitants take as
much pains to adorn their faces and their bodies, to fix their
bracelets of silver, and plait their hair, as our forefathers,
the Picts, used to do in the time of the Romans. Not that I
would wish to see either my wife or daughter adopt those
savage customs; we can live in great peace and harmony with
them without descending to every article; the interruption of
trade hath, I hope, suspended this mode of dress. My wife
understands inoculation* perfectly well; she inoculated all our
children one after another, and has successfully performed
that operation on several scores of people, who, scattered here
and there through our woods, were too far removed from
all medical assistance. If we can persuade but one family to
submit to it, and it succeeds, we shall then be as happy as
our situation will admit of; it will raise her into some degree
of consideration: for, whoever is useful, in any society, will
always be respected. If we are so fortunate as to carry one
family through a disorder, which is the plague among these
people, I trust to the force of example, we shall then become
truly necessary, valued, and beloved: we, indeed, owe every
kind office to a society of men who so readily offer to admit
us into their social partnership, and to extend to my family

the shelter of their village, the strength of their adoption, and
even the dignity of their names. God grant us a prosperous
beginning, we may then hope to be of more service to them
than even missionaries who have been sent to preach to them
a gospel they cannot understand.

As to religion, our mode of worship will not suffer much
by this removal from a cultivated country into the bosom of
the woods; for it cannot be much simpler than that which
we have followed here these many years; and I will, with as
much care as I can, redouble my attention, and, twice a
week, retrace to them the great outlines of their duty to God
and to man. I will read and expound to them some part of
the decalogue; which is the method I have pursued ever
since I married.

Half a dozen of acres on the shores of ——, the soil of
which I know well, will yield us a great abundance of all we
want; I will make it a point to give the overplus to such
Indians as shall be most unfortunate in their huntings; I will
persuade them, if I can, to till a little more land than they
do, and not to trust so much to the produce of the chase.
To encourage them still farther, I will give a quirn* to every
six families; I have built many for our poor back settlers, it
being often the want of mills which prevents them from raising grain. As I am a carpenter, I can build my own plough
and can be of great service to many of them; my example
alone may rouse the industry of some, and serve to direct
others in their labours. The difficulties of the language will
soon be removed; in my evening conversations, I will endeavour to make them regulate the trade of their village in
such a manner as that those pests of the continent, those
Indian traders, may not come within a certain distance; and
there they shall be obliged to transact their business before
the old people. I am in hopes that the constant respect which
is paid to the elders, and shame, may prevent the young
hunters from infringing this regulation. The son of —— will
soon be made acquainted with our schemes, and I trust that

the power of love, and the strong attachment he professes for my daughter, may bring him along with us: he will make an excellent hunter; young and vigorous, he will equal in dexterity the stoutest man in the village. Had it not been for this fortunate circumstance, there would have been the greatest danger; for, however I respect the simple, the inoffensive, society of these people in their villages, the strongest prejudices would make me abhor any alliance with them in blood: disagreeable, no doubt, to nature's intentions, which have strongly divided us by so many indelible characters. In the days of our sickness, we shall have recourse to their medical knowledge, which is well calculated for the simple diseases to which they are subject. Thus shall we metamorphose ourselves, from neat, decent, opulent, planters, surrounded with every conveniency which our external labour and internal industry could give, into a still simpler people, divested of every thing beside hope, food, and the raiment of the woods: abandoning the large framed house, to dwell under the wigwham; and the feather-bed, to lie on the mat or bear's skin. There shall we sleep undisturbed by frightful dreams and apprehensions; rest and peace of mind will make us the most ample amends for what we shall leave behind. These blessings cannot be purchased too dear; too long have we been deprived of them! I would cheerfully go even to the Missisippi to find that repose to which we have been so long strangers. My heart, sometimes, seems tired with beating, it wants rest like my eye-lids, which feel oppressed with so many watchings.

These are the component parts of my scheme, the success of each of which appears feasible; whence I flatter myself with the probable success of the whole. Still the danger of Indian education returns to my mind, and alarms me much; then again I contrast it with the education of the times; both appear to be equally pregnant with evils. Reason points out the necessity of choosing the least dangerous, which I must consider as the only good within my reach; I persuade myself that industry and labour will be a sovereign preservative against the dangers of the former; but I consider, at the same time, that the share of labour and industry which is intended to procure but a simple subsistence, with hardly any superfluity, cannot have the same restrictive effects on our minds as when we tilled the earth on a more extensive scale. The surplus could be then realized into solid wealth, and, at the same time that this realization rewarded our past labours, it engrossed and fixed the attention of the labourer, and cherished in his mind the hope of future riches. In order to supply this great deficiency of industrious motives, and to hold out to them a real object to prevent the fatal consequences of this sort of apathy, I will keep an exact account of all that shall be gathered, and give each of them a regular credit for the amount of it to be paid them, in real property, at the return of peace. Thus, though seemingly toiling for bare subsistence on a foreign land, they shall entertain the pleasing prospect of seeing the sum of their labours one day realised, either in legacies or gifts, equal, if not superior, to it. The yearly expence of the clothes, which they would have received at home, and of which they will then be deprived, shall likewise be added to their credit; thus I flatter myself that they will more cheerfully wear the blanket, the matchcoat,* and the mockassins. Whatever success they may meet with in hunting or fishing shall be only considered as recreation and pastime; I shall thereby prevent them from estimating their skill in the chase as an important and necessary accomplishment. I mean to say to them, "You shall hunt and fish merely to shew your new companions that you are not inferior to them in point of sagacity and dexterity." Were I to send them to such schools as the interior parts of our settlements afford at present, what can they learn there? How could I support them there? What must become of me? Am I to proceed on my voyage and leave them? That I never could submit to! Instead of the perpetual discordant noise of disputes, so common among us, instead of those scolding scenes, frequent in every house, they will observe nothing but silence at home and abroad:

a singular appearance of peace and concord are the first characteristics which strike you in the villages of these people. Nothing can be more pleasing, nothing surprises an European so much, as the silence and harmony which prevail among them, and in each family; except when disturbed by that accursed spirit given them by the wood-rangers in exchange for their furs. If my children learn nothing of geometrical rules, the use of the compass, or of the Latin tongue, they will learn and practise sobriety, for rum can no longer be sent to these people; they will learn that modesty and diffidence for which the young Indians are so remarkable; they will consider labour as the most essential qualification, hunting as the second. They will prepare themselves in the prosecution of our small rural schemes, carried on for the benefit of our little community, to extend them farther, when each shall receive his inheritance. Their tender minds will cease to be agitated by perpetual alarms; to be made cowards by continual terrors: if they acquire, in the village of ——, such an aukwardness of deportment and appearance as would render them ridiculous in our gay capitals, they will imbibe, I hope, a confirmed taste for that simplicity, which so well becomes the cultivators of the land. If I cannot teach them any of those professions which sometimes embellish and support our society, I will shew them how to hew wood, how to construct their own ploughs, and, with a few tools, how to supply themselves with every necessary implement both in the house and in the field. If they are hereafter obliged to confess that they belong to no one particular church, I shall have the consolation of teaching them that great, that primary, worship, which is the foundation of all others. If they do not fear God according to the tenets of any one seminary, they shall learn to worship him upon the broad scale of nature. The Supreme Being does not reside in peculiar churches or communities; he is equally the great Manitou* of the woods and of the plains; and, even in the gloom, the obscurity, of those very woods, his justice may be as well understood and felt as in the most sumptuous temples. Each worship with us hath, you know, its peculiar political tendency; there it has none, but to inspire gratitude and truth: their tender minds shall receive no other idea of the Supreme Being than that of the Father of all men, who requires nothing more of us than what tends to make each other happy. We shall say with them; Soungwanèha, èsa caurounkyawga nughwonshauza neattèwek nèsalanga. —*Our father, be thy will done in earth as it is in great heaven.*

Perhaps my imagination gilds too strongly this distant prospect; yet it appears founded on so few and simple principles, that there is not the same probability of adverse incidents as in more complex schemes. These vague rambling contemplations, which I here faithfully retrace, carry me sometimes to a great distance; I am lost in the anticipation of the various circumstances attending this proposed metamorphosis! Many unforeseen accidents may doubtless arise. Alas! it is easier for me, in all the glow of paternal anxiety, reclined on my bed, to form the theory of my future conduct, than to reduce my schemes into practice. But, when once secluded from the great society, to which we now belong, we shall unite closer together, and there will be less room for jealousies or contentions. As I intend my children neither for the law nor the church, but for the cultivation of the land, I wish them no literary accomplishments; I pray heaven that they may be one day nothing more than expert scholars in husbandry: this is the science which made our continent to flourish more rapidly than any other. Were they to grow up where I am now situated, even admitting that we were in safety, two of them are verging toward that period of their lives when they must necessarily take up the musket, and learn, in that new school, all the vices which are so common in armies. Great God! close my eyes for ever rather than I should live to see this calamity! May they rather become inhabitants of the woods.

Thus then, in the village of ——, in the bosom of that peace it has enjoyed ever since I have known it, connected with mild hospitable, people, strangers to *our* political disputes, and having none among themselves; on the shores of a fine river, surrounded with woods, abounding with game; our little society, united in perfect harmony with the new-adoptive one in which we shall be incorporated, shall rest, I hope, from all fatigues, from all apprehensions, from our present terrors, and from our long watchings. Not a word of politics shall cloud our simple conversation; tired either with the chase or the labours of the field, we shall sleep on our mats without any distressing want, having learnt to retrench every superfluous one: we shall have but two prayers to make to the Supreme Being; that he may shed his fertilizing dew on our little crops, and that he will be pleased to restore peace to our unhappy country. These shall be the only subject of our nightly prayers and of our daily ejaculations: and, if the labour, the industry, the frugality, the union, of men, can be an agreeable offering to him, we shall not fail to receive his paternal blessings. There I shall contemplate Nature in her most wild and ample extent; I shall carefully study a species of society of which I have, at present, but very imperfect ideas; I will endeavour to occupy, with propriety, that place which will enable me to enjoy the few and sufficient benefits it confers. The solitary and unconnected mode of life I have lived in my youth must fit me for this trial; I am not the first who has attempted it: Europeans did not, it is true, carry to the wilderness numerous families; they went there as mere speculators; I, as a man seeking a refuge from the desolation of war. They went there to study the manners of the aborigines; I, to conform to them, whatever they are; some went as visitors, as travellers; I, as a sojourner, as a fellow hunter and labourer, go determined industriously to work up among them such a system of happiness as may be adequate to my future situation, and may be a sufficient compensation for all my fatigues and for the misfortunes I have borne; I have always found it at home, I may hope likewise to find it under the humble roof of my wigwham.

O Supreme Being! if, among the immense variety of planets, inhabited by thy creative power, thy paternal and omnipotent care deigns to extend to all the individuals they contain; if it be not beneath thy infinite dignity to cast thy eyes on us wretched mortals; if my future felicity is not contrary to the necessary effects of those secret causes which thou hast appointed; receive the supplications of a man, to whom, in thy kindness, thou hast given a wife and an offspring: view us all with benignity; sanctify this strong conflict of regrets, wishes, and other natural passions; guide our steps through these unknown paths, and bless our future mode of life. If it is good and well-meant, it must proceed from thee; thou knowest, O Lord, our enterprise contains neither fraud, nor malice, nor revenge. Bestow on me that energy of conduct, now become so necessary, that it may be in my power to carry the young family thou hast given me, through this great trial, with safety and in thy peace. Inspire me with such intentions and such rules of conduct as may be most acceptable to thee. Preserve, O God, preserve, the companion of my bosom, the best gift thou hast given me: endue her with courage and strength sufficient to accomplish this perilous journey. Bless the children of our love, those portions of our hearts: I implore thy divine assistance; speak to their tender minds, and inspire them with the love of that virtue which alone can serve as the basis of their conduct in this world and of their happiness with thee. Restore peace and concord to our poor afflicted country; assuage the fierce storm which has so long ravaged it! Permit, I beseech thee, O Father of nature, that our ancient virtues and our industry may not be totally lost: and that, as a reward for the great toils we have made on this new land, we may be restored to our ancient tranquillity, and enabled to fill it with successive generations, that will constantly thank thee for the ample subsistence thou hast given them!

The unreserved manner in which I have written must give you a convincing proof of that friendship and esteem, of which

I am sure you never yet doubted. As members of the same society, as mutually bound by the ties of affection and old acquaintance, you certainly cannot avoid feeling for my distresses; you cannot avoid mourning with me over that load of physical and moral evil with which we are all oppressed. My own share of it I often overlook when I minutely contemplate all that hath befallen our native country!

FINIS

APPENDIX

INDEX TO THE REVISED 1783 EDITION

A.

THE END.

EXPLANATORY NOTES

I am grateful to Elisabeth Wadge, Caroline Root, and Laura Manning for their help in locating individual references.

3 *the curiosity of a friend*: the 'Mr F. B.' (James's rich patron) referred to a few pages later, was probably William Seton, a Scotsman born in 1746 who had arrived in America about 1766 and settled in New York as an importer of European and Indian merchandise. He later became one of the founders of the Bank of New York. Seton spent the years 1770–3 in England; during this time he corresponded with Crèvecœur, whose descriptive letters on farming life and colonial conditions in America probably form the basis on which the *Letters* were subsequently conceived. Seton helped to gain Crèvecœur's release from detention in New York in 1780, and again aided him on his return to America in 1784. The French edition of *Lettres d'un cultivateur américain* (1784) is subtitled 'adressés à W^mS——on Esqr'.

soon be expected: a second volume was never published; Crèvecœur turned his attention instead to producing an expanded French edition of the *Letters*.

5 *employment at New York*: Crèvecœur's appointment as Louis XVI's consul to New York from September 1783 was a direct result of his literary endeavours, notably his report for the French government on the American colonies' struggle for independence.

7 *Political and Philosophical History . . . pleasure*: the Abbé Guillaume Raynal, FRS (1713–96), a prominent French savant, was one of Crèvecœur's correspondents. His anti-colonialist and anti-clerical *Histoire philosophique et politique des établissements et du commerce des Européens dans les deux Indes*, to which many of the leading writers of the French Enlightenment contributed, was published clandestinely in 1770, and became immensely influential, going through thirty-five French editions and fourteen in English before the end of the century. Its effect on Crèvecœur's thinking may be seen directly in many areas. In particular, Books 17 and 18 of the work discussed 'The Sentiments of a Foreigner on the Disputes of Great-Britain with America', setting America's natural potential against the disastrousness of attempting to pursue independence in the country's current condition of cultural immaturity.

12 *'Navigation of Sir Francis Drake'*, the *'History of Queen Elizabeth'*:
Sir Francis Drake (*c.*1540–96), English courtier, explorer, and cir-
cumnavigator who made piratical raids on the Americas. Elizabeth
I (1538–1603) ruled during the first great era of English exploration
and settlement of the Americas.

Cambridge: one of the oldest and most prestigious universities in
Europe (Peterhouse dates from 1284). The collegiate system of
'Houses' or 'Halls' still exists.

Suvius and town of Pompey underground: the volcano Vesuvius in
the hills above Naples in Italy; the nearby town of Pompeii was
buried within hours when clouds of volcanic ash descended during
an eruption in AD 79. Its rediscovery in 1748 stimulated popular
interest in classical archaeology, and it became an early destination
for tourists in Europe.

13 *the precinct*: district (term for a local administrative subdivision).

viva voce: literally, 'with the living voice' (Lat.); orally, in person.

15 *the Campania*: the region in Southern Italy from the Tyrrhenian Sea
to the Sorrento Peninsula, with Naples as its capital city. Luxuriant
and fertile, it was a notorious breeding-ground for fevers.

16 *the temple of Ceres*: Roman goddess of religion and agriculture,
mother of Proserpine; she was worshipped at Eleusis.

17 *the gown*: clerical robes; the minister suggests that one of James's
sons is destined for a career in the Church.

19 *Yale College, a tabula rasa*: *tabula rasa* meant literally a clean slate
(Lat.). The phrase was made current by John Locke's use of it in
his *Essay Concerning Human Understanding* (1689) to describe the
state of the mind of a new-born child before experience of the world
has given it knowledge or ideas of its own. Locke's empirical theory
of human understanding was a fundamental aspect of eighteenth-
century Anglo-American Enlightenment thinking as studied and
promulgated at institutions like Yale College (now University),
founded in 1717. During the Revolutionary years the idea of the
mind as a *tabula rasa* came to be particularly associated with the
'American' point of view, virtuous and unprejudiced by long affiliation to European tradition, and therefore able to think freshly for
itself from first principles.

21 *friend Edmund*: Edmund Burke (1729–97), British politician, orator,
and writer. His eloquent speeches on American affairs during the
1770s were much reprinted and quoted.

assembly-man: local politician; a member of the legislative assembly.

25 *timothy meadow*: a grass with long cylindrical spikes, widely grown for hay.

28 *the emperor of China . . . his kingdom*: the Confucian *Book of Rites* describes how every year the emperor would plough a few yards as an example of humility and sincerity. This ritual enactment demonstrated that the ruler was maintaining his earthly empire in accordance with the Empire of Heaven. It is likely that Crèvecœur would have been familiar with the oriental example from the works of the Jesuit Jean Baptiste Du Halde, either from his three-volume *Déscription géographique, historique, chronologique, politique, et physique de l'empire de la Chine et de la Tartare Chinoise* (1835), which he would have found to hand at the Collège Royal du Bourbon, or in the popular English translation *The General History of China . . .* (1738–41), which ascribes the high esteem accorded to agriculture in China and the origin of the annual ritual spring ploughing to the Emperor Ven Ti who reigned *c.*179 BC: 'this Prince, perceiving that the Country was become desolate by. . . dreadful Wars, assembled his Council to deliberate on the Means for the Re-establishment thereof, and to engage his Subjects in the Cultivation of the Land; he himself set them an Example by cultivating, with his own Hands, the Land belonging to the Palace.' From Montesquieu (see note to p. 193 below) onwards, both French and British Enlightenment writers looked to the increasing amount of information about the classical civilizations of the Orient for confirmation of their theories; with this quick reference, Crèvecœur is signalling to his reader that the ideas of the physiocrats have an ancient sanction beyond the expected circle of Virgilian literary allusion.

29 *kingbirds*: a form of Tyrant Flycatcher which travels from Central America to the eastern Seaboard to bread.

31 *the N.W.*: the North Wind, perhaps?

35 *shrill cat-birds*: dark grey American songbird, with black cap and reddish under-tail coverts. Named for its call, which sounds like that of a cat.

36 *phebe*: a small bird common in eastern America, also called the pewit or peewee.

42 *ancient college*: Harvard, founded in 1636, is America's oldest institution of learning.

43 *musketoes*: = mosquitos. On the founding of the colony of Nova Scotia, see note to p. 99, below.

Ubi panis ibi patria: 'Where my bread is, there is my homeland' (Lat.).

49 *German Lutheran*: Martin Luther's (1483–1546) followers sub-
scribed to his principle tenet of justification by faith alone, and
relied on thorough personal knowledge of the Bible rather than
clerical mediation. In the Catholic doctrine of transubstantiation,
the whole substance of the bread and wine converted in the Eu-
chartist into the whole substance of the Body and Blood of Christ;
this article of faith was challenged and modified by Lutheran consubstantiation: the belief that after consecration both substances
are present. From the seventeenth century, waves of immigrants
to Canada and America led to a proliferation of strong Lutheran
communities in America.

Seceder: one who has formally withdrawn from affiliation to the
Church, insisting on his right to worship in his own way. The principle of secession, of 'moving on' to one's own territory, has been
important in American culture from the time of the conflicts which
split the first Puritan settlements. Farmer James's decision to leave
his troubled community and take to the woods at the end of the
Letters may be seen as a distant precursor of Huckleberry Finn's
decision to 'light out for the territory' when Aunt Sally's attempts
to 'sivilize' him become too much to bear.

William Penn: (1644–1718), founder of Pennsylvania. Influenced
by Quaker teaching at Oxford, Penn campaigned for freedom of
worship. When, in 1681, he was granted a tract of land the size
of England in America by Charles II in payment of a debt, Penn
set sail with 100 Quakers to found a new state based on religious
teachings of peace. Its capital, Philadelphia, was to be the City of
Brotherly Love. Penn personally negotiated a lengthy peace with
native Indians. He revisited England in 1684, but was ruined
financially when James II's reign ended in disaster and flight. On
returning to America, Penn saw that his experiment had gone
astray in his absence, with political wrangles spoiling previous harmony. He returned to England once more, but fell ill in 1712
when negotiating the sale of his governorship to the Crown, and
died six years later.

Low Dutchman ... synod of Dort: the assembly of the Dutch
Reformed Church convened at Dort in 1618–19 passed five articles of faith asserting unconditional election, a limited atonement,
the total depravity of mankind, the irresistibility of grace, and the
final perseverance of the saints. Low Churchmen minimize the
authority of ecclesiastical hierarchy.

52 *Moravians*: a pietistic Protestant group, the direct continuation of
the Bohemian Brethren. The Moravians had close links with the

Lutheran Church and were active missionaries: in 1732 two brethren went to the Negroes in the West Indies and the following year a mission was begun in Greenland. The Moravians have always maintained a numerically strong presence in America.

54 *Indians took the hatchet against the Virginians in 1774*: in 'Dunmore's War' of that year, the Royal Governor of Virginia, Lord Dunmore, provoked bloody revenge when he violated orders by attacking Shawnee and Mingo Indians from Ohio, who were in their turn making retaliatory strikes following previous atrocities. At the negotiations which succeeded hostilities, the Mingo chief Logan delivered a famously dignified speech conceding defeat and defending his own honour and that of his tribe. It was much admired by Thomas Jefferson, who quoted it in full in his *Notes on the State of Virginia* (written 1781–2, publ. 1787).

59 *sheaves . . . yourselves*: the feudal practice of tithing, in which one-tenth of all produce was claimed by the Church; further segments of the harvest might be appropriated by the farmer's landlord and by the government as taxation. The practice was still widespread in Europe.

61 *technical American knowledge . . . rails and posts*: felling the extensively forested American terrain, clearing the land of tree-roots and undergrowth, and constructing fences and buildings from the lumber were skills unlikely to have been learned by immigrants newly arrived from Scotland, where trees were (in the eighteenth century) notoriously scarce. Samuel Johnson commented acerbically on the treeless wastes of the Highlands in his *Journey to the Western Islands of Scotland* in 1773. Andrew the Hebridean, whose story follows in Crèvecœur's narrative, is a native of this very region.

70 *'to enjoy is to obey'*: from 'The Universal Prayer' by Alexander Pope (1688–1744).

72 *Lancaster six-horse waggons*: large carts for conveying heavy goods.

75 *3000 rails to split*: after felling trees to produce a clearing for settlement and tillage, the next task of settlers was to split the trunks into thin rails for fencing.

77 *calumet*: the American Indian 'pipe of peace'.

80 *pompions*: pumpkins. An archaic word of French derivation; perhaps one of the few occasions on which Crèvecœur's original linguistic nationality shows in his prose.

a frolic: system of mutual aid widely practised in early America, where neighbours joined in the clearing of land and building of dwellings. The occasion was one for revelry and celebration as well as hard labour.

85 *Lycurgus or Solon*: ancient Greek legislators; Lycurgus of Sparta established a constitution following a slave rebellion in the seventh century BC, and is mentioned by Herodotus and Plutarch. Solon (*c*.640–559 BC) was an Athenian political reformer and poet widely credited with being the founder of democracy. Elected chief magistrate *c*.594 BC, he instigated a code of criminal law and reformed the Athenian Constitution.

87–90 *the Island of Nantucket . . . Bermudas*: these map references are wildly incorrect, and indeed mutually inconsistent: distances and directions are closer to 41° 15′ latitude; 60 miles south of Cape Cod; 35 miles SE (or SSE) of Hyannis; 25 miles SE (ESE) of Cape Pog (Poge); 40 miles SE (ESE) of Wood's Hole; 110 miles SE of Boston; 80 miles SE (ESE) of Rhode Island; 1,100 miles NW (NNW) of Bermuda. It is unlikely that Crèvecœur, who was a competent cartographer, would have made such mistakes unwittingly; this, and the fact that he did not correct the errors in either the 1784 or 1787 revised editions of the *Letters*, suggest that he may have intended to make his Nantucket into a kind of mythical 'Happy Isle' unfindable on any map. Thus de-realized, the island becomes as fictional as the Indian village to which Farmer James imagines himself escaping at the end of the book. NB The 'table of references' mentioned in the next sentence is incorporated within the map.

96 *fulling-mill*: new-spun cloth was shrunk and thickened by the 'fulling' process, which involved moisture, heat, and pressure.

loomy: = loamy.

99 *Earl of Sterling*: Sir William Alexander (1567?–1640), Earl of Stirling, poet and statesman. In 1621 he obtained the land of Nova Scotia by charter from James I, who was anxious to further the 'plantation' of North America on the model of Ulster. This prodigious grant was later increased until huge sections of Canada and what would later become the northern United States lay under Alexander's jurisdiction. The charter was renewed by Charles I in 1625. Alexander struggled under formidable difficulties to encourage colonization of his territories.

Duke of York: James II (1633–1701). As Duke of York, in exile during the Protectorate; he returned to England on the accession of his brother Charles II in 1660. He took a keen interest in naval matters and in colonial trade, and in 1664 Charles granted him a patent for the newly subdued Dutch settlement of New Amsterdam on Long Island, which was renamed New York. He subsequently engaged in naval warfare with the Dutch Republic.

100 *Mr. Elliot*: John Eliot (1604–90), prominent New England divine; known as 'Apostle to the Indians', he sailed to Massachusetts in 1631 and settled as pastor in Roxbury. He learned the Nattick or Algonquin language from an Indian servant and translated the Bible into that language in 1663.

102 *wampum*: a string of white shell beads used by the Indians as a medium of exchange and standard of value.

103 *sachem*: Indian chief or ruler.

105 *horse feet (sea spin)*: plant gathered from the seashore and used as fertilizer.

111 *sperma-ceti*: wax product of the head cavity of whales; a valuable prize (along with oil and whalebone) of the whaling industry, it was used in ointments, cosmetics, fine candles, and textile finishing.

113 *the Vineyard*: Martha's Vineyard, an island near to Nantucket. See map pp. 116–17.

129 *scantlings*: small pieces of lumber; the word frequently designated the upright struts in the frame of a house.

133 *galenical medicines*: from the Greek physician Galen (AD 129–?199).

134 *the ambrosial ananas*: pineapple, traditionally good for the digestion.

140 *spoyls*: obsolete form of 'spile', a small piece of wood used to plug a cask or barrel.

145 *patenteed*: i.e., the original recipients of Royal Patents.

149 *Hudibras and Josephus*: Samuel Butler (1620–80) published *Hudibras*, a long satirical and highly allusive poem in three parts (1663, 1664, 1678), written in doggerel octosyllabic couplets, and directed against the hypocrisy and intolerance of the Puritans. Josephus Flavius (*c.*AD37–*c.*100), Jewish historian, was a native of Palestine who subsequently received Roman citizenship. He was best known for his *History of the Jewish War* and *Antiquities of the Jews*.

152 *ne-plus-ultra*: nothing further, perfection (Lat.).

Mosaical portion of the tenth: the title (see note to p. 59, above).

158 *dilaceration*: from the French (see above, note to p. 80); being torn in pieces, rent asunder.

Helotes: or Helots, the indigenous Peloponnesian Greeks who lost their lands and freedom under Spartan (Lacedaemonian) repression. The word became synonymous with slave.

162 *Diarbeck*: possibly Diyarbakir, in Turkey.

169 *trepidation*: archaic use of the word, meaning vibration, disturbance.

reptile state: adjective formed from Lat. *repere* (to creep).

173 *John Bertram*: or Bartram (1699–1777), American Quaker botanist,
known as the father of American botany. He corresponded with
distinguished naturalists in Europe, and in 1765 was appointed
'Botanist to the King' by George III. Bartram travelled extensively
about the American colonies collecting specimens and making
maps, and founded the first American botanical garden in America.
Throughout the *Letters*, Crèvecœur refers to this fellow member
of the American Philosophical Society as 'Bertram'.

Queen Ulrica of Sweden: Ulrika Eleanora (1688–1741) abdicated
in 1720, and subsequently corresponded with many European
literati on a variety of subjects.

176 *musk squash*: spreading trailing plant bearing gourd-like fruits.

177 *nature's God*: from *An Essay on Man* (1733–4) by Alexander Pope.

General Bouquet: (1719–65), British officer who successfully
adapted European army discipline to forest warfare during the
French and Indian War (1754–60). In command of the southern
forces during Pontiac's Rebellion, he defeated the Indians at the
Battle of Bushy Run in 1763 and was subsequently given military
command of the southern colonies in America.

herbarizing: archaic: herbalizing, collecting herb and plant specimens.

180 *Linnæus*: Carl von Linné or Carolus Linnaeus (1707–78), Swed-
ish botanist who established principles for classifying plants and
animals. His *Systema naturae* was published in 1736, followed
by *Genera plantarum* (1737) and *Species plantarum* (1753), which
became the basis for modern systematic botany. The Linnaean system uses a generic and a specific name for each type of plant;
related genera are grouped into classes and related classes into
orders.

187 *Oby . . . Samoyede . . . Laplander . . . Pello . . . Tobolky*: the Oby or
Ob', a river of central Siberia; Samoyeds were the traditionally
nomadic Siberian natives of the northern forest region of central
Russia. Laplanders, also mainly subsistence farmers and trappers,
are natives of a vast northern European area lying mainly within the
Arctic Circle. Pello is in the Lapp area of Finland. Tobolsk, equally
remote, was during the eighteenth century the capital of Siberia.

192 *pervade*: used in archaic sense of 'to pass over', 'go across' (from
Lat. *per-vadere*, to walk over).

193 *pismires*: ants.

Montesquieu: Charles Louis de Secondat, baron de Montesquieu (1689–1755), French philosopher and jurist; he wrote satirical travel letters, the *Letters persanes* (1721), and *Considérations sur les causes de la grandeur et de la décadence des romains* (1734). His masterpiece, *De l'esprit des lois*, appeared in 1748; its comparative study of the three main types of government (republic, monarchy, and despotism) became authoritative for the Enlightenment. Here Crèvecœur is quoting one of his own arbiters against himself, to show how violated feelings supersede the principles of enlightened inquiry and rationality.

201 *àlagrichés*: unidentified; presumablly a French rendering of some kind of Indian cake made from meal.

205 *Apollonius of Chalcis . . . emperor Antoninus*: in his *Meditations* the Roman Emperor Marcus Aurelius Antoninus (AD 121–80) described how the philosopher Apollonius of Chalcedon taught him to meet acute pain, the loss of his son, and the tedium of chronic illness with the same unaltered composure.

209 *inoculation*: smallpox was a great scourge in eighteenth-century America, transmitted by Europeans to the Indians. Even before the scientific procedures pioneered by Edward Jenner in 1796–8, a handful of enlightened men and women practised the prophylactic procedure of introducing inactive disease-causing microorganisms into the body to stimulate the formation of antibodies without producing the disease itself. At first regarded with widespread suspicion, inoculation was also advocated and practised by Benjamin Franklin.

210 *quirn*: or 'quern'; simple apparatus for grinding corn between two flat stones.

212 *matchcoat*: a kind of mantle formerly worn by American Indians, originally made of fur-skins and afterwards of coarse woollen cloth known as match-cloth.

213 *The great Manitou*: 'Great Spirit' of the Indians, the subject of religious awe. The 1782 edition has 'Maniton' here. The Scottish Enlightenment historian William Robertson's influential two-volume *History of America* (1777) describes the Indians' beliefs about the Great Spirit in similar terms, and also expounds the beneficial effects of European settlement and farming on the naturally hostile and unhealthy environment of America.

The Oxford World's Classics Website

www.worldsclassics.co.uk

- Browse the full range of Oxford World's Classics online

- Sign up for our monthly e-alert to receive information on new titles

- Read extracts from the Introductions

- Listen to our editors and translators talk about the world's greatest literature with our Oxford World's Classics audio guides

- Join the conversation, follow us on Twitter at OWC_Oxford

- Teachers and lecturers can order inspection copies quickly and simply via our website

www.worldsclassics.co.uk

American Literature

British and Irish Literature

Children's Literature

Classics and Ancient Literature

Colonial Literature

Eastern Literature

European Literature

Gothic Literature

History

Medieval Literature

Oxford English Drama

Poetry

Philosophy

Politics

Religion

The Oxford Shakespeare

A complete list of Oxford World's Classics, including Authors in Context, Oxford English Drama, and the Oxford Shakespeare, is available in the UK from the Marketing Services Department, Oxford University Press, Great Clarendon Street, Oxford OX2 6DP, or visit the website at www.oup.com/uk/worldsclassics.

In the USA, visit www.oup.com/us/owc for a complete title list.

Oxford World's Classics are available from all good bookshops. In case of difficulty, customers in the UK should contact Oxford University Press Bookshop, 116 High Street, Oxford OX1 4BR.

JANE AUSTEN	**Emma** **Persuasion** **Pride and Prejudice** **Sense and Sensibility**
MRS BEETON	**Book of Household Management**
ANNE BRONTË	**The Tenant of Wildfell Hall**
CHARLOTTE BRONTË	**Jane Eyre**
EMILY BRONTË	**Wuthering Heights**
WILKIE COLLINS	**The Moonstone** **The Woman in White**
JOSEPH CONRAD	**Heart of Darkness and Other Tales** **Nostromo**
CHARLES DARWIN	**The Origin of Species**
CHARLES DICKENS	**Bleak House** **David Copperfield** **Great Expectations** **Hard Times**
GEORGE ELIOT	**Middlemarch** **The Mill on the Floss**
ELIZABETH GASKELL	**Cranford**
THOMAS HARDY	**Jude the Obscure** **Tess of the d'Urbervilles**
WALTER SCOTT	**Ivanhoe**
MARY SHELLEY	**Frankenstein**
ROBERT LOUIS STEVENSON	**Treasure Island**
BRAM STOKER	**Dracula**
WILLIAM MAKEPEACE THACKERAY	**Vanity Fair**
OSCAR WILDE	**The Picture of Dorian Gray**